SFBC 50th
ANNIVERSARY COLLECTION

MEMORY

Other Books by Lois McMaster Bujold

Science Fiction
Falling Free
Shards of Honor
Barrayar
The Borders of Infinity
The Warrior's Apprentice
The Vor Game
Ethan of Athos
Brothers in Arms
Borders of Infinity
Mirror Dance
Cetaganda
Komarr
A Civil Campaign

Fantasy
The Spirit Ring
The Curse of Chalion
Paladin of Souls
The Hallowed Hunt
The Sharing Knife: Beguilement
The Sharing Knife: Legacy

Short Fiction
Dreamweaver's Dilemma

SFBC 50th
ANNIVERSARY COLLECTION

MEMORY

Lois McMaster Bujold

SFBC
SCIENCE
FICTION
35

This SFBC Science Fiction Edition: May 2007.
Publication History: Baen hardcover, October 1996
                      SFBC hardcover, November 1996
                      Baen mass market paperback, October 1997

Visit The SFBC at http://www.sfbc.com

ISBN # 978-0-7394-8343-5

Printed in the United States of America.

For
Trudie Senior
and
Trudie Junior

ONE

Miles returned to consciousness with his eyes still closed. His brain seemed to smolder with the confused embers of some fiery dream, formless and fading. He was shaken by a fearful conviction that he had been killed again, till memory and reason began to place this shredded experience.

His other senses tried to take inventory. He was in null-gee, his short body stretched out flat, strapped to a surface and swathed in what felt like a thin foil med wrap, standard military issue. *Wounded?* All limbs seemed present and accounted for. He was still wearing the soft bodysuit that had lined his now-missing space armor. The straps were not tight. The complex scent of many-times-refiltered air, cool and dry, tickled his nostrils. He secretly snaked an arm free, careful not to rattle the wrap, and touched his bare face. No control leads, no sensors—no blood—*where are my armor, my weapons, my command headset?*

The rescue mission had been going as smoothly as such missions ever did. He and Captain Quinn and their patrol had penetrated the hijackers' ship, found the brig. Blasted through to the captured Barrayaran ImpSec courier officer, Lieutenant Vorberg, still alive though addled with sedatives. The medtech had pronounced the hostage clear of mechanical or chemical boobytraps, and they'd begun the exhilarating trip through the dark corridors back to the waiting Dendarii combat shuttle. The hijackers, very much occupied elsewhere, had made no attempt to jump them. *What went wrong?*

The sounds around him were quiet: the bleep of equipment, the hiss of atmosphere recycling on normal operation, the murmur of voices. One low animal moan. Miles licked his lips, just to be sure that noise wasn't coming from himself. He might not be wounded, but somebody nearby was not in good shape. A tangy whiff of antiseptics escaped filtration. He slitted open his eyes, prepared to play unconscious again and think fast if he found himself in enemy hands.

But he was—safely, he hoped—in his own Dendarii Fleet combat shuttle, strapped to one of the four fold-down bunks toward the rear of the fuselage. The emergency medical station was a familiar sight, though he didn't usually see it from this angle of view. Blue Squad's medtech, his back to Miles, hovered by a bunk across the aisle that held another strapped-down form. Miles couldn't see any body bags. *Only one other casualty.* He would add, *Good,* except that there weren't supposed to be *any* casualties.

Only one casualty, Miles corrected his thought. A violent headache throbbed at the base of his brain. But he bore no plasma arc burns, no nerve-disruptor paralysis. No intravenous tubing or hypospray injector pierced his body, pumping in blood replacements or synergine against shock. He did not float in a narcotic haze of painkillers, and no pressure bandages hampered his slight movements. No sense-blockers. The headache felt like a poststun migraine. *How the hell could I have been stunned through combat armor?*

The Dendarii medtech, still combat-armored but with helmet and gloves off, turned and saw Miles's open eyes. "You're awake, sir? I'll notify Captain Quinn." He hovered briefly over Miles's face, and flashed a light into his eyes, doubtless checking for abnormal pupil response.

"How long . . . was I out? What happened?"

"You had some kind of seizure, or convulsion. No apparent cause. The field kit test for toxins didn't turn up anything, but it's pretty basic. We'll go over you more thoroughly as soon as we're back to the ship's sick bay."

Not dead again. Worse. This is still more of the leftovers from the last time. Oh, hell. What have I done? What have they seen?

He would rather have been—well, no. He would *not* rather have been nerve-disrupted. But almost. "How long?" Miles repeated.

"The seizure seemed to last four or five minutes."

It had certainly taken more than five minutes to get from *there* to *here.* "Then?"

"You've been unconscious for about a half hour, I'm afraid, Admiral Naismith."

He'd never been out so long before. This was the worst attack ever, by far. He'd prayed the last one would *be* the last one. Over two months had passed since his previous unwitnessed, brief collapse. Dammit, he'd been *certain* the new medication had worked.

He made to free himself, fighting out of the heat wrap and bunk straps.

"Please don't try to get up, Admiral."

"I have to go forward and get reports."

The medtech placed a cautious hand upon his chest, and pressed him back onto the bunk. "Captain Quinn ordered me to sedate you if you tried to get up. Sir."

Miles almost barked, *And I countermand that order!* But they did not seem to be in the midst of combat now, and the tech had a medically steely look in his eye, of a man prepared to do his duty whatever the risks. *Save me from the virtuous.* "Is that why I was out so long? Was I sedated?"

"No, sir. I only gave you synergine. Your vital signs were stable, and I was afraid to give you anything else till I had some better idea what we were dealing with."

"What about my squad? Are we all out? The Barrayaran hostage, did we get him out all right?"

"Everybody got out all right. The Barrayaran, um . . . will live. I retrieved his legs; there's a good chance the surgeon will be able to reattach them." The medtech glanced around, as if seeking comradely assistance.

"*What?* How was he injured?"

"Uh . . . I'll call Captain Quinn for you, sir."

"You do that," growled Miles.

The medtech ducked away into free fall, and murmured urgently into an intercom on the far wall. He returned to his patient—Lieutenant Vorberg? IVs were pumping plasma and medications into the man through sites on both an arm and his neck. The rest was concealed by heat foil. At a light-signal from the forward bulkhead, the medtech hastily strapped himself into his station jump seat, and the shuttle went through a quick series of accelerations, decelerations, and attitude adjustments, in preparation for locking on to its mother ship.

Properly, upon docking the injured hostage was rushed out first. In two parts. Miles gritted his teeth in dismay at the sight of the soldier clutching a large cold-container who followed the medtech and float pallet. There did not seem to be much blood smeared around, though. Miles had just given up waiting for

Quinn and was releasing himself from his medical restraints when she appeared from the flight deck and floated down the aisle toward him.

She had doffed the helmet and gloves from her space armor, and pulled back her bodysuit's hood to free her dark, sweat-flattened curls. Her beautifully sculpted face was pale with tension, her brown eyes dark with fear. But his little three-ship fleet could be in no immediate danger, or she would be attending to it, not to him. "Are you all right?" she asked hoarsely.

"Quinn, what—no. Give me a general status report first."

"Green Squad got the hijacked ship's crew out. All of them. There was a bit of equipment damage—the insurance company's not going to be as ecstatic as the last time—but our Life Bonus is safe and warm."

"Praise be to God and Sergeant Taura. And our hijackers?"

"We took their big ship and nineteen prisoners. Three enemy killed. All secured there; our prize crew is aboard cleaning up. Six or eight of the bastards escaped in their jump-pinnance. It's weak on armament—this far from the nearest jump point, the *Ariel* can overtake them at our leisure. Your decision, whether to stand off and blow them up, or attempt capture."

Miles rubbed his face. "Interrogate those prisoners. If this is the same bloody-handed lot that took the *Solera* last year, and murdered all the passengers and crew, Vega Station will pay a reward, and we can collect three times for the same mission. Since the Vegans are offering the same reward for the proof of their deaths, record everything carefully. We'll demand surrender. Once." He sighed. "I take it things did not run exactly according to plan. Again."

"Hey. Any hostage-rescue ploy that gets everyone out alive is a success by any sane standard. Assuming our fleet surgeon doesn't reattach your poor Barrayaran's legs left-to-right or backwards, this is a one-hundred-percenter."

"Er . . . yes. What *happened* when . . . I went down? What happened to Vorberg?"

"Friendly fire, unfortunately. Though it didn't seem all that friendly at the time. You fell over—surprised the hell out of us. Your suit emitted a lot of garbage telemetry, then your plasma arc locked on." She raked her hands through her hair.

Miles glanced at the heavy-duty plasma arc built into the right arm of Quinn's space armor, twin to his own. His heart sank into his churning stomach. "Oh, no. Oh, shit. Don't tell me."

"I'm afraid so. You kneecapped your own rescuee. Neat as could be, right across both legs. Luckily—I guess—the beam cauterized as it sliced, so he didn't bleed to death. And he was so tanked on drugs, I'm not even sure he felt much. For a moment I thought some enemy had taken over remote control of your suit, but the engineers swear that isn't possible anymore. You blew out a bunch of walls—it took four of us to sit on your arm till we could take the medic's can-opener to your armor and get in and get you disconnected. You were thrashing around—you damn near took us out too. In pure desperation, I stunned you on the back of your neck, and you went limp. I was afraid I'd killed you."

Quinn was a little breathless, describing this. Her lovely face was not, after all, the original, but a replacement after her own violent encounter with plasma fire, over a decade ago. "Miles, what the hell was going on with you?"

"I think I had . . . some kind of seizure. Like epilepsy, except that it doesn't seem to leave any neurological tracks. I'm afraid it might be an aftereffect from my cryo-revival last year." *You know damned well it is*. He touched the twin scars on either side of his neck, now grown faint and pale, the lesser souvenirs of that event. Quinn's emergency stunner-treatment explained his lengthy bout of unconsciousness and subsequent headache. So, the seizures were no *worse* than before. . . .

"Oh, dear," said Quinn. "But is this the first—" She paused, and looked at him more closely. Her voice went flatter. "This isn't the first time you've done this, is it."

The silence stretched; Miles forced himself to speak before it snapped. "It happened three or four," *or five* "times soon after I was brought back from stasis. My cryo-revival surgeon said they might go away on their own, the way the memory loss and the shortness of breath have. And after that they seemed to stop."

"And ImpSec let you go out on a covert ops field mission with that kind of time bomb in your head?"

"ImpSec . . . does not know."

"*Miles* . . ."

"Elli," he said desperately, "they'd pull me right off line duty, you know they would. Nail my boots to the floor behind some desk at best. Medical discharge at worst—and that would be the end of Admiral Naismith. Forever."

She froze, stricken.

"I figured if the seizures came back I'd try to solve 'em on my own. I thought I had."

"Does *anybody* know?"

"Not . . . very many. I didn't want to chance it getting back to ImpSec. I told the Dendarii fleet surgeon. I swore her to secrecy. We were working on a causal diagnosis. Haven't got too far yet. Her specialty's trauma, after all." Yes, like plasma arc burns, and limb reattachment. At least Lieutenant Vorberg could not be in better or more experienced hands right now, even if he could have been magically transported in an instant back to Barrayar's own Imperial Military Hospital.

Quinn's lips tightened. "But you didn't tell me. Never mind our personal relationship, I'm your second in command on this mission!"

"I should have told you. Obvious in hindsight." *Blindingly.*

Quinn glanced up the fuselage of the shuttle, where a medtech from the *Peregrine* was wrestling a float pallet in through the hatch. "I still have some mopping up to supervise. You're going to stay in the frigging sick bay till I get back, right?"

"I'm back on track now! It could be months till it happens again. If ever."

"*Right?*" Quinn repeated through her teeth, with an open glare at him.

He thought of Vorberg, and deflated. "Right," he muttered.

"Thank you," she hissed.

He scorned the float pallet, insisting on walking, but otherwise followed the medtech, feeling horribly subdued. *I'm losing control of this. . . .*

As soon as Miles arrived in sick bay, an anxious tech administered a brain scan, drew blood, took samples of every fluid his body could be made to exude, and rechecked every vital sign he possessed. After that, there was not very much to do but wait for the surgeon. Miles withdrew discreetly into a small examining room, where his batman brought him his ship uniform. The man seemed inclined to hover solicitously and Miles, irritated, sent him away.

This left Miles alone in a quiet room with nothing to do but think, possibly a tactical error. Quinn could be trusted with the mopping up, or why else had he made her his second? She had taken over competently enough the last time he had been violently removed from his chain of command, his chest blown out by that sniper's needle grenade on the mission to Jackson's Whole.

He pulled up and fastened his gray trousers, and studied his torso, his fingers tracing the wide spidery burst of scars fading on his skin. The Jacksonian cryo-revival surgeon had done a superb job. His new heart and lungs and assorted other organs were nearly fully grown now, entirely functional. With the latest additions, the brittle bones that had plagued him since his defective birth were almost completely replaced by synthetics throughout his body. The cryo-surgeon had even straightened his spine while she was at it; there was barely a hint left of the hunchback curvature that, along with his dwarfish stature, had made his fellow Barrayarans snigger *Mutant!* when they thought he could not hear. He'd even gained a couple more centimeters in height out of the deal, an expensive little bonus, but it mattered to him. The fatigue didn't show. To the outward eye, he was in better physical shape than he'd ever been in his nearly thirty years of life.

There's just one little hitch.

Of all the threats that had ever shadowed his hard-won career, this was the most elusive, the least expected . . . the most fatal. He'd worked with impassioned concentration, overcoming all doubts as to his physical disabilities, winning his way to premier status as Barrayaran Imperial Security's most creative galactic affairs agent. Where the Barrayaran Empire's regular forces could not reach, past barriers of politics and distance in the chaining network of wormhole jump routes that strung the galaxy together, a supposedly independent mercenary outfit might pop up unimpeded. Miles had spent a decade perfecting his cover identity of "Admiral Naismith," self-styled leader of the Dendarii Free Mercenary Fleet. Daring Rescues Our Specialty.

Such as the current mission. The grotty crew of hijackers had run seriously out of luck the day they'd stolen an unarmed freighter of Zoave Twilight's planetary registry, and found what they thought was the prize in the package in the form of a Barrayaran Imperial Courier, covertly transporting credit chits and vital diplomatic information. If they'd had any sense of self-preservation at all, they should have returned Lieutenant Vorberg and his packets, undamaged and unexamined, immediately to the nearest drop-point, with profuse apologies.

Instead, they'd tried to sell him to the highest bidder. *Slay them all*, ImpSec Chief Simon Illyan had muttered. *The Devil will recognize his own.* Then he'd delegated the details to Miles. The Emperor did not approve of unauthorized persons impeding his couriers. Or torturing them, or attempting to market them like high-information-density slabs of meat. This was one mission where, although the Dendarii Fleet's official sponsor was the insurance company covering the Zoave Twilight ship, it wouldn't hurt to reveal that their cobacker was the Barrayaran Empire. Good publicity, for the protection of the next courier to run into similar bad luck.

Assuming it was luck. Miles itched to go oversee the interrogation of the prisoners; Illyan's second sharpest concern after the retrieval of Vorberg alive was to determine if the courier had been kidnapped by accident or on purpose. If on purpose . . . somebody had some internal investigating to do. In all, Miles was extremely glad that sort of messy job did not fall into his area of expertise.

The surgeon, still dressed in her sterile garb, entered at last. She put her hands on her hips, stared at Miles, and sighed. She looked tired.

"How's the Barrayaran?" Miles ventured. "Will, um . . . he recover?"

"He's not too bad. The cuts were very clean, and luckily just below the knee joints, which saved a world of complications. He'll be about three centimeters shorter after this."

Miles winced.

"But he'll be on his feet by the time he gets home," she added, "assuming that takes about six weeks."

"Ah. Good." But suppose the random blare of the plasma arc had taken Vorberg through the knees. Or about a meter higher, cutting him in half. There were limits to the miracles even his Dendarii surgical expert could perform. It would not have been a career high point, after Miles had airily assured his ImpSec chief that he could rescue Vorberg with scarcely a ripple in his routine, to return him packed in a body bag. Two body bags. Miles felt faint with a weird mixture of relief and horror. *Oh, God, I'm going to hate explaining this to Illyan.*

The surgeon studied Miles's scans, muttering medical incantations. "We're still on baseline, here. No obvious abnormalities show up. The only way I can get any leverage into this is to have you monitored while you undergo an attack."

"Hell, I thought we did every kind of stress and electroshock and stimulus known to science, to try to trigger something in the lab. I thought the pills you gave me had brought it under control."

"The standard anticonvulsant? *Were* you taking it properly?" She eyed him suspiciously.

"*Yes.*" He bit back more profane protestations. "Have you thought of something else to try?"

"No, which is why I gave you that monitor to wear around." Her glance around the examining room did not disclose the device. "Where is it?"

"In my cabin."

Her lips thinned in exasperation. "Let me guess. You weren't wearing it at the time."

"It didn't fit under my combat armor."

Her teeth clenched. "Couldn't you have at least thought to—to disable your weapons?"

"I could hardly be of use to my squad in an emergency, disarmed. I might as well have stayed aboard the *Peregrine*."

"You *were* the emergency. And you certainly *should* have stayed aboard the *Peregrine*."

Or back on Barrayar. But securing Vorberg's person had been the most critical part of the operation, and Miles was the only Dendarii officer ImpSec entrusted with the Barrayaran Imperial recognition codes. "I—" He bit his tongue on futile defenses, and started over. "You are quite correct. It won't happen again, until . . . we get this straightened out. What do we do next?"

She opened her hands. "I've run every test I know. Obviously, the anticonvulsant isn't the answer. This is some kind of idiosyncratic cryonic damage on a cellular or subcellular level. You need to get your head to the highest-powered cryo-neurology specialist you can find."

He sighed, and shrugged into his black tee shirt and gray uniform jacket. "Are we done for now? I urgently need to supervise prisoner interrogation."

"I suppose." She grimaced. "But do us all a favor. Don't go armed."

"Yes, ma'am," he said humbly, and fled.

─── TWO ───

Miles sat before the secured comconsole in his cabin aboard the flagship *Peregrine*, composing what seemed like his thousandth classified field report to the Chief of Barrayaran Imperial Security, Simon Illyan. Well, it wasn't the thousandth, that was absurd. He couldn't have averaged more than three or four missions a year, and he'd been at it less than a decade, really, since the Vervain invasion adventure had made it all official. Less than forty assignments. But he could no longer name the actual number offhand without stopping to think, and add them all up, and it wasn't an effect of lingering cryo-amnesia, either.

Keep organizing, boy. His personal synopsis needed to be no more than a brief guide to the appendices of raw data, drawn from the Dendarii Fleet's own files. Illyan's intelligence analysts liked having lots of raw data to chew upon. It kept them occupied, down in their little cubicles in the bowels of ImpSec headquarters at Vorbarr Sultana. And entertained too, Miles sometimes feared.

The *Peregrine*, the *Ariel*, and the rest of "Admiral Naismith's" select battle group now orbited the planet of Zoave Twilight. His fleet accountant had turned in a busy couple of days, settling up with the insurance company who finally had their freighter and crew back, applying for salvage fees for the hijacker's captured ships, and filing the official claims for bounty to the Vega Station Embassy. Miles entered the costs/returns spreadsheets in full into his report, as *Appendix A*.

The prisoners had been dumped downside, for the Vegan and Zoavan governments to divide between them—preferably in the same sense as poor Vorberg had been. The ex-hijackers were a vile crew. Miles was almost sorry the pinnace had surrendered. *Appendix B* was copies of the Dendarii recordings of the prisoner interrogations. The downside governments would get an edited version of these, with most of the Barrayar-specific queries and answers deleted. Lots of criminal testimony, of little direct interest to ImpSec, though the Vegans ought to be pretty excited about it.

The important thing from Illyan's point of view was that no evidence had been extracted which would indicate that the kidnapping of the Barrayaran courier was anything but an accidental side effect of the hijacking. Unless—Miles made sure to note this in his synopsis—that information had been known only to those hijackers who had been killed. Since that number included both their so-called captain and two of the higher-ranking officers, there were enough possibilities in this direction to keep Illyan's analysts earning their pay. But that lead must now be traced from the other end, through the House Hargraves representatives who had been trying to handle the sale or ransom of the courier for the hijackers. Miles hoped cordially that ImpSec would focus its best negative attentions upon the Jacksonian semicriminal Great House. Though House Hargraves's agents had been extremely, if unwittingly, useful in helping the Dendarii set up their raid.

Illyan ought to like the accountant's report. The Dendarii had not only succeeded in keeping their costs under budget this time—*for a change*—they had made a truly amazing profit. Illyan, who had been willing to spend Imperial marks like water on the principle of the thing, had got his courier officer retrieved effectively for free. *Are we good, yes?*

So—when was the so-efficient ImpSec Lieutenant Lord Miles Vorkosigan finally going to get that longed-for promotion to captain? Odd, how Miles's Barrayaran rank still seemed more real to him than his Dendarii one. True, he had proclaimed himself an admiral first and then earned it later, instead of the more normal other way around, but at this late date no one could say he had not really become what he had once pretended to be. From the galactic point of view, Admiral Naismith was solid all the way through. Everything he advertised himself as being, he really was, now. His Barrayaran identity was simply an extra dimension. An appendix?

There's no place like home.

I didn't say there was nothing better. *I just said there was nothing* like *it*.

This brought him to *Appendix C*, which was the Dendarii

combat armor recordings of the actual penetration and hostage retrieval sequences, Sergeant Taura's Green Squad and its rescue of the freighter's crew, and his own Blue Squad and that whole . . . chain of events. In full sound and color, with all their suits' medical and communications telemetry. Morbidly, Miles ran through all the real-time records of his seizure and its unfortunate consequences. Suit #060's vid recording had some really great close-ups of Lieutenant Vorberg, shocked from his doped stupor, screaming in agony and toppling unconscious in one direction while his severed legs fell in the other. Miles found himself bent over, clutching his chest in sympathy.

This was not going to be a good time to pester Illyan for a promotion.

The convalescent Vorberg had been handed over yesterday to the Barrayaran Counsel's office on Zoave Twilight, for shipment home through normal channels. Miles was secretly grateful that his covert status had let him off the hook for going into sick bay and personally apologizing to the man. Before the plasma arc accident Vorberg had not seen Miles's face, concealed as it had been by the combat armor's helmet, and afterwards, of course . . . The Dendarii surgeon reported Vorberg had only the haziest and most confused memory of his rescue.

Miles wished he could delete the entire Blue Squad record from his report. Impractical, alas. Having the most interesting sequence missing would draw Illyan's attention as surely as a signal fire on a mountaintop.

Of course, if he deleted the entire appendix, all the squad records, it would be camouflaged in the general absence. . . .

Miles considered what could replace *Appendix C*. He had written plenty of brief or vague mission synopses in the past, in the press of events or exhaustion. *Due to a malfunction, the right-arm plasma arc in Suit #032 locked into the "on" position. In the several minutes of confusion surrounding correcting the malfunction, the subject was unfortunately hit by the plasma beam. . . .* Not his fault, if the reader construed this as a malfunction in the suit and not its wearer.

No. He could not lie to Illyan. Not even in the passive voice.

I wouldn't be lying. I'd just be editing my report for length.

It couldn't be done. He'd be sure to miss some tiny corroborative detail in one of the other files, and Illyan's analysts would pick it up, and then he'd be in ten times the trouble.

Not that there was that much in the other sections pertinent to this brief incident. It wouldn't be that hard to run over the whole report.

This is a bad idea.

Still . . . it would be interesting practice. He might have the job of *reading* field reports someday, God forbid. It would be educational to test how much fudging was possible. For his curiosity's sake, he recorded the full report, made a copy, and began playing around with the copy. What minimum alterations and deletions were required to erase a field agent's embarrassment?

It only took about twenty minutes.

He stared at the finished product. It was downright artistic. He felt a little sick to his stomach. *This could get me cashiered.*

Only if I got caught. His whole life felt as if it had been based on that principle; he'd outrun assassins, medics, the regulations of the Service, the constraints of his Vor rank . . . he'd outrun death itself, demonstrably. *I can even move faster than you, Illyan.*

He considered the present disposition of Illyan's independent observers in the Dendarii fleet. One was detached back with the fleet's main body; the second posed as a comm officer on the *Ariel*. Neither had been aboard the *Peregrine* or out with the squads; neither could contradict him.

I think I'd better think about this for a while. He classified the doctored version *top secret* and filed it beside the original. He stretched to ease the ache in his back. Desk work did that to one.

His cabin door chimed. "Yes?"

"Baz and Elena," a woman's voice floated through the intercom.

Miles cleared his comconsole, slipped his uniform jacket back on, and released the door lock. "Enter." He turned in his station chair, smiling a little, to watch them come in.

Baz was Dendarii Commodore Baz Jesek, chief engineer of the Fleet and Miles's nominal second-in-command. Elena was Captain Elena Bothari-Jesek, Baz's wife, and current commander of the *Peregrine*. Both were among the few fellow Barrayarans the Dendarii employed, and both were fully apprised of Miles's dual identity as Admiral Naismith, slightly renegade Betan mercenary, and Lieutenant Lord Miles Vorkosigan, dutiful Barrayaran ImpSec covert ops agent, for both predated the creation of the Dendarii Fleet itself. The lanky, balding Baz had been in on the beginning of it, a deserter on the run whom Miles had picked up and (in his private opinion) re-created. Elena . . . was another matter altogether.

She'd been Miles's Barrayaran bodyguard's daughter, raised

in Count Vorkosigan's household, and practically Miles's foster sister. Barred from Barrayaran military service by her gender, she had longed for the status of a soldier on her army-mad home-world. Miles had found a way to get it for her. She looked all soldier now, slim and as tall as her husband in her crisp Dendarii undress grays. Her dark hair, clipped in wisps around her ears, framed pale hawk features and alert dark eyes.

So how might their lives have been different, if she had only said "Yes" to Miles's passionate, confused proposal of marriage when they were both eighteen? Where would they be now? Living the comfortable lives of Vor aristocrats in the capital? Would they be happy? Or growing bored with each other, and regretting their lost chances? No, they wouldn't even know what chances they had lost. Maybe there would have been children. . . . Miles cut off this line of thought. Unproductive.

Yet somewhere, suppressed deep in Miles's heart, something still waited. Elena seemed happy enough with her choice of husband. But a mercenary's life—as he had recent reason to know—was chancy indeed. A little difference in some enemy's aim, somewhere along the line, might have turned her into a grieving widow, awaiting consolation . . . except that Elena saw more line combat than Baz did. As an evil plot, brooded upon in the recesses of Miles's mind in the secrecy of the night-cycle, this one had a serious flaw. Well, one couldn't help one's thoughts. One could help opening one's mouth and saying something really stupid, though.

"Hi, folks. Pull up a seat. What can I do for you?" Miles said cheerfully.

Elena smiled back, and the two officers arranged station chairs on the other side of Miles's comconsole desk. There was something unusually formal in the way they seated themselves. Baz opened his hand to Elena, to cede her the first word, sure sign of a tricky bit coming up. Miles pulled himself into focus.

She began with the obvious. "Are you feeling all right now, Miles?"

"Oh, I'm fine."

"Good." She took a deep breath. "My lord—"

Another sure sign of something unusual, when she addressed him in terms of their Barrayaran liege relationship.

"—we wish to resign." Her smile, confusingly, crept wider, as if she'd just said something delightful.

Miles almost fell off his chair. "What? *Why?*"

Elena glanced at Baz, and he took up the thread. "I've received a job offer for an engineering position from an orbital shipyard at Escobar. It would pay enough for us both to retire."

"I, I . . . didn't realize you were dissatisfied with your pay grades. If this is about money, something can be arranged."

"It has nothing to do with money," said Baz.

He'd been afraid of that. No, that would be too easy—

"We want to retire to start a family," Elena finished.

What was it about that simple, rational statement that put Miles so forcibly in mind of the moment when the sniper's needle grenade had blown his chest out all over the pavement? "Uh . . ."

"As Dendarii officers," Elena went on, "we can simply give appropriate notice and resign, of course. But as your liege-sworn vassals, we must petition you for release as an Extraordinary Favor."

"Um . . . I'm . . . not sure the Fleet's prepared to lose my two top officers at one blow. Especially Baz. I rely on him, when I'm away, as I have to be about half the time, not just for engineering and logistics, but to keep things under control. To make sure the private contracts don't step on the toes of any of Barrayar's interests. To know . . . all the secrets. I don't see how I can replace him."

"We thought you could divide Baz's current job in half," said Elena helpfully.

"Yes. My engineering second's quite ready to move up," Baz assured him. "Technically, he's better than I am. Younger, you know."

"And everyone knows you've been grooming Elli Quinn for years for command position," Elena went on. "She's itching for promotion. And ready, too. I think she more than proved that last year."

"She's not . . . Barrayaran. Illyan might get twitchy about that," Miles temporized. "In such a critical position."

"He never has so far. He knows her well enough by now, surely. And ImpSec employs plenty of non-Barrayaran agents," said Elena.

"Are you sure you want to formally retire? I mean, is that really necessary? Wouldn't an extended leave or a sabbatical be enough?"

Elena shook her head. "Becoming parents . . . *changes* people. I don't know that I'd want to come back."

"I thought you wanted to become a soldier. With all your heart, more than anything. Like me." *Do you have any idea how much of all this was for you, just for you?*

"I did. I have. I'm . . . done. I know *enough* is not a concept you particularly relate to. I don't know if the wildest successes would ever be enough to fill you up."

That's because I am so very empty. . . .

"But . . . all my childhood, all my youth, Barrayar pounded into me that being a soldier was the only job that counted. The most important thing there was, or ever could be. And that I could never be important, because I could never be a soldier. Well, I've proved Barrayar wrong. I've been a soldier, and a damned good one."

"True . . ."

"And now I've come to wonder what else Barrayar was wrong about. Like, what's really important, and who is really important. When you were in cryo-stasis last year, I spent a lot of time with your mother."

"Oh." On a journey to a homeworld she'd once sworn passionately never to set foot upon again, yes . . .

"We talked a lot, she and I. I'd always thought I admired her because she was a soldier in her youth, for Beta Colony in the Escobar War, before she immigrated and married your father. But once, reminiscing, she went into this sort of litany about all the things she'd ever been. Like astrocartographer, and explorer, and ship's captain, and POW, and wife, and mother, and politician . . . the list went on and on. There was no telling, she said, what she would be next. And I thought . . . I want to be like that. I want to be like her. Not just one thing, but a world of possibilities. I want to find out who *else* I can be."

Miles glanced covertly at Baz, who was smiling proudly at his wife. No question, her will was driving this decision. But Buz was, quite properly, Elena's abject slave. Everything she said would go for him too. Rats.

"Don't you think . . . you might want to come back, after?"

"In ten, fifteen, twenty years?" said Elena. "Do you even think the Dendarii Mercenaries will still exist? No. I don't think I'll want to go back. I'll want to go on. I already know that much."

"Surely you'll want some kind of work. Something that uses your skills."

"I've thought of becoming a commercial shipmaster. It would use most of my training, except for the killing-people parts. I'm tired of death. I want to switch to life."

"I'm . . . sure you'll be superb at whatever you choose to do." For a mad moment, Miles considered the possibility of denying their release. *No, you can't go, you have to stay with me. . . .* "Technically, you realize, I can only release you from this duty. I can't release you from your liege relationship, any more than Emperor Gregor can release me from being Vor. Not that we can't . . . agree to ignore each others' existences for extended periods of time."

Elena gave him a kindly smile that reminded him quite horribly for a moment of his mother, as if she were seeing the whole Vor system as a hallucination, a legal fiction to be edited at will. A look of centered power, not checking outside of herself for . . . for *anything.*

It wasn't fair, for people to go and *change* on him, while his back was turned being dead. To change without giving notice, or even asking permission. He would howl with loss, except . . . *you lost her years ago. This change has been coming since forever. You're just pathologically incapable of admitting defeat.* That was a useful quality, sometimes, in a military leader. It was a pain in the neck in a lover, or would-be lover.

But, wondering why he was bothering, Miles went through the proper Vor forms with them, each kneeling before him to place his or her hands between Miles's. He turned his palms out and watched Elena's long slim hands fly up like birds, freed from some cage. *I did not know I had imprisoned you, my first love. I'm sorry. . . .*

"Well, I wish you every joy," Miles went on, as Elena rose and took Baz's hand. He managed a wink. "Name the first one after me, eh?"

Elena grinned. "I'm not sure she'd appreciate that. Milesanna? Milesia?"

"Milesia sounds like a disease," Miles admitted, taken aback. "In that case, don't. I wouldn't want her to grow up hating me *in absentia.*"

"How soon can we go?" asked Elena. "We are between contracts. The Fleet's scheduled for some downtime anyway."

"Everything's in order in Engineering and Logistics," Baz added. "For a change, no postmission damage repairs."

Delay? *No. Let it be done swiftly.* "Quite soon, I expect. I'll have to notify Captain Quinn, of course."

"Commodore Quinn," Elena nodded. "She'll like the sound of that." She gave Miles an unmilitary parting hug. He stood still, trying to breathe in the last lingering scent of her, as the door whispered closed behind them.

Quinn was attending to duties downside on Zoave Twilight; Miles left orders for her to report to him upon her return to the *Peregrine*. He called up Dendarii Fleet personnel rosters upon his comconsole while he waited, and studied Baz's proposed replacements. There was no reason they shouldn't work out. Promote this man here, move that one and that one to cover the holes. . . . He was not, he assured himself, in shock about this. There were limits even to his capacity for self-dramatization, after all. He was a little *unbalanced*, perhaps, like a man accustomed to leaning on a decorative cane having it suddenly snatched away. Or a sword-stick, like old Commodore Koudelka's. If it weren't for his private little medical problem, he would have to say the couple had chosen their timing well, from the Fleet's point of view.

Quinn blew in at last, trim and fresh in her undress grays, bearing a code-locked document case. Since they were alone, she greeted him with a nonregulation kiss, which he returned with interest. "The Barrayaran Embassy sends you this, love. Maybe it's a Winterfair gift from Uncle Simon."

"We can hope." He decoded and unlocked the case. "Ha! Indeed. It's a credit chit. Interim payment for the mission just concluded. Headquarters can't know we're done yet—he must have wanted to make sure we didn't run out of resources in the middle of things. I'm glad to know he takes personnel retrieval so seriously. It might be me needing this kind of attention, someday."

"It *was* you, last year, and yes he does," agreed Quinn. "You have to give ImpSec that much credit, at least, they do take care of their own. A very old-Barrayaran quality, for an organization that tries to be so up-to-date."

"And what's this, hm?" He fished the second item out of the case. Ciphered instructions, for his eyes only.

Quinn politely moved out of the line of sight, and he ran it through his comconsole, though her native curiosity couldn't help prompting a, "So? Orders from home? Congratulations? Complaints?"

"Well . . . huh." He sat back, puzzled. "Short and uninformative. Why'd they bother to deep-code it? I am ordered to report home, in person, to ImpSec HQ, immediately. There's a scheduled government courier ship passing through Tau Ceti, which will lay over and wait for me—I'm to rendezvous with it by the swiftest possible means, including commercial carrier if necessary. Didn't they learn anything from Vorberg's little adventure? It doesn't even say, *Conclude mission and . . .* , it just says, *Come.* I'm to drop everything, apparently. If it's that urgent, it has to be a new mission assignment, in which case why are they requiring me to spend weeks traveling home, when I'll just have to spend more weeks traveling right back out to the Fleet?" A sudden icy fear gripped his chest. *Unless it's something personal. My father—my mother . . .* no. If anything had happened to Count Vorkosigan, presently serving the Imperium as Viceroy and colonial governor of Sergyar, the galactic news services would have picked it up even as far away as Zoave Twilight.

"What happens"—Quinn, leaning against the far side of the comconsole desk, found something interesting to study on her fingernails—"if you collapse again while you're traveling?"

"Not much," he shrugged.

"How do you know?"

"Er . . ."

She glanced up sharply. "I didn't know psychological denial could drop so many IQ points over the side. Dammit, you've got to do something about those seizures. You can't just . . . ignore them out of existence, though apparently that's exactly what you've been attempting."

"I *was* trying to do something. I thought the Dendarii surgeon could get a handle on it. I was frantic to get back out to the fleet, to a doctor I could trust. Well, I can trust her all right, but she says she can't help me. Now I have to think of something else."

"You trusted her. Why not *me*?"

Miles managed a somewhat pathetic shrug. The palpable inadequacy of this response drove him to add placatingly, "She follows orders. I was afraid you might try to do things for my own good, whether they were the things I wanted or not."

After a moment spent digesting this, Quinn went on a shade less patiently, "How about your own people? The Imperial Military Hospital at Vorbarr Sultana is nearly up to galactic medical standards, these days."

He fell silent, then said, "I should have done that last winter. I'm . . . committed to finding another solution, now."

"In other words, you lied to your superiors. And now you're caught."

I'm not caught yet. "You know what I have to lose." He rose and circled the desk to take her hand, before she started biting her nails; they fell into an embrace. He tilted his face back, slipped an arm up around her neck, and pressed her down to his level for a kiss. He could feel the fear, as suppressed in her as it was in him, in her quick breathing and somber eyes.

"Oh, *Miles*. Tell them—tell them your brains were still thawing out back then. You weren't responsible for your judgments. Throw yourself on Illyan's mercy, quick, before it gets any worse."

He shook his head. "Any time up to last week, that might have worked, maybe, but after what I did to Vorberg? I don't think it can get any worse. *I* wouldn't have any mercy on a subordinate who pulled a trick like that, why should Illyan? Unless Illyan . . . isn't presented with the problem in the first place."

"Great and little gods, you're not thinking you can still conceal this, are you?"

"It drops out of this mission report quite neatly."

She pushed back from him, aghast. "Your brains *did* get frostbitten."

Irritated, he snapped, "Illyan cultivates his reputation for omniscience quite carefully, but it's hype. Don't let those Horus-eye badges"—he mimed the ImpSec insignia by holding his circled thumb and fingers up to his eyes, and peering through owlishly—"affect your mind. We just try to look like we always know what we're doing. I've seen the secret files, I know how screwed up things can really get, behind the scenes. That fancy memory chip in Illyan's brain doesn't make him a genius, just remarkably obnoxious."

"There are too many witnesses."

"All Dendarii missions are classified. The troops won't blab."

"Except to each other. The story's all over the ship, half-garbled. People have asked *me* about it."

"Uh . . . what did you tell them?"

She shrugged a shoulder, angrily. "I've been implying it was a suit malfunction."

"Oh. Good. Nevertheless . . . they're all here, and Illyan's way over there. A vast distance. What can he learn, except through what I tell him?"

"Only half-vast." Quinn's bared teeth had little in common with a smile.

"Come on, use your reason. I know you can. If ImpSec was going to catch this, they should have done it months ago. All the Jacksonian evidence has obviously escaped them clean."

A pulse beat in her throat. "There's nothing reasonable about this! Have you lost your grip, have you lost your frigging *mind*? I swear to the gods, you are getting as impossible to manage as your clone-brother Mark!"

"How did Mark jump into this discussion?" It was a bad sign, warning of a precipitous downhill slide in the tone of the debate. The three most ferocious arguments he'd ever had with Elli were all over Mark, all recently. Good God. He'd avoided—mostly— their usual intimacy this mission for fear of her witnessing another seizure. He hadn't thought he could explain one away as a really terrific new kind of orgasm. Had she been attributing his coolness to their lingering differences about his brother? "Mark has nothing to do with this."

"Mark has *everything* to do with this! If you hadn't gone downside after him, you would never have been killed. And you wouldn't have been left with some damned cryonic short circuit in your head. You may think he's the greatest invention since the Necklin drive, but I loathe the fat little creep!"

"Well, I like the fat little creep! Somebody has to. I swear, you are frigging jealous. Don't be such a damned cast-iron bitch!"

They were standing apart, both with their fists clenched, breathing hard. If it came to blows, he'd lose, in every sense. Instead, he bit out, "Baz and Elena are quitting, did you know that? I'm promoting you to Commodore and Fleet-second in Baz's place. Pearson will take over as Fleet engineer. And you will also be brevet captain of the *Peregrine* till you make rendezvous with the other half of the Fleet. The choice of the *Peregrine*'s new commander will be your first staff appointment. Pick someone you think you can tr . . . work with. Dismissed!"

Blast it, that was *not* how he'd intended to present Quinn with her longed-for promotion. He'd meant to lay it at her feet as a great prize, to delight her soul and reward her extraordinary effort. Not fling it at her head like a pot in the middle of a raging domestic argument, when words could no longer convey the weight of one's emotions.

Her mouth opened, closed, opened again. "And where the hell do you think you're going, without me as a bodyguard?" she bit out. "I know Illyan gave you the most explicit standing orders that you're not to travel alone without one. How much more career suicide do you think you need?"

"In this sector, a bodyguard is a formality, and a waste of resources." He inhaled. "I'll . . . take Sergeant Taura. That ought to be enough bodyguard to satisfy the most paranoid ImpSec boss. And she's certainly earned a vacation."

"Oh! You!" It was seldom indeed that Quinn ran out of invective. She turned on her heel, and stalked to the door, where she turned back and snapped him a salute, forcing him to return it. The automatic door, alas, was impossible to slam, but it seemed to shut with a snakelike hiss.

He flung himself into his station chair, and brooded at his comconsole. He hesitated. Then he called up the short mission file, and ciphered it onto a security card. He punched up the long version—and hit the erase command. *Done.*

He stuffed the ciphered report into the code-locked pouch, tossed it onto his bed, and rose to begin packing for the journey home.

THREE

The only two adjoining cabins left aboard the first Tau Ceti–bound jump-ship heading out of Zoave Twilight happened to be premier-class luxury suites. Miles smiled at this misfortune, and made a mental note to document the security necessity for Illyan's accountants, preferably while pointing out what obscene profits the mission just completed had made. He pottered about, taking his time putting away his sparse luggage, and waiting for Sergeant Taura to finish her meticulous security sweep. The lighting and decor were serene, the beds were spacious and soft, the bathrooms individual and private, and they didn't even have to go out for food; unlimited room service was included in the stiff fare. Once the ship was space-borne, they would be in effect inhabiting their own private universe for the next seven days.

The rest of the trip home would be much less inviting. At the Tau Ceti transfer station he would change uniforms and identities, and step aboard the Barrayaran government vessel in the persona of Lieutenant Lord Miles Vorkosigan, ImpSec courier, a modest young officer with the same rank and duties as the unlucky Lieutenant Vorberg. He shook out his Imperial undress greens, and hung them up in a lockable cupboard along with the uniform boots, their shine protected in a sealed bag. Courier officer always made an excellent cover-identity for Miles's wide-ranging travels to and from the Dendarii Fleet; a courier never had to explain anything. On the debit side, the company aboard the next ship would be all-male, all-military, and, alas, all Barrayaran. No bodyguard required. Sergeant Taura could split off to return to the

Dendarii, and Miles would be left alone with his fellow subjects of the Imperium.

From long experience, he anticipated their reaction to him, to his apparent undersized unfitness for his military duties. They'd say nothing overt—it would be obvious to them that he held this cushy courier's sinecure by virtue of some powerful nepotistic string-pulling on the part of his father the Viceroy Admiral Count Vor-etcetera. It was exactly the reaction he desired, to maintain his deep cover, and Lieutenant Vorkosigan the Dull would do nothing to correct their assumptions. His own slur-sensitive antennae would fill in the blanks. Well, maybe the crew would include men he'd traveled with before, used to him by now.

He locked the cupboard. Let Lieutenant Vorkosigan and all his troubles stay out of sight and out of mind, for the next week. He had more engaging concerns. His belly shivered in anticipation.

Sergeant Taura returned at last, and ducked her head through the open doorway between their two rooms. "All clear," she reported. "No bugs found anywhere. In fact, no new passengers or cargo added at all since we booked passage. We've just left orbit."

He smiled up, and up at her, his most unusual Dendarii trooper, and one of his best. No surprise that she should be good at her job; she'd been genetically engineered for the task.

Taura was the living prototype of a genetic design project of dubious morality conceived and carried out, where else, on Jackson's Whole. They'd wanted a supersoldier, and they'd assigned a research committee to carry out the project. A committee consisting entirely of biological engineers, and not one experienced soldier. They'd wanted something spectacular, to impress the client. They had certainly achieved *that*.

When Miles had first encountered her, the sixteen-year-old Taura had reached her full adult height of eight feet, all of it lean and muscular. Her fingers and toes were tipped with heavy claws, and her outslung mouth made fierce with fangs that locked over her lips. Her body seemed to glow with the radiant heat of a burning metabolism that lent her unnatural strength and speed. That, and her tawny golden eyes, gave her a wolfish air; when fully concentrated upon her work, her ferocious stare could cause armed men to drop their weapons and throw themselves flat on the floor, a psychological-warfare effect Miles had actually witnessed, on one delightful occasion.

Miles had long thought that she was one of the most beautiful women he had ever seen, in her own way. You just had to be able to see her properly. And unlike his blurred-together Dendarii missions, Miles could enumerate every rare occasion they had ever made love, from their very first encounter, six, seven years ago now? From before he and Quinn had ever become a couple, in point of fact. Taura was some kind of very special first for him, as he had been for her, and that secret bond had never faded.

Oh, they'd tried to be good. Dendarii regs against cross-rank fraternization were for the benefit of all, to protect the rankers from exploitation and the officers from losing control of discipline, or worse. And Miles had been quite determined, as the young and earnest Admiral Naismith, to set a good example for his troops, a virtuous resolve that had slipped away . . . somewhere. After the umpteenth we've-lost-count-again time he had been almost killed, perhaps.

Well, if you couldn't be good, at least you could be *discreet.*

"Very good, Sergeant." He held out a hand to her. "You may as well take a break—for the next seven days, eh?"

Her face lit; her lips drew back in a smile that fully exposed her fangs. "Really?" she said, her resonant voice thrilling.

"Really."

She trod over to him, her muscled mass making the deck creak slightly beneath her Dendarii combat boots, and bent to exchange a promissory kiss. Her mouth, as always, was hot and exhilarating. The fangs might be a subliminal trigger to that adrenaline rush, but mostly it was just the sheer wonderful . . . *Taura-ness* of her. She was life-relishing, experience-devouring, living in an eternal Now, and for very good reasons. . . . He forced his mind away from a descending swoop on that future, or any other, and curled his hand around the back of her head to loosen the neatly pinned-up braid of her mahogany hair.

"I'll freshen up," she grinned, breaking away after a time. She twitched at her loosened gray uniform jacket.

"Enjoy the hell out of the bathing facilities," he advised cordially. "It's the most sybaritic setup I've seen since Dyne Station's Ambassadorial Baths."

He retreated to his own facility, to ditch uniform and rank insignia and to engage in a pleasant ritual of leisurely preparation, involving depilation, cleanliness, and cologne. Taura deserved the best. She also deserved all the time she wanted. Seldom could she shed the stern Sergeant, and reveal that feminine self shyly hidden on the inside. Seldom indeed could she trust anyone to guard that vulnerability. The Fairy Princess, he thought of her. *We all have our secret identities, it seems.*

He dressed himself sarong-fashion in a prewarmed fluffy towel, and went to perch on his bed, waiting alertly. Had she anticipated this private space together, and if so, what little garment would she bring out of her valise this time? She *would* insist on trying out these would-be sexy numbers on him, not seeming to realize how like a goddess she was already when dressed in nothing but her streaming hair. Well, all right, not streaming hair; left to its own devices it tended to go stiff and uncooperative and frizzy, tickling his nose, but it looked good on her. He hoped she had managed to lose the horrifying pink thing with the red feathers. It had taken all his tact, last time, to get across the idea that perhaps the color and design choice did not compliment her best features, without ever once intimating any fault in her taste or personal appearance. She might be able to break him with one hand, but he could kill her with a word. *Never.*

His own face lit with unabashed delight at her return. She was wearing something cream-colored and sleek and shimmery-silky, meters of fabric so fine one might with little effort draw it through a ring. The goddess-effect was nicely enhanced, her immense intrinsic dignity unimpaired. "Oh, splendid!" he caroled, with unfeigned enthusiasm.

"Do you really think so?" She spun for him; the silk floated outward, along with a spicy-musky scent that seemed to go straight up his nostrils to his back-brain with no intervening stops. Her bare toes did not click on the floor—prudently, she had trimmed and blunted all her nails, before painting them with gold enamel. He'd have no hard-to-explain need for stitches or surgical glue this time.

She lay down beside him, their ludicrous height-difference obviated. Here at last they might fill their hunger for human, or almost-human, touch until sated, without interruption, without comment. . . . He bristled defensively inside, at the thought of anyone watching this, of some abrupt surprised bark of laughter or sarcastic witticism. Was his edginess because he was breaking his own rules? He didn't expect any outsider to understand this relationship.

Did he understand it himself? Once, he might have mumbled something about the thrill, an obsession with mountain climbing, the ultimate sex fantasy for a short guy. Later, maybe something about a blow for life against death. Maybe it was simpler than that.

Maybe it was just love.

———— ‹(●)› ————

He woke much, much later, and watched her as she slept. It was a measure of her trust, that his slight stirring did not bring her hyperawake, as her genetically programmed drives usually rendered her. Of all her many and fascinating responses, the fact that she *slept* for him was the most telling, if one knew her inside story.

He studied the play of light and shadow over her long, long ivory body, half-draped with their well-stirred sheets. He let his hand flow along the curves, a few centimeters from the surface, buoyed by the feverish heat rising from her golden skin. The gentle movement of her breathing made the shadows dance. Her breathing was, as always, a little too deep, a little too fast. He wanted to slow it down. As if not her days, but her inhalations and exhalations were numbered, and when she'd used them all up . . .

She was the last survivor of her fellow prototypes. They had all been genetically programmed for short lives, in part, perhaps, as a sort of fail-safe mechanism, in part, perhaps, in an effort to inculcate soldierly courage, out of some dim theory that a short life would be more readily sacrificed in battle than a long one. Miles did not think the researchers had quite understood courage, or life. The supersoldiers had died fast, when they died, with no lingering years of arthritic old age to gradually wean them from their mortality. They suffered only weeks, months at most, of a deterioration as fierce as their lives had been. It was as if they were designed to go up in flame, not down in shame. He studied the tiny silver glints in Taura's mahogany hair. They had not been there last year.

She's only twenty-two, for God's sake.

The Dendarii fleet surgeon had studied her carefully, and given her drugs to slow her ferocious metabolism. She only ate as much as two men now, not four. Year by year, like pulling hot gold wire through a screen, they had extended Taura's life. Yet sometime, that wire must snap.

How much more time? A year? Two? When he returned to the

Dendarii next time, would she still be there to greet him, with a proper, *Hello, Admiral Naismith* in public, and a most improper, not to mention rude and raucous, *Howdy, Lover!* in private . . . ?

It's a good thing she loves Admiral Naismith. Lord Vorkosigan couldn't handle this.

He thought a bit guiltily of Admiral Naismith's other lover, the public and acknowledged Quinn. Nobody had to explain or excuse being in love with the beautiful Quinn. She was self-evidently his match.

He was not, exactly, being unfaithful to Elli Quinn. Technically, Taura predated her. And he and Quinn had exchanged no vows, no oaths, no promises. Not for lack of asking; he'd asked her a painful number of times. But she too was in love with Admiral Naismith. Not Lord Vorkosigan. The thought of becoming Lady Vorkosigan, grounded downside forever on a planet she herself had stigmatized as a "backwater dirtball," had been enough to send space-bred Quinn screaming in the opposite direction, or at least, excusing herself uneasily.

Admiral Naismith's love-life was some sort of adolescent's dream: unlimited and sometimes astonishing sex, no responsibilities. Why didn't it seem to be working anymore?

He loved Quinn, loved the energy and intelligence and drive of her, their shared passion for the military life. She was one of the most wonderful friends he'd ever had. But in the end, she offered him only . . . sterility. They had no more future together than did he and Elena, bound to Baz, or he and Taura. *Who is dying.*

God, I hurt. It would be almost a relief, to escape Admiral Naismith, and return to Lord Vorkosigan. Lord Vorkosigan had no sex life.

He paused. So . . . when had that happened, that . . . lack in his life? *Rather a long time ago, actually.* Odd. He hadn't noticed it before.

Taura's eyes half-opened, honey-colored glints. She favored him with a sleepy, fanged smile.

"Hungry?" he asked her, confident of the answer.

"Uh huh."

They spent a pleasant few minutes studying the lengthy menu provided by the ship's galley, then punched in a massive order. With Taura along, Miles realized cheerfully, he might get to try a bite of nearly everything, with no embarrassing wasteful leftovers.

While waiting for their feast to arrive, Taura piled pillows and sat up in bed, and regarded him with a reminiscent gleam in her gold eyes. "Do you remember the first time you fed me?"

"Yes. In Ryoval's dungeons. That repellent dry ration bar."

"Better rat bars than raw rats, let me tell you."

"I can do better now."

"And how."

When people were rescued, they ought to stay rescued. Wasn't that the deal? *And then we all live happily ever after, right? Till we die.* But with this medical discharge threat hanging over his head, was he so sure that it was Taura who would go first? Maybe it would be Admiral Naismith after all. . . . "That was one of my first personnel retrievals. Still one of the best, in a sort of cock-eyed way."

"Was it love at first sight, for you?"

"Mm . . . no, truthfully. More like terror at first sight. Falling in love took, oh, an hour or so."

"Me, too. I didn't really start to fall seriously in love with you till you came back for me."

"You do know . . . that didn't exactly start out as a rescue mission." An understatement: he'd been hired to "terminate the experiment."

"But you turned it into one. It's your favorite kind, I think. You always seem to be especially cheerful whenever you're running a rescue, no matter how hairy things are getting."

"Not all the rewards of my job are financial. I don't deny, it's an emotional kick to pull some desperate somebody out of a deep, deep hole. Especially when nobody else thinks it can be done. I adore showing off, and the audience is always so *appreciative.*" Well, maybe not Vorberg.

"I've sometimes wondered if you're like that Barrayaran fellow you told me about, who went around giving everybody liver patés for Winterfair 'cause he loved them himself. And was always frustrated that no one ever gave *him* any."

"I don't need to be rescued. Usually." Last year's sojourn on Jackson's Whole having been a memorable exception. Except that his memory of it had a big three-month blank in it.

"Mm, not *rescue*, exactly. Rescue's consequence. Freedom. You give freedom away whenever you can. Is it because it's something you want yourself?"

And can't have? "Naw. It's the adrenaline high I crave."

Their dinner arrived, on two carts. Miles sent away the human steward at the door, and he and Taura busied themselves in a brief domestic bustle, getting it all nicely arranged. The cabin was so spacious, the table wasn't even fold-down, but permanently bolted to the deck. Miles nibbled, and watched Taura eat. Feeding Taura always made him feel strangely happy inside. It was an impressive sight in its own right. "Don't overlook those little fried cheese things with the spicy sauce," he pointed out helpfully. "Lots of calories in them, I'm sure."

"Thanks." A companionable silence fell, broken only by steady munching.

"Contented?" he inquired.

She swallowed a bite of something meltingly delicious formed into a dense cake in the shape of a star. "Oh, yes."

He smiled. She had a talent for happiness, he decided, living in the present as she so carefully did. Did the foreknowledge of her death ever ride upon her shoulder like a carrion crow . . . ? *Yes, of course it does. But let us not break the mood.*

"Did you mind, when you found out last year that I was Lord Vorkosigan? That Admiral Naismith wasn't real?"

She shrugged. "It seemed right to me. I always thought you ought to be some sort of prince in disguise."

"Hardly that!" he laughed. *God save me from the Imperium, amen.* Or maybe he was lying now, instead of then. Maybe Admiral Naismith was the real one, Lord Vorkosigan put on like a mask. Naismith's flat Betan accent fell so trippingly from his tongue. Vorkosigan's Barrayaran gutturals seemed to require an increasingly conscious effort, anymore. Naismith was so easy to slip into, Vorkosigan so . . . painful.

"Actually"—he picked up the thread of their previous conversation, confident that she would follow—"freedom is exactly what I don't want. Not in the sense of being aimless, or, or . . . unemployed." *Especially not unemployed.* "It's not *free time* that I want—the present moment excepted," he added hastily. She nodded encouragement. "I want . . . my destiny, I guess. To be, or become, as fully *me* as I possibly can." Hence the invention of Admiral Naismith, to hold all those parts of himself for which there was no room on Barrayar.

He'd thought about it, God knew, a hundred times. Thought of abandoning Vorkosigan forever, and becoming just Naismith. Kick free of the financial and patriotic shackles of ImpSec, go renegade, make a galactic living with the Dendarii Free Mercenary Fleet. But that was a one-way trip. For a Vor lord to possess a private military force was high treason, illegal as hell, a capital crime. He could never go home again, once he went down that road.

Above all, he could not do that to his father. *The-Count-my-Father,* a name spoken all in one breath. Not while the old man lived, and hoped all his old-Barrayaran hopes for his son. He wasn't sure how his mother would react, Betan to the bone as she was even after all these years of living on Barrayar. She'd have no objection to the principle of the thing, but she didn't exactly approve of the military. She didn't exactly disapprove, either; she just made it plain that she thought there were better things for intelligent human beings to do with their lives. And once his father died . . . Miles would be Count Vorkosigan, with a District, and an important vote in the Council of Counts, and duties all day long. . . . *Live, Father. Live long.*

There were parts of himself for which Admiral Naismith held no place, either.

"Speaking of memorable rescues"—Taura's lovely baritone brought him back to the present—"how's your poor clone-twin Mark getting along now? Has he found his destiny yet?"

At least *Taura* didn't refer to his one and only sibling as *the fat little creep.* He smiled at her, gratefully. "Quite well, I think. He left Barrayar with my parents when they departed for Sergyar, stayed with them a bit, then went on to Beta Colony. My Betan grandmother is keeping an eye on him for Mother. He's signed in at the University of Silica, same town as she lives in—studying accounting, of all things. He seems to like it. Sort of incomprehensible. I can't help feeling one's twin ought to share more of one's tastes than an ordinary sib."

"Maybe later in life, you'll grow more alike."

"I don't think Mark will ever involve himself with the military again."

"No, but maybe you'll get interested in accounting."

He glanced up suspiciously—oh, good. She *was* joking. He could tell by the crinkle at the corners of her eyes. But when they uncrinkled, faint crow's feet still tracked there. "As long as I never acquire his girth."

He sipped his wine. Mention of Mark recalled Jackson's Whole, and his cryo-revival, and all his secret problems that were presently spinning out in unwelcome consequence. It also recalled Dr. Durona, his cryo-revival surgeon. Had the refugee Durona sisters actually succeeded in setting up their new clinic on Escobar, far from their unbeloved ex-home? Mark ought to know; he was still channeling money to them, according to his last communication. And if so, were they ready to take on a new, or rather, old patient yet? Very, very quietly?

He could take a long leave, ostensibly to visit his parents on Sergyar. From Sergyar it was only a short hop to Escobar. Once there he could see Rowan Durona. . . . He might even be able to slip it past Illyan even more openly, feigning it was a trip to see a lover. Or at least slip it past the Count. Even ImpSec agents were allowed, grudgingly, to have private lives, though if Illyan himself had one it was news to Miles. Miles's brief love affair with Rowan had been sort of a mistake, an accident that had happened while he was still suffering from cryo-amnesia. But they had parted, he thought, on good terms. Might he persuade her to treat him, yet make no records of it for ImpSec to find?

It *could* be done . . . get his head fixed, whatever the hell was wrong with it, and go quietly on, with no one the wiser. Right?

Part of him was already beginning to regret not decanting both versions of his mission report to ImpSec onto cipher-cards, and saving the final decision for later, when he'd had a bit more time to think it through. Turn in the one, eat the other. But he was committed now, and if he was committed, he needed a better plan than trusting to luck.

Escobar it was. As soon as his schedule allowed. Extremely annoying, that he wasn't being routed through Escobar on this run home.

He sat back, and regarded the triumphant litter of plates, cups, glasses, and bowls crowding the table, looking rather like a battle scene after . . . well, after Taura had been through. No more mopping up required. He glanced past her silk-draped shoulder to their bed. "Well, milady. A nap? Or something?"

She followed his glance. "Something. Then a nap," she decided.

"At your command." He bowed vorishly, sitting, and rose to take her hand. "Seize the night."

FOUR

As was standard operating procedure for returning couriers, an ImpSec groundcar and driver picked up Miles at the military shuttleport outside Vorbarr Sultana, and whisked him directly to ImpSec headquarters downtown. He wished the driver would slow down, or circle the block a few more times, as HQ loomed up around the last corner. As if the frustrating weeks he had spent thinking about his dilemma aboard the government ship on the way home were not enough. He didn't need more thought, he needed *action.*

The driver passed the security checkpoint and pulled through the gates to the massive gray building, vast and grim and foreboding. The impression was not all due to Miles's state of mind; ImpSec HQ was one of the ugliest buildings in Vorbarr Sultana. Tourists from the backcountry, who might otherwise have been expected to avoid the place, drove by just to look at it, in honor of the interesting reputation of the architect, whom legend had it had died insane after the abrupt eclipse of his patron Emperor Yuri. The driver took Miles past the daunting facade, and around to the discreet side entrance reserved for couriers, spies, informers, analysts, secretaries, janitors, and others with real business in the place.

Miles dismissed driver and car with a wave, and stood in the autumn afternoon chill outside the door, hesitating one last time. He had a sinking conviction his carefully crafted plan was never going to work.

And even if it did work, I'd have my head cranked over my shoulder forever, waiting to be caught ex post facto. No. He would not go through with it. He would turn in the doctored cipher-card, yes, he'd left himself no choice there, but then (and before Illyan had a chance to review the thrice-damned thing) he would give Illyan his verbal report and tell him the exact truth. He could feign that he'd felt the news of his medical flaw was too hot to put on record even in cipher. As if he were tossing the problem, promptly and properly, into Illyan's lap for decision. It wasn't physically possible for Miles to have made it home any faster anyway.

If he stood here in the cold any longer, pretending to study the stylized granite monsters carved in low relief on the door lintel— *pressed gargoyles*, some wag had dubbed them—a guard would come up and make polite and pointed inquiries at him. Determined, he slid out of his military greatcoat and folded it neatly over his arm, clutched the cipher-case to his green tunic, and stepped inside.

The clerk at the desk checked him through the usual security ID procedures without comment. It was all very routine. He left his coat—which had never come from any military store, but instead had been tailor-made to fit his very nonstandard size—in the checkroom. It was a measure of his security clearance that he was sent off without an escort to find his own way to Illyan's not-very-accessible office. You had to go up two different lift tubes and down a third to get to that floor.

Once he'd arrived, and passed through the last scanner in the corridor, he found the door of the outer office open. Illyan's secretary was at his desk, talking with General Lucas Haroche, Head of Domestic Affairs. The general's title always put Miles in mind of a gigolo for bored wives, but in fact it was one of the nastier and more thankless jobs in the service, tracking would-be treason plots and antigovernment groups strictly on the Barrayaran side. His counterpart General Allegre had the full-time task of doing the same for restive, conquered Komarr.

Miles usually dealt with the Head of Galactic Affairs (a much more exotic and evocative title, in Miles's opinion) on the rare occasions when he didn't deal with Illyan directly. But the G.A. was stationed on Komarr, and Miles had been routed straight back to Barrayar this time without stopping at the planet that guarded Barrayar's only jump-point gateway to the wormhole nexus. *One must assume it's urgent.* Maybe it would even be urgent enough to divert Illyan's negative attentions from Miles's bad news.

"Hello, Captain. Hello, General Haroche." As the supposedly junior officer present, Miles greeted them both with a vaguely directed salute, which they returned as casually. Miles did not know Illyan's secretary well; the man had held this critical position for about two years, which gave Miles at least six years seniority on him as an Illyan-satellite, if one wanted to think of it in those terms.

The secretary held out his hand for the cipher-case. "Your report, good. Sign it in, please."

"I . . . sort of wanted to hand this one to the boss personally." Miles nodded to Illyan's closed inner door.

"Can't, today. He's not in."

"Not in? I expected . . . there were some things I needed to add verbally."

"I'll pass them on for you, as soon as he gets back."

"Will he be back soon? I can wait."

"Not today. He's out of town."

Shit. "Well . . ." Reluctantly, Miles handed over the case to its proper recipient, and pressed his palm four times to the com-console's read-pad to affirm and document delivery. "So . . . did he leave any orders for me? He must have known when I would arrive."

"Yes, Lieutenant. You are to take leave until he calls you in."

"I thought this was urgent, or why rush me home on the first ship? I've just had several weeks of time off, cooped up on board."

"What can I say?" The secretary shrugged. "Occasionally, ImpSec remembers it is the military. Hurry up and wait."

Miles would get no unauthorized information out of *him.* But if there was that much time . . . his clever little plan to skin off to Escobar for secret treatment, so recently suppressed, reared up out of the mire again. "Leave, huh? Do I have time and permission to visit my parents on Sergyar?"

"I'm afraid not. You are to hold yourself ready to report back here on a one-hour notice. You'd better not depart the city." At Miles's dismayed look, he added, "Sorry, Lieutenant Vorkosigan."

Not half as sorry as I am. He was put forcibly in mind of his own sententious motto about no battle plan surviving first contact with the enemy. "Well . . . tell Illyan I'd like to see him, at his earliest convenience."

"Of course." The secretary made a note.

"And how are your parents, Lieutenant Vorkosigan?" inquired

General Haroche cordially. Haroche was a graying man of fifty-odd, who wore slightly rumpled undress greens. Miles liked Haroche's voice, which was deep and rich and sometimes humorous, with a faint provincial accent from the western districts that his years in the capital hadn't quite smoothed away. Haroche's work had gained him a formidible reputation in ImpSec's inner circles, though it was practically unknown to outsiders, a dilemma Miles appreciated. He predated Miles as a fixture at ImpSec HQ by a year or so; but a decade in Haroche's job, Miles reflected, would give anybody gray hairs, and stomach trouble too.

"You probably have more recent information on them than I do, sir. I think my mail's chasing me back home from the drop at Galactic Affairs HQ on Komarr."

Haroche turned his hands palm-out, and shrugged. "No, not really. Illyan has split out Sergyar from my department, and created a separate Department for Sergyaran Affairs equal with the Komarran."

"Surely there's not that much for a separate department to do," said Miles. "The colony's less than thirty years old. The population isn't even up to a million yet, is it?"

"Just barely," put in the secretary.

Haroche smiled a bit grimly. "*I* thought it was premature, but what the illustrious Viceroy Count Vorkosigan requests . . . has a way of happening." He half-lidded his eyes, as if casting Miles a significant look.

Don't you give me that nepotism crap, Haroche. You know what my real work is. And how well I do it. "Sounds like another cushy ImpSec desk job to me. The colonists are too busy working their tails off to foment rebellion. Maybe I ought to apply for it."

"It's already been filled, I'm afraid. By Colonel Olshansky."

"Oh? I've heard he's a steady man. Sergyar is certainly in a critical strategic position in the wormhole nexus, but I thought that aspect came under Galactic Affairs. Illyan's looking to the future, I suppose." Miles sighed. "I guess I may as well go on home. The office can find me at Vorkosigan House, when it decides it wants me."

The secretary's lips stretched in a sinister smile. "Oh, we can find you wherever you are."

It was an ImpSec-ish in-joke. Miles laughed dutifully, and escaped.

Miles arrived at the last lift-tube foyer on the way back to the exit simultaneously with a captain in undress greens, a dark-haired, middle-aged fellow with intense, hooded, nutmeg-brown eyes and a fleshy blade of a nose sweeping down his roman profile: a familiar but entirely unexpected face.

"Duv Galeni!" said Miles. "What are you doing here?"

"Well, hello, Miles." Galeni smiled as much as Galeni ever smiled, a pleased grimace. He was a little older and a little thicker than when Miles had last seen him, but seemed relaxed and confident. "Working, of course. I requested reassignment here."

"Last we met you were doing that stint in counterintelligence on Komarr. Is this a promotion? Did you develop a sudden hankering for desk work over field work? Did you come to bask in the somewhat radioactive glow from the centers of Imperial power?"

"All of the above, plus . . ." Galeni glanced around, as if to be sure they were alone. What secret was so sensitive it must be whispered here, in the very center of the labyrinth? "There's this woman."

"Good God, that sounds like one of my cousin Ivan's lines. You, a woman, and what?"

"Don't you dare hoot at me. Don't you still have that, ah, enviable arrangement with the formidable Quinn?"

Miles controlled a wince, thinking of his and Quinn's last argument. "More or less." He *had* to get back and fix it with Quinn at his earliest opportunity. She'd relented enough to come to see him off at the *Peregrine*'s shuttle hatch, but their good-byes had been formal and strained.

"There you go," said Galeni tolerantly. "She's a Komarran. From the Toscane family. After she took a doctoral degree in business theory on Komarr, she went into the family transshipping concern. She's now stationed in Vorbarr Sultana as a permanent lobbyist with the trade group representing all the Komarran shipping concessions, as sort of an interface between them and the Imperium. A brilliant woman."

Coming from Galeni, who'd taken an academic doctorate in history himself before becoming one of the first Komarrans ever admitted to the Imperial military service, this was high praise. "So . . . are you romancing her, or thinking of hiring her for your department?"

Miles swore Galeni almost blushed. "This is serious, Vorkosigan."

"Ambitious, too. If she's a scion of *those* Toscanes."

"I was a scion of *those* Galens, once. Back when the Galens rated that particular inflection."

"Thinking of rebuilding the family fortunes, are you?"

"Mm . . . times have changed. And they aren't changing back. But they are changing onward. It's time for a little ambition in my life, I think. I'm almost forty, you know."

"And tottering on the brink of complete decrepitude, obviously." Miles grinned. "Well, congratulations. Or should I say, good luck?"

"I'll take the luck, I believe. Congratulations are still premature. But they will be in order soon, I hope. And you?"

My love-life is entirely too complicated at the moment. Or at any rate . . . Admiral Naismith's is. "Oh! You mean, work. I'm, ah . . . not working, at present. I just got back from a little galactic tour."

Galeni twitched an eyebrow in understanding; his own encounter several years past with the Dendarii mercenaries and "Admiral Naismith" was certainly still vivid in his memory. "Are you headed up and in, or down and out?"

Miles pointed to the down tube. "I'm headed home. I have a few days leave."

"Maybe I'll see you around town, then." Galeni swung into the down tube, and rendered Miles a cheerful parting semisalute.

"I hope so. Take care." Miles descended in turn, exiting at the ground floor.

At the side entrance's security desk, Miles paused in a minor dilemma. Every time he'd ever gone home after a final ImpSec mission debriefing, he'd either called for a car from the Count's garage, driven by an Armsman or servant, or more often found one waiting for him when he emerged from Illyan's lair. But Armsmen, servants, vehicles, and all the rest of the household had decamped with the Count and Countess for the Viceroy's Palace on Sergyar (though his mother had written him dryly that the term "palace" was most misleading). So should he requisition a ride from ImpSec HQ's motor pool? Or order a commercial cab? Though one might be certain that any cab which came here had been vetted by Security first. He'd sent his sparse luggage directly home from the shuttleport.

It was chill and gray out, but not raining. And he'd just spent a great many days stuck aboard a decidedly cramped (if fast) jump-ship. He collected his greatcoat and stepped outside. He was only under orders to keep a bodyguard on duty at all times during his *galactic* travels, after all.

It was about four kilometers from ImpSec HQ to Vorkosigan House, both centrally located in the Old Town. *I do believe I'll walk home.*

⸺◈⸺

He turned the last corner onto the street Vorkosigan House faced just as the gray afternoon darkened into drizzle, and con-gratulated himself on his timing. Four kilometers in . . . well, maybe it wasn't the fastest time he'd ever done, but at least he wasn't gasping for breath as he would have been six months ago.

The brisk walk had been a . . . nonevent. The streets of the central capital were thick with afternoon traffic and clogged with pedestrians, who hurried past on their various businesses, sparing barely a glance for the striding little man in military dress. No long stares, no rude gestures or comments, not even one covert old hex sign against mutation. Had getting rid of his uneven limp, leg braces, and most of the crookedness in his back made that much difference? Or was the difference in the Barrayarans?

Three old-style mansions had once shared the city block. For security reasons the one on this end had been bought up by the Imperium during the period Miles's father had been Regent, and now housed some minor bureaucratic offices. The one on the other end, more dilapidated and with bad drains, had been torn down and replaced only by a little park. In their day, a century and a half ago, the great houses must have loomed magnificently over the horse-drawn carriages and riders clopping past. Now they were overshadowed by taller modern buildings across the street.

Vorkosigan House sat in the center, set off from the street by a narrow green strip of lawn and garden in the loop of the semi-circular drive. A stone wall topped with black wrought-iron spikes surrounded it all. The four stories of great gray stone blocks, in two main wings plus some extra odd architectural bits, rose in a vast archaic mass. All it needed was window slits and a moat. *And a few bats and ravens, for decoration.* Earth-descended bats were rare on Barrayar, as there were not enough earth-descended insects for them to eat, and the native creatures incorrectly called bugs were usually toxic when ingested. A force screen just inside the wall provided the real protection, and eliminated the romantic possibility of bats. A concrete kiosk beside the gate housed the gate guards; in the heyday of the Regency three full platoons of ImpSec guards had traded shifts around the clock, in posts all around the building and for several blocks beyond, watching the important government men hurry in and out.

Now there was one lone gate guard, a young ImpSec corporal who poked his head out the open door at the sound of Miles's steps, emerged, and saluted him. A new man, no one Miles recognized.

"Good afternoon, Lieutenant Vorkosigan," the young man said. "I was expecting you. They brought your valise a couple of hours ago. I scanned it and everything; it's ready to go in."

"Thank you, Corporal." Gravely, Miles returned his salute. "Been any excitement around here lately?"

"Not really, sir. Not since the Count and Countess left. About the most action we've had was the night a feral cat somehow got past the scanner beams and ran into the tangle-field. I never knew cats could make such a racket. She apparently thought she was about to be killed and eaten."

Miles's eye took in an empty sandwich wrapper on the floor, shoved against the far wall, and a small saucer of milk. A flicker of light from the banks of vid displays for the perimeter monitors in the kiosk's second tiny room cast a chilly glow through the narrow doorway. "And, er . . . was she? Killed, I mean."

"Oh, no, sir. Fortunately."

"Good." He retrieved his valise, after an awkward scramble with the guard as he belatedly tried to hand it to Miles. From the shadows under the guard's chair beside the saucer, a pair of yellow-green eyes glinted in feline paranoia at him. The young corporal had an interesting collection of long black cat hairs decorating the front of his uniform, and deep half-healed scratches scoring his hands. Keeping pets on duty was highly unregulation. Nine hours a day stuck in this tiny bunker . . . he must be bored out of his mind.

"The palm-locks have all been reset for you, sir," the guard went on helpfully. "I've rechecked everything. Twice. Can I carry that for you? Do you know how long you will be here? Will there be anything . . . going on?"

"I don't know. I'll let you know." The kid was clearly longing for a little conversation, but Miles was tired. Maybe later. Miles turned to trudge up the drive, but then turned back. "What did you name her?"

"Sir?"

"The cat."

A look of slight panic crossed the young man's face, as that regulation about pets no doubt recalled itself to his mind. "Er . . . Zap, sir."

He was honest, at least. "How appropriate. Carry on, Corporal." Miles gave him a parting ImpSec HQ Analyst's salute, which was a sort of wave of two fingers in the general vicinity of one's temple; ImpSec analysts tended not to have a great deal of respect for anyone whose measured IQ was lower than their own, which included most of the rest of the Imperial Service. The guard returned a snappier grateful version.

When did ImpSec start sending us children for gate guards? The grim men who'd patrolled the place in Miles's father's day would have executed the unfortunate cat on the spot, and sifted its remains for scanning devices and bombs afterwards. The kid must be all of . . . *at least twenty-one years old, if he's ImpSec and that rank in the capital.* Miles controlled a slight twinge of disassociation, and strode up the drive and under the porte cochere, out of the drizzle that was becoming outright rain.

He pressed the palm-lock pad to the right of the front door; its two halves swung out with stately grace to admit him, and closed again behind him as he stepped across the threshold. It felt quite odd, to open the door himself; there had *always* been a Vorkosigan Armsman in the House uniform of brown and silver on duty to admit him. *When did they automate that door?*

The great entry hall with its black-and-white paved floor was chill and shadowy, as the rain and gloom of early evening leached away the light. Miles almost spoke, *Lights!*, to bring up the illumination, but paused, and set down his valise. In his whole life, he'd never had Vorkosigan House entirely to himself.

"Someday, my son, all this will be yours," he whispered experimentally into the shadows. The hard-edged echo of his words seemed to rasp back up from the tessellated pavement. He suppressed a slight shudder. He turned to the right, and began a slow tour of the premises.

The carpet in the next room muffled the lonely clump of his boots. All the remaining furniture—about half seemed to be missing—was covered with ghostly white sheeting. He circled the entire first floor. The place seemed both larger and smaller than he'd remembered, a puzzling paradox.

He checked out the garage occupying the whole eastern wing's sub-basement level. His own lightflyer was tucked neatly into a corner. A barge of an armored groundcar, polished and luxurious but elderly, occupied another. He thought of his combat armor. *I probably ought not to attempt to drive or fly, either, till this damned glitch in my head gets straightened out.* In the lightflyer, he risked killing himself in a seizure; in the land-barge, anyone else on the road. Last winter, before he'd convinced himself that he was healing as promised, he'd gotten really good at apparently casually cadging rides.

He ascended one of the back stairways to the huge kitchen on the lower level. It had always been a lucrative locale for treats and company when he was a child, full of interesting, busy people like cooks and Armsmen and servants, and even an occasional hungry Imperial Regent, wandering through looking for a snack. Some utensils remained, but the place had been stripped of food, nothing left in the pantries or the walk-in freezer or refrigerators, which were tepid and disconnected.

He reset the smallest refrigerator. If he was going to be here very long, he would have to get food. Or a servant. One servant would certainly do. Yet he didn't want a stranger in here . . . maybe one of the recently pensioned folks lived in retirement nearby, and might be persuaded to come back for a few days. But he might not be here very long. Maybe he would buy some ready-meals—*not* military service issue, thank you. There *was* an impressive amount of wine and spirits left to age undisturbed in the climate-controlled cellar, the lock of which opened to his Vorkosigan palm. He brought up a couple of bottles of a particularly chewy red, laid down in his grandfather's day.

Not troubling to switch on the lift-tube, he hauled both bottles and the valise up the curving stairs to his third-floor bedroom in the side wing, which overlooked the back garden. This time he called up the lights, as true night was lending more danger than melancholy angst to his stumbling around in the dark. The chamber was exactly as he'd left it . . . only four months ago? Too neat and tidy; no one had really lived here for a long time. Well, Lord Vorkosigan had dragged in for a good period last winter, but he hadn't been in condition then to make many waves.

I could order in some food. Split it with the gate guard. But he really didn't feel that hungry.

I could do anything I wanted. Anything at all.

Except for the one and only thing he did want, which was to depart tonight aboard the fastest jump-ship available bound for Escobar, or some equally medically advanced galactic depot. He growled, wordlessly. What he did instead was unpack his valise and put everything neatly away, shed his boots and hang up his uniform, and shuck on some comfortable old ship-knits.

He sat on his bed and poured some wine into his bathroom tumbler. He'd avoided alcohol and every other possible drug or druglike substance all the way out to that last mission with the Dendarii; it seemed not to have made any difference to the rare and erratic seizures. If he stayed here quietly alone inside Vorkosigan House until his meeting with Illyan, if an episode occurred again at least no one could witness it.

I'll have a drink, then order some food. Tomorrow, he must form another plan of attack on the . . . the damned *saboteur* lurking in his neurons.

The wine slid down smoky, rich, and warming. Self-sedation seemed to require more alcohol than it used to, a problem easily remedied; the desensitization might be yet another side effect of the cryo-revival, but he was glumly afraid it was simply due to age. He slipped into sleep about two-thirds through the bottle.

———◦《◦》◦———

By noon the next day the problem of food was becoming acute, despite a couple of painkillers for breakfast, and the absence of coffee and tea turning downright desperate. *I'm ImpSec trained. I can figure out this problem. Somebody* must have been going for groceries all these years . . . no, come to think of it, kitchen supplies had been delivered daily by a lift-van; he remembered the Armsmen inspecting it. The chief cook had practically had the duties of a company quartermaster, handling the nutritional logistics of Count, Countess, a couple dozen servants, twenty Armsmen, an assortment of *their* dependents, peckish ImpSec guards not above cadging a snack, and frequent State dinners, parties, or receptions where guests might number in the hundreds.

The comconsole in the cook's cubicle off the kitchen soon

yielded up the data Miles sought. There had been a regular supplier—the account was now closed, but he could surely open it again. Their list of offerings was astonishing in its scope, their prices even more so. *How* many marks had they been paying for eggs?—oh. That was twelve *dozen* eggs to a crate, not twelve eggs. Miles tried to imagine what he could do with a hundred and forty-four eggs. Maybe back when he'd been thirteen years old. Some opportunities just came too late in life.

Instead he turned to the vid directory. The closest purveyor was a small midtown grocery about six blocks away. Another quandary: dare he drive? *Walk there. Take a commercial cab home.*

The place turned out to be an odd little hole in the wall, but it supplied coffee, tea, milk, a reasonable number of eggs, a box of instant groats, and an array of prepackaged items labeled *Reddi-Meals!* He stacked up two of each of the five flavors. On impulse, he also snagged a half-dozen foil packets of expensive squishy cat food, the smelly stuff cats liked. So . . . should he slip it to the gate guard? Or attempt to seduce Zap the Cat to his own following? After the incident with the tangle-field, the beast probably would not be hanging around the back door of Vorkosigan House much.

He gathered up his spoils and took them to the checkout, where the clerk looked him up and down and gave him a peculiar smile. He braced himself inwardly for some snide remark, *Ah, mutant?* He should have worn his ImpSec uniform; nobody dared sneer at that Horus-eye winking from his collar. But what she said was, "Ah. Bachelor?"

His return home and midafternoon breakfast occupied another hour. Five hours till dark. More hours till bedtime. It did not take nearly all that time to look up every cryo-neurology clinic and specialist on Barrayar, and arrange the list in two orders; medical reputation, and the probability of keeping his visit secret from ImpSec. That second requirement was the sticking point. He really didn't want any but the best messing around with his head, but the best were going to be depressingly hard to convince to, say, treat a patient and keep no records. Escobar? Barrayar? Or should he wait until he got out on his next galactic mission assignment, as far from HQ as possible?

He paced the house, restlessly, turning over memories in his mind. This had been Elena's room. That tiny chamber had belonged to Armsman Bothari, her father. Here was where Ivan had slipped through the safety-railing, fallen half a story, and cut his head open, with no discernible effects on his intellect. It had been hoped the fall would make him smarter. . . .

For his evening meal, Miles decided to keep up the standards. He donned his dress greens, pulled all the covers off the furniture in the State dining room, and set up his wine with a proper crystal glass at the head of the meters-long table. He almost hunted up a plate, but reflected he could save the washing up by eating the *Reddi-Meal!* out of its packet. He piped in soft music. Other than that, dinner took about five minutes. When he'd finished, he dutifully put the covers back on the polished wood and fine chairs.

If I'd had the Dendarii here, I could have had a real party.

Elli Quinn. Or Taura. Or Rowan Durona. Or even Elena, Baz and all. Bel Thorne, whom he still missed. All of the above. Somebody. The inner vision of the Dendarii occupying Vorkosigan House gave him vertigo, but there was no doubt they'd know how to liven the place up.

━━━═◉═━━━

By the next evening, he was desperate enough to call his cousin Ivan.

Ivan answered his comconsole promptly enough. Lieutenant Lord Ivan Vorpatril was still wearing undress greens, identical to Miles's except for the symbol of Ops instead of ImpSec pinned to his collar in front of the red lieutenant's rectangles. At least Ivan hadn't changed, still holding down the same desk at Imperial Service headquarters by day, and leading the pleasant life of a Vor officer in the capital by night.

Ivan's handsome, affable face brightened into a genuine smile when he saw Miles. "Well, coz! I didn't know you were back in town."

"I got in a few days ago," Miles confessed. "I've been sampling the somewhat bizarre sensations of having Vorkosigan House to myself."

"Dear God, you're all alone in that mausoleum?"

"Except for the gate guard, and Zap the Cat, who keep to themselves."

"It ought to suit *you*, back from the dead as you are," said Ivan.

Miles touched his chest. "Not really. I never noticed before how much the old place *creaks* at night. I spent this afternoon . . ."

He couldn't very well tell Ivan he'd spent the day plotting a secret medical foray without Ivan asking *why*; he continued smoothly, "looking through the archives. I got to wondering how many people had actually died on the premises, over the centuries. Besides my grandfather, of course. There were a lot more than I'd thought." A fascinating question, actually; he *would* have to scan the archives.

"Yech."

"So . . . what's happening in Town? Any chance of you stopping by?"

"I'm on duty all day, of course . . . there's not too much going on, really. We're at that odd cusp, done with the Emperor's Birthday and not time yet for Winterfair."

"How was the Birthday bash this year? I just missed it. I was still en route, three weeks out. Nobody even got drunk to celebrate."

"Yes, I know. I got stuck delivering your District's bag of gold. It was the usual crush. Gregor retired early, and things sort of trickled off to nothing before dawn." Ivan pursed his lips, looking like he was being seized with a bright idea. Miles braced himself.

"I tell you what, though. In two nights Gregor is having a State dinner. There's two or three major new galactic ambassadors, and a couple of minor counsels, who've presented their portfolios in the last month, and Gregor figured to round them up all at once and get it over with. As usual, Mother is playing hostess for him."

Lady Alys Vorpatril was widely acknowledged as the premier social arbiter of Vorbarr Sultana, not least because of her frequent duties at the Imperial Residence as official welcomer for wifeless, motherless, sisterless Emperor Gregor.

"There's going to be dancing, after. Mother asked me if I couldn't round up some younger people to warm up the ballroom. By *younger* I gather she means under forty. Appropriate ones, you know the drill. If I had known you were in town, I'd have nailed you before this."

"She wants you to bring a date," Miles interpreted this. "Preferably, a fiancée."

Ivan grinned. "Yeah, but for some reason most fellows I know won't lend me theirs."

"Would I be supposed to provide a dance partner too? I hardly know any women here anymore."

"So, bring one of the Koudelka girls. I am. Sure, it's like taking your sister, but they are decorative as hell, especially en masse."

"Did you ask Delia?" said Miles thoughtfully.

"Yeah. But I'll cede her to you if you like, and take Martya. But if you're escorting Delia, you have to promise not to make her wear high heels. She hates it when you make her wear high heels."

"But she's so . . . impressive in them."

"She's impressive out of them, too."

"True. Well . . . yes, all right." Miles entertained a brief flashing vision of himself having a seizure right on the Imperial ballroom floor, in front of half the Vorish social cream of the capital. But what was the alternative? Stay home by himself yet another night with nothing to do but dream about his after-the-next-mission escape to Escobar, evolve nineteen more impractical ways to defeat ImpSec's observation of him on ImpSec's home turf, or brainstorm how to steal the gate guard's cat for company? And Ivan might solve his transportation dilemma.

"I don't have a car," Miles said.

"What happened to your lightflyer?"

"It's . . . in the shop. Adjustments."

"Want me to pick you up?"

His brains were lagging. That would leave *Ivan* driving, to the terror of all prudent passengers, unless Miles could bully Delia Koudelka into taking over. Miles sat up, seized with a bright idea of his own. "Does your mother really want extra bodies?"

"She says so."

"Captain Duv Galeni is in town. I saw him the other day at ImpSec HQ. He's stuck down in the Analysis section, except that he seems to regard it as a rare treat."

"Oh, yeah, I knew that! I would have remembered to tell you eventually. He came over to our side of town a few weeks ago in tow of General Allegre, for some consultation by the upper-ups. I meant to do something to welcome him to Vorbarr Sultana, but I hadn't got around to it yet. You ImpSec boys tend to keep to yourselves over there in Paranoia Central."

"But anyway, he's trying to impress this Komarran girl," Miles forged on. "Not girl, woman I suppose, some kind of high-powered wheel in a trade delegation. She's strong on brains rather than beauty, I gather, which doesn't surprise me, knowing Galeni. And she has interesting Komarran connections. How many points d'you think he would score for getting her into an Imperial State dinner?"

"Many," said Ivan decisively. "Especially if it's one of my mother's exclusive little soirees."

"And we both owe him one."

"More than one. And he's not nearly as sarcastic as he used to be, either, I noticed. Maybe he's mellowing out. Sure, invite him along," said Ivan.

"I'll give him a call, and get back to you, then." Happy in his inspiration, Miles cut the com.

FIVE

Miles climbed from Captain Galeni's groundcar, which was stopped at the east portico of the Imperial Residence, and turned to assist Delia Koudelka, who scarcely needed help. She swung out her long athletic legs, and bounced to her feet. The flowing skirts of her dress, in her favorite blue, revealed a glimpse of her matching dancing slippers, sensible, comfortable, and flat. She was the tallest of Commodore Koudelka's four daughters; the top of Miles's head was a good ten centimeters below the level of her shoulder. He grinned up at her. She returned a somewhat twisted smile, companionable and sporting.

"I don't know why I let you and Ivan talk me into this," she sighed to his ear.

"Because you like to dance," Miles stated with certainty. "Give me the first two, and I promise I'll find you a nice tall galactic diplomat for the rest of the evening."

"It's not that," she denied, eyeing his shortness.

"What I lack in height, I make up in speed."

"*That's* the trouble." She nodded vigorously.

Galeni turned over his modest vehicle to the waiting Imperial servant, who drove it away, and arranged his own lady's hand upon his arm. It took some knowledge of Galeni to read his saturnine features; Miles made him out as a little proud, a little smug, and a little embarrassed, as a man who arrives at a party wildly over-dressed. Since Galeni, albeit almost painfully neat, scrubbed, shaved, and polished, wore the same dress green Service uniform with glittering insignia as Miles did, it could only be the effect of his companion.

He ought to be smug, thought Miles. *Wait'll Ivan sees this.*

If Laisa Toscane possessed more brains than beauty, she had to be some kind of genius. Yet the exact source of her intense physical impression was elusive. Her face was softly molded and pleasant, but not nearly as striking as, say, Elli Quinn's expensive sculpture. Her eyes were unusual, a brilliant blue-green, though whether the color was cosmetically or genetically conferred Miles could not tell. She was short even for a Komarran woman, two handspans shorter than Galeni, who was almost as tall as Delia. But her most distinctive feature was her skin, milk-white and almost seeming to glow—*zaftig*, Miles thought, was the word for that rich flesh. *Plump* was misleading, and not nearly enthusiastic enough. He had never seen anything so edibly female outside a Cetagandan haut-lady's force screen.

Wealth did not always confer taste upon its possessor, but when it did, the results could be impressive. She wore dark red, loose trousers in the Komarran style and a matching, low-cut top, made subtle with a boxy open jacket in cream and blue-green. Understated jewelry. Her hair was too dark to be called blond, too silvery to be called brown, and curled in short wisps in a forthrightly Komarran fashion. Her smile seemed pleased and excited, as she glanced up at her escort, but by no means overwhelmed. *If she makes it past Aunt Alys,* Miles decided, *she's going to do just fine.* He lengthened his stride to match Delia's, and bowed his little party indoors, as if Emperor Gregor's State dinner was his personal gift to them.

They were vetted through by the Imperial guards, and a majordomo who determined that they had no wraps to be relieved of, nor, under Miles's escort, further need of guidance. The next person they encountered was indeed Lady Alys Vorpatril, who stood at the foot of the staircase. Tonight she'd chosen a gown of dark blue velvet trimmed with gold, in salute perhaps to the Vorpatril colors of her long-deceased husband. She'd worn a widow's dove gray all through Miles's childhood, he seemed to recall, but had at length given it up, possibly about the same time she had finally forgiven Lord Vorpatril for getting himself killed in that particularly outrageous fashion during the War of Vordarian's Pretendership.

"Hello, Miles dear, Delia," she greeted them. Miles bowed over her hand, and introduced Captain Galeni and Dr. Toscane with more formality. Lady Alys nodded approval—Miles was relieved that Ivan had indeed followed through and arranged their addition to the guest list as promised, and not forgotten till some embarrassing last minute, or later. "Gregor is receiving everyone in the Glass Hall as usual," Lady Alys went on. "You'll be seated at his table for dinner, down from the Escobaran Ambassador and her husband—I thought we ought to intersperse the galactics with a few natives this time."

"Thanks, Aunt Alys." Miles glanced past her shoulder at a slight, familiar figure in officer's dress greens, standing in the shadows in the door to the left of the staircase and talking in low tones with an ImpSec guard. "Uh, Delia, would you show Duv and Laisa to the Glass Hall? I'll be right along."

"Sure, Miles." Delia smiled at Laisa, swept up her long skirts with the ease of practice, and led the Komarrans up the wide stairs.

"What a lovely young woman," stated Lady Alys, gazing after them.

"Ah, you mean Dr. Toscane?" Miles hazarded. "She was all right to bring, I take it."

"Oh, yes. She is the principal heiress of *those* Toscanes, you know. Quite appropriate," Alys spoiled this encomium somewhat by adding, "for a Komarran."

We all have our little handicaps. Lady Alys was employed by the Emperor to see that the Right people were admitted; but Miles had spotted the other member of the team, the man Gregor employed to see that the Safe people were admitted. Chief of Imperial Security Simon Illyan glanced up at last from his conversation with the ImpSec guard, who saluted him and disappeared through the doorway. Illyan did not smile or beckon Miles, but Miles ducked around Lady Alys and made for him anyway, trapping him before he could follow the guard.

"Sir." Miles gave him an analyst's salute; Illyan returned an even more modified version, a slightly frustrated wave more repelling than acknowledging. The ImpSec chief was a man in his early sixties, with brown hair going gray, a deceptively placid face, and a permanent habit of blending quietly into the background. Illyan was clearly on duty tonight supervising the Emperor's personal security, evidenced by the comm link earbug in his right ear and the charged lethal weapons on both hips. This meant either that there was more going on here tonight than Miles had been briefed about, or that there wasn't much going on anywhere else to nail Illyan down at HQ, and he'd left the routine to his bland and steady second-in-command Haroche. "Did your secretary give you my message, sir?"

"Yes, Lieutenant."

"He'd told me you were out of town."

"I was. I came back."

"Have you . . . seen my latest report?"

"Yes."

Damn. The words, *There's something important I left out of it* seemed to choke in Miles's throat. "I need to talk with you."

Illyan, always closed, seemed more expressionless than usual. "This is neither the time nor the place, however."

"Quite, sir. When?"

"I'm waiting on further information."

Right. If it wasn't hurry up and wait, it was wait and hurry up. But something must be about to break soon, or Illyan wouldn't have Miles dancing attendance in Vorbarr Sultana on a one-hour report-for-duty notice. *If it's a new mission, I wish to hell he'd let me in on it. I could at least be starting some contingency planning.* "Very good. I'll be ready."

Illyan nodded dismissal. But as Miles turned away, he added, "Lieutenant . . ."

Miles turned back.

"Did you drive here tonight?"

"Yes. Well, Captain Galeni did."

"Ah." Illyan seemed to find something mildly interesting to look at over the top of Miles's head. "Sharp man, Galeni."

"*I* think so." Giving up on prying anything further out of Illyan tonight, Miles hurried to catch up with his friends.

He found them all waiting for him in the broad corridor outside the Glass Hall; Galeni was chatting amiably with Delia, who seemed in no hurry to go in and find Ivan and her sister. Laisa was gazing around with obvious fascination at the handmade antiques and subtly colored patterned carpets lining the corridor. Miles strolled along with her to study the elaborate and painstaking inlay on a polished tabletop, a scene of running horses in the natural hues of the various woods.

"It's all so *very* Barrayaran," she confided to Miles.

"Does it meet your expectations?"

"Indeed, yes. How old do you suppose that table is—and what went through the mind of the craftsman who made it? Do you suppose he ever imagined us, imagining him?" Her sensitive-looking fingers ran over the polished surface, aromatic with fine scented wax, and she smiled.

"About two hundred years, and no, at a guess," said Miles.

"Hm." Her smile grew more pensive. "Some of our domes are

over four hundred years old. And yet Barrayar seems older, even when it isn't. There is something intrinsically archaic about you, I think."

Miles reflected briefly upon the nature of her home-world. In another four hundred years, the terraforming on Komarr *might* begin to make it habitable for humans outdoors without breath masks. For now, the Komarrans lived all together in domed arcologies, as dependent upon their technology for survival against the choking chill as the Betans were on their screaming hot desert world. Komarr had never had a Time of Isolation, never been out of touch with the galactic mainstream. Indeed, it made its living fishing out of that stream, with its one vital natural resource—six important wormhole jump points in close practical proximity to one another. The jumps had made Komarran local space a nexus crossroads, and eventually, unfortunately, a strategic target. Barrayar had exactly one wormhole jump route connecting it to the galactic nexus—and it went through Komarr. If you did not hold your own gateway, those who did control it would own you.

Miles pulled his thoughts back to a smaller and more private human scale. Obviously, Galeni ought to take his lady out in the open Barrayaran air. She'd surely enjoy all those kilometers of un-Komarran wilderness. Hiking, say, or, if she truly favored the archaic—

"You ought to get Duv to take you horseback riding," Miles suggested.

"Goodness. Can he ride, too?" Her amazing turquoise eyes widened.

"Er . . ." Good question. Well, if not, Miles could give him a crash course. "Sure."

"Intrinsically archaic seems so . . ." She dropped her voice to a secretive tone—"intrinsically romantic. But don't tell Duv I said so. He's such a stickler for historical accuracy. The first thing he does is blow off all the fairy dust."

Miles grinned. "I'm not surprised. But I thought you were the practical businesswoman type, yourself."

Her smile grew more serious. "I'm a Komarran. I have to be. Without the value-added, from our trade, labor, transport, banking, and remanufacturing, Komarr would dwindle again to the desperate subsistence—and less-than-subsistence—level from which it rose. And seven out of ten of us would die, one way or another."

Miles twitched an interested brow; he thought her figures exaggerated, if obviously sincerely felt. "Well, we shouldn't hold up the parade. Shall we go in?"

He and Galeni rearranged themselves at the sides of their respective ladies, and Miles led the way through the nearby double doors. The Glass Hall was a long reception chamber lined on one side with tall windows, on the other with tall antique mirrors, hence its name, acquired when glass was a lot harder to come by.

Playing host rather than liege lord tonight, Gregor stood near the door in company with a few high government Ministers roped in for the occasion, greeting his guests. The Emperor of Barrayar was a lean, almost thin man in his mid-thirties, black-haired and dark-eyed. Tonight he wore well-cut civilian clothes, in the most conservative formal Barrayaran style, with a hint of the Vorbarra colors in the trim and side-piping on the trousers. Gregor was preternaturally quiet by choice when permitted to be. Not now, of course, when he was in Social Mode, a duty he disliked but, as with all his duties, did well anyway.

"Is that him?" Laisa whispered to Miles, as they waited for the group ahead of them to finish their pleasantries and move on. "I thought he would be in that fantastical military uniform one sees him wearing in all the vids."

"Oh, the parade red-and-blues? He only puts them on for the Midsummer Review, Birthday, and Wintefair. His grandfather Emperor Ezar was a real general before he was ever Emperor, and wore uniforms like a second skin, but Gregor feels he never was, despite his titular command of the Imperial forces. So he goes for his Vorbarra House uniform or something like this whenever etiquette permits. We all appreciate it vastly, because it lets *us* off the hook for wearing the damned things. The collar chokes you, the swords trip you, and the boot tassels catch on things." Not that the collar of the dress greens was much lower, and except for the tassels the tall boots were similar, but at his height Miles found the long sword of the pair a particular trial.

"I see," said Laisa. Her eyes twinkled in amusement.

"Ah. We're up." Miles shepherded his flock forward.

Delia had known Gregor all her life, and except for a brief word and smile of greeting stepped back to give the newcomers a chance.

"Yes, Captain Galeni, I've heard of you," Gregor said gravely, when Miles introduced the Komarran-born officer to him. Galeni looked for a split second as if he wasn't sure how to process this alarming tidbit of information, and Gregor added quickly, "Good things."

Gregor turned to Laisa, his gaze, for a moment, rather arrested. He recovered quickly, and bowed slightly over her hand, murmuring something polite and hopeful about Komarr as a welcome part of the Empire's future.

Once through the formalities, Delia led off in a search for Ivan and her sister among the thinly scattered, brilliantly dressed guests. The room was not nearly so jammed as for the Birthday or Winterfair. Laisa glanced back over her shoulder at Gregor. "Heavens. I nearly felt he was apologizing for conquering us."

"Well, not really," said Miles. "We didn't have much choice, after the Cetagandans invaded us through you. He was merely expressing sorrow for any personal inconveniences it may have caused which, all things considered, seem to be tailing off, thirty-five years after the fact. Multiplanet empires are a tricky balancing act. Though the Cetagandans have managed theirs for centuries, not that they would be my first pick as political role models."

"He doesn't seem exactly the stern personality your official news services project, does he?"

"More glum than stern, really—that's just how he comes out on the vid. Fortunately, perhaps."

They found their way temporarily blocked by a skinny old man doddering along with a cane; his ultraformal parade red-and-blues, correct right down to the two swords banging on his bony hips, hung loosely on him, and were oddly faded in color. Miles grabbed his guests and stepped back hastily to let him pass.

Laisa watched with interest. "Now who's the old General?"

"One of the most famous relics of Vorbarr Sultana," said Miles. "General Vorparadijs is the last surviving Imperial Auditor to have been personally appointed by Emperor Ezar."

"He looks rather military, for an auditor," said Laisa doubtfully.

"That's Imperial Auditor, with a capital A," Miles corrected. "And a capital Imp. Um . . . every society has to face the question, Who will guard the guardians? The Imperial Auditor is the Barrayaran-style answer. The Auditors are sort of a cross between, oh, a Betan Special Prosecutor, an Inspector General, and a minor deity.

"It doesn't necessarily have anything to do with accounting, though that's the origin of the title. The original counts were Voradar Tau's tax collectors. With that much money floating past my illiterate ancestors, they tended to grow sticky fingers. The Auditors policed the Counts for the Emperor. The unexpected arrival of an Imperial Auditor, usually with a large Imperial cavalry force, frequently triggered messy and unusual suicides. The Auditors used to get assassinated more in those days, too, but the early Emperors were really consistent in following those up with spectacular mass executions, and the Auditors became remarkably untouchable. It's said they used to be able to ride the countryside with bags of gold hanging off their saddles and almost no guards, and the bandits would secretly ride point to clear their paths, just to make sure the Auditors were sped out of their districts with no irritating delays. I think that's a legend, myself."

Laisa laughed. "It's a great story, though."

"There are supposed to be nine of them," put in Galeni. "A traditional number with several possible Old Earth origins. It's a favorite topic for undergraduate history papers. Though I believe there are only seven living Auditors at present."

"Are they appointed for life?" asked Laisa.

"Sometimes," said Miles. "Others are just appointed on a case-by-case basis. When my father was Regent, he only appointed acting Auditors, though Gregor confirmed several of their appointments when he reached his majority. In all matters pertaining to their investigations, they actually speak with the Emperor's Voice. That's another very Barrayaran thing. I once spoke with the Count my Father's Voice, in a little murder investigation in my own District. It was a strange experience."

"It sounds really interesting, from a sociological view," said Laisa. "Do you suppose we could corner General Vorparadijs, and get him talking about old times?"

"No, no!" said Miles in horror. "It's the *office* that's interesting. Vorparadijs himself is the deadliest senile old Vor bore in Vorbarr Sultana. All he does is this monologue about how standards have gone to hell since Ezar's day," *with pointed looks at me, usually,* "interspersed with detailed accounts of his bowel troubles."

"Yes," agreed Delia Koudelka. "He interrupts you constantly to tell you Youth Have No Manners. Youth is anybody under sixty."

"Seventy," Miles corrected. "He still refers to my *father* as 'Piotr's younger boy.' "

"Are all Auditors that old?"

"Well, not *that* old. But they tend to pick retired admirals and generals in case they have to put the wind up nonretired admirals and generals."

They avoided the deadly General, and caught up with Ivan and

Martya Koudelka only to be parted from them again by the major-domo, who seated them for dinner in the ornate Lesser Dining Hall. The meal went well, Miles thought. Miles exerted himself to ask leading questions of the Escobaran ambassador, and to patiently endure the usual spate of inquiries about his famous father. Laisa, across from him, held her own in conversation with an elderly gentleman of the Escobaran's retinue. Gregor and Captain Galeni managed a few exquisitely polite exchanges about Barrayaran-Komarran relations suitable for the tender ears of galactic guests; it wasn't just for Miles's sake that they had been seated at Gregor's table, Miles judged.

Laisa's bright eyes rose at what Miles recognized was a straight-line about Komarran shipping deliberately handed her by Galeni. She addressed Gregor directly, across the Escobarans. "Yes, Sire. In fact, the Komarr Shippers' Syndicate, for which I work, is very concerned about the issue before the Council of Ministers right now. We've petitioned for tax relief on profits directly reinvested in capital improvements."

Inwardly, Miles applauded her nerve, to lobby the Emperor himself over the entree—*Yeah, go for it! Why not?*

"Yes," said Gregor, smiling a little. "Minister Racozy mentioned it to me. I'm afraid it will find stiff opposition in the Council of Counts, whose more conservative members feel our large military expenditures on Komarr's jump-point defenses should be, er, proportionally shared by those on the front lines."

"But capital growth will provide a much bigger base to tax on the next round. To siphon it off too soon is like . . . like eating your seed corn."

Gregor's brows rose. "An ˙extremely useful metaphor, Dr. Toscane. I shall pass it on to Minister Racozy. It might make a better appeal to some of our backcountry Counts than the more complex discussions of jump technologies on which he's been attempting to tutor them."

Laisa smiled. Gregor smiled. Galeni looked downright smug. Laisa, having made her point, had the good sense to back off and turn the conversation immediately to lighter matters, or at least, to Escobaran policies on jump technologies, less potentially volatile than Barrayaran-Komarran taxation issues.

Music for the dancing afterwards in the ballroom downstairs was provided as usual by the Imperial Service Orchestra, surely among the less martial, if more talented, soldiers of Barrayar. The elderly colonel who directed them had been a fixture in the Imperial Residence for years. Gregor opened the dancing formally by taking Lady Alys for a spin around the floor, then, as etiquette demanded, a string of female guests in order of rank starting with the Escobaran ambassadoress. Miles claimed his two dances with the tall, blond, beautiful Delia. Having made whatever point that made to the onlookers, he went on to practice an Illyan-like blending with the walls to watch the show. Captain Galeni danced, if not well, at least earnestly. He had an eye on a political career after his twenty years in the Service were up, and was methodically collecting all possible pertinent skills.

One of Gregor's Armsmen approached Laisa; when Miles next spotted her, dipping and sliding in a mirror dance, she was opposite Gregor. Miles wondered if she'd get in a few more good lines about trade relations while she was at it. An exhilarating opportunity, and she wasn't wasting it; the Komarr Shippers' Syndicate should give her a bonus for this night's work. Glum Gregor actually laughed at something she said.

She returned to Galeni, temporarily holding up the wall along with Miles, with her eyes shining. "He's more intelligent than I imagined," she said breathlessly. "He listens . . . very intently. You feel as though he's taking it all in. Or is that an act?"

"No act," said Miles. "He's processing everything. But Gregor has to watch what he says very closely, given that his word can be literally law. He'd be shy if he could, but he's not allowed."

"Not allowed? How *odd* that sounds," said Laisa.

She had the chance to test Gregor's reserve three more times on the marquetry dance floor before the evening drew to a close at a proper and conservative hour before midnight. Miles wondered if Gregor was giving him the lie about his shyness, because he actually made Laisa laugh once or twice, too.

The party was breaking up before Miles finally found himself in Gregor's orbit for a quiet, private word. Unfortunately, the first thing Gregor said was, "I hear you managed to get Our courier back to Us almost in one piece. A bit below your usual standards, wasn't it?"

"Ah. So Vorberg's home, is he?"

"So I'm told. What exactly happened?"

"A . . . very embarrassing accident with an automated plasma arc. I'll tell you all about it, but . . . not here."

"I look forward to it."

Which put Gregor on the growing list of people for Miles to try to avoid. Damn.

"Where did you find that extraordinary young Komarran woman?" Gregor added, gazing off into the middle distance.

"Dr. Toscane? Impressive, isn't she? I admired her courage as much as her cleavage. What all did you find to talk about out there?"

"Komarr, mostly . . . Do you have her, um, the Shippers' Syndicate's address? Oh, never mind, Simon can get it for me. Along with a complete Security report, whether I want it or not, no doubt."

Miles bowed. "ImpSec lives to serve you, Sire."

"Behave," Gregor murmured. Miles grinned.

———=◉=———

Upon their return to Vorkosigan House, Miles invited the two Komarrans in for a drink, before reflecting upon the present logistical complications of entertaining. Galeni started to politely decline, mentioning something about work tomorrow, but simultaneously Laisa said, "Oh, yes please. I'd love to see the house, Lord Vorkosigan. It's imbued with so much history." Galeni immediately swallowed whatever he'd been about to add, and followed her in, smiling slightly.

All the ground-floor rooms seemed too vast and shadowed and foreboding for just three people; Miles led them upstairs instead to a more humanly scaled small parlor, then had to zip around the room whisking the covers off the furniture before anyone could sit down. He set the lights to a reasonably romantic late-evening glow, then galloped downstairs again two and three flights respectively in search of three wineglasses and a suitable bottle of wine. He arrived back upstairs rather out of breath.

He returned to the small parlor to find Galeni had not taken advantage of his opportunity. Miles should have uncovered only the small sofa, forcing the two into closer proximity than the separate, admittedly comfortable, chairs they had chosen. Staid old rule-following Galeni seemed unconscious of his lady's secret yen for a little romantic idiocy. Miles was oddly reminded of Taura, forced by her size and work and rank into a permanent public persona too dangerous to mock. Laisa was not too big, but perhaps was too bright, too conscious of her public and social duties. She'd never ask directly. Galeni made her smile, but not laugh. The lack of any sense of *play* between them worried Miles. You had to have a keen sense of humor to do sex and stay sane.

But Miles did not feel particularly qualified just now to give Galeni advice on how to run his love-life. He thought again of Taura's comment: *You try to give away what you want yourself.* Hell. Galeni was a big boy, let him find his own damnation.

It wasn't hard to lead Laisa into conversation about her work, though it made things a little one-sided; Miles and Galeni naturally couldn't say much in return about their own highly classified business. This segued into what seemed to be the topic of the evening, Komarr-Barrayaran relations and history. The Toscane family had been notable cooperators after the conquest, hence their premier position today.

"But you can't," Miles maintained stoutly when the subject came up, "properly call them collaborators. I think that term ought to be reserved for those who cooperated *before* the Barrayaran invasion. No reflection upon the Toscanes' patriotism that they declined to embrace the scorched earth, or rather, scorched Komarr position of the later resistance. Quite the reverse." The Barrayaran invasion hadn't exactly been a win-win situation, but at least the cooperators had known how to cut their losses and go on. Now, a generation later, the success of the Toscane-led resurgent oligarchy demonstrated the validity of their reasoning.

And unlike Galeni, whose father Ser Galen had spent his life pursuing a futile Komarran revenge, the Toscane position had left Laisa with no embarrassing connections to live down. Ser Galen was a topic neither Miles nor Galeni broached; Miles wondered how much Galeni had told her of his late, mad father.

It was halfway between midnight and dawn, with another bottle of the best wine killed among them, before Miles could bring himself to let his yawning company go home. He watched reflectively as Galeni's groundcar turned out of the drive and down the night-quiet street, saluted on its way by the lone ImpSec night guard. Galeni, like Miles, had spent the last decade pursuing an all-consuming career; its secret strains had left him, perhaps, a bit romantically retarded. Miles hoped, when the time came, Galeni didn't put his proposal to Laisa as some sort of business proposition, but he was very much afraid that would be the only mode Galeni could allow himself. Galeni didn't have enough forward momentum. That desk job suited him.

That one won't be lingering for you very damned long, Galeni. Someone with more nerve will move in and snap her up, and carry her off to keep greedily for himself. As a would-be Baba, a traditional Barrayaran marriage-broker, Miles did not feel the evening had advanced Galeni's agenda nearly enough. Sexually frustrated enough by proxy for both his friends, Miles went back inside. The door secure-locked itself.

He undressed slowly, and sat on his bed, watching his com-console with the same malignant intensity with which Zap the Cat eyed a human bearing food. It remained silent. *Chime, damn you.* In the natural perversity of things, this ought to be the hour Illyan called him in, when he was tired and half-drunk and unfit to report. *Now, Illyan. I want my mission!* Every hour that passed seemed a greater strain. Every hour, another hour wasted. If enough time went by before Illyan called him in that he might have made it to Escobar and back, he'd be fit to chew the carpet even when not having a seizure.

He considered hauling up another bottle, and getting *really* drunk, in an act of sympathetic magic to make Illyan *really* likely to call. But nausea and vomiting tended to make time move subjectively slower, not faster. An unattractive prospect. *Maybe Illyan's forgotten me.*

A thin joke; Illyan never forgot anything. He couldn't. Sometime back when *he'd* been an ImpSec lieutenant in his late twenties, then-Emperor Ezar had sent him off to distant Illyrica, to have an experimental eidetic memory-chip installed in his brain. Old Ezar had fancied owning a walking recording device answerable to himself alone. The technology had not caught on as a commercial development, due to the 90% incidence of iatrogenic schizophrenia the chip had subsequently induced in its wearers. Ruthless Ezar had been willing to take that 90% risk for the 10% reward, or rather, had been willing for a disposable young officer to take it for him. Ezar in pursuit of his policies had disposed of thousands of soldiers like Illyan, in his lifetime.

But Ezar had died soon after, and left Illyan, like a wandering planetoid, to fall into orbit around Admiral Aral Vorkosigan, who proved to be one of the major political stars of the century. Illyan had worked Security for Miles's father, one way or another, for the next thirty years.

Miles wondered what it would be like to have thirty-five years of memories at your beck and call, as sharp and instantaneous as if just experienced. The past would never be softened by that welcome roseate fog of forgetfulness. To be able to rerun every mistake you'd ever made, in perfect sound and color . . . it had to be something like eternal damnation. No wonder the chip-bearers had gone mad. Although maybe remembering *other* people's mistakes was not so painful. You learned to watch your mouth, around Illyan. He could quote you back every idiotic, stupid, or ill-considered thing you'd ever said, verbatim, with gestures.

In all, Miles didn't think he'd care for a chip, himself, even if he were medically qualified. He felt close enough to schizoid dementia already without any further technological boost in that direction, thanks.

Galeni, now, seemed the bland unimaginative sort who would qualify; but Miles had reason to believe Galeni harbored hidden depths, as hidden as his father Ser Galen's terrorist past. No. Galeni was not a suitable candidate either. Galeni would just go insane so quietly, he would rack up huge damages before anyone caught on.

Miles stared at his comconsole, willing it to light up. *Call. Call. Call. Give me my goddamn mission. Get me out of here.* Its silence seemed almost mocking. At length, he gave up and went to get another bottle of wine.

— SIX —

It was evening two full days later before the personal comconsole in his bedchamber chimed again. Miles, who had been sitting next to it all day, nearly flinched out of his chair. He let it chime again, deliberately, while he tried to slow his racing heart and catch his breath. *Right. This has to be it. Cool, calm, and collected, boy. Don't let Illyan's secretary see you sweat.*

But to his bitter disappointment, the face that formed over the vid plate was only his cousin Ivan. He'd obviously just blown in from his day's work at Imperial Service Headquarters, still wearing his undress greens . . . with blue, not red, rank rectangles on the collar behind his bronze Ops pins. *Captain's tabs? Ivan is wearing captain's tabs?*

"Hi, coz," said Ivan cheerily. "How was your day?"

"Slow." Miles fixed his features into a polite smile, hoping to conceal the sinking feeling in his gut.

Ivan's smile broadened; he ran a hand over his hair, preening. "Notice anything?"

You know damned well I noticed instantly. "You have a new hairstylist?" Miles feigned to hazard uncertainly.

"Ha." Ivan tapped a tab with a fingernail, making it click.

"You know, impersonating an officer is a crime, Ivan. True, they've never caught you yet. . . ." *Ivan got promoted to captain before me . . . ?!*

"Ha," Ivan repeated smugly. "It's all official, as of today. My new pay grade started at reveille this morning. I knew this was in the pipeline, but I've been sitting on the news. Thought you all deserved a little surprise."

"How come they promoted *you* before *me*? Who the hell have you been sleeping with?" boiled off Miles's lips before he could bite it back down. He hadn't meant his tone of voice to come out quite that harsh.

Ivan shrugged, smirking. "I do my job. And I do it without going around bending all the rules into artistic little origami shapes, either. Besides, you've spent I don't know how much time on medical leave. Deduct that, and I've probably got *years* of seniority on you."

Blood and bone. Every bit of that unwelcome leave had been bought with blood and bone and endless pain, laid down willingly enough in the Emperor's service. *Blood and bone and they promote Ivan? Before me . . . ?!* Something like rage choked him, clotting words in his throat like cotton.

Ivan's face, watching his, fell. Yes, of course, Ivan had expected to be applauded, in some suitably backhanded way, expected Miles to share his pride and pleasure in his achievement, which truly made a sad dish when eaten alone. Miles struggled for better control of his face, his words, his thoughts. He tried to return his voice to the proper tone of light banter. "Congratulations, coz. Now that your rank and pay grade have become so exalted, what excuse are you going to give your mother not to get married to some fine Vor bud?"

"They have to catch me first," grinned Ivan, lightening again in response. "I move fast."

"Mm. Better not wait too long. Didn't Tatya Vorventa give up and get married recently? Though there's still Violetta Vorsoisson, I suppose."

"Well, no, actually, she got married last summer," Ivan admitted.

"Helga Vorsmythe?"

"Picked off by one of her Da's industrialist friends, of all things. He wasn't even Vor. Wealthy as hell, though. That was three years ago. God, Miles, you are out of it. No problem. I can always go for someone younger."

"At this rate, you're going to end up courting embryos." *We all will.* "That skewed male-female birth ratio about the time we were being born is catching up with us. Well, good going with your captaincy. I know you worked for it, even though you pretend not to. You'll be Chief of Ops before I turn around, I wager."

Ivan sighed. "Not unless they break down and finally give me some ship duty to go on my resume. They're awfully stingy with it, these days."

"They're pinching half-marks in the training cycles, I'm afraid. Everyone's complaining on that score."

"*You've* had more ship duty than anyone I know up to the rank of commodore, in your own inimitable, ass-backwards way," Ivan added enviously.

"Yeah, but it's all classified secret. You're among the very few who know."

"The point is, you haven't let the lack of half-marks stop you. Or the rules. Or respect for reality, as far as I can tell."

"I never let *anything* stop me. That's how you get what you want, Ivan. No one's just going to hand it to you." Well . . . no one was going to just hand it to Miles. Things fell out of the sky onto Ivan, and had done so all his charmed life. "If you can't win, change the game."

Ivan twitched a brow upward. "If there's no game, isn't winning a pretty meaningless concept?"

Miles hesitated. "Out of the mouths of . . . Ivans. I'll . . . have to think about that one."

"Don't strain yourself, little genius."

Miles managed an unfelt smile. Ivan looked as though this whole conversation was leaving as bad a taste in his mouth as it was in Miles's. Better to cut the losses. He would make it up with Ivan later. He always did. "I think I'd better go now."

"Yes. You have so much to do." With a grimace, Ivan cut the com even as Miles's hand reached for the off-key.

Miles sat in his comconsole's station chair in silence, for a full minute. Then, being quite alone, he threw back his head and spat his frustration at his bedroom ceiling, in a string of all the blue galactic curses he knew. Afterwards, he felt slightly better, as if he'd managed to eject something poisonous from his soul along with the foul words. He didn't begrudge Ivan his promotion, not really. It was just . . . it was just . . .

Was winning all he really wanted? Or did he still want also to be *seen* to have won? And by whom? ImpSec was the wrong damned department to be working for, if you hungered for fame along with your fortune. Yet Illyan knew, Miles's parents knew, Gregor, all the close people who really counted knew about Admiral Naismith, knew what Miles really was. Elena, Quinn, all the Dendarii. Even Ivan knew. *Who the hell am I twirling for, if not for them?*

Well . . . there was always his grandfather General Count Piotr Vorkosigan, dead these thirteen years. Miles's eye fell on his grandfather's ceremonial dagger in its elaborate sheath, sitting in a place of honor, or at least uncluttered by other detritus, on its own shelf across the room. Miles had actually insisted on carrying it around with him at all times, earlier in his career. Proving . . . what? To whom? *Nothing to no one, now.*

He rose, walked over to the shelf, and lifted the weapon, drawing the fine blade from its sheath and watching the light play over the textured steel. It was still a fabulous antique, but it lacked . . . some former geas it had once held upon him; the magic was gone, or at least, the curse was lifted. It was just a knife. He slid it back into its sheath, opened his hand, and let it fall back to its place.

He felt out of balance. He had felt that way increasingly, when at home, but this trip the sensation was acute. The strange absence of the Count and Countess was like a preview of their deaths. This was a taste of what it would be like to be Count Miles Vorkosigan, all day long. He wasn't sure he liked the flavor.

I need . . . Naismith. This eviscerated Vor life unnerved him. But Naismith was an expensive hobby. To get ImpSec to pay for Naismith required a reason, literally a mission in life. *What have you done to justify your existence today?* was a question to which Admiral Naismith had better be able to supply a daily answer, or risk being snuffed out. ImpSec's accountants were as dangerous to his continuation as enemy fire. *Well . . . almost.* His hand traced the spray of scars on his chest, under his shirt.

There was something wrong with his new heart. It pumped blood all right, all the ventricles and valves were in order . . . it was supposed to have been grown from his own tissues, but it seemed a stranger's mismatch. . . . *You're going looney, all alone in this empty house.*

A mission. A mission was what he needed. Then everything would be all right again. It wasn't that he wished harm on anyone, but he longed for a hijacking, a blockade, a small colonial war . . . better still, a rescue. Free the prisoners, yeah.

You've done all that. If that's what you wanted, why aren't you happy?

The taste for adrenaline, it appeared, was an appetite that grew by what it fed upon. Naismith was an addiction, a craving that required ever-stronger and more toxic doses for the same level of satisfaction.

He'd tried a few dangerous sports, by way of experiment, to soothe that hunger. He wasn't all that good at them, lacking, among other things, the time to acquire true expertise. And besides . . . that extra edge was missing. It wasn't very interesting to risk only himself. And a trophy seemed a tawdry bit of junk, when he'd played for and won ten thousand human lives in a single round.

I want my frigging mission. Call me, Illyan!

———▶◀———

The call, when it came at last, literally caught him napping. The chime brought him abruptly out of an exhausted afternoon doze, after a night of almost no sleep at all, racked with circular patterns of worry and useless speculation. He had practiced in his mind, Miles estimated, about three hundred versions of his up-coming interview with Illyan. The only certainty he held was that the three hundred and first would be something totally different.

The face of Illyan's secretary formed over the vid plate.

"Now?" Miles said, before the man could get his first word out. He rubbed his hand through sleep-bent hair, and over his slightly numb face.

The secretary blinked, cleared his throat, and started in with his own practiced sentences. "Good afternoon, Lieutenant Vorkosigan. Chief Illyan requests that you report to his office in one hour."

"I could make it quicker."

"One hour," the secretary repeated. "HQ will send a car for you."

"Oh. Thanks." Useless to ask for more information over a comconsole; Miles's machine was more secured than a commercial model, but not that much more.

The secretary cut the com. Well, it would give him time to take another cold shower, and dress properly.

After his second bath of the day he pulled a set of fresh-pressed undress greens out of his closet, and set about transferring his ImpSec silver eyes to their place on the collar, in front of the— ahem!—battered red lieutenant's tabs he'd been wearing for eight bleeding years. The rank tabs were duplicates, but the eye-of-Horus pins, built up in molecular layers of tarnish-proof silver in a hidden pattern, were issued one set (right-and left-facing) to a soldier. Name and serial number were engraved on the back, and woe to the man who lost his. ImpSec eyes were as hard to counterfeit as money, and as powerful. When Miles was finished, his appearance was as neat as for any interview with the Emperor. Neater. Gregor had less immediate control over his destiny than Illyan did.

It was all sympathetic magic. When you couldn't do some-thing truly useful, you tended to vent the pent-up energy in something useless but available, like snappy dressing. Still he was downstairs and waiting ten minutes before the ImpSec groundcar showed up at the front portico.

When he arrived this time at Illyan's office, the door to the inner chamber was open. The secretary waved him through.

Illyan looked up from his own oversized, overworked comconsole desk, and nodded in return to Miles's slightly-sharper-than-analyst's salute. He reached for a control, and the door to the outer office slid closed, and secure-locked itself. The locking was an unusual gesture, and Miles quelled a rising hope that it meant that this time, something bloody big was in the works, something really challenging.

There was a chair waiting, good. Illyan had been known, when particularly furious, to keep one standing till the yelling part was done. Not that Illyan ever raised his voice; he tended to the devastatingly well-chosen word to convey his emotions, a style Miles admired and hoped to emulate. But there was a peculiar tension in the ImpSec chief today. Grim, much more so than normal. Miles seated himself, and gave Illyan a short nod, signifying his commander had all his attention: *I'm ready. Let's go.*

Illyan leaned not forward, but back, studying Miles across the wide black surface of the desk. "You told my secretary you had something you wanted to add to your last report?"

Shit. Now or never. But the confession of his little medical problem would be certain to totally derail whatever mission assignment was coming up. *Never it is, then. I'll fix it myself, later. As soon as possible.* "Nothing important now. What's up?"

Illyan sighed, and drummed his fingers once, introspectively, on the black glass before him. "I received a disturbing report from Jackson's Whole."

Miles's breath drew in. *I died there once.* "Admiral Naismith is notably unwelcome in those parts, but I'm ready for a rematch. What have the bastards done now?"

"This is not a new mission, nor a new report. This is in relation to your last . . . I can hardly call it a mission, since I never ordered it. Your last adventure there." Illyan looked up at him.

"Oh?" said Miles cautiously.

"Complete copies of your cryo-revival surgeon's medical records finally surfaced. It took some time, due to the confusion of the Durona Group's hurried departure from Jackson's Whole, with their records scattered between Escobar and House Fell.

House Fell, needless to say, was not forthcoming with extra data. It took even more time for the records to be received and processed by my analysis section, and to finally be read in detail by someone who realized their significance and implications. Some months, in fact."

Miles's belly went abruptly very cold, as if in memory of his freezing death. He had a sudden insight as to the exact state of mind of a person who fell/jumped/was pushed from the top of a very tall building, in that subjectively stretched eternity it took for them to reach the pavement below. *We have just made a major mistake. Oh, yes.*

"What bothers me most, of course," Illyan went on, "is not your seizures themselves, but the fact that you concealed them from the ImpSec physicians who were trying to return you fit for duty. You lied to them, and through them, to me."

Miles swallowed, searching his paralyzed consciousness for a defense for the indefensible. What couldn't be defended could only be denied. He pictured himself chirping brightly, *What seizures, sir?* No. "Dr. Durona . . . said they would go away on their own." She *had*, dammit, she had. "Or . . . they might," he corrected. "At that time, I thought they had."

Illyan grimaced. He picked a cipher-card from his desktop, and held it up between thumb and forefinger. "This," he stated, "is my latest independent report from the Dendarii. Including *your* fleet surgeon's medical reports. The ones she kept in her cabin, not in her sick bay office. They were not easy to obtain. I've been waiting for them. They came in last night."

He had a third observer. I might have known. I should have figured it.

"Do you want to try to play any more little guessing games about this?" Illyan added dryly.

"No, sir," Miles whispered. He hadn't meant it to come out a whisper. "No more games."

"Good." Illyan rocked slightly in his station chair, and tossed the card back to the desktop. His face looked like death itself. Miles wondered what his own face looked like. As wide-eyed as an animal in the headlights, as viewed from a groundcar traveling toward it at a hundred kilometers an hour, he suspected.

"This"—Illyan pointed to the cipher-card—"was a betrayal of the subordinates who depended on you as well as of the superiors who trusted you. And it was a *knowing* betrayal, proved on

Lieutenant Vorberg's body. Do you have anything to say in your defense?"

If the tactical situation was bad, change your ground. *If you can't win, change the rules.* Miles's internal tension shot him up out of his chair, to pace back and forth before Illyan's desk. His voice rose. "I have served you, body and blood—and I've bled plenty—for nine years, sir. Ask the Marilacans how well I've served you. Ask a hundred others. Over thirty missions, and only two that could remotely be classified as failures. I've laid my life on the line dozens of times, I've literally laid it *down*. Does that suddenly count for *nothing* now?"

"It counts"—Illyan inhaled—"for much. That's why I am offering you a medical discharge without prejudice, if you resign now."

"Resign? *Quit?* This is your idea of a *favor*? ImpSec has made worse scandals than this disappear—I know you can do more than that, if you choose!"

"It's the best way. Not just for you, but for your name's sake. I have thought this through from every angle. I've been thinking about it for weeks."

This is why he called me home. No mission. There never was. Only this. I was screwed from before the beginning. No chance.

"After serving your father for thirty years," Illyan continued, "I can do no less. And no more."

Miles froze. "My father . . . asked for this? He knows?"

"Not yet. Apprising him is a task I leave to you. This is one last report I do not care to make."

Rare cowardice on Illyan's part, and a fearsome punishment. "My father's influence," said Miles bitterly. "Some favor."

"Believe me, without your record you so justly quote, even your father could not gain you this mercy from me. Your career will end quietly, with no public scandal."

"Yeah," Miles panted. "Real convenient. It shuts me up, and gives me no appeal."

"I advise—with all my heart—against your forcing this to a court-martial. You will never get a more favorable judgment than this private one, between us. It is with no intent to be humorous that I tell you, you haven't a leg to stand on." Illyan tapped the cipher-card, for emphasis. Indeed, there was no amusement at all in his face. "On the documented evidence here alone, never mind the rest of it, you'd be lucky to get out with only a dishonorable discharge, and no further sentence atop it."

"Have you discussed this with Gregor?" Miles demanded. Imperial favor, his last emergency defense, the one he'd sworn he'd die rather than call upon—

"Yes. At great length. I was closeted with him all this morning over nothing but this."

"Oh."

Illyan gestured at his comconsole. "I have your records ready, for you to sign out here and now. Palm-print, retina-scan, and it's done. Your uniforms . . . didn't come from military stores, so need not be returned, and it is traditional to keep one's insignia, but I'm afraid I must ask you to hand in your silver eyes.

Miles, turning on his heel, aborted the half-gesture of his agitated hands reaching to clamp defensively to his collar. "Not my *eyes*! It's . . . not true, I can explain, I can—" The edges and surfaces of the objects in the room, the comconsole desk, the chairs, Illyan's face, seemed suddenly sharper than before, as if imbued with some heightened measure of reality. A nimbus of green fire broke up into colored confetti, closing over him, *No—!*

He came to consciousness flat on his back on Illyan's carpet. Illyan's blood-drained face hovered over him, tense and worried. Something was lodged in Miles's mouth—he turned his head and spat out a stylus, a light-pen from Illyan's desk. His collar was unfastened—his hand reached to touch it—but his silver eyes were still in place. He just lay there, for a moment.

"Well," he said thinly at last. "I imagine that was quite a show. How long?"

"About"—Illyan glanced at his chrono—"four minutes."

"About standard."

"Lie still. I'll call a medic."

"I don't need a goddamn medic. I can walk." He tried to get up. One leg buckled, and he went down again, face mashed in the carpet. His face was sticky—he'd evidently hit his mouth, which was swelling, on the first fall, and his nose, which was bleeding. Illyan handed him a handkerchief, and he pressed it to his face. After about a minute, he suffered Illyan to help him back into the chair.

Illyan half-sat on the edge of his desk, watching him. Watching over him, always. "You knew," said Illyan. "And you lied. To *me*. In *writing*. In that damned falsified report, you pissed away . . . everything. I'd have mistrusted my memory chip before I mistrusted you. *Why*, Miles? Were you that panicked?" The anguish leaked into that level voice like blood into a bruise.

Yes. I was that panicked. I didn't want to lose Naismith. I didn't want to lose . . . everything. "It doesn't matter now." He fumbled at his collar. One pin tore the green fabric, coming off in his shaking hands. He thrust the pins blindly at Illyan. "There. You win."

Illyan's hand closed over them. "God save me," he said softly, "from another such victory."

"Fine, good, give me the read-pad. Give me the retinal scan. Let's get this the hell over with. I'm sick of ImpSec, and eating ImpSec shit. No more. Good." The shaking didn't stop, radiating outward in hot waves from the pit of his belly. He was terrified he was about to start crying in front of Illyan.

Illyan sat back, his closed hand turning inward. "Take a couple of minutes to compose yourself. Take as long as you need. Then go into my washroom and wash your face. I'm not unlocking my door till you're fit to go out."

Strange mercies, Illyan. You kill me so courteously. But he nodded, and stumbled to Illyan's little lavatory. Illyan followed him to the door, then, apparently deciding he would stay on his feet this time, left him alone. The face in the mirror was indeed unfit to be seen, bloody and ravaged. It was very like the face he had last seen looking back at him the day Sergeant Beatrice had been killed, except about a hundred years older now. *Illyan will not shame a great name. Neither should I.* He washed carefully, though he failed to get all the bloodstains out of his torn collar and the cream-colored shirt opened under it.

He returned, to sit docilely, and let Illyan hand him the read-pad for his palm-print, administer the retinal scan, and record his brief, formal words of resignation. "All right. Let me out," he said quietly.

"Miles, you're still shaking."

"I will be, for a while yet. It will pass. Let me out, please."

"I'll call a car. And walk you to it. You shouldn't be alone."

Oh, yes I should. "Very well."

"Do you wish to go directly to a hospital? You ought to. As a properly discharged veteran, you're entitled to ImpMil treatment in your own right, not just in your father's name. I . . . figured that would be important."

"No. I wish to go home. I'll deal with it . . . later. It's chronic, not critical. Probably be another month before it happens again, if it runs to form."

"You should go to a hospital."

"You"—Miles eyed him—"have just lost your authority over my actions. May I remind you. Simon."

Illyan's hand opened in troubled acquiescence. He walked back around his desk, and pressed the keypad that unlocked his door. He rubbed his hand over his own face, for a moment, as if to wipe away all emotion. And the water standing in his eyes. Miles fancied he could almost feel the coolness of that evaporation, across Illyan's round cheekbones. When Illyan turned back, his face was as bland and closed as Miles had ever seen it.

God, my heart hurts. And his head. And his stomach. And every other part of him. He climbed to his feet, and walked to the door, shrugging away Illyan's hesitant hand under his elbow.

The door hissed open revealing three men, standing in anxious guard near it: Illyan's secretary, General Haroche, and Captain Galeni. Galeni's brows rose, looking at Miles; Miles could tell exactly when he noticed the insignia-stripped collar, for his eyes widened in shock.

Cripes, Duv, what d'you think? That he'd had a fistfight with Illyan, along with the screaming match? That an enraged Illyan had torn those ImpSec eyes forcibly from Miles's tunic? *Circumstantial evidence can be so convincing.*

Haroche's lips parted in a breath of disturbed surprise. "What the hell . . . ?" His hand opened in question to Illyan.

"Excuse us." Illyan met no one's eyes, pushing through. The assembled ImpSec officers all wheeled to stare after the pair, as they made it to the corridor and turned left.

SEVEN

Conscious of the ImpSec driver's eyes following him, Miles walked carefully through the front door of Vorkosigan House. He did not let his shoulders sag until the doors closed safely behind him. He fell into the first chair he came to, on top of its cover. It was another hour before he stopped shivering.

Not the growing darkness but bladder pressure at last drove him to his feet. *Our bodies are our masters, we their prisoners. Free the prisoners.* Once up and moving, his only desire was to be still again. *I should get drunk. It's traditional, for situations like this, isn't it?* He collected a bottle of brandy from the cellar. Wine seemed inadequately poisonous. This burst of activity dwindled to rest in the smallest room he could find, a fourth-floor chamber which, but for its window, might have passed for a closet. It was a former servant's room, but it had an old wing chair in it. After going to all the trouble to find the brandy, he had not the ambition left to open the bottle. He crouched down small in the big chair.

On his next trip to his bathroom, sometime after midnight, he picked up his grandfather's dagger, and brought it back with him to set it beside the sealed brandy bottle on the lamp table by his left hand. The dagger tempted him as little as the drink, but toying with it did provide a few moments of interest. He let the light slide over the blade, and pressed it against his wrists, his throat, along the thin scars from his cryonic prep already slashed there. *Definitely the throat, if anything.* All or nothing, no playing around.

But he'd died once already, and it hadn't helped. Death held neither mystery nor hope. And there lurked the horrible possibility that those who had sacrificed so much to revive him the last time would be inspired to try it again. And botch it. Or rather, botch it even worse. He'd seen half-successful cryo-revivals, vegetable or animal minds whining brokenly in once-human bodies. No. He didn't want to die. At least not where his body could ever be found. He just couldn't bear being alive right now.

The sanctuary in between the two organic states, sleep, refused to come to him. But if he sat here long enough, eventually he must sleep, surely.

Get up. Get up and run, as fast as you can. Back to the Dendarii, before ImpSec or anyone could stop him. Now was his chance, Naismith's chance. Naismith's last chance. *Go. Go. Go.*

He sat on, muscles knotted, the litany of escape beating in his head.

He discovered that if he drank no water, he didn't need to get up so often. He still didn't sleep, but in the predawn his thoughts began to slow. A thought an hour. That was all right.

Light seeped into the room again through the window, making the lamplight grow pale and wan. A quadrangle of sun crept slowly across the worn patterned rug, as slowly as his thoughts, left to center to right, then gone.

The sounds of the city outside softened with the oncoming twilight. But his little bubble of personal darkness remained as insulated from the world as any cryo-chamber.

━━━◉━━━

Distant voices were calling his name. *It's Ivan. Blech. I don't want to talk to Ivan.* He did not respond. If he said and did nothing, maybe they wouldn't find him.

Maybe they'd go away again. Dry-eyed, he stared at a crack in the aging plastered wall, which had been in his line of sight for hours.

But his ploy didn't work. Booted footsteps sounded in the corridor outside the little chamber. Then Ivan's voice, shouting much too loud, hurting his ears: "In here, Duv! I found him!"

More footsteps, a quick, heavy stride. Ivan's face wove into his field of vision, blocking the wall. Ivan grimaced. "Miles? You in there, boy?"

Galeni's voice. "My God."

"Don't panic," said Ivan. "He's just gone and got himself sensibly drunk." He picked up the sealed bottle. "Well . . . maybe not." He prodded the unsheathed knife beside it. "Hm."

"Illyan was right," muttered Galeni.

"Not . . . necessarily," said Ivan. "After about the twenty-fifth time you see this, you stop getting excited about it. It's just . . . something he does. If he were going to kill himself, he'd have done it years ago."

"You've seen him like this before?"

"Well . . . maybe not quite like this . . ." Ivan's strained face occluded the plaster again. He waved a hand in front of Miles's eyes.

"He didn't blink," Galeni noted nervously. "Perhaps . . . we ought not to touch him. Don't you think we should call for medical help?"

"You mean psychiatric? Absolutely not. *Real* bad idea. If the psych boys ever got hold of him, they'd never let him go. No. This is a family matter." Ivan straightened decisively. "*I* know what to do. Come on."

"Is it all right to leave him alone?"

"Sure. If he hasn't moved for a day and a half, he isn't going far." Ivan paused. "Bring the knife along, though. Just in case."

They clattered out again. Miles's slow thoughts worked through it, one thought per quarter hour.

They're gone.

Good.

Maybe they won't come back.

But then, alas, they reappeared.

"I'll take his shoulders," Ivan directed, "you take his feet. No, better pull his boots off first."

Galeni did so. "At least he's not rigid."

No, quite limp. Rigidity would require effort. The boots thumped to the floor. Ivan took off his own uniform tunic, rolled up the sleeves of the round-collared shirt under it, slipped his hands under Miles's armpits, and lifted. Galeni took his feet as instructed.

"He's lighter than I thought," said Galeni.

"Yeah, but you should see Mark, now," said Ivan.

The two men carried him down the narrow servant's stairs between the fourth floor and the third. Maybe they were going to put him to bed. That would save him a bit of trouble. Maybe he would go to sleep there. Maybe, if he were very lucky, he wouldn't wake up again until the next century, when there would be nothing left of his name and his world but a distorted legend in men's minds.

But they continued on past Miles's bedroom door, and bumped him through into an old bathroom down the hall, one that had never been remodeled. It contained an antique iron tub large enough for small boys to swim in, at least a century old.

They plan to drown me. Even better. I shall let them.

"One two three, on three?" said Ivan to Galeni.

"Just three," said Galeni.

"All right."

They swung him over the edge; for the first time, Miles glimpsed what waited for him below. His body tried to spasm, but his unused locked muscles foiled him, and his dry throat blocked his cry of outrage.

About a hundred liters of water. With about fifty kilos of ice cubes floating in it.

He plunged downward into the crashing cold. Ivan's long arms thrust him under all the way.

He came up yelling "*Ice* wat—" Ivan shoved him back in again.

On his next breath, "Ivan, you goddamn fri—"

On the third emergence his voice found expression in a wordless howl.

"Ah, ha!" Ivan chortled happily. "I thought that would get a rise out of you!" He added aside to Galeni, who had ducked away out of range of the wild splashing, "Ever since that time he spent at Camp Permafrost as a weather officer, there's nothing he hates worse than cold. Back you go, boy."

Miles fought his way out of Ivan's grip, spat freezing water, clambered up, and fell out over the side of the tub. Ice cubes stuck here and there to the outside of his sodden uniform tunic, and slithered down his neck. His hand drew back in a fist, and shot upward at his cousin's grinning face.

It connected with Ivan's chin with a satisfying meaty thunk; the pain was delicious. It was the first time in his life he'd ever successfully slugged Ivan.

"Hey!" Ivan yelped, ducking backwards. Miles's second swing missed, as Ivan now prudently held him at arm's length, out of Miles's range. "I thought that sort of thing broke your arm!"

"Not anymore," Miles panted. He stopped swinging, and stood shivering.

Ivan rubbed his jaw, brows rising. "Feeling better now?" he asked after a moment.

Miles answered with a spate of swearing, plucking off and throwing a few last clinging ice cubes from his tunic at Ivan's head along with the curses.

"Glad to hear it," said Ivan genially. "Now I'm going to tell you what you're going to do, and you're going to do it. First thing is, you're going to go to your room and take off that wet uniform. Then depilate that repellent beard stubble and get a hot shower. And then you're going to get dressed. And then we're going to take you out to dinner."

"Don't want to go out," Miles mumbled, surly.

"Did I ask for an argument? Did you hear me ask for a Betan vote, Duv?"

Galeni, watching in fascination, shook his head.

"Right," Ivan continued. "I don't want to hear it, and you don't have a choice. I've got another fifty kilos of ice tucked in the freezer downstairs, and you know I won't hesitate to use it."

Miles could read the utter, indeed, enthusiastic sincerity of this threat in Ivan's face. His bad words trailed off into a disagreeable, but not disagreeing, hiss. "You enjoyed that," he grumbled at last.

"Damn straight," said Ivan. "Now go get dressed."

⇒═◉═

Ivan made few further demands upon Miles until he had dragged him out to a nearby restaurant. There he made *sotto voce* threats until Miles put a few bites of food into his mouth, chewed, and swallowed. Once he started eating, he found he was very hungry, and Ivan desisted, satisfied with his performance.

"Now," said Ivan, shoveling in the last bite of his own dessert. "What the hell is going on with you?"

Miles glanced up at the two captains, at Galeni's eye-of-Horus pins. "You first. Did Illyan send you both?"

"He asked me to check on you," said Galeni, "having got the idea that we were friends of a sort. Since the gate guard reported you had gone in, but never come out, and you didn't answer your com-console after repeated calls and messages, I thought I'd better take a look in person. I felt . . . less than comfortable invading Vorkosigan House by myself, so I rounded up Ivan, whom I construed as having a family right to be there. On the authorization I had from Illyan, the gate guard overrode your locks and let us in, so we didn't have to break a window." Galeni hesitated. "I also didn't fancy having to pull your body down from a rafter somewhere all by myself."

"Told you not," said Ivan. "Not his style. If he ever does do himself in, I'm betting it'll be something that involves large explosions. And lots of innocent bystanders, probably."

Miles and Ivan exchanged sneers.

"I . . . wasn't so sure," said Galeni. "You didn't see him, Ivan, when he came out of Illyan's office. The last time I saw anybody who looked that shocky was a fellow I helped pull out of his crashed lightflyer."

"I'll explain it," Miles sighed, "but not here. Some more private place. Too much of it has to do with business." He glanced away from Galeni's silver eyes. "My former business."

"Right," agreed Galeni blandly.

They ended up back in the kitchen at Vorkosigan House. Miles hoped dimly Ivan would help him get drunk, but his cousin brewed tea, instead, and made him drink two cups for rehydration, before settling down astride a chair, his arms crossed on the back, and saying, "All right. Give. You know you have to."

"Yes. I know." Miles closed his eyes briefly, wondering where to begin. The beginning would probably do. Excuses and denials, all so well practiced, boiled up in his head. The taste of them, balanced on his tongue, was more loathsome than clean confession, and more lingering. The shortest way between two points was a straight line. "After my cryo-revival last year . . . I had a problem. I started getting these seizures. Convulsions, lasting two to five minutes. They seemed to be triggered by moments of extreme stress. My surgeon stated that, like the memory loss, they might right themselves. They were rare, and seemed to be tailing off as promised. So I . . . didn't mention it to my ImpSec doctors, when I came home."

"Oh, shit," murmured Ivan. "I see where this is going. Did you tell *anyone*?"

"Mark knew."

"You told Mark, but not *me*?"

"I could trust Mark . . . to do what I asked of him. I could only trust you to do what you thought was right." He'd said almost the same thing to Quinn, hadn't he. God.

Ivan's lips twitched, but he did not deny it.

"You can see why I was afraid it might be a one-way ticket to a medical discharge, at worst. A desk job at best, and no more Dendarii Mercenaries, no more field work. But I thought if I, or rather my Dendarii surgeon, could fix it quietly, Illyan need never be the wiser. She gave me some medication. I thought it was working." *No. No excuses, dammit.*

"And Illyan caught up with you and canned you for it? Isn't that a little extreme, after all you've done for him?"

"There's more."

"Ah."

"My last mission . . . we went to pry a kidnapped ImpSec courier out of the hands of some hijackers out past Zoave Twilight. I wanted to supervise the rescue personally. I was wearing my combat armor. I . . . had an episode right in the middle of the operation. My suit's plasma arc locked on. I damn near cut the poor courier in half, but he was lucky. I just lopped off his legs, instead."

Ivan's jaw dropped, then closed. "I . . . see."

"No, you don't. Not yet. That was merely criminally stupid. What I did next was fatal. I falsified my mission report. Claimed the accident with Vorberg was an equipment malfunction."

Galeni's breath drew in sharply. "Illyan said . . . you'd resigned by request. But he didn't say whose request or why, and I didn't dare ask. I didn't believe it. I thought it might be the start of some new scam, an internal investigation or something. Except I don't think even you could have faked the look on your face."

Ivan was still processing it. "You lied to *Illyan?*"

"Yeah. And then I documented my lie. Anything worth doing is worth doing well, yes? I didn't resign, Ivan. I was fired. On all of Barrayar right now, there is no one more fired than I am."

"Did he really rip off your silver eyes?" Ivan's own eyes were round.

"Who said that?"

Galeni grunted. "Looked like it. Haroche thought so."

Worse. He was crying, Ivan. In all his life, Miles had never seen Illyan weep. "No. I did that myself. I did it all to myself." He hesitated. "I had my last seizure in his office. Right in front of him. I think I mentioned they seem to be triggered by stress."

Ivan's face screwed up in a sympathetic wince.

Galeni blew out his breath. "Haroche couldn't believe it either. He said everyone at ImpSec HQ knew Illyan thought you shit gold bars."

Naismith was the best, oh yes. "After the Dagoola IV operation, he damn well should have thought so." But the Dagoola rescue had been almost four years ago. *So what have you shit for me lately?* "I take it that's a direct quote from Haroche."

"Mm, he can be blunt. He doesn't exactly suffer fools gladly. I'm told he came up through the ranks. He said you were being groomed as Illyan's successor."

Miles's brows rose in startlement. "Impossible. Being a desk driver requires very different qualities than being a field agent. A diametrically opposed attitude to the rules, for starters. I'm not . . . wasn't nearly ready for Illyan's job."

"So Haroche said. Your next posting was to be his assistant, it seems. Five years on the domestic side, and you'd have been ready to step up when Illyan was ready to retire."

"Rubbish. Not Domestic Affairs. Now, if I had to fly a desk, Galactic Affairs on Komarr would actually make sense. I have some experience there."

"That gap in your experience was exactly what they hoped to target by harnessing you with Haroche. Illyan once told me Haroche was personally responsible while he was a Domestic Affairs agent for derailing no less than four serious plots against the Emperor's life. Not including the *Yarrow* incident, which won him his chiefship. Maybe Illyan hoped whatever Haroche has would rub off on you."

"I don't need—" Miles began, and shut his mouth.

"What's the *Yarrow* incident," asked Ivan, "and if it's that important, why haven't I heard of it?"

"A textbook case in counterterrorism," said Galeni. "Illyan has all his new analysts study it."

"The case is famous inside ImpSec," Miles explained. "Being a success, however, it's practically unknown outside ImpSec. It's the nature of the job. Successes are secret and thankless, failures are splashy and gain you only blame." *Take my career, for example. . . .*

"It was a close call," said Galeni. "A hyperisolationist faction aligned with Count Vortrifrani plotted to suicide-drop an old jump-freighter named the *Yarrow* square on the Imperial Residence. It would have taken out most of the place even without the explosives they'd packed it with. The explosives were their one mistake, since that was the loose thread that led Haroche's team to them. Vortrifrani distanced himself like crazy, but it broke up his support, and the Imperium has been less, ah, embarrassed by him since."

Ivan blinked. "My mother's flat isn't far from the Residence. . . ."

"Yes, one wonders how many people in Vorbarr Sultana they'd have taken out if they'd missed their drop point."

"Thousands," Miles muttered.

"I'll have to remember to thank Haroche, next time I see him," said Ivan, sounding impressed.

"I was off-world, at the time," Miles sighed. "As usual." He suppressed an irrational twinge of jealousy. "Nobody ever said anything to me about this proposed promotion. When . . . was this vile little surprise supposed to be sprung?"

"Within the year, apparently."

"I thought I'd made the Dendarii too valuable for ImpSec to even dream of doing anything else with me."

"So, you did a little too good a job."

"Chief of ImpSec at age thirty-five. Huh. God be praised, I'm saved from *that* at least. Well. No joy to Haroche, to be required to paper train some Vor puppy for the express purpose of being promoted over his head. He ought to be quite relieved."

Galeni said apologetically, "I gather he was, actually."

"Ha," said Miles blackly. He added after a moment, "By the way, Duv. I trust it's obvious that what I've told you is private information. The official version, for ImpSec HQ and everywhere else, was that I was medically discharged without prejudice."

"So Illyan said, when Haroche asked. Illyan was tight-lipped as hell. But you could see there had to be more to it."

Ivan excused himself. Miles brooded into his teacup. He thought he could sleep, now. In fact, there was nothing he wanted more. Ivan returned all too soon, and dumped down a valise beside the kitchen table.

"What's that?" Miles asked suspiciously.

"My things," said Ivan. "For a couple of days."

"You're not moving in!"

"What, don't you have enough space? You've got more rooms than a hotel, Miles."

Miles slumped again, recognizing an argument he wasn't going to win. "There's a thought, for my next career. Vorkosigan's Bed and Breakfast."

"Rooms cheap?" Ivan cocked an eyebrow.

"Hell, no. Charge 'em a fortune." He paused. "So when are you planning to move back out?"

"Not until you get some people in here. Till you get your head fixed, you certainly need a driver, at the very least. I saw your lightflyer downstairs in the garage, by the way. In the shop for adjustments, my ass. And somebody to cook meals and stand over you and see you eat them. And somebody to clean up after you."

"I don't make that much mess—"

"And clean up after all the other somebodies," Ivan went on relentlessly. "This place needs a *staff*, Miles."

"Just like any other museum, eh? I don't know."

"If you're saying you don't know if you want them, guess what. You don't have a choice. If you're saying you don't know how to hire them . . . want my mother to do it for you?"

"Er . . . I think I'd rather select my own personnel. She'd make it all too right and proper, to use Sergeant Bothari's old phrase."

"There it is. Do it, or I'll have her do it for you. How's that for a threat?"

"Effective."

"Right, then."

"Don't you think I could get by with just one person? To do everything, drive, cook . . ."

Ivan snorted. "—chase after you and make you take your nasty medicine? For that, you'd need to hire a Baba to find you a wife. Why don't you just start with a driver and cook, and go on from there."

Miles grimaced tiredly.

"Look," said Ivan. "You're a bleeding Vor lord in Vorbarr Sultana. We *own* this town. So live like one! Have some fun for a change!"

"Have you lost your mind, Ivan?"

"You're not a *guest* in Vorkosigan House, Miles. You're its only child, or you were till Mark came along, and he has his own private fortune. At least widen your possibilities! You grew so narrow, working for Illyan. It's like you hardly had a life at all, lately."

That's quite right. Naismith had all the life. But Naismith was dead now—killed by that needle grenade on Jackson's Whole after all, though the double-take of realization had required a full year to run its course.

Miles had read of mutants, twins born joined together inseparably in their bodies. Sometimes, horrifically, one died first, leaving the other attached to a corpse for hours or days until they died too. Lord Vorkosigan and Admiral Naismith, body-bound twins. *I don't want to think about this anymore. I don't want to think at all.*

"Let's . . . go to bed, Ivan. It's late, isn't it?"

"Late enough," said Ivan.

EIGHT

Miles slept till midmorning the next day. To his dismay, when he threaded the labyrinth of the house down to the kitchen, he found Ivan sitting drinking coffee, his breakfast dishes piled in the sink.

"Don't you have to go to work?" Miles inquired, pouring the chewy dregs from the coffeemaker into his cup.

"I have a few days personal leave," Ivan informed him.

"How many?"

"As many as I need."

As many as he needed, that is, to satisfy himself that Miles was going to behave properly. Miles thought it through. So . . . if he hired that unwanted staff, Ivan, relieved of the deathwatch, would slope off home to his neat little flat—which, incidentally, had no staff underfoot, only a discreet cleaning service. Then Miles could fire the staff . . . that is, discharge them again, with suitably glowing recommendations and a bonus. Yeah. That would work.

"Have you communicated to your parents about this yet?" Ivan asked.

"No. Not yet."

"You ought to. Before they get some garbled version through some other source."

"So I ought. It's . . . not easy." He glanced up at Ivan. "I don't suppose you could . . . ?"

"Absolutely not!" cried Ivan in a tone of horror. After a moment of silence, he relented to the measure of a, "Well . . . if you really can't. But I'd rather not."

"I'll . . . think about it."

Miles slopped the last of the greenish coffee into his cup, trudged back upstairs, and dressed in a loose, embroidered backcountry-style shirt and dark trousers, which he found in the back of his closet. He'd last worn them three years ago. At least they weren't tight. While Ivan wasn't around, he pulled all his Barrayaran uniforms and boots out of his closet and bundled them into storage in an unused guest room down the hall, so he wouldn't have to look at them every time he opened his closet door. After a long hesitation, he exiled his Dendarii mercenary uniforms likewise. The few clothes left hanging seemed lonely and forlorn.

He settled himself at his comconsole in his bedroom. A message to his parents, ah God. And he ought to send one to Elli Quinn, too. Would he ever get the chance to make it right again with her? Face-to-face, body to body? It was a horribly complex thing to attempt via a comconsole message: just his thin electronic ghost, mouthing words ill-chosen or misunderstood, weeks out of synchrony. And all his messages to the Dendarii were monitored by ImpSec censors.

I can't face this now. I'll do it later. Soon. I promise.

He turned his thoughts instead to the less daunting problem of Vorkosigan House staffing. So what was the budget for this project? His lieutenant's medical-discharge half-pay would barely cover the salary and board of one full-time servant, even with a free room thrown in, at least of the sorts of superior folk normally employed by the aristocracy in the capital—he would be competing with sixty other District Counts' households in that labor market here, a host of lesser lordlings, and the sort of new industrial wealthy non-Vor who were presently carrying off such a distressing percentage of eligible Vor maidens to preside over their homes in the style to which they aspired.

Miles tapped in a comconsole code. The pleasant, smiling face of the Vorkosigans' business manager, Tsipis, appeared with startling promptness over the vid plate upon Miles's call reaching his office in Hassadar. "Good morning, Lord Vorkosigan! I was not aware you had returned from your off-planet duty. How may I serve you?"

He was not yet aware of Miles's medical discharge, either, apparently. Miles felt too weary to explain even the edited-for-public-consumption version of events, so only said, "Yes. I got in a few weeks ago. It . . . looks like I'm going to be downside longer than I'd anticipated. What funds can I draw upon? Did Father leave you any instructions?"

"All of it," said Tsipis.

"Excuse me? I don't understand."

"All of the accounts and funds were made joint with you, just before the Count and Countess departed for Sergyar. Just in case. You are your father's executor, you know."

"Yes, but . . ." He hadn't thought Sergyar was that wild a frontier. "Um . . . what can I do?"

"It's much easier to say what you can't do. You can't sell the entailed properties, namely the residence at Hassadar and Vorkosigan House. You can buy whatever you wish, of course, or sell anything your grandfather left you solely in your own name."

"So . . . can I afford to hire a full-time driver?"

"Oh, my, yes, you could afford to staff Vorkosigan House in full. The funds are there, piling up."

"Aren't they needed for the Viceroy's Palace on Sergyar?"

"Countess Vorkosigan has tapped a certain amount of her private moneys, apparently for some redecorating project, but your father is only maintaining his twenty Armsmen at present. Everything else on Sergyar comes out of the Imperial budget."

"Oh."

Tsipis brightened. "Are you thinking of reopening Vorkosigan House, my lord? That would be splendid. It was such a fine sight, last year at Winterfair, when I dined there."

"Not . . . at present."

Tsipis drooped. "Ah," he murmured, in a tone of disappointment. Then a look of belated enlightenment came over his face. "My lord . . . do you need *money*?"

"Er . . . yes. That was what I had in mind. To, like, pay a driver, maybe a cook, pay bills, buy things . . . a suitable living allowance, you know." His ImpSec pay, accumulating in his lengthy absences on duty, had always been more than enough. He wondered how much to ask Tsipis for.

"But of course. How would you like it? A weekly deposit into your Service account, perhaps?"

"No . . . I'd like a new account. Separate. Just . . . to me as Lord Vorkosigan."

"Excellent thinking. Your father is always very careful to keep his personal and Imperial funds identifiably separated. It's a good habit to start. Not that the most foolhardy Imperial Auditor would ever have dared to take him on, of course. Nor have looked anything but a fool afterwards, when the numbers were laid out." Tsipis tapped on his comconsole, and glanced aside at some data readout. "Suppose I transfer the entire accumulated unused Household fund over into your new account, for seed money. And then just send the usual weekly allotment to follow."

"Fine."

"Now, if you need any more, do call me right away."

"Sure."

"I'll send you your new account chit by courier within the hour."

"Thank you." Miles reached to cut the com, then added as an afterthought, "How much is it?"

"Five thousand marks."

"Oh, good."

"And eighty thousand marks to start," Tsipis added.

Miles did a quick mental reversal, and calculation. "This place was sucking down five thousand marks a *week*?"

"Oh, much more than that, with the Armsmen, and the Countess's personal account. And this does not include major repairs, which are budgeted separately."

"I . . . see."

"Now, should you take an interest, I should be happy to go over all your financial affairs with you in *much* more detail," Tsipis added eagerly. "There's so much that could be done with a somewhat more aggressive, entrepreneurial, and, dare I say, less conservative and more attentive approach."

"If . . . I ever have the time. Thank you, Tsipis." Miles cut the com much less casually.

Good God. He could buy . . . damn near anything he wanted. He tried to think of something he wanted.

The Dendarii.

Yeah. We know. But their price, for him, wasn't measured in money. *What else?*

Once, in his increasingly distant youth, he'd lusted briefly after a lightflyer, faster and redder than Ivan's. A particularly fine model, albeit several years old now, sat in the garage downstairs, only lightly used. Of course, he couldn't fly it at all now.

It was never what I wanted to buy that held my heart's hope. It was what I wanted to be.

What had that been? Well, an admiral, of course, a real one, a Barrayaran one, by age 35, one year younger than when his father had become the youngest in post-Isolation history at age 36. Despite Miles's height, and in the teeth of his handicaps. But even had he been born normal of body, his era had brought him no convenient major wars to speed promotion. ImpSec covert ops had been the best he could do, not just the one branch of the Service that would take him, but the only one that could put him in the forefront of the only significant action presently available. How could you be a Great Man if history brought you no Great Events, or brought you to them at the wrong time, too young, too old? *Too damaged.*

He turned to his list of five retired Vorkosigan Armsmen living in the Vorbarr Sultana area. Though elderly, an Armsman, with his wife perhaps to cook, would be the ideal solution to his problem. He wouldn't have to teach them anything about Vorkosigan House's routine, and they'd have no objection to a short-term gig. He began coding his calls. *Maybe I'll get lucky on the first try.*

One was too doddering to drive anymore himself. The other four's wives all said no, or rather, *No!*

It wasn't as if he were in the heat of battle; he could not justify invoking certain archaic loyalty oaths. With a snort, he gave it up, and went to collect last night's scraps from the kitchen in his on-going campaign to convince Zap the Cat to not snatch food with razor claws, run under a chair, and growl through her gorge, but rather, eat daintily, and sit on one's lap and purr gratefully afterwards, like a proper Vor cat. In all, there was a lot about Zap that reminded Miles of his clone-brother Mark, and he'd done all right with Mark in the end. It wouldn't hurt to let the gate guard know about Tsipis's courier, too.

———◆———

Miles arrived to find the gate guard had a visitor, a tall, blond young man who bore a notable, if softer, resemblance to the sharper-featured Corporal Kosti. He also bore a large lacquered box.

"Good morning, or should I say, afternoon, sir," the guard greeted him with a vague aborted salute almost worthy of an HQ analyst, belatedly recognizing the fact that Miles wore no uniform. "Um . . . may I introduce my younger brother Martin?"

You're not old enough to have a younger brother. "Hello." Miles stuck out his hand.

The blond youth shook it without hesitation, though his eyes did widen a bit, looking down at Miles. "Uh . . . hello. Lieutenant. Lord Vorkosigan."

Nobody'd briefed Kosti either, it appeared. The corporal was too far down in the hierarchy, maybe. Miles glanced away from the ImpSec silver eyes on Kosti-the-elder's stiff collar. Well, get it over with. "No more the lieutenant, I'm afraid. I've just mustered out of the Service altogether. Medical discharge."

"Oh. I'm sorry to hear that, si—my lord." The gate guard sounded quite sincere. But he did not demand embarrassing explanations. Nobody, looking at Miles, would question the medical discharge story.

Zap oozed from under the kiosk's chair, and growled slightly at Miles, whom she was growing to recognize. "That hairy beast isn't getting any friendlier, is she?" said Miles. "Just fatter."

"I'm not surprised," said Corporal Kosti. "Every time we change shifts she tries to convince whoever's coming on duty she's been starved by the last man."

Miles offered a scrap, which Zap deigned to accept in the usual manner, and then retreated to scarf her spoils. Miles sucked on the scratch on the back of his thumb. "Clearly, she's training to be a guard cat. If only we could teach her to tell friend from foe." He stood up again.

"Nobody wants to hire me for just two months," Martin said to his brother, evidently continuing a conversation Miles's arrival had interrupted.

Miles's brow rose. "Looking for work, are you, Martin?"

"Looking to turn eighteen, and apply to the Service," said Martin stoutly. "I've two more months to wait. But my mother said if I don't find something for me to do the meanwhile she will. And I'm afraid it has something to do with cleaning."

Wait till you meet your first master sergeant, kid. You'll find out about cleaning. "I cleaned drains on Kyril Island, once," Miles reminisced. "I was quite good at it."

"You, my lord?" Martin's eyes grew round.

Miles's lips crimped. "It was exciting. I found a body."

"Oh." Martin settled. "ImpSec business, right?"

"Not . . . at the time."

"His first sergeant will straighten him out," the corporal confided confidently to Miles.

He treats me as an honorable veteran. He does not know. "Oh, yes." The two insiders grinned malevolently at the would-be apprentice. "The Service is getting pickier with its recruits, these days. . . . I hope you didn't slack your schoolwork."

"No, my lord," said Martin.

If true, this one would be a shoo-in. He had the physique for a ceremonial guard; his brother, obviously, had the brains to be a real one. "Well, good luck to you." *Better luck than mine.* No, unjust to use his daily gift of breath to complain about his luck. "So, Martin . . . can you drive?"

"Of course, my lord."

"Lightflyer?"

A slight hesitation. "I've done a bit."

"I happen to be in temporary need of a driver."

"Really, my lord? Do you think—could I—?"

"Perhaps."

The corporal's forehead crinkled in mild dismay. "It's part of my job to keep him alive, Martin. You wouldn't embarrass me, would you?"

Martin gave him a brotherly curl of the lip, but disdained, interestingly, to rise to the bait. His attention was on Miles. "When could I start?"

"Any time, I suppose. Today, if you like." Yes, he needed to at least go to the grocery and get another crate of *Reddi-Meals!* "There probably wouldn't be much to do at first, but I wouldn't know in advance when I wanted you, so I'd like you to live in. You could spend your spare time studying up for your Service entrance evaluations." Plus, of course, the medical watch. Would the acquisition of the possibly-more-pliable Martin be enough to displace Ivan? He would have to apprise Martin of that extra little detail of his job later.

No. Sooner. The next attack could happen any time. Unfair, to hit the kid with a convulsing employer and no warning. Elli Quinn would agree. "I can't drive myself. I've been having trouble with seizures. An aftereffect of an acute case of death I picked up last year, courtesy of . . . a well-aimed needle grenade. The cryorevival almost worked."

The corporal looked enlightened. "I never thought a courier's job was the feather bed some people make it out to be."

Martin stared down at him in utter fascination, almost as impressed as he'd been by the drain-cleaning confession. "You were *dead*, my lord?"

"So they tell me."

"What was it like?"

"I don't know," said Miles shortly. "I missed it." He relented slightly. "Being alive again hurt, though."

"Wow." Martin shoved the lacquer box toward his brother. Zap the Cat emerged again to roll backwards across the mirror-polished toes of the corporal's boots, purring wildly, waving her claws in the air, and glaring at the box.

"Calm down, Zap, you'll set off the alarms," said the corporal, amused. He set the box down on the kiosk's tiny table and released the lid. Somewhat absently, he tore off the cover of his Service-issue ready-meal lunch, and set it on the floor; Zap sniffed it, and returned to clawing his booted leg and looking longingly at the lacquered box.

The inside of the box lid turned into a clever tray or plate, with little compartments. Onto it Kosti placed two temperature-controlled jugs, a bowl, and cups; there followed an assortment of sandwiches on two different kinds of bread with variously colored fillings, cut into circle, star, and square shapes, the crusts removed; carved fruit on a stick; buttery cookies; and round tarts with flaky, fluted, sugar-sprinkled crusts, oozing dark, thick fruit syrups. From one of the jugs Kosti poured a pinkish cream soup into the bowl; from the other, some spicy hot drink. Both steamed in the cool air. For Zap the Cat there was a wad of prettily tied green leaves that unfolded to reveal a meat paste of some kind, apparently the same as filled one of the sandwiches. Zap dived in the moment Kosti spread it on the floor, growling ecstatically, tail lashing.

Miles stared in amazement, and swallowed saliva. "What *is* all that, Corporal?"

"My lunch," said Kosti simply. "M' mother sends it over every day." He batted away a brotherly paw descending on one sandwich. "Hey. You can get yours at home. This is mine." He glanced up a little uncertainly at Miles.

Technically, ImpSec personnel on duty were not supposed to eat anything but ImpSec-issued rations, to avoid any attacks through ingestible drugs or poisons. But if you couldn't trust your mother and brother, who could you trust? Besides . . . it wasn't Miles's officerly job to enforce ImpSec regs in idiotic situations anymore. "Your mother makes all that? Every day?"

"Mostly," said Kosti. "With my sisters married—"

Of course.

"—and just Martin left in the house, I think she's getting a little bored."

"Corporal Kosti. Martin." Miles took a deep breath, laden with delectable aromas. "Do you think your mother would like a *job*?"

"Things are looking up," said Ivan judiciously over their lunch the next day. Ma Kosti had deposited her artistic offering and withdrawn from the Yellow Parlor, possibly to bring the next load. Several minutes later he added, muffled around a full mouth, "What are you paying her?"

Miles told him.

"Double it," said Ivan decisively. "Or you'll lose her after your first dinner party. Someone will hire her away. Or kidnap her."

"Not with her son as my gate guard. Besides, I'm not planning any dinner parties."

"That would be a shame. Want me to?"

"No." Miles weakened, possibly a subtle and sinister effect of the spiced peach tart melting in his mouth. "Not at present, anyway." He smiled slowly. "But in the department of great leaders of history . . . you can tell everyone with perfect truth that Lord Vorkosigan eats the same food as his gate guard and driver."

A contract with Ivan's cleaning service to send in people twice a week completed the staffing of Vorkosigan House to Ivan's convenience. But as a ploy to get rid of Ivan, Miles realized, the acquisition of Ma Kosti had proved a slight miscalculation. He should have hired a *bad* cook.

If Ivan would only leave, Miles could go back to brooding in peace. He couldn't lock his bedroom door and not answer it without it being an invitation to Ivan to break it down; and there was a limit to how much he could snarl and sulk without risking another ice-water dip.

At least Ivan could start going back to work in the daytime, Miles thought. He tried a broad hint over dinner.

" 'Most men,' " he quoted, " 'are of naught more use in their lives but as machines for turning food into shit.' "

Ivan cocked an eyebrow at him. "Who said that? Your grandfather?"

"Leonardo da Vinci," Miles returned primly. But was compelled to add, "Grandfather quoted it to me, though."

"Thought so," said Ivan, satisfied. "Sounds just like the old General. He *was* a monster in his day, wasn't he?" Ivan put another bite of roast dripping with wine sauce into his mouth, and started chewing.

Ivan . . . was a pain. The last thing a monster wanted was a fellow to follow him around all day long with a mirror.

———◈———

The days had blended formlessly into a week before Miles found a message from the outside world on his comconsole. He hit the replay, and the fine-boned face of Lady Alys Vorpatril composed itself over his vid plate.

"Hello, Miles," she began. "I was very sorry to hear about your medical discharge. I know it must be a great disappointment to you, after all your efforts."

Credit to Ivan, he had certainly not told her the whole story, or her condolences would have been much differently phrased. She dismissed his utter destruction with an airy wave, and went on to her own concerns. "At Gregor's request I am hostessing an intimate luncheon in the Residence's south garden tomorrow afternoon. He has asked me to invite you. He asks you to come an hour early for a personal conference. I'd take that as *Requests and Requires your Attendance*, rather than just *invites*, if I were you, on that first matter. Or so I read it between the lines, though he was all soft-voiced about it, the way he gets sometimes, you know. RSVP immediately you get this message, please." She cut the com.

Miles bent, and rested his forehead on the cool edge of the comconsole. He'd known this moment must come; it was inherent in choosing to live. Gregor was giving him the opportunity to formally apologize. They had to clear the air sooner or later. If only as Count of his District someday, Miles was going to be around Vorbarr Sultana for a long time yet. He wished he might render his apology in the old archaic belly-sticking sense. *In absentia.* It would be easier and less painful.

Why didn't they just leave me dead the first time?

He sighed, sat up, and punched in Lady Alys's number on the com.

—◦— NINE —◦—

Count Vorkosigan's armored groundcar sighed to the pavement under the east portico of the Imperial Residence. Martin looked nervously back over his shoulder toward the gates, and the gesturing guards clustered around them. "Are you sure that's going to be all right, my lord?"

"Don't worry about it," said Miles, seated beside him in the driver's compartment. "They'll have that little bit of wrought-iron straightened back up and repainted before I'm ready to be picked up again, I wager."

Martin made to pop the canopy, or at least, hunted valiantly for the control to do so in the gleaming array before him. Miles pointed. "Thanks," Martin muttered.

The canopy rose; Miles escaped with his life. "Martin . . . tell you what. While I'm engaged in here, why don't you take this barge for a practice spin around the city." He dropped the groundcar's comm link into his pocket. "I'll call you back when I need you. If you"—Miles deleted *run into a*—"have a problem, call me . . . no." He suspected he would shortly be praying for interruptions to his upcoming interview with Gregor, but it was cheating to prearrange them. "Call this number." He leaned over and tapped a code into the car's elaborate console. "This will get you a very competent gentleman named Tsipis, nice fellow, he'll tell you what to do."

"Yes, my lord."

"Watch your forward momentum. The power in this beast fools you. The heavy-duty fuel cells add mass almost as badly as the armoring does. The handling is quite deceptive. Take it out someplace where you have a lot of space, and experiment, so it won't surprise you again."

"Uh . . . thank you, sir." The canopy hissed shut; through the polarized half-mirroring Miles could see Martin suck on his lip in concentration, as the car rose and moved forward once more. The car's silvery-gleaming left rear edge was undamaged, Miles noted without surprise. Another trainee, ah yes. If he'd had his wits about him, he could have sent the boy out to practice all last week, and avoided that minor embarrassment with Gregor's gate. But Martin would do all right, once he'd been permitted enough experience, and the better for not having the unnerving presence of his lordly little new employer at his elbow.

One of the Residence's liveried servants met Miles at the door, and escorted him to the north wing; they were headed for Gregor's private office, then. The north wing was the only section of the sprawling Imperial Residence less than two hundred years old. It had been burned to the ground during the War of Vordarian's Pretendership, the year of Miles's soltoxin-gas-damaged birth, and subsequently rebuilt. The Emperor's ground-floor office was one of Gregor's few truly private and personal spaces. The decoration was spare, the limited artwork all purchased from rising young artists who were actually still alive, and there wasn't an antique in it.

Gregor was standing by a tall, heavily draped window, staring out at his garden, as Miles entered. Had he been pacing? He wore his Vorbarra House uniform today, very sharp; Miles, presently feeling allergic to uniforms, was underdressed for the Residence in some slightly outdated street wear he'd rummaged from the back of his closet.

The servant announced, "Lord Vorkosigan," and bowed himself out. Gregor nodded, and waved Miles to a chair. Miles returned a somewhat leaden smile as Gregor seated himself across from him, and leaned forward, hands clasped on his knees.

"This is as difficult for me as I'm sure it must be for you," Gregor began.

Miles's smile grew dryer. "Not . . . quite, I fancy," he murmured.

Gregor grimaced; one hand flipped outward, as if to bat away the bait. "I wish you hadn't done it."

"I wish I hadn't done it too."

Gregor continued inconsistently, "We cannot undo what's done. No matter how we might wish it."

"Mm. If I could—one of those one-wish things—I don't even know that I'd choose this. Maybe go back instead to the death of

Sergeant Bothari, and undo that, right at the beginning. I don't know . . . maybe it wouldn't have worked out any better. Probably not. But that was a more innocent mistake, if more lethal. I've graduated to more calculated stupidities, these days." His voice was stiff.

"You were on the verge of such great things."

"What, a desk job in Domestic Affairs? I beg to differ." That was, perhaps, the sharpest bite in all this tangle: that he'd sacrificed everything up to and including his integrity to save an identity that was scheduled to be taken away from him within a year anyway. If he had known, he would have . . . what? *What, huh?*

Gregor's lips thinned in serious displeasure. "I've spent a lifetime having my affairs managed by old men. You were the first man of my generation I thought I might successfully place in a position of real power and responsibility in the upper echelons of what is ironically called *my* government."

And I screwed up, yes, we know, Gregor. "You have to give them this much credit, they weren't old when they started serving you. Illyan's brevet field promotion to Chief of ImpSec was at what, age thirty? And he was going to make *me* wait to thirty-five, the hypocrite."

Gregor was shaking his head. *If he says, "Miles, Miles, whatever are we going to do with you?", I'm walking out of here.* But what he said instead was, "So what are you planning to do now?"

Almost as bad. But Miles stayed seated. "I don't know. I need . . . some time off, serious time off. Time to think. Medical leave and travel time aren't really the same thing."

"I . . . request, that you not attempt to make independent contact with the Dendarii Mercenaries. I realize that I and ImpSec combined probably couldn't stop you, if you were determined to hijack them and take off. But there's no way I'd be able to save you from a treason charge this time."

Miles, managing not to swallow guiltily, nodded perfect understanding. He'd always known that would be a one-way trip. "The Dendarii don't need a commander with convulsions either. Till I get my head fixed—if it can be fixed—it's a null temptation." Perhaps fortunately. He hesitated, then let his primary anxiety surface in the most neutral wording he could muster. "What will the status of the Dendarii Fleet be now?"

"That would seem to depend on its new commander. How will Quinn want to play it?"

So, Gregor was *not* planning to unilaterally dispose of all of

Miles's creative efforts. Miles sighed inward relief, and chose his next words carefully. "She'd be a fool to throw away our—her—Imperial retainer. And she's nobody's fool. I see no reason the fleet cannot continue to be the same resource for ImpSec under her that they were under me."

"I'm willing to wait and see how it works out. See if she can deliver the successes. Or not."

God help you, Quinn. But the Dendarii could remain the Emperor's Own, even without him, yes, that was the important part. They were not to be abandoned. "Quinn's been my apprentice for damn near a decade. She's in her mid-thirties, at the peak of her performance. She's creative, she's determined, and she gets amazingly streamlined in emergencies, of which she's encountered a fair number, in my wake. If she's not ready to move up . . . then I'm not the commander I thought I was."

Gregor nodded shortly. "Very good." He inhaled, almost visibly changing tack; his face grew lighter. "Will you join me for lunch now, m'lord Vorkosigan?"

"I appreciate the gesture, Gregor. But must I stay?"

"There's someone I want you to meet. Or rather, observe."

He still values my opinion? "My judgment lately has been nothing to write home about."

"Mm . . . speaking of that . . . have you told your parents about this yet?"

"No," said Miles, and added cautiously, "Have you?"

"No . . ."

A glum silence fell for a moment.

"It's your job," said Gregor at last, firmly.

"I don't deny it."

"*Do* see to your medical treatment promptly, Miles. I am willing to make that an Imperial order, if necessary."

"Not . . . necessary, Sire."

"Good." Gregor rose; Miles perforce rose too.

They were halfway to the door when Miles managed a small-voiced "Gregor?"

"Yes . . . ?"

"I'm sorry."

Gregor hesitated, then returned a very tiny nod. They continued on together.

In a grassy nook in the South Garden, enclosed by trees and flowering shrubs, a table for four had been set under a fringed muslin awning. The weather was cooperating, the autumn sun dappling a shade that was perfectly cooled by a faint breath of breeze. The noises of the surrounding city seemed muffled and distant, as if the garden were embedded in a dream. Miles, slightly disturbed, eyed the arrangement as he seated himself at Gregor's left hand. *Surely he does not mean to honor me with this. That would be a mockery, right now.* Gregor waved away an anxious liveried servant offering a prelunch selection of drinks; they were waiting for someone, it appeared.

Enlightenment arrived simultaneously with Lady Alys Vorpatril, very correctly dressed for a Vor woman in the afternoon in a blue bolero and skirt trimmed with silver that seemed— deliberately?—to bring out the faint streaks of silver in her dark hair. She escorted Dr. Laisa Toscane, neat and stylish in Komarran trousers and jacket. Servants leapt to seat the women, then faded discreetly out of sight again.

"Good afternoon, Dr. Toscane," Miles said, as greetings were exchanged all around. "We meet again. Is this your second trip to the Residence, then?"

"My fourth." She smiled. "Gregor very kindly invited me to a luncheon meeting last week with Minister Racozy and some of his staff, where I had a chance to present some of my Trade Group's views. And then there was a ceremonial reception for some retiring District officers, that was just fascinating."

Gregor? Miles glanced at Alys Vorpatril, seated on his own left; she returned a very bland look.

The servants began presenting food and the conversation commenced, not surprisingly, with a few platitudes about Komarran affairs. It took an almost immediate hard left turn, however, as Gregor and Laisa began comparing families and childhoods; they were both only-children, a fact they seemed to find mutually engrossing and worthy of much comparison-analysis. Miles had the strong sense of having come in on Part 2, or perhaps Part 4, of an ongoing serial. Miles's own role seemed limited to occasional confirming murmurs about incidents of the distant past he barely remembered. Alys, normally chatty, said almost as little.

Gregor exerted himself to draw Laisa out; but she held her own, gently insisting on a point-for-point trade of information. It was more than Miles had heard Gregor talk at one time in ages.

When the cream cakes appeared, along with an offering of

five kinds of dessert coffees and teas, Gregor said shyly, "I've arranged a small surprise for you, Laisa." He made a covert hand-motion, down at his side, an obviously prearranged signal immediately picked up by an attentive liveried man, who promptly disappeared around the shrubbery. "You said you'd never seen a horse except in vids. The horse is such a symbol of the Vor, I thought you might like a ride."

On cue, the liveried man returned leading the most gorgeous little white mare Miles had ever seen in his life, not barring his grandfather's stables of expensive bloodstock. Big-eyed, dainty-footed . . . the hooves were all polished black, and the long silvery mane and flowing tail had scarlet ribbons braided in, to match the saddlecloth, not to mention the scarlet embroidered lead-line attached to the gilt bridle.

"Oh, my." Laisa's breath was quite taken away, as she ogled the beast. "May I pet it? But I have no idea how to ride!"

"But of course." Gregor escorted her to the mare's side; she laughed as her hands flew to touch the glossy neck, and ran through the shining mane. The mare's placid eyes half-closed in calm acceptance of these just attentions. "I'll lead you myself," said Gregor. "Just at a walk. She's very gentle." The mare was next door to somnolent, in fact, in Miles's judgment; Gregor was obviously taking no chances on any unpleasant horsy accidents spoiling his show.

Laisa made doubtful, fascinated, please-talk-me-into-it noises. Miles leaned over to Lady Alys and whispered, "*Where* did Gregor ever find that *horse?*"

"Three Districts away," she murmured back. "It was flown in to the Residence's stables yesterday. Gregor has been driving his domestic staff to distraction for four days, planning every detail of this luncheon."

"I'll give you a leg up," Gregor went on, as the groom held the embroidered lead-line. "Here, let me show you how. You bend your leg and I cup it in my hand. . . ."

It took three tries and a good deal of laughter to boost Laisa aboard. If Gregor was trying to cop a feel, he'd managed to do so with stunning savoir faire. She settled into the velvet-padded saddle looking delighted, self-conscious, and a little proud of herself. Gregor recovered the line from the groom, motioned him away, and led off for a tour of the garden paths, talking and gesturing.

Miles, wide-eyed, swallowed a large gulp of scalding tea. "So, Aunt Alys . . . are you playing Baba, or what?"

"It's beginning to look like it," she said dryly, her own eyes following the delicate little cavalcade.

"When did this happen?"

"I'm not quite sure. I looked around, and . . . there it was. I've been scrambling to catch up ever since."

"But Alys . . . a Komarran, for Empress?" It had to be an Empress that Gregor had in mind; Alys would never have leant herself as a procurer. "Aren't the conservative-wing Vor lords going to shit themselves? Not to mention the remaining radical revolutionary Komarrans. They'll shit themselves sideways."

"Please do not use barracks-language at the table, Miles. But in answer to your question . . . perhaps. The Centrist Coalition will like it, though. Or could be persuaded to."

"By you? Or by their wives, through you, do you mean? Do *you* approve?"

Her eyes narrowed thoughtfully. "Taking it all in all . . . yes, I think I do. Since your mother would not bestir herself in that department, I have by default been supervising Gregor's bride-search for the last decade. And a frustrating task it has been. I mean, he'd just *sit* there, and stare at me, with this dreadful, doleful, *Why are you doing this to me?* look on his face. I think I've paraded every tall, slim, Vor beauty on the planet past him at one time or another, to the great disruption of their lives and the routines of their families; I've offered dozens of resumes . . . nothing worked. I swear, Gregor has been even more frustrating than Ivan, and Ivan has lost so many good opportunities. . . . A certain nameless wit, or half-wit, even whispered I ought to start trying boys, but I pointed out that would *not* solve the heir problem, which is the whole point of the exercise in the first place."

"Not without a great deal of unprecedented genetic engineering interference," Miles agreed. "No, not boys, not Gregor. But not a Vor either. I had that figured out years ago—I wish you'd have asked me. Gregor's even more closely related to Mad Emperor Yuri than I am. And, um . . . he knows more about his father, the late unlamented Crown Prince Serg, than I think my parents might wish. He has these historically well-founded genetic paranoias about—well—paranoia. And about Vor inbreeding. He'd never let himself fall in love with another Vor."

Alys's fine dark brows twitched. "I eventually figured out the Vor part for myself. It left me with a dilemma, as you may imagine."

"So . . . what does he see in Dr. Toscane, d'you think? Besides brains, beauty, a nice personality, a good sense of humor, social grace, wealth, and non-Vor genetics, that is?"

Alys vented a small, ladylike snort. "I think it's even simpler and more fundamental than that, though I doubt Gregor is conscious of it. Not to imitate one of your mother's annoying Betan-style instant psychoanalyses, but . . . Gregor's mother was murdered when he was five years old." Her red lips crimped briefly in old pain; Lady Alys had known Princess Kareen, back then. "Look at Dr. Toscane's figure. It's . . . maternal. Not a bone in sight anywhere. All that time I wasted herding tall, slender beauties past him, when I should have been rounding up short, *plump* beauties. I could cry." She ate a decisive bite of cream cake, instead.

Miles cleared his throat, neutrally. Gregor and Laisa rounded a corner, turned away, and passed up an alley of topiaried yew trees. Tall, thin Gregor strode at Laisa's stirrup, gesturing animatedly, smiling and talking. Laisa leaned half-toward him, over the saddle-bow, eyes shining, lips parted, listening with . . . all her heart, Miles feared.

"So, Miles," Alys went on, her voice cooler, "tell me about your Captain Galeni. It's not clear to me where he fits in all this."

"He's not my Captain," Miles said. "He's Gregor's Captain."

"But he's your friend, according to Ivan."

"Ivan worked with him much longer than I did."

"Quit evading the question. I have a feeling it's important, or could be. It's as much my job to prevent domestic disasters for Gregor as it is Simon's to prevent security ones or as it was your father's—it's Minister Racozy's job now, I suppose—to prevent political ones. Simon's ImpSec report claims Galeni and Dr. Toscane are not lovers."

"I . . . no. I don't think so either. He was courting her, though. That's why I invited them along to the Imperial State dinner in the first place. To help him out." Miles's Imperial luncheon was turning heavy, in his belly.

"But they are not formally engaged?"

"I don't think so."

"Had they talked about matrimony?"

"*I* don't know. I'm not exactly intimate with Galeni, y'know. We've just . . . worked together, thrown together once by accident in that mess with Mark on Earth, later by assignment during an ImpSec investigation of a certain nasty incident on Komarr. I think Galeni had marriage on his mind, yes. But he's a very closed man, for a lot of good reasons. I think it's been hard for him to try to get close to Laisa. Not because of what she is, but because of how he is, or how he's made himself. Slow, and deliberate, and careful."

Lady Alys tapped one long enameled fingernail on the lace tablecloth, unmarred, around her place, by crumbs or spills. "I need to know, Miles. Is Captain Galeni likely to be a problem over this? I don't want any more surprises."

"What do you mean by problem? Be a problem, or make a problem?"

Alys's softly modulated voice grew edged. "That's exactly what I'm asking you."

"I . . . don't know. I think he could be hurt. I'm sorry." Galeni was about to get frigging mangled, was what. *God, Duv . . . this wasn't what I'd meant to do for you. Sorry, sorry, this is my day to be one sorry sod, all right.*

"Well, ultimately, it's Laisa's choice," said Alys judiciously.

"How can poor Galeni compete with the *Emperor*?"

She gave him a slightly pitying look. "If she loves Galeni . . . there's no contest. If she doesn't . . . then there's no problem. Right?"

"I think my head hurts."

Lady Alys's lip curled slightly, in covert agreement; but her expression returned to its usual pleasant calm, as Gregor and the pony show approached again. Gregor helped Laisa down, managing something suspiciously close to an embrace in the process. He handed the horse off to its groom again, and another servant brought silver basins for the pair to wash the horse residue, if any, off their hands. A redundant gesture: the beast had to have been shampooed to within an inch of its life this morning. Miles would have had no hesitation about eating his lunch off its gleaming haunches.

Alys made a show of checking her chrono. "I'm sorry to break up this delightful afternoon, Gregor, but your meeting with Count Vortala and Minister Vann is only twenty minutes from now."

"Oh," Laisa, pink-cheeked and conscience-stricken, scrambled up from the chair she'd just reoccupied. "I'm keeping you from your work."

"Not with Lady Alys here to remind me of it," Gregor returned, with a glint that made Alys's smile thin, in turn. But Gregor rose obediently, and bowed over Laisa's hand—was he . . . ?

Yes. He was going to kiss it. In fact, he turned it over and brushed his lips on her palm. Miles crossed his arms, and put his own hand over his mouth, and bit his tongue. Laisa closed her hand over the kissed spot like a woman capturing a butterfly, and smiled. Actually, she grinned. Gregor grinned back, looking exhilarated. Alys cleared her throat. Miles bit harder. Gregor and Laisa exchanged a long and remarkably idiotic look. Alys broke it up at last, took Laisa in hand, and bore her away, saying something brightly about a walk through the lower salons to view the inlaid panels along the way.

Gregor flung himself back half-sideways in his chair, one booted leg hooked over the arm, swinging. "Well. What do you think of her?"

"Dr. Toscane?"

"I wasn't asking your opinion of your Aunt Alys."

Miles studied Gregor's eager smile. No . . . this man was not asking for a critique. "Lovely."

"Isn't she?"

"Very intelligent."

"Brilliant. I wish you could have attended Racozy's staff meeting. Her presentation was a model of clarity."

No doubt, with every expert the trade association owned doubtless up all night to help prepare it . . . still, Miles had run a staff briefing or two himself, in his day. He respected the effort involved. But Gregor was not so much soliciting Miles's opinion as asking for a confirmation of his own. *I was never a yes-man.*

"Very patriotic," Gregor burbled on, "in just the forward-looking, cooperative way your father had always hoped to achieve on Komarr."

"Yes, Sire."

"Beautiful eyes."

"Yes, Sire," Miles sighed. "Very, um, blue-green." *Why is he doing this to me?* Because the Count and Countess Vorkosigan weren't here, perhaps. He was using Miles as a stand-in for his parents, who, after all, were orphaned Gregor's foster parents as well. Good God, how were they going to react to this?

"Quick-witted . . ."

"Yes, Sire. Very."

"Miles?"

"Yes, Sire?"

"Stop that."

"Um." Miles tried the tongue-biting trick again.

Gregor's boot stopped swinging; his face grew more serious, shadowed. He added quietly, "I'm terrified."

"Of rejection? I'm not the expert on women Ivan claims to be, but . . . all the preliminary signs looked like go-aheads to me."

"No. Of . . . what could happen later. This job could be the death of me. And of those closest to me."

The shade of Princess Kareen, not the vagrant breeze, chilled the air. It was perhaps as well for Gregor's untrusted sanity that the north wing where his mother had died *had* burned flat, and been rebuilt ghost-free.

"Ordinary men and women . . . die every day. For all sorts of reasons, from random chance to inexorable time. Death is not an Imperial monopoly."

Gregor looked at him. "So it's not," he said softly. He nodded decisively, as if Miles had just said something useful. *What?*

Miles tried to change the subject. "So what's up at your meeting with Vortala and Vann?"

"Oh, the usual. Their Imperial Lands Distribution committee wants favors for friends. I want their friends to present proof of competent usage plans."

"Ah." All South Continent matters, of no direct interest to the Vorkosigan's District. Miles wondered if he ought to pass the word to his father's Deputy that this would be the ideal week to lobby Gregor for favors for the District. In his current state of dreamy idiocy and sexual fog, the love-stricken Gregor might well grant anything. No . . . better for the Imperium to keep this temporary insanity a State secret. Marriage would cure Gregor quickly enough.

A Komarran Empress. God. What a nightmare for ImpSec. Illyan really would have that stroke he'd been threatening for years. "Have you warned Illyan about this yet?"

"I thought I'd send Lady Alys to apprise him, if things seemed hopeful. Fairly soon. She seems to have made it her department."

"She's the best ally and go-between you could have. Behave, and you'll keep her on your side. But have you thought through the political ramifications of this . . . marriage?" It was the first time anyone had spoken that word out loud, Miles realized.

"I've thought about nothing else for the past week. It could be a good thing, you know, Miles. A symbol of Imperial unity and all that."

It was more likely the Komarran underground would make it a symbol of Komarr being screwed again by Barrayar. Miles imagined the potential for vicious political satire, and winced. "Don't get your hopes up on that score."

Gregor shook his head. "At the last . . . none of that matters. I've finally found something for me. Really for me, not for the Imperium, not even for the Emperor. Just for me."

"Then grab it with both hands. And don't let the bastards take it away from you."

"Thank you," Gregor breathed.

Miles bowed himself out. He wondered if his new driver had killed anyone yet, and if the Count's car was still right-side-up. But mostly, he wondered how he could avoid Duv Galeni for the next few weeks.

TEN

It took Miles several days to extract himself from Ivan's clutches and escape south to the Vorkosigan's District alone, or almost alone. In the end, he formally pledged his word as Vorkosigan to Ivan that he wouldn't attempt either active or passive suicide stunts while gone. Ivan had reluctantly accepted this, but it was obvious from Martin's new wariness that Ivan had chosen to put an extra word in his ear about problems besides seizures to watch for in his employer, and, probably, some com numbers to call in case of emergencies or excessive weirdness. *Now the kid thinks I'm crazy. Or at any rate, discharged because I was crazy, not crazy because I was discharged. Thanks, Ivan.* But perhaps a few days in the peace and calm of Vorkosigan Surleau would ease Miles's mind, and Martin's too.

Miles knew they'd crossed the northern border of his home District when the first blue shadows of the Dendarii Mountains colored the horizon ahead of them, appearing out of the wavering air as suddenly as a mirage. "Turn to the east, here," Miles told Martin. "I've a mind to quarter the District. We'll pass just north of Hassadar. Have you ever been down this way before?"

"No, my lord." Dutifully, Martin banked the lightflyer into the morning sun; the canopy's polarization compensated for the glare. As Miles had suspected, Martin was shakier as a lightflyer pilot than a groundcar chauffeur. But the fail-safe systems made a lightflyer, a small, highly maneuverable, stripped-down cross between an antigrav sled and an airplane, almost impossible to crash. Somebody having a five-minute seizure might possibly manage the feat, though.

Sometimes the best way across a square was around three

sides. . . . Not that the Vorkosigan's District was a square, exactly, more of a squashed, irregular parallelogram, some 350 kilometers from the northern strip of lowlands to the southern mountain passes, and about 500 kilometers east-to-west, skirting the mountain chain along its highest ranges. Only about the northern fifth was flat fertile plains, and of that, of course, only half was usable. The city of Hassadar appeared on their near-right; Miles directed Martin wide around the high-traffic areas, avoiding the complications of the city computer's navigational control of the lightflyer traffic.

"Hassadar's all right, I guess," said Vorbarr Sultana—born-and-bred Martin, gazing out over the city's earnest little effort at urban sprawl.

"It's as modern as any city on Barrayar," said Miles. "More modern than Vorbarr Sultana. Almost all of it was built after the Cetagandan Invasion, when my grandfather chose it for the new District capital."

"Yeah, but Hassadar's about *all* the District has," said Martin. "I mean, there's hardly anything else here."

"Well . . . if by *anything* you mean cities, no. It's landlocked away from any chance at the coastal trade. It's always been agricultural, as much so as the mountains permit."

"There's not much to do up there in the mountains, judging from the number of hillmen who come to Vorbarr Sultana looking for work," said Martin. "We make jokes about them. Like, what do you call a Dendarii hillgirl who can outrun her brothers? A virgin." Martin chuckled.

Miles did not. A distinct chill fell in the cabin of the lightflyer. Martin glanced sideways, and shrank in his seat. "Sorry, m'lord," he muttered.

"I've heard it before. I've heard them all." In fact, his father's Armsmen, all District men, used to make them up, but that was different, somehow. Some of them had been hillmen themselves, and not lacking in wit. "It's true that the Dendarii mountain folk have a lot fewer ancestors than you Vorbarr Sultana slugs, but that's because they failed to roll over and surrender to the Cetagandans." A slight exaggeration: the Cetagandans had occupied the lowlands, where they'd made handy targets for the hillmen led by the terribly young General Count Piotr Vorkosigan to descend upon. The Cetagandans should have moved their lines back fifty kilometers, instead of trying to push them up into the treacherous hills. The Vorkosigan's District had subsequently lagged behind others in development because it was among the most war-torn on Barrayar.

Well . . . that had been a good excuse two generations ago, even one generation ago. But now?

The Imperium plucks us Vorkosigans from our District, and uses us up, and never replaces what it borrows. And then makes jokes about our impoverishment. Odd . . . he'd never thought of his family's ardent service as a hidden tax on the District before.

Miles waited an extra ten minutes more than he'd originally intended to, then said, "Turn south here. Give us a thousand meters more of altitude, though."

"Yes, m'lord." The flyer banked to the right. After a few more minutes, the automated beacon on the ground detected them, and issued the standard bleat over the lightflyer's com, a recorded voice intoning, "Warning. You are entering a high radiation area. . . ."

Martin paled. "M'lord? Should I continue on this heading?"

"Yes. We're all right at this altitude. But it's been years since I flew over the center of the wastelands. It's always interesting to check and see how things are progressing down there."

The farmland had given way to woodland many kilometers back. Now the woodland grew more sparse, the colors odder and grayer, scraggly and blighted in some areas, strangely dense in others. "I own almost all of that, y'know," Miles went on, gazing down at it. "I mean, personally. Not a figure of speech because my father's the District Count. My grandfather left it to me. Not to my father like most of the rest of our property. I've always wondered what sort of a message to me that was supposed to be." Blighted land for a blighted scion, a comment on his early disabilities? Or resigned realization that Count Aral's life would run its course long before the blasted land recovered? "I've never set foot on it. I plan to put on radiation gear and visit it, sometime after I have children. They say there are some very strange plants and animals down there."

"There's no *people,* are there?" said Martin, staring downward in palpable unease. Without being told, he added a few hundred more meters of altitude.

"A few squatters and bandits, who don't expect to live long enough to have cancer or children. The District rangers round them up and run them out, from time to time. It looks deceptively recovered, in spots. In fact, the radioactivity levels in some areas have dropped by half in my lifetime. When I'm old, this will just begin to be usable again."

"Ten more years, m'lord?" said Martin.

Miles's lips twitched. "I was thinking, like, fifty more years, Martin," he said gently.

"Oh."

After a few more minutes, he craned his neck and stared out the canopy past Martin. "There on your left. That blotch is the site of Vorkosigan Vashnoi, the old District capital. Huh. It's going gray-green now. It used to be all black, still, when I was a kid. I wonder if it still glows in the dark?"

"We can come back after dark and look," Martin offered, after a slight pause.

"No . . . no." Miles settled back in his seat, and stared ahead at the mountains rising to the south. "That's enough."

"I could power up some more," said Martin presently, as the moldy colors on the landscape below fell behind to be replaced by healthier greens and browns and golds. "See what this flyer can do." His tone was decidedly longing.

"I know what it can do," said Miles. "And I have no reason to hurry, today. Another time, perhaps."

Martin had dropped a number of such hints, obviously finding his employer's taste in travel staid and dull. Miles itched to take over the controls and give Martin a real thrill-ride, through the Dendarii Gorge. That triple-dip through the wild up-and-down drafts beside, and under, the main waterfall could force a sufficiently white-knuckled passenger to throw up.

Alas, even without the seizures, Miles didn't think he was physically or mentally—or morally—up to it anymore, not the way he and Ivan had used to do it, when slightly younger than Martin here. It was a miracle they hadn't killed themselves. At the time they had been convinced it was their superior Vorish skill, but in retrospect it looked more like divine intervention.

Ivan had started the game. Each cousin took a turn at the light-flyer's controls on runs through the deep winding gorge till the other either tapped out, martial arts—fashion, by banging on the dash, or else lost their last meal. For a proper run one had to disable several of the lightflyer's fail-safe circuits first, a trick Miles would just as soon Martin not learn about. Miles had pulled ahead of Ivan in the score early by the simple precaution of not eating first, till Ivan twigged to it and insisted they eat breakfast together, to assure fairness.

Miles won the final round by challenging Ivan to a night run. Ivan took the first turn, and brought them through alive, though he was white and sweating when they popped up over the last rim and leveled out.

Miles lined up for his run, and turned off the flyer's lights. All credit to Ivan's nerve, he didn't break and claw, screaming, for the (disabled) emergency-eject button till he realized his cousin was also flying the speed-pattern through the gorge with his eyes closed.

Miles, of course, didn't bother to mention he'd flown the identical pattern over sixty times in daylight during the prior three days, gradually darkening the canopy until fully opaqued.

That had been the last round of *that* game. Ivan never challenged him again.

"What are you smiling about, m'lord?" Martin inquired.

"Ah . . . nothing, Martin. Bank right here, and head up across the middle of that wooded area. I'm curious to see how my forest is getting along."

The absentee Vorkosigan sires had gone in heavily for low-supervision sorts of farming. After fifty years of forestry, the fine hardwood trees were almost ready for sustained selective cutting. In another ten years, say? Patches of oak, maple, elm, hickory, and vesper-birch vied in brilliance in the autumn sun. A dark green grace note was added here and there on the steep hillsides by the genetically engineered winter-hardy ebony, a new strain—or rather, new to Barrayar—imported just three decades ago. Miles wondered where it would all end up: in furniture, houses, and other common things? He hoped some of it at least would be used beautifully. For musical instruments, say, or sculpture or inlay.

Miles frowned at a column of smoke rising several ridges away. "Go over there," he told Martin, pointing. But upon arrival he discovered it was all right; it was just his terraforming crew, burning off another hillside of poisonous native scrub prior to treating the soil with organic waste of Earth-DNA origin and planting the tiny saplings.

Martin circled above them, and the half-dozen men in breath masks looked up and waved cordially, all unknowing who observed them. "Give them a wing-waggle back," Miles told Martin, who complied. Miles wondered what it would be like, to do that job all day every day, terraforming Barrayar the old low-tech way, meter by meter. But at least it would be easy to look back and measure your life's accomplishment.

They left the forest plantation and continued west over the rugged red-brown hills, all patched and embroidered here and there with Earth-descended colors, marking human habitation or feral growth. The gray mountains, snow-dusted, marched ever higher to their left. Miles settled back and closed his eyes a while, weary for no reason; he was eating and sleeping as well as he ever did. At last, at an inquiring murmur from Martin, he opened them to spot the distant glimmer of the long lake at Vorkosigan Surleau, winding some 40 kilometers westward through the patchy hills.

They passed over the village at the lake's foot, and the ruined and burned-out castle occupying the headland above it, that had been the original reason for the village's existence. Miles had Martin fly all the way to the headwaters and back before they circled to land on the Vorkosigans' property. There were easily a hundred new residences dotting the lakeside further up, around the curve of the few kilometers of shoreline belonging to his family, that were now owned by people from Hassadar or Vorbarr Sultana. They were the source of the population explosion of . . . well, at least a dozen boats marring, or decorating depending on your point of view, the blue surface of the waters. The village was growing too, serving the vacationers and retirees as well as the few Old Vor estates nearby.

The Vorkosigans' summer place had formerly been a long, two-story stone guard barracks for the castle, now converted to a graceful residence with a fine view over the lake. Miles had Martin bring the lightflyer down on the landing pad by the garage, over the ridge.

"To the house, my lord?" Martin inquired, unloading their bags.

This house at least had a caretaker couple in residence to keep it alive and maintain the extensive grounds; it would not have the dark and tomblike atmosphere of the mansion in the capital.

"No . . . leave those for now. I want to visit the stables first."

Miles led off down the path to the collection of outbuildings and Earth-green pastures in the first little valley back from the lake. The teenaged girl from the village who looked after the handful of remaining horses came out to greet them, and Martin, who had obviously been dutifully prepared to endure several days of unalleviated rural boredom in his eccentric lord's company, brightened right up. Miles left them to get acquainted, and went to the pasture gate.

His horse, who had picked up the rather unfortunate name of Fat Ninny from Miles's grandfather in the first few weeks of his life as a foal, came to greet Miles at his call, nickering, and Miles faithfully rewarded him with peppermints from his pocket. He

petted the big roan's wide velvety nose. The beast, rising . . .
twenty-three years old now?—had more gray among his red hairs,
and wheezed from his canter across the pasture. So . . . dare he
ride, with this seizure-thing? Probably not the sort of days-long
camping trips up into the hills he most enjoyed. If he trained Martin to be his spotter, he could perhaps risk a few turns around the
pastures. He wasn't likely to break any of his synthetic bones,
falling off, and he trusted Ninny not to step on him.

Swimming, the other main pleasure of life at Vorkosigan
Surleau, was right out. Sailing was dubious; he'd have to wear a
life jacket constantly and take Martin. Could Martin even swim,
let alone play lifeguard to a seizuring man overboard while simultaneously not letting the boat get away from him? It seemed rather
a lot to ask. Well . . . the lake's waters were chilling with the onset
of autumn anyway.

It was not by accident that Miles's thirtieth birthday came up
the week following, while he lingered in quiet ennui by the lakeside. It was the best place to ignore the event, unlike the capital
where he was likely to be plagued with acquaintances and relatives, or at least Ivan, ragging him on the topic, or worse, inflicting
a party on him. Though Ivan would doubtless be restrained by the
knowledge that his turn would be next, in a couple of months.
Anyway, Miles would really only be one day older, just like any
other day. Right?

The day in question dawned foggy and damp from the previous day's melancholy rains that had so suited Miles's mood, but it
was apparent from the high pale blue directly overhead that the
weather would develop into something warm and hazy and perfect. It was also apparent that he was not going to be permitted to
ignore it all, when the first call of congratulations came over the
house's comconsole from a primly amused Lady Alys. Could Ivan
be far behind? If he didn't find some way to hide, he risked being
tied up all day on the blasted thing.

He snagged a prebreakfast roll from the kitchen on the way
through, and walked out along the hillside path to the garden-and-
graveyard. Formerly the last resting place of the barracks's
guardsmen, it had been taken over by the Vorkosigans as their
family plot after the destruction of Vorkosigan Vashnoi. Miles sat
companionably for a while beside Sergeant Bothari's grave, nib-

bling the roll and watching the rising sun burn redly through the morning mists above Vorkosigan Surleau.

Then he strolled over to old General Piotr's plot, and stared down at it for long minutes. Time was he had stamped and shouted to that mockingly silent stone, whispered and pleaded. But the old man and he seemed to have nothing further to say to each other. Why not?

I'm talking to the wrong damned grave, is the problem, Miles decided abruptly. Ruthlessly, he turned and strode back to the house to wake up Martin, who would sleep till noon if allowed. He knew someplace he could go where the comconsole could not pursue him. And he desperately needed to talk to a certain small lady there.

———◆———

"So where are we headed, m'lord?" Martin inquired, settling into the lightflyer's pilot's seat, and flexing his fingers.

"We're going to a little mountain community called Silvy Vale." Miles leaned over and entered instructions into the vid map/navigator program, which projected a color-enhanced 3-D grid for them. "There's a particular spot I want you to land, in this little valley here, just above this narrow fork. It's a cemetery, actually. There should be just enough space between the trees to put the lightflyer down. Or there was, the last time I was up there. It's a pretty place, beside the brook. The sun comes down through the trees . . . maybe I should have packed a picnic. It's about a four day-walk from here, or two and a half days on horseback. Or something under an hour by lightflyer."

Martin nodded, and powered up; they rose above the ridge, and turned southeast. "I bet I could get you there faster," Martin offered.

"No . . ."

"Are we going the long way around again?"

Miles hesitated. Now that he was in the air, his urgency was slackening, to be replaced by seeping dread. *And you thought apologizing to the Emperor was hard.* "Yeah. I've been meaning to show you a few facts of life about mountain downdrafts and lightflyers. Head south and west here, toward those peaks."

"Very good, sir," said Martin, practicing his best Vor lord's servant's style, though spoiling the effect immediately thereafter by adding, "A hell of a lot better than another riding lesson." Martin and Ninny had not gotten along as well as Miles had expected them to. Martin clearly preferred lightflyers.

There followed an hour of interesting moments in and around Dendarii Gorge. Even city-boy Martin was impressed by the grandeur of place, Miles was pleased to note. They took it a lot slower than he and Ivan ever had; the lessons made their breakfasts merely a mild regret, and not an immediate emergency. But eventually, Miles ran out of delays to offer, and they turned due east again.

"So what's to do in this Silvy Vale place?" asked Martin. "Friends? Scenery?"

"Not . . . exactly. When I was about your brother's age—I'd just graduated from the Imperial Service Academy, in fact—the Count-my-Father stuck me, that is, assigned me to be his Voice in a case that was brought before the Count's Court. He sent me up to Silvy Vale to investigate and judge a murder. An infanticide for mutation, very much in the old traditional style."

Martin made a face. "Hillmen," he said in revulsion."

"Mm. It turned out to be more complex than I'd thought, even after I managed to tag the right suspect. The little girl—it was a little girl four days old who was killed, for being born with the cat's mouth—her name was Raina Csurik. She'd be getting close to ten years old by now, if she'd lived. I want to talk to her."

Martin's brows rose. "Do you, uh . . . talk to dead people a lot, m'lord?"

"Sometimes."

Martin's mouth crooked in an uncertain, we-hope-this-is-a-joke smile. "Do they ever talk back?"

"Sometimes . . . what, don't you ever talk to dead people?"

"I don't know any. Except you, m'lord," Martin modified this slightly.

"I was only a would-be corpse." *Give yourself time, Martin. Your acquaintance will surely expand in time.* Miles knew lots of dead people.

But even on that long list, Raina held a special place. After he'd peeled away all the Imperial pomp and nonsense, exhausted all the vying for promotion, waded through all the idiot regulations and dark nasty corners of military life . . . when it wasn't a goddamn game anymore, when things went real, and really scary, with lives and souls too going down the flash-disposer for it . . . Raina was the one symbol of his service that still made sense. He had a horrible feeling he'd somehow lost touch with Raina too, lately, in all this mess.

Had he got so wound up with playing Naismith, and with winning that game, that he'd forgotten what he was playing for? Raina was one prisoner Naismith would never rescue, down underground these ten years.

There was a probably apocryphal tale told of Miles's ancestor Count Selig Vorkosigan, collecting—or more likely, attempting to collect—taxes from his District's people, no more thrilled by the prospect then than they were now. One impoverished widow, left with her feckless late husband's debts, offered up the only thing she had, her son's drum-playing, son included. Selig, it was said, accepted the drumming but gave back the boy. Self-serving Vorish propaganda, no doubt. Naismith had been Miles's own best sacrifice, his all in all, what he came up with when he turned himself inside-out with the trying. Barrayar's galactic interests seemed very far away in this mountain morning light, but serving those interests had been his part. Naismith was the drum-song he'd played, but Vorkosigan was the one who'd played it.

So he knew exactly how he'd lost Naismith, misstep by misstep. He could touch and name every link in that disastrous chain of events. Where the hell had he lost Vorkosigan?

When they landed, he would tell Martin to take a walk, or go fly the lightflyer around some more. This was one conversation with the dead he didn't want a witness to. He'd failed Gregor, yet faced him, failed his family, and would have to face them soon. But facing Raina . . . that was going to hurt like needle grenade fire.

Oh, Raina. Small lady. Please. What do I do now? He hunched away from Martin, very silent, his forehead leaning against the canopy, eyes closed, head aching.

Martin's voice broke into his increasingly agonized reverie. "M'lord? What should I do? I can't land in the valley where you said, it's all water."

"What?" Miles sat up, and opened his eyes, and stared out in astonishment.

"There seems to be a lake there," said Martin.

Indeed. Across the narrow shoulder where the two descending streams had met now sat a small hydroelectric dam. Behind it, filling the steep valleys, a winding sheet of water reflected the hazy morning blue. Miles rechecked the vid map, just to be sure, and then the date on the map. "This map's only two years old. But this sure as hell isn't on it. But . . . this is the place, all right."

"Do you still want to land?"

"Yes, um . . . try to set down on the shore there on the east side, as close to the mark as you can."

It wasn't an easy task, but Martin at last found a spot and eased the lightflyer down among the trees. He popped the canopy, and Miles climbed out, and stood on the steep bank, and peered down at the clear brown water. He could only see a few meters into it. A scattering of white tree stumps stuck up out of it like bones. Martin, curious, followed him, and stood by his side, as if to help him look.

"So . . . is the cemetery still under there, or have the folk of Silvy Vale moved their graves? And if so, where have they moved them to?" Miles muttered.

Martin shrugged. The blank and placid mirror of the water gave no answer either.

ELEVEN

After Martin jockeyed the lightflyer up out of the trees, Miles located the clearing he sought about a kilometer away. He had Martin put them down in the yard in front of a cabin built of weathered silvery wood. The cabin, with its familiar full-length porch giving a fine view over the valley and the new lake, appeared unchanged, though there were a couple of new outbuildings downslope.

A man came out onto the porch to see what was landing in his yard. It was not the balding, one-armed Speaker Karal. This was a total stranger, a tall fellow with a neatly trimmed black beard. But he leaned, interested, on the porch railing of bark-peeled sapling as if he owned the place. Miles climbed out of the lightflyer, and stood by it for an uncertain moment, staring up at the man, rehearsing explanations for himself and secretly glad of Martin's bulk. Perhaps he should have brought a trained bodyguard.

But the stranger's face lit with recognition and excitement. "Lord Vorkosigan!" he cried. He ran down off the porch two steps at a time, and strode toward Miles, his hands out in greeting, smiling broadly. "Great to see you again!" His smile faded. "Nothing wrong, I hope?"

Well, this one remembered *Miles*, all right, from that judgment of nearly a decade ago. "No, this is purely a social visit," Miles offered, as the man came up and shook his hand—both his hands—with enthusiastic cordiality. "Nothing official."

The man stepped back, looking down at his face, and his smile turned into a sly grin. "Don't you know who I am?"

"Um . . ."

"I'm Zed Karal."

"Zed?" Zed Karal, Speaker Karal's middle son, had been twelve years old. . . . Miles did a little quick math. Twenty-two, or thereabouts. Yeah. "The last time I saw you, you were shorter than me."

"Well, my ma was a good cook."

"Indeed. I remember." Miles hesitated. "Was? Are your parents, um . . ."

"Oh, they're fine. Just not here. My older brother married this lowlander girl from Seligrad, and went there to work and live. Ma and Da go down to live with them for the winter, 'cause the winters are getting hard for them up here. Ma helps with their kids."

"Is . . . Karal not the Speaker of Silvy Vale anymore, then?"

"No, we have a new Speaker, as of about two years ago. A young hotshot full of Progressive ideas he picked up living in Hassadar, just your type. I think you'll remember him all right. Name's Lem Csurik." Zed's smile broadened.

"Oh!" said Miles. For the first time today a smile tugged at his own lips. "Really. I'd . . . like to see him."

"I'll take you to him right now, if you'll give me a lift. He's probably working on the clinic today. You won't know where that is, it's bright-new. Just a second." Zed dashed back into his cabin to put something in order, a hint of that former twelve-year-old in his run. Miles felt like banging his head on the lightflyer's canopy, to try to force his spinning brain back into gear.

Zed returned, to hop into the lightflyer's backseat, and give Martin a string of directions interspersed with running commentary as they rose into the air and passed over the next ridge. He brought them down about two kilometers away in front of the rising frame of a six-room building, the biggest structure Miles had ever seen in Silvy Vale. Power lines were already strung to it, feeding a rack of pack-rechargers for power tools. Half a dozen men paused in their labors to watch them land.

Zed clambered out and waved. "Lem, hey Lem! You'll never guess who's here!" Miles followed him toward the building site; Martin sat at the controls and watched in bemusement.

"My lord!" Lem Csurik's recognition was instantaneous too; but then, Miles's appearance was, ah, distinctive. Miles could probably have picked Lem out of the crowd in turn with a moment's study. He was still the wiry hillman of about Miles's age that Miles remembered, though obviously much happier than the day a decade back when he'd been falsely accused of murder, and even more confident-looking than the time Miles had briefly seen him in Hassadar six years ago. Lem too went for an engulfing two-handed greeting.

"Speaker Csurik. Congratulations," Miles said in return. "I see you've been busy."

"Oh, you don't know the half of it, my lord! Come see. We're getting our own clinic—it's going to serve the whole area. I'm pushing to have it undercover before the first snow flies, and all ready by Winterfair. That's when we're getting our doctor, a real one, not just the medtech who flies the circuit once a week. The doc's one of your lady mother's scholarship students from the new school in Hassadar; he's going to serve us here four years in exchange for his schooling. Winterfair's when he's supposed to graduate. We're fixing him up a cabin, too, upslope; it's got a real nice view—"

Lem introduced his crew all around, and took Miles on a tour of, if not the clinic yet, the dream of the clinic that burned in his imagination so hotly, Miles could see its ghostly outlines all complete.

"I saw the electric dam in the valley, coming in," Miles said, when Lem at last paused for breath. "Where did that come from?"

"We built it," said Lem proudly. "You can bet that was a job and a half, with so few power tools. Had to make the power to have the power, of course. We'd been waiting and waiting for the powersat receptor the District promised us, but we were so far down the list, we'd still be waiting. Then I got to figuring. I went over to Dos'tovar and looked at their hydro plant, which they'd had for years. It was low-tech, but it worked. I got a couple of the fellows from there to come help us with the dam, picking the best site and all, and got an engineer from Hassadar whose house I'd helped build to come help us with the electrical system guts. He gets the use of a cabin up from the new lake for a vacation place in the summer in return. We still owe for the generators, but that's all."

"That was the best site, was it?"

"Oh, yes. The shortest span and the biggest drop available, and the most water-flow. We'll outgrow it in time, but that's the whole point. Without basic power, this place was in stasis. Now we *can* grow. Couldn't have won the lottery from the District for the doctor without power for the clinic, for one thing."

"You didn't let anything stop you, did you?"

"Well, m'lord, you know who I learned *that* from."

Harra, his wife, of course. Raina's mother. Miles nodded. "Speaking of Harra, where is she today?" He had come up here wanting only to stand silent before the dead, but he was now beginning to want very much to talk to Harra.

"Teaching at the school. I built on another room—we have two teachers now, you know. There's a girl Harra trained who does the little ones, and Harra teaches the older ones."

"Can I, ah, see it?"

"Harra'd skin me alive if I let you get away without seeing her! Come on, I'll take you over there now."

Zed, having turned Miles over to the responsible authority, waved good-bye and headed back home, disappearing among the trees. Lem spoke briefly to his crew, and took over Zed's place as native guide in the back seat of the lightflyer.

Another short hop brought them to an older and more traditional structure: a long cabin with two doors and fieldstone fireplaces on both ends. A large hand-carved sign with scrolling letters above the porch labeled it *The Raina Csurik School*. Lem led Miles through the door on the left, Martin trailing to linger uncertainly just outside. About twenty teenagers of various sizes sat at handmade wooden desks with comconsole lap-links atop them, listening to the vigorously gesturing woman at the head of the room.

Harra Csurik was still tall and lean, as Miles remembered her. Her straight straw-blond hair was tied back neatly at the nape of her neck, hill-woman fashion, and she wore a hill woman's simple dress, though clean and well made. Like the majority of her students, her feet were bare in this mild weather. But her protuberant gray eyes were lively and warm. She broke off her lecture abruptly as she saw Miles and Lem.

"Lord Vorkosigan! Well, I never expected this!" She advanced upon him much as Zed and Lem had, but not content with a handshake, she hugged him. At least she didn't pick him up bodily. Miles concealed his startlement, recovered his wits quickly enough to hug her back, and took both her hands in a half-swing around as she released him.

"Hello, Harra. You look splendid."

"I haven't seen you since Hassadar."

"Yes, I . . . should have been round long before this. But they kept me busy."

"I have to tell you, it meant the world to me, when you came to my graduation from the teacher's college there."

"That was a piece of good luck, that I was on-planet at the time. No merit in it."

"That's a matter of opinion. Come, see. . . ." She towed him toward the front of the room. "See, kids, who's come to see us! It's your own Lord Vorkosigan!"

They stared at him with interest, rather than suspicion or revulsion, their eyes shifting to check the odd little man in the flesh before them against the picture on the wall at the front of their classroom. Above the vid projection space three still-portraits were lined up, two by mandate: one of Emperor Gregor in the splendid and gaudy parade dress uniform, and one of their District Count, Miles's father, staring out sternly in the most formal brown-and-silver livery of the Vorkosigans. The third portrait was nonregulation—public offices were not normally required to display a portrait of their Count's heir as well, but Miles's own face smirked back at him from up there. It was one of his younger and stiffer scans, wearing Imperial Service dress greens with light blue ensign's rectangles on the collar. It had to date from his Academy graduation, because no silver Eye-of-Horus pins yet glittered there. Where the devil had Harra obtained it?

She displayed him as proudly to her students as any show-and-tell exhibitor, excited as a six-year-old with a jar of pet bugs. He hadn't come to Silvy Vale expecting to see anyone, let alone speak publicly, and felt decidedly underdressed in an old backcountry-style tunic and worn black trousers left over from a set of Service fatigues, not to mention the battered Service boots he'd muddied by the reservoir. But he managed a few generic, hearty *Well done, well done,* comments that seemed to please everyone. Harra took him around the front porch into the next room and repeated the show, throwing the young woman teaching there into terminal flusterment, and raising the younger students' wriggle-quotient to something near explosion.

As they were coming back around on the porch, Miles seized Harra's hand to slow her down for a moment. "Harra—I didn't come up here for a surprise inspection, for heaven's sake. I just came up to . . . well, to tell you the truth, I just wanted to do a little memorial burning on Raina's grave." The tripod and brazier and aromatic wood were stashed in the back of the lightflyer.

"That was good of you, m'lord," said Harra. Miles made a small throwaway gesture, but she shook her head in denial of his denial.

Miles went on, "It seems I'd need a boat to do it now, and I don't want to risk setting fire to the boat I'm sitting in. Or did you folks move the graveyard?"

"Yes, before it was flooded, people moved some of the graves, those who wanted to. We picked a real nice new spot up on the ridge, overlooking the old site. We didn't move my mother's grave, of course. I left her down there. Let even her burial be buried, no burnings for her." Harra grimaced; Miles nodded understanding. "Raina's grave . . . well, I guess it was because the ground was so damp down there by the creek, and she only had that bit of a makeshift crate for a coffin, and she was so tiny anyway . . . we couldn't find her to move. She's gone back to the soil, I guess. I didn't mind. It seemed right, when I thought about it. I really think of this school as her best memorial, anyway. Every day I come here to teach is like burning an offering, only better. Because it makes, instead of destroys." She nodded once, resolute and calm.

"I see."

She looked at him more closely. "You all right, m'lord? You look really tired. And all pale. You haven't been sick or something, have you?"

He supposed three months of death qualified as about as sick as one could get. "Well, yes. Or something. But I'm recovering."

"Oh. All right. Are you headed anywhere, after this?"

"Not really. I'm sort of . . . on holiday."

"I'd like you to meet our kids, mine and Lem's. Lem's Ma or his sister take care of them while I'm teaching. Won't you come home for lunch with us?"

He'd intended to be back at Vorkosigan Surleau by lunchtime. "Kids?"

"We've two, now. A little boy four and a little girl one."

No one was using uterine replicators up here yet; she'd borne them in her body like her lost firstborn. Dear God but this woman worked. It was an invitation he could not possibly escape. "I'd be honored."

"Lem, show Lord Vorkosigan around a minute—" Harra went back inside, to consult with her team teacher and then with her students, and Lem dutifully took Miles on an outside tour of the architectural highlights of the school. A couple of minutes later, children exploded from the building, shrieking off happily in all directions in early dismissal.

"I didn't mean to disrupt your routine," Miles protested futilely. He was in for it now. He could not for three worlds betray those smiles of welcome.

They descended by lightflyer unannounced upon Lem's sister,

who rose to the challenge smoothly. The lunch she provided was, thank God, light. Miles dutifully met and admired Csurik children, nieces, and nephews. He was hijacked by them and taken on a stroll through the woods, and viewed a favorite swimming hole. He waded gravely along with them on the smooth stones with his boots off, till his feet were numb with the chill, and in a voice of Vorish authority pronounced it a most excellent swimming hole, perhaps the finest in his District. He was obviously an anomaly of some fascination, an adult almost their own size.

What with one thing and another, it was late afternoon before they arrived back at the school. Miles took one look at the mob of people streaming into the wide yard, bearing dishes and baskets and flowers, musical instruments and pitchers and jugs, chairs and benches and trestles and boards, firewood and tablecloths, and his heart sank. Despite all his efforts to avoid such things today, it seemed he was in for a surprise party after all.

Phrases like, *We should go before dark, Martin's not used to flying in the mountains,* died on his lips. They'd be lucky if they got out of here before tomorrow morning. Or—he noted the stone pitchers of Dendarii Mountain maple mead, the deadliest alcoholic beverage ever invented by man—tomorrow afternoon.

It took him a meal, sunset, a bonfire, and rather a lot of carefully rationed sips of maple mead, but eventually, he actually relaxed and began to enjoy it. Then the music began, and enjoyment became no effort at all. Off to the side Martin, at first inclined to turn up his nose a bit at the rustic homemade quality of it all, found himself teaching city dances to a group of eager teens. Miles bit back inflicting any prudent warnings on the boy, such as *Maple mead may go down smooth and sweet, but it destroys cell membranes coming back up.* Some things you had to learn for yourself, at certain ages. Miles danced traditional steps with Harra, and other women until he lost count. A couple of older folk, who'd been there at his judgment of a decade ago, nodded respectfully at him despite his capering. It was not, after all, a party for him, despite the bombardment of birthday congratulations and jokes. It was a party for Silvy Vale. If he was the excuse for it, well, it was the most use he'd been to anybody for weeks.

But as the party died down with the bonfire's embers, his sense of incompletion grew. He'd come up here to . . . what? To try to bring his dragging depression to some kind of head, perhaps, like lancing a boil, painful but relieving. Disgusting metaphor, but he was thoroughly sick of himself. He wanted to take a jug of mead, and finish his talk with Raina. Bad idea, probably. He might end up weeping drunkenly by the reservoir, and drowning himself as well as his sorrows, poor repayment to Silvy Vale for the nice party, and betrayal of his word to Ivan. Did he seek healing, or destruction? *Either.* It was this formless state in between that was unbearable.

In the end, somehow, after midnight, he fetched up by the waterside after all. But not alone. Lem and Harra came with him, and sat on logs too. The moons were both high, and made faint silky patterns on the wavelets, and turned the rising mist in the ravines to silver smoke. Lem had charge of the jug of mead, and distributed it judiciously, otherwise keeping a mellow silence.

It was not the dead Miles needed to talk to, in the dark, he realized. It was the living. Useless to confess to the dead; absolution was not in their power. *But I'll trust your Speaking, Harra, as you once trusted mine.*

"I have to tell you something," Miles said to Harra.

"Knew there was something wrong," she said. "I hope you're not dying or something."

"No."

"I was worried it might be something like that. A lot of muties don't live very long lives, even without someone to cut their throats."

"Vorkosigan does it backwards. I had my throat cut all right, but it was for life, not for death. It's a long story and the details are classified, but I ended up in a cryo-chamber out in the galactic backbeyond last year. When they thawed me out, I had some medical problems. Then I did something stupid. Then I did something really stupid, which was to lie about the first thing. And then I got caught. And then I got discharged. Whatever it was about my achievements you admired, that inspired you, it's all gone now. Thirteen years of career effort down the waste-disposer in one flush. Hand me that jug." He swallowed sweet fire, and handed it back to Lem, who passed it to Harra and back to himself. "Of all the things I thought I might be by age thirty, *civilian* was never on the list."

The moonlight rippled on the water. "And you told *me* to stand up straight and speak the truth," said Harra, after a long pause. "Does this mean you'll be spending more time in the District?"

"Maybe."

"Good."

"You're ruthless, Harra," Miles groaned.

The bugs sang their soft chorus in the woods, a tiny organic moonlight sonata. "Little man"—Harra's voice in the dark was as sweet and deadly as maple mead—"my mother killed my daughter. And was judged for it in front of all of Silvy Vale. You think I don't know what public shame is? Or waste?"

"Why d'you think I'm telling all this to you?"

Harra was silent for long enough for Lem to pass around the stone jug one last time, in the dim moonlight and shadows. Then she said, "You go on. You just go on. There's nothing more to it, and there's no trick to make it easier. You just go on."

"What do you find on the other side? When you go on?"

She shrugged. "Your life again. What else?"

"Is that a promise?"

She picked up a pebble, fingered it, and tossed it into the water. The moon-lines bloomed and danced. "It's an inevitability. No trick. No choice. You just go on."

—————◦◉◦—————

Miles got Martin and the lightflyer in the air again by noon the next day. Martin's eyes were red and puffy, and his face had a pale greenish cast worthy of a speed run through the Dendarii Gorge. He flew very gently and carefully, which suited Miles exactly. He was not very conversational, but he did manage a, "Did you ever find what you were looking for, m'lord?"

"The light is clearer up here in these mountains than anywhere else on Barrayar, but . . . no. It was here once, but it's not here now." Miles twisted in his seat straps, and stared back over his shoulder at the rugged receding hills. *These people need a thousand things. But they don't need a hero. At least, not a hero like Admiral Naismith. Heroes like Lem and Harra, yes.*

Martin squinted, perhaps not appreciating that light just at present.

After a time, Miles asked, "How old is middle-age, Martin?"

"Oh . . ." Martin shrugged. "Thirty, I guess."

"That's what I'd always thought, too." Though he'd once heard the Countess define it as ten years older than whatever you were, a moveable feast.

"I had a professor at the Imperial Service Academy once," Miles went on, as the hills grew more gentle beneath them, "who taught the introduction to tactical engineering course. He said he never bothered changing his tests from term to term to prevent cheating, because while the questions were always the same, the answers changed. I'd thought he was joking."

"Unh?" said Martin dutifully.

"Never mind, Martin," Miles sighed. "Just go on."

— TWELVE —

After their return to the lake house, and a sparing lunch from which Martin excused himself altogether, Miles locked himself into the comconsole chamber and prepared to face the expected spate of messages forwarded from Vorbarr Sultana. The birthday congratulations were each the measure of their senders; grave and straight from Gregor, tinged with cautious mockery from Ivan, and falling into a range in between from the handful of acquaintances who knew he was on-planet.

Mark's tight-beam recording from Beta Colony was . . . Markian. His mockery was an awkward imitation of Ivan's, edgier and more self-conscious. From the stilted would-be flippancy Miles gathered this was not the message's first draft. But it was, Miles realized upon reflection, very probably the first time in his life Mark had ever had to compose a birthday greeting to *anyone*. *Keep trying, Mark, you'll learn how to be a human being yet.*

Miles's judicious smugness faded as he realized this compelled him to compose a return message. It was obvious Mark hadn't heard the news about Miles's change of status yet. How the devil was he going to tell Mark about it in a way his clone-brother couldn't construe as blame? He set the problem aside, temporarily.

He saved the one from his parents for last. It had been beamed, not mailed. Therefore it would have left Sergyar in the government data tight-beam, and been express-jumped through the wormhole barriers between receivers, taking little more than a day en route; shipped message disks took as long to travel between the two worlds as a person, almost two weeks. This was, therefore, the latest news, and would contain their reactions to the latest news they'd had. He took a deep breath, and keyed it up.

They'd sat back from the vid receptor, to both fit into the scan, and so appeared as small smiling half-figures over his vid plate. Count Aral Vorkosigan was a thick-bodied, white-haired man in his early seventies, dressed in his brown-and-silver Vorkosigan House uniform; this message must have been recorded sometime during his working day. The Countess wore a Vor lady's afternoon-style jacket and skirt in green, ditto. Red roan hair, like Ninny's even to the having of more gray in it, was held back from her broad forehead by fancy combs in her usual style. She was as tall as her husband, and her gray eyes danced with amusement.

They do not know. No one's told them yet. Miles knew this with sinking certainty before either even opened their mouth.

"Hello, love," the Countess began. "Congratulations for reaching thirty alive."

"Yes," the Count seconded. "We truly wondered if you would make it, many times. But here we all are. Somewhat the worse for wear, but after a deep contemplation of the alternative, happy to be so. I may be far from you here on Sergyar, but I can look in the mirror every morning, and remember you by all these white hairs."

"It's not true, Miles," objected the Countess, grinning. "He was already going gray when I met him, at age forty-odd. I didn't get *my* gray hairs till after, though."

"We miss you," the Count continued. "Do insist your travel to your next mission assignment be routed through Sergyar, coming or going or both, and plan at least a short layover. There's so much going on here of significance to the future of the Imperium. I know you'd be interested in seeing some of it."

"I'll light up Simon's life if he doesn't send you by," the Countess added. "You can pass that on to him as my personal threat. Alys tells me you've been home for several weeks. Why haven't we heard from you? Partying too hard with Ivan to take ten minutes out to talk to your aged parents?"

Lady Alys too had declined, it appeared, to be the bearer of even the nonclassified version of the bad news, and she was ordinarily the Countess's main gossip-pipeline to everything of Vorish interest in Vorbarr Sultana and Gregor's court.

"Speaking of Alys," the Countess went on, "she tells me Gregor has met This Girl—and you can just hear the capital letters in her voice. What do you know about this? Have you met her? Should we be happy, or worried, or what?"

"An Imperial marriage to a Komarran," said Count Vorkosigan—once nicknamed "the Butcher of Komarr" by his political enemies, most of whom he'd survived—"is fraught with potential complications. But at this late date, if Gregor will only do his duty and produce a proper Crown Prince *somehow*, I'll do whatever I can to support the project. And all of us in my generation who were in the pool of potential heirs will breathe a great sigh of relief. Assure Gregor of my full support. I trust his judgment." The Count's face grew oddly wistful. "Does she seem like a nice girl? Gregor deserves a little personal happiness, to make up for all the nonsense on the other side that he bears for us all."

"Alys said she'll do," said the Countess, "and I trust Alys's judgment. Though I don't know if the young lady quite realizes what she's getting into. Please assure Dr. Toscane of *my* full support, Miles, whatever she decides to do."

"Surely she'll accept, if Gregor asks her," said the Count.

"Only if she's so head-over-heels in love as to have lost all sense of self-preservation," said the Countess. "Believe me, you have to have lost your mind to marry a Barrayaran Vor. Let's hope she has." Miles's parents exchanged peculiar smiles.

"So let's see," the Count went on. "What were we doing at age thirty? Can you remember back that far, Cordelia?"

"Barely. I was in the Betan Astronomical Survey, screwing up my first chance at being promoted to captain. It came around again the next year, though, and you bet I grabbed it then. Without which I would never have met Aral when and where I did and you wouldn't exist, Miles, so I don't wish to change a bit of it now."

"I was a captain by twenty-eight," the Count reminisced smugly. The Countess made a face at him. "Ship duty suited me. I didn't get stuck at a desk for another four or five years, when Ezar and the Headquarters hotshots began planning the annexation of Komarr." His face grew serious again. "Good luck to Gregor on this thing of his. I hope he can succeed where . . . I did not succeed so well as I'd hoped to. Thank God for a new generation and clean starts." He and the Countess glanced at each other and he finished, "So long, boy. Communicate, dammit."

The Countess added, "Take good care of yourself, kiddo,

please? Communicate, dammit." Their forms twinkled into thin air.

Miles sighed. *I can't put this off much longer, I really can't.*

———◦◦◦———

He did manage to put it off one more day, by having Martin fly him back to Vorbarr Sultana the following morning. Ma Kosti served Miles lunch in splendid isolation in the Yellow Parlor; she'd obviously worked hard to make it as proper as possible, perhaps studying up on her new job from etiquette manuals, or getting tips from other Vors' servants in the area. He ate dutifully, despite an urge to gather up his plates and go join Martin and his mother in the kitchen. Certain aspects of the Vor lord role seemed remarkably stupid, at times.

Afterwards, he went to his room to finally face the task of composing a message to his parents. He'd recorded and erased three different tries—one too glum, one too flippant, one way too full of ugly sarcasms—when an incoming call interrupted his endeavors. He welcomed it despite the fact that it was Ivan. Ivan was in uniform, calling on his lunch break, perhaps.

"Ah, you're back in town. Good," Ivan began. That *Good* seemed quite heartfelt, apparently on more than one level. "Feeling better for the little vacation in the hills, I trust?"

"Somewhat," Miles said cautiously. How had Ivan found out so soon that he was back?

"Good," Ivan repeated. "Now. I've been wondering. Have you done anything toward getting your head looked at yet? Seen a doctor?"

"Not yet."

"Made an appointment anywhere?"

"No."

"Hm. Mother asked me. Gregor'd asked her, it seems. Guess who's at the bottom of that chain of command, and gets delegated to actually do something about it. I said I didn't think you'd done anything yet, but I'd ask. Why haven't you?"

"I . . ." Miles shrugged. "There didn't seem to be any rush. I wasn't bounced out of ImpSec for having seizures, I was bounced out of ImpSec for falsifying a report. And not one on a minor matter, either. Even if the medicos could do something to get me back into guaranteed peffect working order tomorrow, which if they could my Dendarii surgeon would have already done it, it wouldn't . . . change anything." *Illyan won't take me back. He*

*can't. It's a matter of frigging principle, and Illyan is one of the
most principled men I know.*

"I'd wondered . . . if it was because you didn't want to go to
ImpMil," said Ivan. "Didn't want to deal with the military docs. If
that's the case, I understand, I suppose—I think you're being silly,
mind you, but I can understand. So I've looked up three different
civilian clinics that specialize in cryo-revival cases, that seem to
have good reputations. One's here in Vorbarr Sultana, one's over
in Weienovya in Vordarian's District, and one's on Komarr, if you
think closer proximity to galactic medicine is an advantage that
would offset any lingering animosity toward your name there. You
want me to make you an appointment at one of them?"

Miles thought he could guess the names of all three, from his
prior search. "No. Thanks."

Ivan sat back, his lips twisting in puzzlement. "You know . . .
I'd figured that would be the first thing you'd do, once the little
ice-water bath brought you up out of the fog. You'd get your legs
under yourself and be off and running, just like always. I never
saw you face a wall that, if you couldn't go over it, you'd not try to
find some way around, through, or under, or blow it up with sap-
per's charges. Or just bang your head against it till it fell down.
And then they'd stick *me* with chasing you. Again."

"Running where, Ivan?"

Ivan grimaced. "Back to the Dendarii, of course."

"You know I can't do that. Without my official position in
ImpSec, under due Imperial authority, my command of the Dendarii becomes a Vor lord, a Count's heir for God's sake, running a
private army. Treason, Ivan, lethal treason. We've been all through
that before. If I went, I could never come back. I gave my word to
Gregor I wouldn't do it."

"Yeah?" said Ivan. "If you're not coming back, what does your
word as Vorkosigan have to do with anything ever again?"

Miles sat silent. So. That business with having Ivan underfoot
in Vorkosigan House hadn't been only a deathwatch after all. It
had been an escape-watch as well.

"I'd have bet money you'd bolt," Ivan went on, "if there'd
been anybody who had a high enough security classification to bet
with. Besides Galeni, of course, and he's not the wagering sort. 'S
why I've been dragging my feet despite Gregor and Mother about
harassing you to get your head fixed. Why borrow trouble? It's a
bet I'm glad to lose, by the way. So when *are* you going to get an
appointment?"

". . . Soon."

"Too vague," Ivan rejected this. "I want a straight answer. Something like, *Today*. Or maybe, *Tomorrow before noon*."

Ivan wouldn't go away till he extracted a response that satisfied him. "By . . . the end of the week," Miles managed.

"Good." Ivan nodded shortly. "I'll check back at the end of the week and expect to hear all about it. 'Bye—for now." He cut the com.

Miles sat staring at the empty vid plate. Ivan was right. He hadn't done a thing more about pursuing a cure since he'd been fired. Once freed from his constraining need for secrecy from ImpSec, why hadn't he been all over this seizure disorder, attacking it, tearing it apart, or at least riding some hapless medico as hard as he'd ever ridden the Dendarii Mercenaries to successfully complete their missions?

To buy time.

He knew it for the right answer, but it only brought him to a new level of self-bafflement. *Time for what?*

Keeping himself on self-inflicted medical leave allowed him to avoid facing certain unpleasant realities square-on. Such as the news that the seizures couldn't be cured, and that the death of hope was permanent and real; no cryo-revival for that corpse, just a warm and rotting burial.

Yeah? Really?

Or . . . was he just as afraid his head *could* be fixed—and then he'd be logically compelled to grab the Dendarii and take off? Back to his real life, the one that soared out far, far away into the glittering galactic night, escaping all the dirtsuckers' petty little concerns. Back to heroing for a living.

More afraid.

Had he lost his nerve, after that hideous episode with the needle grenade? He had a clear flash-vision in his memory of his odd angled view of his own chest blowing outward in a lumpy red spray, and pain beyond measure, and despair beyond words. Waking up afterward hadn't been a picnic, either. *That* pain had dragged on for weeks, without escape. Suiting up again to go out with the squad after Vorberg had been hard, no question, but he'd been doing all right until the seizure.

So . . . was the whole thing, from end to end, from seizure to falsification to discharge, a tricky dance to save himself from ever having to look down the wrong end of a needle-grenade launcher again, without having to say *I quit* out loud?

Hell, of course he was afraid. He'd have to be a frigging idiot not to be. Anyone would, but he'd *done* death. He knew how bad it was. Dying hurt, death was just nothing, both were to be avoided by any sane man. Yet he'd gone back. He'd gone back all the other times, too, after the little deaths, his legs smashed, his arms smashed, all the injuries that had left a map of fine white scars over his body from head to toe. Again and again and again. How many times did you have to die to prove you weren't a coward, how much pain were you required to consume to pass the course?

Ivan was right. He'd always found a way over the wall. He imagined it through, the whole scenario. Suppose he got his head fixed, here or on Komarr or on Escobar, it didn't matter where. And suppose he took off, and ImpSec declined to assassinate their renegade Vor, and they achieved some unspoken agreement to ignore each other forevermore. And he was all and only Naismith.

And then what?

I face fire. Climb that wall.

And then what?

I do it again.

And then what?

Again.

And then what?

It's logically impossible to prove a negative.

I'm tired of playing wall.

No. He needed neither to face nor avoid fire. If fire came his way, he'd deal with it. It wasn't cowardice, dammit, whatever it was.

So why haven't I tried to get my head fixed yet?

He rubbed his face and eyes, and sat up, and attempted once more to compose a coherent account of his new civilian status and how he'd come by it for the Admiral Count and his Lady, the woman whom his father routinely addressed as *Dear Captain*. It came out very stiff and flat, he was afraid, worse even than Mark's birthday message, but he refused to put it off until yet another tomorrow. He recorded and sent it.

Albeit not by tight-beam. He let it go the long way, by ordinary mail, though marked *Personal*. At least it was gone, and he would not be able to call it back again.

Quinn had sent a birthday greeting too, demurely worded so as not to provide too much entertainment for the ImpSec censors. A strong tinge of anxiety leaked through her casual facade nonetheless. A second inquiry was more openly worried.

With enormous reluctance, he repeated a truncated version of his message for Quinn, minus the backfill and cutting straight to the results she had predicted. She deserved better, but it was the best he could do right now. She did not deserve silence and neglect. *I'm sorry, Elli.*

———————

Ivan invited himself to dinner the next night. Miles feared he would have to endure more of the campaign to get him to address his medical problems, about which, admittedly, he had still done nothing, but instead Ivan brought flowers to Ma Kosti, and hung around the kitchen during dinner preparations, making her laugh, until she ran him out. At that point Miles began to fear it was the opening of a campaign to hire away his cook, though whether in Ivan's own right or on behalf of Lady Alys he was not yet sure.

They were halfway through dessert—by Ivan's request, a reprise of the spiced peach tart—when they were interrupted by a comconsole call, or rather, by Martin lurching in to announce, "There's some ImpSec stiff-rod on the com for you, Lord Vorkosigan."

Illyan? Why would Illyan call me? But when, Ivan following in curiosity, he'd trooped to the nearest com on that floor, the one sited in his grandfather's old sitting room overlooking the back garden, the face that formed over the vid plate at his touch was that of Duv Galeni.

"You smarmy goddamn little pimp," said Galeni, in a dead-level voice.

Miles's own bright, innocent, panicked, "Hi, Duv, what's up?" tripped over this and fell very flat, and just lay there, withering under Galeni's glare. Galeni's face was neither red nor pale, but livid, gray with rage. *I should have stayed at Vorkosigan Surleau one more week, I think.*

"You *knew*. You set this up. You set *me* up."

"Um . . . just checking." Miles swallowed. "What are we talking about?"

Galeni didn't even bother to dignify this with an answer, but glared on, his lips curling back on his long teeth in an expression that had nothing to do with a smile.

"Gregor and Laisa, by chance?" Miles hazarded. More thick silence, broken only by Galeni's breathing. "Duv . . . I didn't know it would come out like this. Who would have guessed it, after all these years? I was trying to do you a favor, dammit!"

"The one good thing that's ever come my way. Taken. Stolen. Vor *does* mean thief. And you goddamn Barrayaran thieves stick together, all right. You and your fucking precious Emperor and the whole damned pack of you."

"Uh," put in Ivan from the side, "is this comconsole secured, Miles? Sorry, Duv, but if you're going to express yourself so, um, frankly, wouldn't it be better to do it in person? I mean, I hope this isn't over your ImpSec channel. They have ears in the damnedest places."

"ImpSec can take its ears and the flat head between them and shove them up its collective ass." Galeni's accent, normally elusively urbane, was going not only distinctly Komarran but street-Komarran.

Miles signaled Ivan to shut up. Remembering what had happened to two unlucky Cetagandans the last time Miles had seen Galeni this upset, a personal visit seemed like a singularly bad idea just now. There was Corporal Kosti to protect him, of course, but could Kosti handle one of his own superiors? In a homicidal trance? It seemed rather a lot to ask of the poor fellow.

"Duv, I'm *sorry*. I didn't mean it to come out this way. It was nothing I'd planned. It took everyone by surprise, even Lady Alys. Ask Ivan."

Ivan shrugged, hands out. "'S true."

Miles cleared his throat, cautiously. "How, um . . . did you find out about this?"

"She called me."

"When?"

"About five minutes ago."

She's just dumped him. Oh great.

"They *both* called me," Galeni groaned. "She said I was her best friend here, and she wanted me to be the first Komarran to hear the news."

Gregor's really gone and done it, then. "And, uh . . . what did you say?"

"Congratulations, of course. What else could I say? With the pair of 'em sitting there grinning at me?" Miles breathed relief. Good. Galeni *hadn't* lost all control. He'd just called Miles to have a shoulder to gnash his teeth on. Looked at in a certain light, it was a measure of immense trust. *Terrific. Thanks, Duv.*

Ivan rubbed his neck. "You've been chasing this woman for five months, and all you got was that she thinks you're her friend? Duv, what the hell were you doing all that time?"

"She's a *Toscane*," said Galeni. "I'm just an impoverished collaborator, by her family's standards. I had to persuade her that I had a future worthy of her, nothing to look at now, no, but later . . . then *he* came along, and just, just swept her up with no trouble at all."

Miles, having watched Gregor practically turning handsprings in an effort to be pleasing to Laisa, said only, "Um."

"Five months is *way* too slow," said Ivan, continuing his tone of earnest critique. "God, Duv, I wish you'd asked me for some advice earlier."

"She's *Komarran*. What can one of you damned Barrayaran sugar-plum-fairy-soldier-bloody-buffoons know about a Komarran woman? Intelligent, educated, sophisticated—"

"Almost thirty . . ." Miles mused.

"I had a timetable," said Galeni. "When she'd known me six months exactly, I was going to ask her."

Ivan winced.

Galeni seemed to be calming down, or at least beginning a downward slide from his immediate reaction of rage and pain into a less energy-intensive despair. Perhaps his violent words were going to be safety-vent enough for his boiling emotions, without violent actions this time. "Miles . . ."—at least he didn't preface the name with a string of pejoratives now—"you're nearly Gregor's foster brother."

No *nearly* about it. "Um?"

"Do you think . . . could you possibly persuade him to relinquish . . . no." Galeni ran down altogether.

No. "I owe Gregor . . . from too far back. On a personal as well as a political level. This heir business is essential to my future health and safety, and Gregor's been dragging his feet on it forever. Till now. I can't do anything but support him. And anyway"—he remembered his Aunt Alys's words—"it's Laisa's decision, not yours or mine *or* Gregor's. I can't help it if you forgot to tell *her* about your timetable. I'm sorry."

"Shit." Galeni cut the com.

"Well," said Ivan thinly into the silence that followed. "At least that's over with."

"Have you been avoiding him too?"

"Yes."

"Coward."

"*Who* was it spent the last two weeks hiding out in the mountains?"

"It was a strategic withdrawal."

"Well. I believe our dessert is drying out back in the dining room."

"I'm not hungry. Besides . . . if this is Gregor and Laisa's night to start informing selected personal friends, prior to the official announcement . . . I may as well stay here for a few more minutes."

"Ah." Ivan nodded, and pulled up a chair, and seated himself.

Three minutes later, the comconsole chimed. Miles keyed it on.

Gregor was trimly dressed in dark and distinctly civilian gear; Laisa was lovely as usual in bluntly Komarran style. Both were smiling, eyes alight with the glow of their mutual infatuation.

"Hello, Miles," Gregor began, to which Laisa added a, "Hello again, Lord Vorkosigan."

Miles cleared his throat. "Hi, folks. What can I do for you?"

"I wanted you to be among the first to know," said Gregor. "I've asked Laisa to marry me. And she said yes." Gregor was looking quite blitzed, as if this prompt assent had come as a surprise to him. Laisa's smile, to her credit, was at least equally blitzed.

"Congratulations," Miles managed.

Ivan leaned over his shoulder into the vid pickup to add a second to the motion, and Gregor said, "Oh, good, you're here. You were next." Going down his list of profoundly relieved heirs in official order of rank? Well . . . it was the Barrayaran thing to do. Laisa murmured greetings to Ivan too.

"Am I the first to know?" Miles trolled.

"Not quite," said Gregor. "We've been taking turns. Lady Alys was first, of course; she's been in on this from the start, or nearly so."

"I sent the message to my parents yesterday. And I've told Captain Galeni," added Laisa. "I owe him so much. He and you both."

"And, ah, what did he say?"

"He agreed it might be good for planetary accord," said Gregor, "which, considering his background, I find most heartening."

In other words, you asked him point-blank, and he said, Yes, Sire. Poor, excellent Duv. No wonder he called me. It was that or explode. "Galeni . . . is a complex man."

"Yes, I know you like him," said Gregor. "And I sent a message to your parents that should arrive tonight. I expect to hear back from them by tomorrow."

"Oh," Miles said, reminded. "Aunt Alys was ahead of you, I think. My father asked me to send on his personal assurance of support. And my mother asked me to tell you the same particularly, Dr. Toscane."

"I'm looking forward to meeting the legendary Cordelia Vorkosigan," Laisa said, with evident sincerity. "I think I could learn a lot from her."

"I think you could too," admitted Miles. "Good God. They'll be coming home for this, won't they."

"I can think of no one I want more to stand on my wedding circle than them, except you," said Gregor. "I trust you will be my Second?"

Just like a duel. "Certainly. Uh . . . what's the timetable on the public-circus part of this?"

Gregor sagged slightly. "Lady Alys seems to have some very definite ideas on that score. I wanted the betrothal ceremony immediately, but she's insisting it not even be announced till after her return from Komarr. I'm dispatching her to be my Voice to Laisa's parents, all the proper forms, you know. And the formal betrothal not for two months. And the wedding not for nearly a year! We compromised on one month after her return to the betrothal, and are still arguing about the other. She says if we don't give the Vor ladies time to dress properly, they'll never forgive me. I didn't see why it should take them two months to get dressed."

"Mm. I'd give her a free rein in this, if I were you. She could have the conservative Old Vor faction eating out of her hand for you without them ever knowing what hit them. Which is half your problem solved. I can't speak for the radical Komarran half, I'm afraid."

"Alys thinks we should have two weddings, one here, one on Komarr," said Gregor. "A double ordeal." He glanced aside, and squeezed Laisa's hand. "But worth it."

Staring down the social gauntlet opening with increasing complexity before them, they both looked like they were thinking of eloping. "You'll get through it all right," Miles assured them heartily. "We'll all help, won't we, Ivan?"

"My mother's already volunteered me," Ivan admitted glumly.

"Have you, ah, told Illyan?" Miles asked.

"I sent Lady Alys to break the news to him before anyone else," said Gregor. "He called on me in person to assure me of his personal and professional support—that phrase about support keeps cropping up. Do I look like I'm about to faint? I couldn't tell if he was pleased or horrified, but then, Illyan can be hard to read sometimes."

"Not that hard. I'd guess he was personally pleased, and professionally horrified."

"He did suggest I do all I could to expedite the return of your lady mother before the betrothal, to, as he put it, lend her clout to Lady Alys. I wondered if you'd add your voice to that plea for us, Miles. She's so hard to detach from your father."

"I'll try. Actually, it would probably take a wormhole blockade to keep her away."

Gregor grinned. "Congratulations to you too, Miles. Your father before you needed a whole army to do it, but you've changed Barrayaran history just with a dinner invitation."

Miles shrugged helplessly. *God, is everybody going to blame me for this? And for everything that follows?* "Let's try to avoid making history on this one, eh? I think we should push for unalleviated domestic dullness."

"With all my heart," Gregor agreed. With a cheery salute, he cut the com.

Miles laid his head down on the table, and moaned. "It's not my fault!"

"Yes, it is," said Ivan. "It was all your idea. I was there when you came up with it."

"No, it wasn't. It was yours. You're the one who dragooned me into attending the damned State dinner in the first place."

"I only invited *you*. *You* invited Galeni. And anyway, my mother dragooned me."

"Oh. So it's all her fault. Good. I can live with that."

Ivan shrugged agreement. "Well, should we drink to the happy couple? There are things in your cellars with more dust on them than an old Vor."

Miles thought it over. "Yeah. Let's go exploring."

Over the racks downstairs, just after violently rejecting

Miles's diffident suggestion of maple mead as the after-dinner poison of choice, Ivan added reluctantly, "D'you think Galeni will try to do anything he'd regret? Or that we'd regret?"

Miles hesitated a long time before saying, "No."

THIRTEEN

Ivan did not make good his threat to follow up his harassment about Miles's medical treatment, or lack of it, because he was press-ganged into assisting Lady Alys's departure for Komarr. She paused in passing Vorkosigan House to drop off several kilos of historical references about previous Imperial weddings, with orders for Miles to study up. When she returned, she'd doubtless have a lengthy list of chores for everyone from Ivan outward. And the next man outward from Ivan was Miles.

Miles leafed through the old books in some dismay. How many of these dusty ceremonies were they going to drag out of the museum? It had been forty years since the last Imperial wedding, between Prince Serg of glorious/dubious memory and the ill-fated Princess Kareen. That had been a circus of monumental proportions, and Serg had only been the heir, not the reigning Emperor. Still, Miles supposed such a renewal of the forms of the Vor cemented their fraying identity as a class. Perhaps a well-conceived and conducted ceremony would act as a kind of social immuno-suppressant, to keep the Vor from rejecting the transplanted Komarran tissue. Alys certainly seemed to think so, and she ought to know; the Vorpatrils were as old-Vor as they came.

Glumly, he contemplated his future duties. He supposed being the Second to the Emperor at his wedding was politically as well as socially important, given the degree to which the two modes could run together in Vorbarr Sultana, but it still made him feel about as useful as a plaster lawn statue holding up a flambeau. Well . . . duty had brought him much stranger tasks before this. Would he rather be back cleaning freezing drains under Camp

Permafrost? Or running around Jackson's Whole one step ahead of some psychotic local baron's goon squads?

Don't answer that, boy.

Lady Alys had found a temporary replacement for herself as Gregor's social chaperone in Drou Koudelka, the Commodore's wife and Delia's mother. Miles discovered this when Madame Koudelka called to issue an invitation/command for him to come be Vorishly ornamental at another of Gregor's courting picnics. Miles arrived a trifle early at the Residence's east portico only to run into a mob of men in parade red and blues just leaving some ultraformal morning ceremony. He stood aside to let the uniformed officers pass, trying to keep the naked envy out of his face.

One man stepped down the stairs slowly and carefully, leaning on the railing. Miles recognized him instantly, and quelled an impulse to try to duck behind the nearest topiaried bush. Lieutenant Vorberg. Vorberg had never seen Admiral Naismith, only a sawed-off suit of combat armor. It had apparently been Gregor's day to hand out various Imperial recognitions, for a new decoration gleamed on Vorberg's chest, the one for being wounded in the Emperor's Service. Miles had half a jar full of similar ones at home in a drawer; at some point Illyan had stopped issuing them to him anymore, perhaps fearing that Miles's threat to don them all at once sometime was not facetious. But it was clearly the first serious honor Vorberg had ever had occasion to collect, for he wore it with a bemused self-consciousness.

Miles couldn't help himself. "Ah—Vorberg, is it?" he essayed, as the lieutenant passed him.

Vorberg blinked uncertainly at him, then his face cleared. "Vorkosigan, yes? I've seen you around Galactic Affairs HQ on Komarr, I believe." He nodded cordially, one ImpSec courier and fellow Vor to another.

"Where'd you collect the bad luck charm?" Miles nodded to Vorberg's chest. "Or should I not ask?"

"It's not that classified. I was on a routine—fairly routine—run out past Zoave Twilight. Bunch of goddamn hijackers captured the ship I was on."

"Not one of our courier ships! Surely I'd have heard about that. It would have been a major flap."

"I wish it had been. ImpSec might have sent a proper force after me for that. It was just a commercial freighter of Zoavan registry. So anyway, ImpSec in its infinite wisdom, and doubtless under the advice of the same budget-pinching accountants who booked me on that damned ship in the first place, scraped up some low-bidder merc outfit to try and spring me. It was a real foul-up." He lowered his voice confidentially. "If you're ever out that way yourself, avoid the collection of clowns calling itself the Dendarii Free Mercenary Fleet. They're deadly."

"Isn't that the idea?"

"Not to your *own side* it's not."

"Oh." Someone must have told Vorberg he'd been hit by friendly fire. The surgeon, probably: she was incurably honest. "But I've heard of the Dendarii. I mean, obviously they have some renegade Barrayarans in their ranks, or they wouldn't have named themselves after my District's chief geographical feature. Unless they had some military history buff who was impressed by my grandfather's guerrilla campaigns."

"Their exec officer was some expatriate Barrayaran, yes. I met him. Their commander's rumored to be Betan. Apparently he escaped Betan therapy."

"I thought the Dendarii were supposed to be good."

"Not notably."

"You're here, aren't you?" said Miles, nettled. He controlled himself. "So . . . are you going back on duty?"

"I get to ride a desk or something at HQ for a couple of weeks, after this." Vorberg's vague nod indicated the ceremony just concluded. "Make-work. I don't see why my legs can't finish healing while I travel, but evidently the docs think I ought to be able to run away at full speed if required."

"*That's* the truth," Miles admitted ruefully. "If I had only moved a little faster myself . . ." He cut off his words.

For the first time, Vorberg seemed to become aware of Miles's subdued civilian garb. "Are you on medical leave too?"

Miles's voice went curt. "I'm on medical discharge."

"Oh." Vorberg had the grace to look embarrassed. "But—I thought you had some kind of special dispensation from, um, above." Vorberg might be a little vague on who Miles was, but he knew exactly who Miles's father was.

"I exceeded it. Courtesy of a needle grenade."

"Ouch," said Vorberg. "That sounds even more unpleasant than plasma fire. I'm sorry to hear it. What do you plan to do, then?"

"I really don't know."

"Will you go back to your District?"

"No . . . I have, um, social duties that will keep me in Vorbarr

Sultana for a while." The general announcement of Gregor's betrothal had not yet been made; there would doubtless be a leak sometime, but Miles was determined it wouldn't be from him. ImpSec HQ was going to be a very busy place, once these nuptial preparations went into full swing. If Miles were still working there, now would be a wonderful time to seek some extended and very distant galactic mission. But he couldn't very well warn Vorberg of that. "Vorkosigan House is . . . home enough."

"Perhaps I'll see you around. Good luck to you."

"You too." Miles gave him an analyst's salute, and passed on. Vorberg, of course, did not return the salute-like gesture to a civilian, but merely nodded politely.

Gregor's majordomo ushered Miles through to another garden party, minus the horse this time, and not so intimate. Gregor's close friend Count Henry Vorvolk and his Countess were present, and a couple of other of Gregor's cronies. The social agenda of the afternoon seemed to be to introduce the prospective bride to the next circle of Imperial acquaintances, outward from foster family such as Alys, Miles, and Ivan. Gregor arrived a little late, obviously having just changed from the parade uniform of this morning's award ceremony.

Drou Koudelka, Delia's mother, presided cheerfully in the absent Alys's place. Drou had formerly been Gregor's own bodyguard in his childhood, before she'd married Koudelka, and had also run security for Miles's mother. Miles could see that Gregor was anxious that Drou and Laisa hit it off well.

Gregor needn't have worried. Madame Koudelka, immensely experienced in the Vorbarr Sultana scene, got on well with everyone. As a close observer of the Vor while not one of them, she was very well placed to pass on private advice to Laisa, which seemed to be Gregor's idea.

Laisa did well too, as usual. She had the instincts of an ambassador, was observant, and never made the same mistake twice. Dropping her down in a Barrayaran city slum or the far backcountry and expecting her to survive might be optimistic, but it was clear she could handle Barrayar's galactic interface quite comfortably.

Despite the agenda, Gregor did manage to get his fiancée to himself for a while, when at his broad Imperial hint the group broke up for a postprandial stroll through the grounds. Miles ducked out with Delia Koudelka to sit on a bench overlooking the formal section of the gardens, and watch the minuet as the diligent strollers charitably tried to avoid Gregor and Laisa along the branching paths.

"How's your da?" Miles asked her, when they'd settled. "I should go see him, I suppose."

"Yes, he'd wondered why you seemed to be avoiding him this home leave. Then we heard about your medical discharge. He told me to tell you he was awfully sorry about that. Did you already know it was coming up that night we went to the State dinner? You never let on. But it couldn't have been a surprise to you."

"I was still desperately hoping I might skin out of it somehow." Not strictly true; he'd been in a state of complete denial, not thinking about it at all. Bad mistake, in retrospect.

"How's your Captain Galeni?"

"Despite everyone's assumption to the contrary, Duv Galeni is not my personal property."

She pursed her lips impatiently. "You know what I mean. How's he taking Laisa's engagement to Gregor? I was sure he was sweet on her, that night."

"Not real well," Miles admitted, "but he'll get over it. He was just courting too slowly, I guess. She must have decided he wasn't that interested."

"It would be a nice change from louts trying to crawl all over you," Delia sighed.

Miles pictured himself with pitons, and lots and lots of rope, attempting Mount Delia. A very dangerous face, that one. "And how are you getting on with Ivan these days? I didn't know if I ought to apologize for hijacking you from him, that night."

"Oh, Ivan."

Miles smiled faintly. "Are you looking forward to this Imperial wedding?"

"Well, *Mother's* all excited, at least for Gregor's sake. She's planning all our clothes already, and wondering if my sister Kareen can get back from Beta Colony for it. I wonder if she thinks weddings are contagious. We keep getting these little hints that Ma and Da would like the house back for themselves someday. Or at least the bathrooms."

"And you?"

"Well, there will be dancing." She brightened. "And maybe interesting men."

"Ivan's not an interesting man?"

"I said men, not boys."

"He's almost thirty. You're what, twenty-four?"

"It's not the years, it's the attitude. Boys just want to get laid. Men want to get married, and get on with their lives."

"I'm pretty sure men want to get laid too," Miles said rather apologetically.

"Well, yes, but it's not such an all-encompassing desire. They have some brain cells left over for other functions."

"You can't tell me women don't reciprocate."

"Maybe we're more selective."

"Your argument is not supported by the statistics. Almost everybody seems to get married. They can't be that selective."

She looked thoughtful, apparently struck by this. "Only in our culture. Kareen says on Beta Colony they do it differently."

"They do everything differently on Beta Colony."

"So maybe it is just contagious."

So how come I seem immune? "I'm surprised none of you girls have been snapped up yet."

"It's because there's four of us, I think," Delia confided. "Fellows get close to the herd, and then get all confused as to who's their target."

"I can see that," Miles allowed. En masse, the Koudelka blondes were a most unnerving phenomenon. "Looking to ditch your sisters, are you?"

"Any time," Delia sighed.

The Vorvolks strolled by, and stopped to chat; Miles and Delia ended up drifting back to Madame Koudelka in their wake, and the party broke up. Miles returned to Vorkosigan House, to scrounge around diligently for any task other than the homework the departing Lady Alys had dropped on him.

———※———

Miles was ensconced in the Yellow Parlor after dinner in a close review of Tsipis's monthly financial report, making notes and still ignoring the pile of leather-bound, dusty volumes in the corner, when Martin barged in.

"Somebody came to the door," Martin announced in a tone of mild amazement. As an apprentice butler, a chore he had picked up by default in addition to his duties as driver and occasional dishwasher, Martin had received instructions on the appropriate methods for ushering visitors inside, and guiding them through the labyrinth of the house to its living inhabitant. It was perhaps time for a short review of the principles involved.

Miles set down his reader-unit. "So . . . did you let him, her, or it in? Not a salesperson, I trust; the gate guard's usually good about keeping them out. . . ."

Duv Galeni stepped in behind Martin. Miles swallowed his patter. Galeni was in uniform, still the undress greens of his day's office duties. He did not appear to be armed. In fact, he mostly looked just tired. And a little disturbed, but without that subtle manic edge that Miles had learned to red-flag. "Oh," Miles managed. "Come in. Have a seat."

Galeni's hand opened dryly, acknowledging the invitation despite the fact that he was in already. He settled stiffly into a straight chair.

"Would you . . . care for a drink?"

"No, thank you."

"Ah, that will be all, then, Martin. Thank you." After a beat, Martin took the hint, and decamped.

Miles had no idea where this was going, so merely raised his brows.

Galeni cleared his throat uncomfortably. "I believe I owe you an apology. I was out of line."

Miles relaxed. Perhaps it was going to be all right. "Yes, and yes. But it was understandable. Which is enough said."

Galeni nodded shortly, back to his normal cool mode.

"Um . . . I hope I was your only confidant, that night."

"Yes. But that is only the preamble to what I came for. Something rather more difficult has come up."

Now what? Please, no more complicated love-lives . . . "Oh? What sort of something?"

"It's a professional dilemma, not a personal one this time."

I'm out of ImpSec, Miles carefully did not point out. He waited, curiosity aroused.

Galeni frowned more deeply. "Tell me . . . have you ever caught Simon Illyan in a mistake?"

"Well, he fired *me*," said Miles wryly.

Galeni's hand twitched, rejecting the joke. "No. I mean an error."

Miles hesitated. "He's not superhuman. I've seen him get led astray, down some incorrect line of reasoning, though not too often. He's pretty good about constantly rechecking his theories against new data."

"Not complex mistakes. Simple ones."

"Not really." Miles paused. "Have you?"

"Never before this. I haven't worked intimately with him, you understand. There's a weekly briefing with my department, and the occasional special request for information. But there have been four . . . odd incidents in the last three days."

"Incidents, eh? What sort?"

"The first one . . . he asked me for a digest I was preparing. I finished it and sent it upstairs, then two hours later he called down and requested it again. There was a moment of confusion, then his secretary confirmed from the office log I had delivered it, and said he'd already handed it in to him. Illyan then found the code card on his desk, and apologized. And I didn't think anything more about it."

"He was . . . impatient," Miles suggested.

Galeni shrugged. "The second thing was so small, just a memo from his office with the wrong date. I called his secretary and had it corrected. No problem."

"Mm."

Galeni took a breath. "The third thing was a memo with the wrong date, addressed to my predecessor, who hasn't been there for five months, and asking for the latest report on a certain joint Komarran-Barrayaran trade fleet that had gone on a long circuit out past Tau Ceti. And which had returned to home orbit six months ago. When I called up to find out just what kind of information he wanted, he denied asking for any such thing. I shot the memo back to him, and he got real quiet, and cut the com. That was this morning."

"That's three."

"Then there was the weekly briefing this afternoon with my department, the five of us Komarran affairs analysts and General Allegre. You know Illyan's normal delivery style. Long pauses, but very incisive when he does speak. There were . . . more pauses. And what came out in between seemed to jump around, sometimes bewilderingly. He dismissed us early, before we were half done."

"Um . . . what was today's topic?"

Galeni's mouth shut.

"Yes, I understand, you really can't tell me, but if it was Gregor's upcoming matrimonial project—maybe he was editing out things for your benefit, on the fly or something."

"If he didn't trust me, he shouldn't have had me there at all," snapped Galeni. He added reluctantly, "It's a good theory. But it doesn't quite . . . I wish you had been there."

Miles set his teeth against the obvious quips. "What are you suggesting?"

"I don't know. ImpSec spent quite a lot of money and time training me as an analyst. I look for changes in patterns. This is one. But I'm the new face in town, and a Komarran to boot. You've known Illyan all your life. Have you seen this before?"

"No," Miles admitted. "But those all sound like normal human errors."

"If they'd been more spread out, I doubt I'd have noticed. I don't need—or want—to know details, but is Illyan under any special strain in his personal life right now, that none of us in the office know about?"

Like you are, Duv? "I don't think Illyan *has* a personal life. Never married . . . lived in the same little apartment six blocks from work for fifteen years, till they tore the building down. He moved into one of the witness apartments on the lower level of HQ as a temporary stopgap two years ago, and still hasn't bothered to move out. I don't know about his early life, but there haven't been any women lately. Nor men, either. Nor sheep. Though I suppose I could see sheep. They can't talk, even under fast-penta. That's a joke," he added, as Galeni failed to smile. "Illyan's life is regular as a clock. He likes music . . . never dances . . . notices perfumes, and flowers with a lot of scent, and odors generally. It's a form of sensory input that isn't routed through his chip. I don't think it does somatic stuff either, no touch, just audio and visual."

"Yes. I was wondering about that chip. Do you know anything about that supposed chip-induced psychosis?"

"I don't think it can be the chip. I don't know that much about its tech specs, but all those folks were supposed to have gone wonky within a year or two of its installation. If Illyan was going to go nuts, he should have done it decades ago." Miles hesitated. "One does wonder about . . . stress? Ministrokes? He's sixty-plus . . . hell, maybe he's just *tired.* He's had that damned job for thirty years. I know he was planning to retire in five years." Miles decided not to explain how he knew that.

"I cannot imagine ImpSec without Illyan. The two are synonyms."

"I'm not sure he actually likes his job. He's just very good at it. He's had so much experience, he's almost impossible to surprise. Or panic."

"He has a very personal system for running the place,"

Galeni observed. "It's quite Vorish, really. Most non-Barrayaran organizations attempt to define their tasks so as to make the people who hold them interchangeable parts. It assures organizational continuity."

"And eliminates inspiration. Illyan's leadership style isn't very flashy, I admit, but he's flexible and infinitely reliable."

Galeni cocked an eyebrow. "Infinitely?"

"Usually reliable," Miles corrected quickly. For the first time, Miles wondered if Illyan was naturally drab. He'd always assumed it was a response to the high-security aspects of Illyan's job—a life with no handles for enemies to grab and twist. But maybe instead his colorless approach was how he dealt with whatever it was about the memory chip that had overwhelmed others?

Galeni placed his hands out flat across his knees. "I've told you what I've observed. Do you have any suggestions?"

Miles sighed. "Watch. Wait. What you've got here so far isn't even a theory. It's a handful of water."

"My theory is there's something very wrong with this handful of water."

"That's an intuition. Which is not an insult, by the way. I've learned a deep respect for intuition. But you mustn't confuse it with proof. I don't know what to say. If Illyan is developing some sort of subtle cognitive problems, it's up to his department heads to . . ." What? Mutiny? Go over Illyan's head? The only two people on the planet with that kind of elevation were Prime Minister Racozy and Emperor Gregor. "If this is something real, other people are going to notice it eventually. And it's better that it should be pointed out first by anyone else in ImpSec but you. Except me. *That* would be worse."

"What if they all feel that way?"

"I . . ." Miles rubbed his forehead. "I'm glad you talked to me."

"Only because you were the one person I knew whose knowledge of Illyan had a really long baseline. Otherwise . . . I'm not sure I should be talking about it at all. Not outside of ImpSec."

"Nor inside of ImpSec either. Though there's Haroche. He's worked directly under Illyan for almost as long as I did."

"That may be why I found it difficult to approach him."

"Well . . . talk to me again, huh? If anything else disturbs you."

"Maybe it's all hot air," said Galeni, not very hopefully.

Miles could recognize denial at a hundred meters, these days. "Yeah. Um . . . you want to change your mind about that drink?"

"Yeah," sighed Galeni.

Two mornings after this, Miles was deeply involved in an inventory of his closets' limited civilian contents, making a list of gaps and wondering if it would be simpler to just hire a valet and say "Take care of it," when his bedroom comconsole chimed. He ignored it for a minute, then clambered up off the floor next to the pile of discarded clothing and slouched to answer it.

Illyan's stern face appeared, and Miles's spine automatically straightened. "Yes, sir?"

"Where are you?" Illyan asked abruptly.

Miles stared. "Vorkosigan House. You just rang me here."

"I know that!" said Illyan irritably. "Why weren't you *here*, at 0900 as ordered?"

"Excuse me. What orders?"

"*My* orders. 'Be there at 0900 sharp and bring your notepad. You'll like this one. It's a breakout.' I thought you'd be early."

Miles recognized the style of an Illyanesque verbatim self-quote, all right. The content rang a very faint bell. It was an alarm bell. "What's this all about?"

"Something my Cetagandan analysts have cooked up, and spent a week pitching to me. It could be a very high-result, low-cost bit of tactical judo. There's a gentleman by the name of Colonel Tremont whom they think may be the best man to give the fading Marilacan resistance a shot in the arm. There's just one little hitch. He's presently a guest in the Cetagandan prison camp on Dagoola IV. The experience should have given him lots of motivation, if he can be freed. Anonymously, of course. I plan to give you considerable discretion as to the method, but those are the results I want: a new leader for Marilac, and no connection with Barrayar."

Miles didn't merely recognize the mission, he could swear those had been the exact words that Illyan had first used to describe it. At a highly secret morning conference at ImpSec HQ, long ago . . .

"Simon. The Dagoola mission was completed five years back. The Marilacans threw the last of the Cetagandans off their planet last year. You fired me over a month ago. I don't work for you anymore."

"Have you lost your mind?" Illyan demanded, and stopped abruptly. They stared at one another.

Illyan's face changed. Froze. "Excuse me," he muttered, and cut the com.

Miles just sat, staring at the empty vid plate. He'd never before felt his heart pound like this while sitting perfectly still in an empty room. Galeni's report had worried him.

Now he was terrified.

FOURTEEN

Miles sat unmoving for ten minutes. Galeni had been right. Hell, Galeni hadn't guessed the half of it. Illyan wasn't just forgetting things that were there, he was remembering things that weren't. Flashbacks?

Hey, if the man can't tell what year it is, I see a way you could get your old job back. . . .

It wasn't very funny.

What to do? Miles was surely the one person on Barrayar who dared not say a word in criticism of Illyan. It would be attributed instantly to a post-termination snit, or worse, attempted vengeance.

But he could not ignore the situation, not knowing what he knew now. Orders flowed from Illyan's office, and people *obeyed* them. Trustingly. Thirty years of accumulated trust was a bank it would take time to break. How much damage could Illyan do in the meantime? Now, of all times? Suppose Illyan flashed back to some of the messier moments of the Komarr Revolt?

And how long had this been going on, before Galeni noticed? It seemed sudden, but perhaps it was only suddenly visible. How many weeks—months—of orders were tainted with this unreliability? Somebody was going to have to go back over every message that had emanated from Illyan's office all the way back to—when? *Someone. But not me.*

And was the malfunction sited in the chip, or in Illyan's own neural tissue? Or was it some subtle synergistic dysfunction? That was a medical and bioengineering question, and it would take a technical expert to answer it. *Again, not me.*

In the end, he turned to exactly the solution, if you could call it that, which Galeni had fallen back on. *Bounce the information to Someone Else, and hope they'll do something.* So how long was it going to take the committee of concerned Illyan-observers to stop tossing the hot ball back and forth, and unite in effective action? *It's not my decision. I wish to hell it were.*

Reluctantly, he punched in a comconsole code. "This is Lord Vorkosigan. Connect me to the Office of Domestic Affairs, please," he told the ImpSec corporal who answered.

General Haroche wasn't in. "Have him call me as soon as you can reach him," Miles told the office clerk. "It's urgent."

He turned back to his piles of clothing while he waited. He scarcely knew which ones to pitch and which ones to put back. Haroche didn't call. Miles tried his office two more times before he finally ran the man down.

Haroche frowned impatiently at him from the comconsole imager. "Yes? What is it, Lord Vorkosigan?"

Miles took a deep breath. "Simon Illyan called me a short time ago. I think you should review the call."

"Excuse me?"

"Go up to Illyan's office, and get his secretary to replay the call for you. In fact, you should both see it. I know it was recorded; it's standard operating procedure."

"Why?"

Indeed. Why should Haroche take the word of a security pariah whom he had witnessed his respected superior Illyan not only discharge, but personally escort from his HQ? "General, it's really important, it's really urgent, and I really would rather you judged it for yourself."

"You're being theatrically mysterious, Lord Vorkosigan." Haroche frowned unamused disapproval.

"I'm sorry." Miles kept his voice flat and level. "You'll understand when you see it."

Haroche raised one eyebrow. "Oh? Maybe I will, then."

"Thank you." Miles cut the com. No use in asking Haroche to call back after viewing the vid; it would be out of Miles's hands for certain, then.

There. He'd done it, done the right thing, as nearly as possible under the circumstances.

He felt quite sick.

Now: should he call Gregor? It was unfair to let the Emperor be blindsided in this, but God . . .

Haroche would do so soon enough, Miles supposed. As soon as he caught up with events and put Illyan under proper medical care, Haroche would by default and the chain of command become acting Chief of ImpSec, and his immediate next duty would be to notify Gregor of this unpleasant turn of events, and determine the Emperor's will in the matter. It would all be over before the day was done.

Maybe the cause of Illyan's confusion was something simple, easily fixed; maybe he'd be back on duty within days. A short circuit in his chip, say. *There's nothing simple about that chip.* But ImpSec would take care of its own.

Miles sighed, and returned to his list of self-imposed little chores, barely attentive. He tried to read, but could not concentrate. It wasn't possible for Illyan to be covering his tracks in this, was it? Suppose Haroche had gone up to view that call, and it wasn't on the log anymore? But if Illyan had that degree of self-awareness, he ought to have turned *himself* in for medical treatment.

The day dragged on interminably. In the evening, when he broke and called both Gregor and Haroche, he could not reach either. Mutually tied up on this crisis, perhaps. He left messages requesting return calls, which did not come. He slept badly.

———※———

He *hated* being out of the information circuit. By the following evening Miles was ready to go in person to pound on ImpSec's back door and demand secret reports to which he had no entitlement whatsoever, when Galeni turned up at Vorkosigan House. He'd obviously come straight from work, still in uniform, and looked grim even by his own morose standards.

"Drink?" said Miles after one look at his face, when Martin ushered him into the Yellow Parlor, with a proper announcement this time. "Dinner?"

"Drink." Galeni flung himself into the nearest armchair, and leaned his head back, as if his neck ached right down to the base of his spine. "I'll think about dinner. I'm not hungry yet." He waited until Martin had departed to add, "It's over."

"Talk. What happened?"

"Illyan broke down completely in the middle of the all-departments briefing this afternoon."

"This afternoon? You mean General Haroche didn't turn him over to the ImpSec medical department yesterday?"

"What?"

Miles described his disturbing call from Illyan. "I notified Haroche immediately. Please don't tell me the man didn't do what I told him to."

"I don't know," said Galeni. "I can only report what I saw." As a trained analyst, not to mention historian, Galeni had a keen sense of the difference between eyewitness testimony, hearsay, and speculation. You always knew which category whatever he was recounting fell into.

"Illyan's under medical care *now*, isn't he?" Miles demanded in worry.

"Oh, God, yes," sighed Galeni. "The briefing started out almost normally. The department heads gave their weekly précis reports, and listed all the red flag items they want the other departments to watch out for. Illyan seemed nervous, more restless than usual, fiddling with objects on the table . . . he snapped a data card in half, then muttered some apology. He stood up to give his usual list of chores for everyone, and it came out . . . one line never tracked another. He was all over the map. Not as if he thought it were the wrong day, but as if it were the wrong twenty days. Every sentence was grammatically correct and completely incoherent. And he didn't even seem to be aware of it, till he began looking at all of us staring at him with our jaws hanging open, and ran down.

"Then Haroche stood up—I swear it was the bravest thing I ever saw. And said, *Sir, I believe you should present yourself for medical evaluation immediately.* And Illyan barked back that he wasn't sick, and told Haroche to sit the hell down . . . except the look in his eyes kept flashing back and forth between rage and bewilderment. He was shaking. Where is that hulking teenager of yours with the drinks?"

"Probably took a wrong turn again, and is lost in the other wing. He'll sort himself out eventually. Please go on."

"Ah." Galeni rubbed his neck. "Illyan didn't want to go. Haroche called for a medic. Illyan countermanded him, said he couldn't leave in the middle of a crisis, except the crisis he seemed to think we were in the middle of was the Cetagandan invasion of Vervain, ten years ago. Haroche, who was about the color of milk by then, took him by the arm, and tried to steer him out—that was a mistake, because Illyan started to fight him. Haroche yelled, *Oh, shit, get a medic and hurry!* Which was bright of him. Damn, but Illyan fights dirty when he fights. I'd never seen that."

"Neither have I," said Miles, sickly fascinated.

"Two other men needed medics by the time the medic got there. They sedated Illyan to the eyeballs and tied him down in the ImpSec HQ clinic. And that was the end of *that* committee meeting. And to think I used to complain that they were boring."

"Ah, God." Miles pressed his hands to his eyes, and massaged his face. The scenario could hardly have been worse had it been deliberately engineered for maximum chaos and humiliation. And number of witnesses.

"Haroche is staying late at work tonight, needless to say," Galeni went on. "The whole building's in a suppressed uproar. Haroche gave us all orders not to talk to anyone, of course."

"Except me?"

"He forgot to except you, for some reason," said Galeni dryly. "So you didn't get this from me. You didn't get this, period."

"Quite. I understand. I assume he's reported this to Gregor by now."

"One hopes."

"Dammit, Haroche should have had Illyan under medical care before quitting time last night!"

"He looked pretty scared. We all did. Arresting the Chief of Imperial Security in the middle of ImpSec HQ is . . . not an easy task."

"No. No . . . I shouldn't criticize the man who's in the line of fire, I suppose. He would have had to take enough time to make sure. It's not the sort of thing you dare make a mistake on, if you value your career. Which Haroche does." Taking Illyan down in such a public arena seemed needlessly cruel. *At least Illyan fired me in private.* But on the other hand it was absolutely clear, no ambiguity about it, no room for confusion or rumor or innuendo. Or argument.

"Bad timing for this," Miles went on. "Though I don't suppose there is such a thing as a good time to have a biocybernetic breakdown. I wonder . . . if the strain of all these upcoming, um, Imperial demands was causal? It hardly seems possible. Illyan's weathered much worse crises than a wedding."

"A strain doesn't have to be the worst, to be the last," Galeni pointed out. "This thing could have been hanging by a thread since who knows when." Galeni hesitated. "I don't suppose this could have already been underway when he fired you? I mean . . . might you argue that his judgment was already impaired?"

Miles swallowed, not certain he was grateful to Galeni for saying out loud something he scarcely dared think. "I wish I could say so. But no. There was nothing wrong with his judgment then. It followed quite logically from his principles."

"So when did this start? It's a critical question."

"Yes. I've asked it of myself. Everyone else will be asking too, I'm sure. We'll all have to wait on the ImpSec physicians to tell us, I guess. Speaking of which, was there any word yet as to exactly what did cause this thing?"

"Nothing that trickled down to me. But they can hardly have started to examine the problem yet. I suppose they'll have to fly in obscure experts."

Martin appeared at last with their drinks, and Galeni elected to stay to dinner, a bit of news that made Martin's face fall. Since Ma Kosti served the two men elegantly and abundantly on zero notice, Miles could only assume Martin had been forced to give up his portion to the guest, and been required to subsist on sandwiches. Having seen Ma Kosti's idea of a quick snack, Miles did not feel overly guilty about this, though her art tonight was somewhat wasted on his and Galeni's distraction.

Still . . . the worst was over, with Illyan, and the larger dangers averted. The rest would just be cleanup.

⸻⸻◈⸻⸻

The pressed gargoyles on the lintel over the side door to ImpSec HQ were looking particularly suffused this morning, Miles thought, as if weighed down with sorrow and about to burst from the internal pressure of their sinister secrets. And the expressions on the faces of some of the men he passed bore a subtle resemblance to those of their granite mascots. The clerk at the security desk in the lobby looked up at him with a harried blink. "May I help you, sir?"

"I'm Lord Vorkosigan. I'm here to see Simon Illyan."

The clerk checked his comconsole. "You aren't on my roster, my lord."

"No. I just dropped by to visit him." The clerk, and everyone else, had to at least know that Illyan was off duty, if only because they had to have been informed that Haroche was now their acting chief. "In the clinic. Give me a tag and let me in, please."

"I can't do that, my lord."

"Of course you can. It's your job. Who's duty officer today?"

"Major Jarlais, my lord."

"Good. He knows me. Call him for your authorization, then."

Jarlais's face appeared on the clerk's comconsole within a couple of minutes. "Yes?"

The clerk explained Miles's request.

"I don't think that's possible, my lord," Jarlais said uncertainly to Miles, who was leaning into range of the vid pickup over the clerk's shoulder.

Miles sighed. "Call your boss . . . no, hell, it's going to take thirty minutes to work my way up the entire chain of command. Let's cut out the middlemen, eh? I hate to bother him when he's as busy as he undoubtedly is this morning, but just call General Haroche."

Jarlais, obviously, was equally reluctant to interrupt his superior, but a Vor lord in one's lobby was hard to dismiss, and impossible to ignore. They got through to Haroche's comconsole in a mere ten minutes, good work under the circumstances, Miles thought.

"Good morning, General," Miles said to Haroche's image over the desk clerk's vid plate. "I came in to see Simon."

"Impossible," rumbled Haroche.

Miles's voice grew edged. "It's *impossible* only if he's dead. I think you are trying to say that you don't wish to allow it. Why not?"

Haroche hesitated. "Corporal, set your cone of silence and give up your comconsole seat to Lord Vorkosigan for a moment, please."

The clerk obediently slid aside; a shadow fell around Miles and Haroche's image from the security generator over the station chair.

"Where did you hear about this?" Haroche demanded suspiciously, as soon as their privacy was assured.

Miles raised his brows, and switched gears without a moment's pause. "I was worried. When you didn't call me back after my call to you of day before yesterday, and didn't return any of my other messages, I finally called Gregor."

"Oh," said Haroche. His suspicion faded into mere irritation.

That was a close one, Miles realized. If Haroche hadn't reported to Gregor yet, it could have been a major stumble, potentially very damaging to Galeni. He'd better be carefully vague about when he'd supposedly talked to the Emperor, until he actually did. "I want to see Illyan."

"Illyan may not even be able to recognize you," said Haroche, after a long pause. "He's babbling classified material at a meter a minute. I had to assign guards of the highest security levels."

"So what? I'm cleared at the highest security levels." Hell, he *was* classified material.

"Surely not. Your clearance must have been revoked when you were . . . discharged."

"Check it." Ah, hell. Haroche had access to all of Illyan's files, now; he could look up the full true story of Miles's termination any time he had a minute. Miles hoped he hadn't had too many spare minutes to devote to such inquiries in the last day.

Haroche, after a narrow-eyed look at Miles, tapped out a code on his comconsole. "Your clearance is still on file," he said in some surprise.

"There you go."

"Illyan must have forgotten to alter it. Was he growing confused as early as that? Well . . ." His hand tapped on. "I revoke it now."

You can't do that! Miles bit back the outraged scream. Haroche most certainly could. Miles stared at him, frustrated. So what was he going to do? Flounce out of ImpSec with an angry cry of, *We'll just see about that! I'm going to tell my big brother on you!* No. Gregor was a card he dared only play once, and only in the direst emergency. He let out his breath, and his anger, in a carefully controlled sigh. "General. Prudence is one thing. Paranoia that can't tell friend from foe is quite another."

"Lord Vorkosigan," said Haroche, equally tightly. "We don't yet know what we have here. I don't have *time* to spend entertaining idly curious civilians this morning, friendly or not. Please do not pester my staff any more. Whatever the Emperor chooses to pass on to you is his business. My only duty is to report to him. Good *day.*" He cut the com with a firm swipe; the cone of silence vanished from around Miles, leaving him in the lobby again, with the clerk staring earnestly at him.

That did not go well.

⎯⎯⎯⎯◦◉◦⎯⎯⎯⎯

The first thing he did upon returning to Vorkosigan House was lock himself in his bedroom and call Gregor. It took forty-five minutes to get through. If it had taken forty-five hours, he would have persisted just the same.

"Gregor," Miles began without preamble, when the Emperor's face appeared over his vid plate. "What the hell is going on with Illyan?"

"Where did you hear about it?" asked Gregor, unconsciously echoing Haroche, and looking worried.

Miles summed up Illyan's call to him, and his call to Haroche, of two days ago. He again left Galeni out of it. "And then what happened? Something's happened, obviously."

Gregor gave him a brief précis of Illyan's breakdown, minus most of the harrowing details supplied by Galeni. "Haroche had him admitted to ImpSec's own clinic, which makes sense under the circumstances."

"Yes, I tried to see Illyan this morning. Haroche wouldn't let me in."

"They can bring whatever equipment or experts they need in there. I've personally granted funds and authority for anything Haroche wants to requisition."

"Gregor, track this for a moment. Haroche wouldn't let *me* in. To see *Illyan.*"

Gregor's fingers spread in a frustrated gesture. "Miles, give the man a break. He has his hands full, suddenly taking over all Illyan's duties, transferring his own department to the administration of his second—let him settle for a few days, without jogging his elbow, please. When he feels more in control, I'm sure he will relax. You have to admit, Simon would be the first to approve a cautious approach to such an emergency."

"True. Simon would prefer to be in the hands of people who really cared about security. But I'm beginning to think I would prefer it if there were any signs he was in the hands of people who really cared about Simon Illyan." He remembered the lingering nightmare of his own bout of post-cryo-revival amnesia. It had been one of the most terrifying periods of his life, to have so lost his memories, himself . . . was Illyan experiencing something like that right now? Or something even more grotesque? Miles had been lost among strangers. Illyan seemed lost among what should have been friends.

Miles sighed. "All right, I'll leave poor Haroche alone. God knows I don't envy him his job. But would you keep me posted on the medical bulletins? I find all this . . . unexpectedly dismaying."

Gregor looked sympathetic. "Illyan really was a mentor to you, wasn't he?"

"In his own acerbic and demanding way, yes. It was an excellent way, in retrospect. But before that, even . . . he served my father for thirty years, my whole life. Until I was eighteen years old, I called him "Uncle Simon," till I was admitted to the Service

Academy, after which I just called him "Sir." He had no surviving
family of his own by then, and his job and, I'm beginning to think,
that damned chip in his head ate any chance of his starting a new
one for himself."

"I didn't realize you thought of him as some sort of foster father, Miles."

Miles shrugged. "A foster uncle, anyway. It's . . . a family
matter. And I am Vor."

"Pleased to hear you admit it," murmured Gregor. "One wonders if you realize the fact, sometimes."

Miles flushed. "What I owe to Illyan is something all mixed up
between a foster uncle and a family retainer . . . and I'm the only
Vorkosigan on the planet at the moment. It feels like . . . no, it *is*
my responsibility."

"The Vorkosigans," granted Gregor, "were always nothing if
not loyal."

"It gets to be kind of a habit."

Gregor sighed. "Of course I'll keep you informed."

"Once a day? Haroche will be giving you bulletins once a day,
I know, with your morning ImpSec briefing."

"Yes, Illyan and my coffee always used to arrive together.
Sometimes, if he came in person, he'd bring the coffee himself. I
always felt it was a polite hint: *Sit up and pay attention.*"

Miles grinned. "That's Illyan. Once a day, yes?"

"Oh, very well. Look, I must go now."

"Thanks, Gregor."

The Emperor cut the com.

Miles sat back, partially satisfied. He had to give events and
people time to sort themselves out. He thought of his own placid
advice to Galeni about intuition versus proof. His intuition demon
could just go back in its box—he pictured himself stuffing a small
Naismith-shaped gnome into a trunk, and fastening the lid with
straps. And little tiny meeping and banging noises coming from
inside . . . *I didn't become Illyan's top agent because I was better
at following the rules than anybody else.* But it was too damned
early to say *There's something wrong with this picture*, or even to
think it very loudly.

ImpSec would take care of its own; it always did. And he wasn't
going to make a fool of himself in public again. He would wait.

FIFTEEN

The week dragged past. The daily short briefings via comconsole from Gregor seemed all right at first, but as each one fell atop the last with little sense of progress, ImpSec's caution began to seem downright glacial to Miles. He complained of this to Gregor.

"You're always impatient, Miles," Gregor pointed out. "Nothing ever goes fast enough to suit you."

"Illyan shouldn't have to wait on doctors. Other people must, maybe, but not him. Don't they have any conclusions yet?"

"They ruled out stroke."

"They ruled out stroke the first day. Then what? What about the chip?"

"There is apparently some evidence of deterioration or damage to the chip."

"We guessed that already, too. What kind? When? How? Why? What the hell are they doing in there all this time?"

"They're still working on ruling out other neurological problems. And psychological ones. It's apparently not easy."

Miles hunched, grouchily. "I don't buy the iatrogenic psychosis idea. He's had that chip in too long without any signs of problems like this before."

"Well . . . that's just the point, it seems. Illyan has had this particular neural augmentation in place and running for longer than any other human being ever. There are no standards for comparison. He's the baseline. No one knows what thirty-five years of accumulated artificial memory does to a personality. We may be finding out."

"I still think we ought to be finding out faster."

"They're doing all they can, Miles. You'll just have to wait like the rest of us."

"Yeah, yeah . . ."

Gregor cut the com; Miles stared unseeing into the empty space over the vid plate. The trouble with synopsized information was that it was always so nebulous. The devil was in the details, the raw data; embedded therein were all the tiny clues that fed the intuition demon until it became strong and fat and, sometimes, grew up to become an actual Theory, or even a Proof. Miles was at least three layers away from reality; the ImpSec physicians synopsized it to Haroche, who boiled it down for Gregor, who filtered it to Miles. There weren't enough facts left in the clarified drippings by that time to color an opinion.

———※◎※———

Lady Alys Vorpatril returned from her official journey to Komarr the following morning; that afternoon, she called Miles on his comconsole. He braced himself for the impact of descending social duties; some repressed inner voice cried *Incoming!*, and dove for cover, uselessly. The inner man would simply have to be dragged out again by the heels and propped upright to march on her orders.

But instead her first words were, "Miles, how long have you known about this dreadful nonsense going on with Simon?"

"Um . . . a couple of weeks."

"Did it never occur to any of you three young louts that *I* would wish to be informed?"

Young louts—Ivan, Miles, and . . . Gregor? She *was* upset.

"There was nothing you could do. You were halfway to Komarr. And you already had a top-priority job. But no, I confess I didn't think of it."

"Fools," she breathed. Her brown eyes smoldered.

"Um . . . how did things go, by the way? On Komarr."

"Not terribly well. Laisa's parents are rather upset. I did what I could to soothe their fears, given that I judge some of their anxieties to be quite well founded. I asked your mother to stop on her way and speak to them some more."

"Mother's on her way home?"

"Soon, I hope."

"Ah . . . are you sure my mother is the best person for that job? She can be awfully blunt in her opinions of Barrayar. And she's not always the most diplomatic."

"No, but she's absolutely honest. And she has this peculiar trick of making the most outlandish things seem perfectly sensible, at least for the duration of the time she's talking to you. People end up agreeing with her, and then spending the next month wondering how it happened. I have, at any rate, accomplished all the proper forms and duties of Gregor's Baba."

"So . . . is Gregor's wedding on, or off?"

"Oh, on, of course. But there is a difference between things done in a scramble, and things done superbly well. There will be enough tensions that I can't ease. I don't intend to leave any hanging that I can eliminate. Goodwill is going to be at a premium." She frowned fiercely. "Speaking of goodwill, or the lack of it— they told me Simon was in the ImpSec Headquarters clinic, so *of course* I went immediately to see him. That idiot general what's-his-name wouldn't let me in!"

"Haroche?" ventured Miles.

"Yes, that was it. Not a Vor, that fellow, and it shows. Miles, can't you do something?"

"Me! I have no authority."

"But you worked with those, those, those . . . *men* for years. You understand them, presumably."

I am ImpSec, he'd once told Elli Quinn. He'd been quite proud to identify himself with that powerful organization, as if they'd flowed together to become some sort of higher cyborg. Well, he was amputated now, and ImpSec seemed to be stumping along without him in perfect indifference. "I don't work for them anymore. And if I did, I'd still be just a lowly lieutenant. Lieutenants don't give orders to generals, not even Vor lieutenants. Haroche wouldn't let me in either. I think you need to talk to Gregor."

"I just did. He was quite maddeningly vague about it all."

"Maybe he didn't want to distress you. I gather Illyan is in a pretty disturbing mental state right now, not recognizing people and so on."

"Well, how can he, if no one he knows is allowed to see him?"

"Um. Good point. Look, I have no intention of defending Haroche to you. I'm pretty annoyed at him myself."

"Not annoyed enough," snapped Lady Alys. "Haroche actually had the nerve to tell me—*me!*—that it was no sight for a lady. I asked him what *he* had been doing during the War of Vordarian's Pretendership." Her voice trailed off in a hiss—Miles's ear was not quite sure, but he thought it detected suppressed barracks language. "I can see Gregor is thinking he may have to work with

Haroche for a long time yet. He didn't say it in so many words, naturally, but I gather Haroche has persuaded Gregor that his status as acting Chief of ImpSec is too new and fragile to bear interference from such dangerously unauthorized—and female—persons such as myself. *Simon* never had any such qualms. I wish Cordelia were here. She was always better than I at cutting through masculinist drivel."

"So to speak," said Miles, thinking of Vordarian's fate at his mother's hands. But Lady Alys was quite correct: Illyan had always treated her as a valued, though different, member of Gregor's support team. Haroche's new and tighter professional order must have come as a bit of a shock to her. Miles went on, "Haroche is in an excellent position to persuade Gregor. He's in total control of the flow of all information to him." Though you couldn't call that a change in how things were done; it had always been that way, but when Illyan had been the sluice keeper it had somehow never bothered Miles.

Alys's dark brows twitched; she said nothing aloud to this. Beneath her speculative frown the silence grew . . . noticeable.

To break the discomfort his unguarded words had engendered, Miles said lightly, "You could go on strike. No wedding till Gregor twists Haroche's arm for you."

"If something sensible isn't done and done soon, I just might."

"I was joking," he said hastily.

"I was not." She gave him a curt nod, and cut the com.

━━◈━━

Martin cautiously shook Miles awake shortly after dawn the next morning.

"Um . . . m'lord? You have a visitor downstairs."

"At this ungodly hour?" Miles rubbed his sleep-numbed face, and yawned. "Who?"

"Says his name's Lieutenant Vorberg. One of your ImpSec sticks again, I guess."

"Vorberg?" Miles blinked. "Here? Now? Why?"

"He wants to talk to you, so I guess you'd better ask him."

"Quite, Martin. Um . . . you didn't leave him standing on the doorstep, did you?"

"No, I put him in that big downstairs room on the east side."

"The Second Receiving Room. That's fine. Tell him I'll be

down in just a minute. Make some coffee. Bring it there on a tray with two cups, and the usual trimmings. If there's any of your mother's pastries or breads left over in the kitchen, stuff 'em in a basket or something and bring them too, right? Good."

Curiosity aroused, Miles pulled on the first shirt and trousers that came to hand, and padded barefoot down two flights of the curving front staircase, then turned left and made his way through three more rooms till he came to Second Rec. Martin had pulled a cover off one chair for the guest, and left it in a white heap on the floor. Fingers of sunlight poked through the heavy curtains, leaving the shadows in which Vorberg sat somehow denser. The lieutenant was wearing undress greens, but his face was gray with a faint beard stubble. He frowned wearily at Miles.

"Good morning, Vorberg," said Miles, cautiously polite. "What brings you to Vorkosigan House so early in the day?"

"It's late in the day for me," said Vorberg. "I just came off night shift." His brows lowered.

"They found you a job, did they?"

"Yes. I'm night guard commander for the close security on the clinic."

Miles sat down on a covered chair, abruptly awake even without coffee. *Vorberg* was one of Illyan's guards? But of course, as a courier, he already had the kind of clearance required. He was at loose ends, readily requisitionable for a physically light, if mentally demanding duty. And . . . he was an HQ outsider. No close old friends there to gossip with. Miles tried to keep his tone level, noncommittal. "Oh? What's up?"

Vorberg's voice went tight, almost angry. "I do think it's bad form of you, Vorkosigan. Almost petty, under the circumstances. Illyan was your father's man for years. I passed the message on at least four times. Why haven't you come?"

Miles sat very still. "Excuse me. I think I've missed the first half of something. What, ah . . . could you please tell me *exactly* what's been going on in there? How long have you been on this duty?"

"Since the first night they brought him in. It's been pretty ugly. When he's not sedated, he babbles. When he is sedated, if he's been combative again, he still babbles, but you can't make out what he's saying. The medics keep him restrained almost all the time. It's as if he's wandering through history, in his mind, but every once in a while, he seems to pass through the present. And when he does, he asks for you. At first I thought it was the Count your father he wanted, but it's definitely you. *Miles*, he says, and *Get that idiot boy in here,* and *Haven't you found him yet, Vorberg? It's not like you can mistake the hyperactive little shit.* Sorry," Vorberg added as an afterthought, "that's just what he said."

"I recognize the style," whispered Miles. He cleared his throat, and his voice grew stronger. "I'm sorry. This is the first I've heard of this."

"Impossible. I've passed it on in my night report four or five nights in a row, now."

Gregor would not have failed to redirect such a word. Gregor hadn't a hint of this. The break was somewhere else up in Vorberg's chain of command. *We will find out. Oh yes, we will.* "What kind of medical treatment or tests is he receiving?"

"I don't know. Nothing much happens on my shift."

"I suppose . . . that's reasonable."

They both fell silent as Martin brought the coffee and rolls on a baking sheet for a makeshift tray—*Make a note for Lesson Six in butlering, Finding the Serving Utensils*—snagged a roll for himself, smiled cheerily, and strolled back out. Vorberg blinked at this odd turn of service, but sucked down coffee gratefully. He frowned again at Miles, more speculatively this time. "I've been hearing a lot of strange things from the man, in the deep night. Between the times the sedatives wear off, and before he goes, uh, goes noisy and wins another dose."

"Yes. I would imagine so. Do you know why Illyan is asking for me?"

"Not exactly. Even in his more lucid moments, it comes out sounding pretty garbled. But I've been getting the damnedest unpleasant feeling that the problem is half in me. Because I don't know the background, I can't decipher what may be perfectly clear statements. I *have* figured out you were never a bloody courier."

"No. Covert ops." A sunbeam was creeping over his chair arm, making the coffee in the thin cup perched there glow red.

"High level covert ops," said Vorberg, watching him in the shadows and light beams.

"The highest."

"I don't quite know why he discharged you—"

"Ah." Miles smiled bleakly. "I really must tell you, someday. It's true about the needle grenade. Just not complete."

"Part of the time he doesn't seem to know he discharged you. But part of the time he does. And he still asks for you, even then."

"Have you ever reported this directly to General Haroche?"

"Yes. Twice."

"What did he say?"

"Thank you, Lieutenant Vorberg."

"I see."

"I don't."

"Well . . . neither do I, completely. But now I think I can find out. Ah . . . I think perhaps this conversation had better not have taken place."

Vorberg's eyes narrowed. "Oh?"

"That conversation we had on the steps outside the Residence will do instead, if anyone inquires."

"Ho. And just what are you to the Dendarii Mercenaries, Vorkosigan?"

"Nothing, now."

"Well . . . you covert ops fellows were always the worst bunch of weasels I ever met, so I don't know even now if I trust you, but if you're being straight with me . . . I'm glad for the sake of the Vor that you haven't just abandoned your father's liegeman. There's not many of us left who care enough to, enough to . . . I don't know how to say it."

"Who care enough to make Vor real," suggested Miles.

"Yes," said Vorberg gratefully. "That's right."

"Damn straight, Vorberg."

———◦◉◦———

An hour later, Miles strode through the graying morning to the side portal of ImpSec HQ. Clouds were blowing in from the east, chilling the promise of the early sun; he could smell rain in the air. The granite gargoyles looked blank and surly in the shadowless light. The building above them rose big and closed and blocky. And ugly.

Haroche's first concern had been to place guards with the highest security clearances around Illyan. Not a word about *doctors* with the highest clearances, or *medtechs*, or, God forbid, *the best experts possible, cleared or not.* He wasn't treating Illyan so much as a patient as a prisoner. A prisoner of his own organization—did Illyan appreciate the irony? Miles suspected not.

So was Haroche paranoid and thickheaded by nature, or

merely temporarily panicked by his new responsibilities? Haroche couldn't have arrived where he was by being stupid, but his new and complex job had fallen into his lap suddenly and with little warning. Haroche had started his career in Service Security, as a military policeman. As Domestic Affairs assistant and then chief, he'd largely interfaced downward and inward, dealing with predictable military subordinates. Illyan had been ImpSec's upward and outward face, dealing smoothly with the Emperor, the Vor lords, all the unwritten and sometimes unacknowledged rules of the idiosyncratic Vor system. Illyan's handling of Alys Vorpatril, for example, had been subtly brilliant, giving him a wide-open pipeline of information into the private side of Vor society in the capital that had more than once proved an enormously valuable supplement to more official dealings. In his first encounter with her, Haroche had deeply offended this potential ally, as if the fact that she didn't appear in the government's organizational flow chart meant her power didn't exist. Chalk up a big one in favor of the thickheaded hypothesis.

But as for the paranoia—Miles had to acknowledge, Illyan's head was so stuffed with the hottest Barrayaran secrets of the last three decades it was a wonder it hadn't melted down long before this. You couldn't let him go wandering off down the street not knowing what year it was. Haroche's caution was in fact commendable, but it ought to have been tinged with more . . . what? Respect? Courtesy? *Grief*?

Miles took a breath and marched through the doors. Martin, who had been unusually fortunate in finding a big enough parking place quite nearby for the Count's armored groundcar, trailed him uncertainly, clearly awed by the sinister building despite his family connection. Miles planted himself before the security desk, and frowned at the clerk, the same fellow who'd been on duty last week.

"Good morning again. I'm here to see Simon Illyan."

"Um . . ." The clerk tapped his comconsole. "You're still not on my roster, Lord Vorkosigan."

"No, but I am on your doorstep. And I intend to stay here until I get some results. Call your chief."

The clerk hesitated, but came down in favor of letting someone with more status face down a Vor lord, even so short and odd a one as Miles. They hung up briefly at the level of Haroche's, formerly Illyan's, secretary, but Miles evicted the clerk from his station chair and bulled through to Haroche himself.

"Good morning, General. I'm here to see Illyan."

"Again? I thought I'd settled that. Illyan is in no condition to socialize."

"I didn't think he was. I request admittance to see him."

"Request denied." Haroche's hand moved to cut the com.

Miles controlled his temper, and tried to muster soft words and weasely arguments. He was willing to talk all day, till he talked himself inside. No, not soft words—Haroche favored a blunt aproach, for all that he assiduously tailored his own speech to Vorbarr Sultana upper-class standard. "Haroche! Talk to me! This is getting old. What the devil's going on in there that has the hairs up your butt so bad? I'm trying to help, dammit."

For a moment, Haroche frowned less deeply, but then his face hardened again. "Vorkosigan, you have no business in this place now. Please remove yourself."

"No."

"Then I will have you removed."

"Then I will return."

Haroche's lips thinned. "I don't suppose I can have you shot, considering who your father is. And besides, it's known that you have . . . mental problems. But if you go on making a nuisance of yourself, I might have you arrested."

"On what charge?"

"Trespass in a restricted area alone is good for a year in detention. I imagine I could come up with others. Resisting arrest is almost a sure bet. But I wouldn't hesitate to have you stunned."

He wouldn't dare. "How many times?"

"How many times do you propose to make it necessary?"

Miles said through his teeth, "You can't count past twenty-two even with your boots off, Haroche." It was serious insult to imply extra digits, on this mutation-scarred planet. Both Martin and the listening clerk watched the rising temperature of this exchange with increasing alarm.

Haroche's face reddened. "That does it. Illyan was soft in the head to discharge you—I'd have had you court-martialed. Get out of my building now."

"Not until I see Illyan."

Haroche cut the com.

About a minute later, two armed guards appeared around the corner, and marched toward Miles, who was badgering the clerk to try Haroche's secretary again. *Dammit, he wouldn't dare— would he . . . ?*

He would. Without preamble, each guard took an arm and began hustling him toward the door. They didn't quite care if his toes touched the ground or not. Martin trailed after them like an overexcited puppy, not sure whether to bark or bite. Through the door. Through the outer gates. They deposited him on the sidewalk outside the perimeter wall, on his feet but only just barely.

The senior officer said to the gate guards, "General Haroche has just given a direct order that if this man tries to enter the building again, he is to be stunned."

"Yes, sir." The senior guard saluted, and stared uneasily at Miles. Miles, face flushed, gulped for breath against a chest tight with humiliation and rage. The guards wheeled and marched back inside.

A rather bare strip-park across the street had benches viewing ImpSec's infamous architecture, empty now in the gathering chill mist. Miles, shaken, walked across to one and sat down, staring up at the building that had defeated him for the second time. Martin followed him uncertainly, and sat down gingerly on the far end, awaiting orders. Not daring to speak.

Wild visions of a Naismith-style covert ops raid coursed through Miles's mind. He pictured himself leading gray-uniformed mercenaries descending ninja-style over the side of ImpSec HQ . . . crap. He really would get himself shot, wouldn't he? Scorn puffed from his lips. Illyan was one prisoner who was outside of Naismith's range.

How dare Haroche threaten me, Miles had raved inwardly. Hell, why shouldn't Haroche dare? Mad to be judged solely on his own supposed merits, Miles himself had spent the last thirteen years eviscerating Lord Vorkosigan. He'd wanted to be seen as himself, not his father's son, nor his grandfather's grandson, nor the descendant of any other Vorkosigan for the last eleven generations. Trying so hard, no wonder he'd succeeded in convincing everyone, even himself, that Lord Vorkosigan didn't . . . count.

Naismith was obsessed with winning at all costs, and being seen to have won.

But Vorkosigan . . . Vorkosigan couldn't surrender.

It wasn't quite the same thing, was it?

Failing to surrender was a family tradition. Vorkosigan lords through history had been stabbed, shot, drowned, trampled, and burned alive. Most recently and spectacularly, one had even been blown nearly in half, then quick-frozen, thawed out, sewn up, and pushed off to stagger punch-drunkenly on his way again. Miles wondered if the Vorkosigans' legendary obduracy wasn't partly luck, whether good or bad he could not say. Maybe one or two had actually tried to surrender, but missed their chance, as in the tale of the general whose last words were reputed to have been, *Don't worry, Lieutenant, the enemy can't possibly hit us at this ran—*

The joke about the Dendarii District was that they'd wanted to give in, but no one could be found who was literate enough to decipher the Cetagandan amnesty offer, so they'd fought on to a bewildered victory. *There is more hillman in me than I'd thought.* He should have suspected it of a man who secretly *liked* the taste of maple mead.

Naismith could, demonstrably, get Vorkosigan killed. He could strip-mine the little lord for every positive human trait down to bare and naked Dendarii bedrock, cold and sterile. Naismith had embezzled his energy, ransacked him for time, nerve, wit, leached the very volume from his voice, even stolen his sexuality. But at that point, even Naismith could go no further. A hillman, dumb as his rocks, just didn't know how to quit. *I am the man who owns Vorkosigan Vashnoi.*

Miles threw back his head and laughed, tasting the metallic tang of the misting rain sifting into his open mouth.

"My lord?" said Martin uneasily.

Miles cleared his throat, and tried to rub the weird smile back off his face. "Sorry. I just figured out why it was I hadn't gone to get my head fixed yet." And he'd thought *Naismith* was the sly one. Vorkosigan's Last Stand, eh? "It struck me as funny." Hilarious, in fact. He stood up, stifling another giggle.

"You're not going to try and go back in there, are you?" asked Martin in alarm.

"No. Not directly. Vorkosigan House first. Home, Martin."

⸻※⸻

He showered again, to wash off the morning's accumulation of rain and city grime, but mostly to scrub out the unpleasant, lingering scent of shame. His mother's people's custom of the baptism crossed his thoughts, as well. A towel around his waist, he visited several closets and drawers to lay out his clothing for inspection.

He had not worn his Vorkosigan House uniform for several years, not even for the Emperor's Birthdays or the Winterfair Balls, casting it aside in favor of what had seemed, to him, the higher status of real Imperial military Service uniforms, dress greens or parade red-and-blues. He laid the brown fabric out on his bed, empty as a snake's shed skin. He inspected the seams and the silver embroidery of the Vorkosigan logos on collar and shoulders and sleeves carefully for wear or damage, but some meticulous servant had put it all away clean and covered, and it was in excellent shape. The dark brown boots too came out of their protective bag still softly gleaming.

Counts and their heirs, honorably retired from more active Imperial service, were permitted by ancient custom to wear their military decorations on their House uniforms, in recognition of the Vor's official and historical status as—what was that dippy phrase? "The Sinews of the Imperium, the Emperor's Right Arm." Nobody'd ever called them the Brains of the Imperium, Miles noted dryly. So how come no one had ever claimed to be, say, the Gall Bladder of the Imperium, or the Emperor's Pancreas? Some metaphors were best left unexamined.

Miles had never once worn all his accumulated honors, in part because four-fifths of them related to classified activities, and what fun was a decoration you couldn't tell a good story about, and in part because . . . why? Because they'd belonged to Admiral Naismith?

Ceremoniously, he laid them all out on the brown tunic in what would be the correct order. The bad luck badges like the one Vorberg had just won for getting wounded filled one whole row and part of another. His very first medal ever was from the Vervani government. His most recent high honor had drifted in rather belatedly from the grateful Marilacans, by jump-mail. He'd loved covert ops; it had taken him to such *very* strange places. He laid out no less than five Barrayaran Imperial Stars in metals of various denominations, depending more on how much salt Illyan had sweated back at HQ during the particular missions they represented than the amount of blood Miles personally had shed on the front lines. Bronze only represented his commander's nails bitten to the second knuckle; gold signified gnawing to the wrist.

He hesitated, then arranged the gold medallion of the Cetagandan Order of Merit on its colorful ribbon, properly, around the tunic's high collar. It was cool and heavy under his hand. He could be one of the few soldiers in history ever to be decorated by both sides in the same war . . . though to be truthful, the Order of Merit had come later, and actually had been presented to Lord Vorkosigan, not the little Admiral for a change.

When they were all arranged, the effect was just short of looney.

Separated into all the little secret compartments, he hadn't realized just how much he'd accumulated, till he put it all together again. No, not again. For the first time.

Let's lay it all on the line. Smiling grimly, he fastened them down. He donned the white silk shirt that went underneath, the silver-embroidered suspenders, the brown trousers with the silver side-piping, the gleaming riding boots. Lastly, the heavy tunic. He fastened his grandfather's dagger in its cloisonné sheath, with the Vorkosigan seal in the jeweled hilt, on its proper belt around his waist. He combed his hair, and stepped back to regard himself, glittering in his mirror.

Going native, are we? The sarcastic voice was growing fainter.

"If you expect to open a can of worms," he spoke aloud for the first time, "you'd best trouble to pack a can-opener."

———※———

Martin, engrossed in reading a hand-viewer, looked up at the sound of Miles's booted step, and did a gratifying double-take.

"Bring my car round to the front portico," Miles instructed him coolly.

"Where are we going? My lord."

"To the Imperial Residence. I have an appointment."

——◦◉◦— SIXTEEN ——◦◉◦—

Gregor received Miles in the serene privacy of his office in the Residence's north wing. He was seated behind his comconsole desk, perusing some visual display, and didn't look up till after the majordomo had announced Miles and withdrawn. He tapped a control and the holovid vanished, revealing the small, smoldering, brown-uniformed man standing across from him.

"All right, Miles, what's this all ab—good God." Gregor sat up, startled; his brows climbed as he began to take in the details. "I don't think I've ever seen you come the Vor lord with *intent*."

"At this point," said Miles, "*intent* should be steaming out both my ears. I would bet"—his catch-phrase used to be, *I would bet my ImpSec silver eyes*—"anything you please that there is a bigger mess with Illyan than Haroche has reported to you."

Gregor said slowly, "His reports are necessarily synopses."

"Ha. You've sensed it too, haven't you. Did Haroche ever once pass on the word that Illyan had requested to see me?"

"No . . . has he? And how do you know?"

"I had it from a, how shall I say it, a reliable anonymous source."

"How reliable?"

"To imagine he set me up with a false tale would be to attribute a mind bordering on the baroque to a person I judge to be almost painfully straightforward. And then there's the problem of motivation. Let's just say, reliable enough for practical purposes."

Gregor said slowly, "As I understand it, Illyan is at present . . . well, to be blunt, dangerously out of his mind. He's been demanding a lot of impractical things. A jump-ship raid on the Hegen Hub to turn back an imaginary invasion was mentioned to me."

"It was real once. You were there."

"Ten years ago. How do you know this isn't just more of the same hallucinatory raving?"

"That's just the point. I can't judge, because I haven't been permitted to see him. No one has. You heard from Lady Alys."

"Er, yes."

"Haroche has now blocked me twice. This morning he offered to have me stunned if I continued to make a pest of myself."

"How much of a pest were you?"

"You can doubtless request—I'd make that request and require, if I were you—a review of Haroche's comconsole recording of our last conversation. You might even find it entertaining. But Gregor—I have a *right* to see Illyan. Not as his ex-subordinate, but as my father's son. A Vor obligation that passes completely around ImpSec's military hierarchy and comes in through another door. To their dismay, no doubt, but that's their problem. I suspect . . . I don't know what I suspect. But I can't sit still till I figure it out."

"Do you think there's something smoky?"

"Not . . . necessarily," Miles said more slowly. "But stupidity can be just as bad as malice, sometimes. If this chip crash is anything like my cryo-amnesia, it has to be hell for Illyan. To lose yourself inside your own head . . . it was the loneliest I've ever been in my life. And nobody came for me, till Mark bulled through. At the very least, Haroche is mishandling this due to nerves and inexperience, and needs to be gently, or maybe not so gently, straightened out. At the worst—the possibility of deliberate sabotage *has* to have crossed your mind, too. Even though you haven't talked about it much with me."

Gregor cleared his throat. "Haroche asked me not to."

Miles hesitated. "Finally read my files, has he?"

"I'm afraid so. Haroche has . . . rigorous standards of loyalty."

"Yeah, well . . . it's not his standards of loyalty I'm questioning. It's his judgment. I still want in."

"To see Illyan? I can order that, I suppose. It's getting to be time, in my estimation."

"No, more than that. I want to go over every scrap of raw data pertaining to the case, medical or otherwise. I want *oversight.*"

"Haroche will not be pleased."

"Haroche will go mulish, I expect. And I can't be calling you every fifteen minutes to reiterate your backup. I want some real authority. I want you to assign me an Imperial Auditor."

"What?!"

"Even ImpSec has to bend and spread 'em for an Imperial Auditor. An Auditor can legally requisition *anything*, and all Haroche or anyone else can do is fume—and hand it over. An Auditor speaks with your Voice. They have to listen. You can't pretend this isn't important enough to justify an Auditor's attentions."

"No, indeed, but . . . what would you be looking for?"

"If I knew already, I wouldn't have to look. All I know is that this thing has a . . ."—he spread his hands—"a wrong shape. The reasons may turn out to be trivial. Or not. Don't know. Gotta know."

"Which Auditor did you have in mind?"

"Um . . . can I have Vorhovis?"

"My top man."

"I know. I think I could work with him."

"Unfortunately, he's on his way to Komarr."

"Oh. Nothing too serious, I hope."

"Preventive maintenance. I sent him along with Lord and Lady Vorob'yev to help grease the arrangements with the Komarran oligarchy for announcing my upcoming marriage. He has considerable diplomatic talents."

"Hm." Miles hesitated. He'd really had Vorhovis in mind, when this inspiration had struck. "Vorlaisner, Valentine, and Vorkalloner are all a trifle . . . conservative."

"Afraid they'd side with Haroche against you?"

"Um."

Gregor's eyes glinted. "There's always General Vorparadijs."

"Oh, God. Spare me."

Gregor rubbed his chin, thoughtfully. "I foresee a problem here. Whatever Auditor I assign to you, there's about a fifty percent chance you'd be back here the following morning demanding another one to keep the first one under control. You don't really want an Auditor; you want an Auditor-shaped shield to cover your back while you do your very own investigating."

"Well . . . yes. I don't know. Maybe . . . maybe I could do something with Vorparadijs after all." His heart sank, contemplating this vision.

"An Auditor," said Gregor, "is not just my Voice. He's my eyes and ears, as well, very much in the original sense of the word. My listener. A probe, though most surely not a robot, to go places I can't, and report back with an absolutely independent angle of view. You"—Gregor's lip twisted up—"have the most independent angle of view of any man I've ever met."

Miles's heart seemed to stop. Surely Gregor couldn't be thinking of—

"I think," said Gregor, "it will save ever so many steps if I simply appoint *you* as an acting Imperial Auditor. With the usual broad limits on a Ninth Auditor's powers of course; whatever you do has to be at least dimly related to the event you are assigned to evaluate, in this case, Illyan's breakdown. You can't order executions, and in the unlikely event you direct any arrests . . . well, I would appreciate it if they came attached to sufficient evidence for successful prosecutions. One expects a certain, um, traditional decorum in an Imperial Auditor's investigations, and due care."

"Anything worth doing," Miles quoted Countess Vorkosigan, "is worth doing well." He wondered if his eyes were starting to glow. They felt like embers.

Gregor recognized the source, and smiled. "Just so."

"But Gregor—Haroche will know it's a scam."

Gregor's voice went soft. "Then Haroche will be dangerously mistaken." He added, "I was not happy with the way events seemed to be progressing either, but short of going down there in person, I didn't see what to do. Now I do. Does that satisfy you—Lord Vorkosigan?"

"Oh, Gregor. You can't begin to guess how much. Working in the chain of command for the last thirteen years has been like trying to waltz with an elephant. Slow, lumbering, ready to step on you at any moment and reduce you to grease. D'you have any idea how nice it would be *just once* to be able to dance on top of the damned elephant, instead of under it?"

"I thought you'd like it."

"Like it? It'll be downright orgasmic."

"Don't get carried away," Gregor cautioned, his eyes crinkling.

"No." Miles caught his breath. "But . . . I think this will work just fine. Thank you. I accept your charge, my liege."

Gregor called in his majordomo, and sent him off to the Residence's vault for an Auditor's symbolic chain of office, and the very nonsymbolic electronic seal that went with it. While they were waiting for him to return, Miles ventured, "It's traditional for an Auditor to make his first visit unannounced." He added reflectively, "Probably a hell of a lot of fun for them, too."

"I have long suspected it," agreed Gregor.

"But I would rather not be stunned walking through ImpSec's front gate. D'you think you ought to personally call Haroche, and set up my first appointment?"

"Do you want me to?"

"Mm . . . I'm not sure."

"In that case . . . go with tradition." Gregor's voice took on a cool scientific tinge. "Let's see what happens."

Miles stopped, seized with suspicion. "You sound just like my mother when you say that. What do you know that I don't?"

"I know less than you do right now, I'm increasingly sure. But . . . I've been thinking about Haroche. Watching him. Except for this business with Illyan, about which he seems understandably rattled, he seems to be taking over ImpSec's normal routine smoothly. If Illyan . . . does not recover, sooner or later I must be faced with the decision of whether to confirm Haroche in his job, or appoint another man. I'm curious to see what he's made of. You could be a test for him on more than one level."

"Are you saying you want to give him an opportunity to screw up?"

"Better sooner than later."

Miles grimaced. "Does that work in reverse, as well? Are you giving me a chance to screw up too?"

A very slight smile curved Gregor's mouth. "Let's just say . . . a parallax view of the problem could be most revealing." He added, "I did have a thought about the question of sabotage versus some natural deterioration in Illyan's neural augmentation."

"Yes?"

"Sabotage ought to have been followed up promptly by some sort of attack, during the confusion immediately after Illyan went down."

"Or better still, just before he went down," said Miles.

"Right. But nothing out of the ordinary except Illyan's, I'm not sure what to call it . . . illness, indisposition?"

"Indisposed is a good term," Miles allowed. "Illness implies an internal cause. Injury implies an external cause. I'm not sure I could use either word with certainty right now."

"Quite. Anyway, nothing else unusual *except* Illyan's indisposition has so far occurred."

Illyan's destruction. "Noted," said Miles. "Unless the motivation was something like, say, personal revenge. Not a one-two punch, just a one-punch."

"Have you started to develop a list of potential suspects, by chance?"

Miles groaned. "If you start allowing personal motivations, as well as political ones—it could have been in return for anything ImpSec has done to anyone any time in the last thirty years. It doesn't even have to be sane—someone could have been nursing a grudge all out of proportion to the original injury. That is not the end of the problem to start with, it's too damned vast. I'd prefer to start with the chip. There's only one of it." He cleared his throat. "There's still the problem of not getting stunned at the door. I hadn't intended to take on ImpSec single-handed. I'd assumed I'd have a real Auditor to hide behind, one of those portly retired admirals, say—and I still think I would like to have a witness. An assistant, to be sure, but really, a witness. Someone I can trust, and *you* can trust, someone with the requisite amount of security clearance but who is not himself in ImpSec's hierarchy."

"Do you have someone in mind?" asked Gregor.

———————

"My God," said Ivan, unconsciously echoing Gregor, as he gaped at Miles. "Is that *real*?" His finger reached out to tick the heavy gold chain of the Imperial Auditor's rank and office now hanging around Miles's neck. Its thick links connected big square enameled plaques chased with the Vorbarra arms and logos. It ran over Miles's shoulders and dipped across his chest, and weighed about a kilo, Miles judged. The electronic seal appended from the center in a gold clasp, also engraved with Gregor's arms.

"You want to try to peel off the foil wrapping and eat the chocolate inside?" Miles inquired dryly.

"Urgh." Ivan looked around Gregor's office. The Emperor sat on the edge of his comconsole desk, one leg swinging. "When Gregor's liveried man came galloping into HQ and yanked me off work, I thought the damned Residence was burning down, or my mother'd had a heart attack, or something. But it was only you, coz?"

"That's Lord Auditor Coz to you, for the duration."

Ivan appealed to Gregor. "Tell me this is a joke."

"No," said Gregor. "Quite real. An audit is exactly what I want. I, or to put it more officially, *We* are not happy with current progress. As you know, an Imperial Auditor may request anything he pleases. The first thing he requested was an assistant. Congratulations."

Ivan rolled his eyes. "He wanted a donkey to carry his luggage, and the first ass he thought of was me. So flattering. Thanks, Lord Auditor Coz. I'm sure this is going to be just a joy."

Miles said quietly, "Ivan, we're going in to audit ImpSec's handling of Illyan's breakdown. I don't know what kind of load I'll be asking you to carry, but there's at least a chance it'll be high explosives. I need a donkey I can rely on absolutely."

"Oh." Ivan's irony dropped abruptly away; he straightened. "Oh. Illyan, huh?" He hesitated, then added, "Good. About time somebody lit a fire under somebody over that. Mother will be pleased."

"I hope so," said Gregor sincerely.

Ivan's lip curled up despite the new seriousness in his eyes. "Well, well, Miles. I must say, it does look right on you. I always thought you needed a choke-chain."

⸺◈⸺

Miles had Martin pull the groundcar up to ImpSec's front gates this time. He let the two Imperial Armsmen in Vorbarra livery Gregor had loaned him get out first, then motioned them to flank him as he approached the gate guards. Ivan trailed, watching in fascination. Miles allowed the two Armsmen and Ivan to present their identifications to be scanned and confirmed first.

"Good afternoon, gentlemen," Miles addressed the guards cordially, the moment these rituals were complete and the lights on their machines flashed green. Uncertainly, eyes narrowing, they braced. Searching their consciences, Miles hoped. Miles focused on the senior sergeant. "Please get on your comconsole and tell General Haroche that the Imperial Auditor is here. I request and require him to meet me in person at his front gate. Now."

"Aren't you the same fellow we threw out of here this morning?" asked the sergeant in worry.

Miles smiled thinly. "Not exactly, no." *I've been through a few changes since then.* He held out his empty hands. "Note, please, that I am not trying to enter your premises. I have no intention of throwing you into the dilemma of trying to choose whether to disobey a direct order, or else commit an act of treason. But I do know it takes approximately four minutes to physically get from the Chief's office to the front gate. At that point, *your* troubles will be over."

The senior sergeant withdrew into his kiosk, and spoke urgently into his com, with interesting hair-tearing gestures. When he exited again, Miles noted the time on his chrono. "Now let's see what happens, as Gregor would say." Ivan sucked on his lower lip, and kept his mouth shut.

At length, a flurry of uniforms appeared around the side of ImpSec's oversized front steps; Haroche marched quickly forward across the rain-slicked cobblestones, trailed himself by a minion of note, Illyan's secretary. "Four minutes, twenty-nine seconds," murmured Miles to Ivan. "Not bad."

"Can I go behind the bushes and throw up now?" Ivan muttered back, watching ImpSec's power bearing down on them.

"No. Quit thinking like a subordinate."

Miles came to a parade rest, and waited for Haroche to puff to a halt before him. He permitted himself one brief, glorious moment of enjoyment of the appalled expression on the General's face, as Haroche too took in the details, then set it aside. He could take the memory out and treasure it later. His inner vision of the medically tormented Illyan drove him forward now. "Good afternoon, General."

"Vorkosigan. I told you not to come back here."

"Try again," Miles said grimly.

Haroche stared at the chain glittering across his chest. Despite the flanking Vorbarra Armsmen, both personally known to him, he choked, "That can't be real."

"The penalty for counterfeiting an Imperial Auditor's credentials," Miles stated flatly, "is death."

Miles felt he could almost hear the gears grinding in Haroche's head. Some long seconds crawled past, then Haroche corrected himself in a slightly cracked voice, "My Lord Auditor."

"Thank you," Miles husked. Now they were on-script, his new authority formally recognized and acknowledged, and they could proceed. "My Imperial master Gregor Vorbarra requests and requires me to audit ImpSec's handling of the current situation. I request and require your full cooperation in this examination. Shall we continue this in your office?"

Haroche's brows drew down; a faintly ironic light started in his eye. "Oh, I think we should. My Lord Auditor."

Miles dismissed his two Vorbarra outriders to be driven back to the Imperial residence by Martin, and led Haroche inside.

The flat filtered air of Illyan's office was fraught with memory. Miles had sat or stood in here a hundred times, to receive orders or deliver results. He'd been fascinated, excited, certainly challenged, occasionally triumphant, sometimes exhausted, sometimes defeated, sometimes in pain. Sometimes in great pain. This room had been the center from which his life had radiated. All that was gone now. Miles's position across from Illyan's comconsole desk was the same, but the flow of authority was reversed. He'd have to watch out for old reflexes.

Haroche pulled up a chair from the side wall for him with his own hands; after a moment, Ivan retrieved one for himself, and sat flanking Miles. Haroche settled his bulk in Illyan's chair, tented his hands above the black glass, and waited cautiously.

Miles leaned forward, and counted off with his right hand, fingers pressing the cold surface. "All right. As you should have deduced by now, Gregor is seriously displeased with the way this organization has been treating Simon Illyan's breakdown. So this is what I want, and this is the order I want it in. First, I want to see Illyan. Then, I want a conference with his full medical staff. I want them to bring everything they have learned so far, and be prepared to brief me. After that . . . I'll figure out what else after that."

"You have, necessarily, my full cooperation. My Lord Auditor."

"Now that we're down to business, you can shelve the formalities."

"But you've given me a dilemma."

And a moment of near heart failure, too, Miles hoped nastily. But no. There was no place for personal animosities now. "Oh?"

"It was, and remains, premature to accuse any man of sabotage in the matter of Illyan's chip failure before the cause of the chip failure is determined. Potentially very embarrassing, if the cause turns out to be natural."

"I'm conscious of this too."

"Yes . . . you would be. But I can't help thinking ahead. In fact, it's my job. So I have a little list, that I'm holding in limbo pending the arrival of some data with which to pin it to reality."

"Only a little list?"

"Illyan always divided his lists into the short one and the long one. A kind of triage, I suppose. Seems a good system. But on my short list—you are very near the top."

"Oh," Miles echoed. Suddenly, Haroche's obstructionism fell into place.

"And now you've made yourself untouchable," Haroche added.

"The full phrase is, untouchable Vor bore," Miles said. "I . . . see." This was exactly the sort of humiliating suspicion he'd most dreaded, in taking on Illyan's rescue. Well . . . too bad.

They stared steadily at one another, across the black glass. Haroche continued, "So the very last thing in the world I want is to admit you to Illyan's presence where you can get off some kind of second shot. Now, it appears, I must do so. But I want to formally register the fact that I do so under protest. My Lord Auditor."

"Noted." Miles's mouth was dry. "Do you have a motive, to go along on your list with my opportunities and the as-yet-nonexistent method?"

"Isn't it obvious?" Haroche's hands opened. "Illyan terminated you, very abruptly. Destroyed your career."

"Illyan helped create me. He had a right to destroy me." Under the circumstances—of which Haroche was fully apprised by now, Miles could see it in his eyes—almost an obligation.

"He terminated you for falsifying your reports. A documented fact that I would also like to formally register, my Lord Auditor." Haroche glanced at Ivan, who remained wonderfully bland, a defensive response he'd spent a lifetime perfecting.

"One report. Once. And Gregor already knows all about it." Miles could almost feel the ground shifting under his feet. How had he ever classified this man as thickheaded? He was losing his momentum almost as fast as he'd gained it. But he tightened his jaw against all temptation to defend, explain, protest, apologize, or otherwise be diverted from his goal.

"I don't trust you, Lord Vorkosigan."

"Well, you're stuck with me. I can't be removed except by the Emperor's own Voice which appointed me, or a three-quarters vote of impeachment by the Council of Counts and the Council of Ministers in full joint session assembled, something I don't think you can arrange."

"Then it would likely be useless for me to go to Gregor and request a different Auditor for this case."

"You can try."

"Ha. That answers that. And even if you were guilty . . . I'm starting to wonder if I could do anything about it. The Emperor is the only appeal, and you appear to already have him sewn up. Would attempting to take you out be career suicide?"

"Well . . . if our positions were reversed, I wouldn't give up

till I'd nailed you to the wall with the biggest spikes available."
Miles added after a moment, "But if, after I go in to see Illyan,
some sort of second shot occurs . . . you can bet I'll be measuring
its trajectory with utmost care."

Haroche vented a long sigh. "This is premature. I'll be more
relieved than anyone if the medics bring in a diagnosis of natural
causes. It would short-circuit a world of trouble."

Miles grimaced reluctant agreement. "You've got that right,
General."

They regarded each other with a certain steady reserve. In all,
Miles thought he felt more relieved than unnerved. Haroche had
certainly been as blunt as Miles could have desired about clearing
the air. Maybe he could work with this man after all.

Haroche's study of Miles hung up on the magpie collection of
military baubles on his tunic. His voice went unexpectedly plaintive.
"Vorkosigan, tell me—*is* that really a Cetagandan Order of Merit?"

"Yeah."

"And the rest of it?"

"I didn't clean out my father's desk drawer, if that's what
you're asking. Everything here is accounted for, in my classified
files. You may be one of the few men on the planet who doesn't
have to take my word for it."

"Hm." Haroche's brows quirked. "Well, my Lord Auditor,
carry on. But I'll be watching you."

"Good. Watch closely." Miles rapped the black glass, and rose.
Ivan scrambled up behind him.

———◈———

In the corridor on their way downstairs to the HQ clinic, Ivan
murmured, "I've never seen a general tap-dance sitting down,
before."

"It feels like a minuet in a minefield, to me," Miles admitted.

"Watching you come the little Admiral at him was worth the
price of admission, though."

"What?" He almost stumbled.

"Wasn't it on purpose? You're acting just like you do when
you play Admiral Naismith, except without the Betan accent. Full
tilt forward, no inhibitions, innocent bystanders scramble for their
lives. I suppose you'll say terror is good for me, clears the arteries
or something."

Were Admiral Naismith's decorations acting as some kind of

magic talisman for him? Miles didn't even want to try to digest the implications of this right now. Instead he said lightly, "Do you consider yourself an innocent bystander?"

"God knows I try to be," sighed Ivan.

———◉———

The air of the clinic, which along with the forensic laboratories occupied a whole floor of ImpSec HQ, was thick with familiar odors too, Miles thought as he entered: unpleasant medical ones. He'd spent all too many hours in here himself, over the years, from his very first visit with incipient pneumonia from hypothermia, to his most recent physical exam, the one that had returned him to the ill-fated duty of rescuing Lieutenant Vorberg. The smell of the place gave him the shivers.

All the four private rooms save one had been cleared of other patients, and stood dark and empty and open. A green-uniformed guard stood stolid duty outside the one closed door.

An ImpSec colonel with medical tags on his tunic popped up breathlessly at Miles's elbow as he entered. "My Lord Auditor. I'm Dr. Ruibal. How may I serve you?" Ruibal was a short, round-faced man with furry eyebrows, pinched together now in one crooked line of worry.

"Tell me about Illyan. No, take me to Illyan. We'll talk after."

"This way, my lord." The doctor gestured the guard aside, and led Miles into the windowless room.

Illyan lay faceup on the bed, half-covered by a sheet, his wrists and ankles bound with what the medics dubbed "soft restraints." He breathed heavily. Was he sedated? His eyes were open, glazed and unfocused. Heavy beard stubble shadowed his normally clean face. The warm room smelled of dried sweat, and worse organics. Miles had spent a week forcing his way in here, using some of the most extreme methods he'd ever dared attempt. Now all he wanted to do was turn tail and run out again.

"Why is this man naked?" he asked the colonel. "Is he incontinent?"

"No," said Ruibal. "Procedures."

Miles didn't see any tubes, probes, or machines. "What procedures?"

"Well, none at present. But he isn't easy to handle. Getting him in and out of clothes as well as the other . . . presents problems for my staff."

Indeed. The guard, now hovering inside the door, sported a maroon-purple black eye. And Ruibal's own mouth was bruised, his lower lip split. "I . . . see."

He forced himself nearer, and half-knelt by Illyan's head. "Simon?" he said uncertainly.

Illyan's face turned toward him. The glazed eyes flickered, focused. Lit with recognition. "Miles! Miles. Thank God you're here." His voice cracked with urgency. "Lord Vorvane's wife and children—did you get them out alive? Commodore Rivek at Sector Four is going frantic."

Miles recognized the mission. It was about five years old. He moistened his lips. "Yeah. It was all taken care of. We got them out, all right and tight." He'd been awarded a gold star for that one. It hung third from the left in its row on him now.

"Good. Good." Illyan sighed, lay back; his eyes closed. His stubbled lips moved. His eyes opened and lit, again, with recognition. "Miles! Thank God you're here." His hands moved, and came up short against their restraints. "What is this? Get me out of this."

"Simon. What day is this?"

"It's the Emperor's Birthday tomorrow. Or is it today? You're dressed for it . . . I have to be there."

"No," said Miles. "The Emperor's Birthday was weeks ago. Your memory chip is malfunctioning. You have to stay in here till they figure out what's wrong, and fix it."

"Oh." Four minutes later, Illyan turned his head back to Miles; his lips rippled in startlement. "Miles, what the hell are you doing here? I sent you to Tau Ceti. Why can't you ever obey an order?"

"Simon, your memory chip is malfunctioning."

Illyan hesitated. "What day is it? Where am I?"

Miles repeated the information.

"Dear God," whispered Illyan. "Now, that's a bitch." He lay listlessly, looking dismayed.

Five minutes later, Illyan looked up at him and said, "Miles! What the hell are you doing here?"

Shit. He had to stand up, and turn around for a minute. *I don't know how much of this I can take.* He became aware that Dr. Ruibal was watching him closely.

"Has it been this bad all week?" he asked.

Ruibal shook his head. "There has been a definite and measurable progression. His . . . how can I describe it. His moments of temporal confusion have been getting steadily closer together.

The first day I thought I noted six perceptual jumps. Yesterday they were coming six an hour."

It was twice that now. Miles turned back. In a little while, Illyan looked up at him, and his face lit with recognition. "Miles. What the hell's going on?"

Patiently, Miles explained again. It didn't matter if he repeated the wording, he realized. Illyan wasn't going to get tired of it. Or remember it, five minutes later.

On the next round, Illyan frowned across at him. "Who the devil are you?"

"Miles. Vorkosigan."

"Don't be absurd. Miles is five years old."

"Uncle Simon. Look at me."

Illyan stared earnestly at him, then whispered, "Watch out. Your grandfather wants to kill you. Trust Bothari."

"Oh, I do," sighed Miles.

Three minutes later: "Miles! What the hell's going on? Where am I?"

Miles repeated the drill.

The guard with the black eye remarked, "How come he believes you all the time? He only believes us about one time out of five. The other four times he tries to kill us."

"I don't know," said Miles, feeling harried beyond measure.

Again. "Miles! Vorberg found you!"

"Yes . . . yes?" Miles sat up straight. "Simon, what day is this?"

"God, I don't know. My damned chip is fucked up beyond repair. It's turning to snot inside my head. It's driving me crazy." He grasped Miles's hand, hard, and stared into his eyes with the uttermost urgency. "I can't stand this. If the thing can't be fixed . . . swear you'll cut my throat for me. Don't let it go on forever. I won't be able to do it for myself. Swear to me. Your word as Vorkosigan!"

"God, Simon, I can't promise that!"

"You have to. You can't abandon me to an eternity of *this*. Swear."

"I can't," Miles whispered. "Is this . . . what you sent Vorberg to get me for?"

Illyan's face changed again, the desperation unfocusing into bewilderment. "Who's Vorberg?" Then a sudden hard suspicion. "Who the hell are you?" Illyan shook free of his hand.

Miles went five more rounds, then walked out into the corridor. He leaned against the wall, head down till the nausea passed. His body shook, suppressed shudders that traveled from bottom to top. Dr. Ruibal hovered. Ivan too took the opportunity to step out, and breathe deeply.

"You see what we're up against," said Ruibal.

"This is . . . *graceless.*" Miles's voice was a whisper, but Ruibal flinched. "Ruibal. You get him washed. Shaved. Give him some clothes back. There's a complete supply of civvies in his apartment downstairs, I know." Maybe if Illyan didn't look so much like an animal, they wouldn't treat him so much like one.

"My lord," said the colonel. "I'm reluctant to ask my corpsmen to risk losing more teeth. But if you'll stay for it, we'll try. You're the only person I've seen he hasn't tried to slug."

"Yes. Of course."

Miles saw the process through. Having a familiar person present did seem to be a calming influence on Illyan. People he'd known for the longest time would be best; then whatever day and year he opened his eyes, every five minutes, he would see a known face, who could tell him a story he might trust. Clothed again, Illyan sat up in a chair, and ate from a tray a corpsman brought, apparently the first meal for a couple of days that he had not tried to turn into a projectile weapon.

An officer appeared at the door, and spoke to Ruibal.

"The briefing you requested has been prepared, my Lord Auditor," Ruibal told Miles. His obsequious tone wasn't just in honor of Miles's Auditor's menace, because he added wistfully, "Will you came back, afterwards?"

"Oh, yes. Meantime . . ." Miles's eye fell on Ivan.

"I would rather," stated Ivan quietly, "charge a laser-cannon site naked than be in here by myself."

"I'll keep it in mind," said Miles. "In the meanwhile—stay with him till I get back."

"Yeah." Ivan took over the chair at Illyan's elbow as Miles vacated it.

As Miles followed Ruibal out the door, he heard Illyan's voice, for a change more amiable than stressed: "Ivan, you idiot. What are you doing here?"

SEVENTEEN

The clinic's conference chamber bore a strong generic resemblance to every other ImpSec briefing room in which Miles had ever spent endless hours. A round black table featured a secured holovid projector with a control panel that looked like a jump-ship navcomp. Five station chairs were presently set closely around it, occupied by three men who rose hastily and stood at attention when Ruibal ushered Miles inside. When they were all assembled, there was no one in the room below the rank of colonel except Miles. This was not all that unusual for Vorbarr Sultana; at Imperial Service HQ across town where Ivan worked, the joke was that the colonels carried the coffee.

No: he was neither above nor below them in rank, Miles reminded himself. He was outside them altogether. It was apparent that however accustomed they might be to generals and admirals, this was their first close encounter with an Imperial Auditor. The last Imperial Audit ImpSec had suffered had been almost five years ago, and more traditionally financial in scope. Miles had brushed up against it on the opposite side that time, as the Auditor had choked on certain aspects of mercenary accounting. That investigation had had a dangerous political tinge, from which Illyan had insulated him.

Ruibal introduced the team. Ruibal himself was the neurologist. Next, or perhaps first, in importance was a rear admiral, Dr. Avakli, the biocyberneticist. Avakli was on loan from the medical group who did all the Imperial Service jumpship pilots' neural implants, the one neuroenhancement technology up and running on Barrayar with any resemblance to that which had produced

Illyan's eidetic chip. Avakli, in nice contrast to the rounder Ruibal, was long, thin, intense, and balding. Miles hoped the last was a sign of a high intellectual temperature. The other two men were tech support assistants to Avakli.

"Thank you, gentlemen," Miles said when introductions were complete. He sat; they sat, except for Ruibal, who was apparently elected spokes-goat.

"Where would you like me to begin, my Lord Auditor?" Ruibal asked Miles.

"Um . . . the beginning?"

Obediently, Ruibal began to rattle off a long list of neurological tests, illustrated with holovids of the data and results.

"Excuse me," said Miles after a few minutes of this. "I did not phrase myself well. You can skip all the negative data. Go directly to the positive results."

There was a short silence, then Ruibal said, "In summation, I did not find evidence of organic neurological damage. The physiological and psychological stress levels, which are quite dangerously high, I judge to be an effect rather than a cause of the biocybernetic breakdown."

"Do you agree with that assessment?" Miles asked Avakli, who nodded, though with a little judicious lip-pursing to indicate the ever-present possibility of human error. Avakli and Ruibal exchanged a nod, and Avakli took Ruibal's place at the holovid projector.

Avakli had a detailed holovid map of the chip's internal architecture, which he began to display. Miles was relieved. He'd been a little afraid they were going to tell him ImpSec Medical had lost the owner's manual in the intervening thirty-five years, but they appeared to have quite a lot of data. The chip itself was an immensely complex sandwich of organic and inorganic molecular layers about five by seven centimeters broad and half a centimeter thick, which rested in a vertical position between the two lobes of Illyan's brain. The number of neurological connections that ran from it made a jump-pilot's control headset look like a child's toy. The greatest complexity seemed to be in the information retrieval net, rather than the protein-based data storage, though both were not only fiendishly ornate, but largely unmapped—it had been an autolearning-style system which had assembled itself in a highly non-linear fashion *after* the chip had been installed.

"So is the . . . damage or deterioration we're seeing confined to the organic or the inorganic parts? Or both?" Miles asked Avakli.

"Organic," said Avakli. "Almost certainly."

Avakli was one of those scientists who never placed an unhedged bet, Miles realized.

"Unfortunately," Avakli went on, "it was never originally designed to be downloaded. There is no single equivalent of a dataport to connect to; just these thousands and thousands of neuronic leads going into and out of the thing all over its surface."

In view of the chip's history as Emperor Ezar's ultra-secure data dump, this made sense. Miles would not have been surprised to learn the thing had been customized to be especially nondownloadable.

"Now . . . I was under the impression the thing worked in parallel with Illyan's original cerebral memory. It doesn't actually replace it, does it?"

"That is correct, my lord. The neurological input is only split from the sensory nerves, not shunted aside altogether. The subjects apparently have dual memories of all their experiences. This appears to have been the major contributing factor to the high incidence of iatrogenic schizophrenia they later developed. A sort of inherent design defect, not of the chip so much as of the human brain."

Ruibal cleared his throat in polite theoretical, or perhaps theological, disagreement.

Illyan must have been a born spy. To hold more than one reality balanced in your mind until proof arrived, without going mad from the suspense, was surely the mark of a great investigator.

Avakli then went into a highly technical discussion of three projected ideas for extracting some kind of data download from the chip. They all sounded makeshift and uncertain of result; Avakli himself, describing them, didn't sound too happy or enthusiastic. Most of them seemed to involve long hours of delicate micro-neurosurgery. Ruibal winced a lot.

"So," Miles interrupted this at length, "what happens if you take the chip out?"

"To use layman's terminology," said Avakli, "it goes into shock and dies. It's evidently *supposed* to do so, apparently to prevent, um, theft."

Right. Miles pictured Illyan mugged by chip-spies, his head hacked open, left for dead . . . someone else had anticipated that picture too. They'd been a paranoid lot, in Ezar's generation.

"It was never designed to be removed intact from its organic electrical support matrix," Avakli continued. "The chance of any coherent data retrieval is vastly reduced, anyway."

"And if it's not taken out?"

"The protein chain arrays show no signs of slowing in their dissociation."

"Or, in scientists' language, the chip is turning to snot inside Illyan's head. One of you bright boys apparently used just that phrase in his hearing, by the way."

One of Avakli's assistants had the grace to look guilty.

"Admiral Avakli, what are your top theories as to what is causing the chip to break down?"

Avakli's brows narrowed. "In order of probability— senescence, that is, old age, triggering an autodestruction, or some sort of chemical or biological attack. I'd have to have it apart to prove the second hypothesis."

"So . . . there is no question of removing the chip, repairing it, and reinstalling it."

"I hardly think so."

"And you can't repair it *in situ* without knowing the cause, which you can't determine without removing it for internal examination. Which would destroy it."

Avakli's lips compressed in dry acknowledgment of the inherent circularity of the problem. "Repair is out of the question, I'm afraid. I've been concentrating on trying to evolve a practical downloading scheme."

"As it happens," Miles went on, "you misunderstood my initial question. What happens to *Illyan* if the chip is removed?"

Avakli gestured back to Ruibal, a toss-the-hot-ball spasm.

"We can't predict with certainty," said Ruibal.

"Can you guess with reasonable odds? Does he, for example, instantly go back to being twenty-seven years old again?"

"No, I don't think so. A plain removal, with no attempt to save the chip, would in fact be a reasonably simple operation. But the brain is a complex thing. We don't know, for example, to what extent it has rerouted its own internal functions around the artifact in thirty-five years. And then there's the psychological element. Whatever he's done to his personality that has allowed him to work with it and stay sane will be unbalanced."

"Like . . . taking away a crutch, and discovering your legs have atrophied?"

"Perhaps."

"So how much cognitive damage are we talking about? A little? A lot?"

Ruibal shrugged helplessly.

"Have any aging galactic experts in this obsolete technology been located yet?" Miles asked.

"Not yet," said Ruibal. "That may take several months."

"By which time," said Miles grimly, "if I understand this, the chip will be jelly and Illyan will be either permanently insane or dead of exhaustion."

"Ah," said Ruibal.

"That about sums it up, my lord," said Avakli.

"Then why haven't we yanked the damned thing?"

"Our orders, my lord," noted Avakli, "were to save the chip, or as much of the chip's data as could be retrieved."

Miles rubbed his lips. "Why?" he said at length.

Avakli's brows rose. "I would presume, because the data is vital to ImpSec and the Imperium."

"Is it?" Miles leaned forward, staring into the brightly colored, biocybernetic nightmare chip-map hanging before his eyes above the table's central vid plate. "The chip was never installed to make Illyan into a superman. It was just a toy for Emperor Ezar, who fancied owning a vid recorder with legs. I admit, it's been handy for Illyan. Gives him a nice aura of infallibility that scares hell out of people, but that's a crock and he knows it even if they don't.

"The chip has nothing to do with running ImpSec, really. He was promoted to the job because he was standing at my father's right hand the day Vordarian's forces murdered his predecessor, and my father liked and trusted him. There was no time for a talent search, in the middle of a raging civil war. Of all the qualities that made Illyan the best chief in ImpSec's history . . . the chip is surely the most trivial." His voice had fallen to nearly a whisper. Avakli and Ruibal were leaning forward to hear him. He cleared his throat, and sat up.

"There are only four categories of information on that chip," Miles went on. "Old and obsolete. Current, which is all backed up in reality—Illyan has always had to function with the ever-present assumption that he could drop or be dropped dead at any time, and Haroche or somebody would have to take over in midstream. Then there's trash data, personal stuff of no use to anyone except Illyan. Maybe not even to Illyan. Thirty-five years of showers, meals, changing clothes, filling out forms. Not too damned many sex acts, I'm afraid. Lots of bad novels and holovid dramas, all in there, verbatim. A thousand times more of that than anything else. And, somewhere in all the billions of images, maybe a dozen hot secrets that no one else knows. Or perhaps even ought to know."

"What do you wish us to do, my Lord Auditor?" asked Ruibal, into the silence that stretched after this soliloquy.

You wanted authority. Now you've got it, boy. Miles sighed. "I want to talk with one more man. In the meanwhile . . . assemble everything you need for the surgical removal of the chip. Equipment, to be sure, but mostly, the man. I want the best pair of hands you can get, in ImpSec or out of it."

"When should we start, my lord?" asked Ruibal.

"I'd like you to be *finished* in two hours." Miles rapped the table, and rose. "Thank you, gentlemen. Dismissed."

———◦(◦)◦———

Miles called Gregor on a secured comconsole right from the clinic level.

"So have you found what you wanted?" Gregor asked.

"I didn't *want* any of this. But I've made progress. I'm pretty sure it won't be a surprise to you to learn the problem's not in Illyan's brain, it's in the damned chip. It's doing uncontrolled data dumps. About every five minutes it floods his mind with a new set of crystal-sharp memories from random times in the past. The effect is . . . hideous. Cause unknown, they can't fix it, removal will destroy the data still on it. Leaving it in will destroy Illyan. You see where this is heading."

Gregor nodded. "Removal."

"It seems indicated. It should have been . . . well, if not done already, at least proposed and prepared for. The problem is, Illyan's in no condition to consent to the operation."

"I see."

"They also don't know what the effects of removing it will be. Full recovery, partial recovery, personality changes, cognitive changes—they're rolling dice down here. What I'm saying is, you still may not get your chief of Imperial Security back."

"I see."

"Now. Is there anything you want saved off that chip that I don't know about?"

Gregor sighed. "Your father is perhaps the only other person who would be able to answer that question. And in the over fifteen years since I reached my majority, he hasn't seen fit to confide any to me. The old secrets appear to be keeping themselves."

"Illyan is your man now. Do you consent to pulling the chip, my liege?"

"D'you advise it, my Auditor?"

Miles blew out his breath. "Yes."

Gregor chewed on his lower lip for a moment; then his face set. "Then let the dead bury their dead. Let the past go. Do it."

"Yes, Sire."

Miles cut the com.

———◉———

This time Miles was admitted to Haroche's/Illyan's office without delay or a murmur of protest. Haroche, studying something on his comconsole display, waved him to a chair. Miles pulled it wrong-way-around and sat astride it, his arms across its back.

"Well, my Lord Auditor," said Haroche, turning off his vid. "I trust you found the cooperation of my subordinates to be fully satisfactory."

Illyan did irony better, but you had to give Haroche credit for trying. "Yes, thank you."

"I admit"—Haroche gestured to the comconsole—"I misestimated you. I'd seen you flitting in and out of here for years, and I was aware you were covert ops. But I was not always fully aware of *which* covert ops, or how many. No wonder you were Illyan's pet." His gaze, on Miles's decorated tunic, was now more calculating than disbelieving.

"Reading my record, were you?" Miles refused to flinch in front of Haroche.

"Scanning the synopses, and some of Illyan's annotations. A full study would take a week. My time is at a premium at the moment."

"Yes. I've just talked with Gregor." Miles inhaled. "We've concluded that the chip has to be removed."

Haroche sighed. "I'd hoped that could be avoided. It seems so permanent. And so crippling."

"Not nearly as crippling as what's going on right now. Incidentally, Illyan definitely should have had someone familiar by him from the start, for his comfort. It seems to make a tremendous difference in his level of combativeness. He could possibly have avoided most of the sedation. And the humiliating restraints. Not to mention the wear and tear on the corpsmen."

"Much earlier, I still wasn't sure what we were dealing with."

"Mm. But it was wrong to leave him alone in agony."

"I . . . admit, I had not gone down to the clinic to inspect in person. The first day was bad enough."

Understandable, if cowardly. "Ivan and I were able to do a lot, just by being there. I've thought of another person who could do even more. I think Lady Alys Vorpatril should sit with him until the surgery is prepared."

Haroche frowned, his forehead wrinkling. "You and Lieutenant Vorpatril are, or at least were, oath-sworn military personnel. She's a civilian, and barred by her gender from most oaths."

"But hardly a nonperson, for all of that. If I must, I will order her admittance on my authority as Auditor, but I wanted to give you a chance to mend your mistake. If nothing else, you should be alive to the fact that as Gregor's Baba and closest senior female relative, she will be in charge of all the social arrangements for the Emperor's wedding. You may still be acting head of ImpSec at that time. How this fits into your security . . . challenges, should be obvious. The Empress Laisa may make new arrangements once she's installed, but in the meantime, Lady Alys is the old guard, in charge of the transition. It's Vor custom.

"The military, in an admirable effort to promote merit before blood, spends a lot of time pretending that Vor is not real. The high Vor, whose safety and good behavior are going to be your particular charge as long as you sit behind that desk, spend at least as much energy pretending Vor *is* real."

Haroche's brows rose. "So which are right?"

Miles shrugged. "My mother would call it the clash of two competing fantasies. But whatever your personal opinion of the merits and defects of the Vor system—and I have a few thoughts of my own about it that I wouldn't necessarily spout on the floor of the Council of Counts—it's the system we are both oath-sworn to uphold. The Vor really are the sinews of the Imperium. If you don't like it, you can emigrate, but if you stay, this is the only game in town."

"So how did Illyan get along so well with you all? He was no more Vor than I."

"Actually, I think he rather enjoyed the spectacle. I don't know what he thought when he was younger, but by the time I re-

ally came to know him, in the last ten years or so . . . I think he'd
come to feel that the Imperium was a creation he helped to maintain. He seemed to have a vested interest in it. An almost Cetagandan attitude, in a weird way; more of an artist to his medium
than a servant to his master. Illyan *played* Gregor's servant with
great panache, but I don't think I've ever met a less servile human
being."

"Ah." Haroche's eyes were alert, as he took this in. His fingers
drummed once on the black glass, a downright Illyanesque gesture. The man was actually listening, by God. And learning? A
heartening thought.

Haroche's lips compressed with decision, and he tapped out a
code on his comconsole. Lady Alys's secretary appeared; after a
few murmured words of greeting and explanation, Alys's own face
formed over the vid plate. She frowned at Haroche.

"Milady." He nodded shortly to her. His hand gesture might be
interpreted either as a modified analyst's salute, or a man tugging
his forelock; the nuance was nicely vague. "I've reconsidered your
request for admittance to the ImpSec clinic. Chief Illyan may be
facing surgery shortly. I'd take it as a personal favor if you would
be willing to come down here and stay with him for a while beforehand. Familiar faces seem to help him to, um, stay calm with
fewer drugs."

Alys straightened. "I told you *that* yesterday!"

"Yes, milady," said Haroche meekly. "You were right. May I
send a car to your residence for you? And how soon?"

"For this," Alys stated, "I can be ready in fifteen minutes."

Miles wondered if Haroche appreciated what an awesome
statement this was. It could take a high Vor lady fifteen *hours* to
get ready to go places, sometimes.

"Thank you, milady. I think this could be a great help."

"Thank you, General." She hesitated. "And thank Lord
Vorkosigan too." She cut the com.

"Huh," said Haroche; his mouth twitched lopsidedly. "She *is*
sharp."

"In certain areas within her personal expertise, one of the
sharpest."

"One wonders how Lord Ivan . . . ah, well. How was that, my
Lord Auditor?"

Extraordinary. "A noble apology. She had to accept. You
won't be sorry."

"As hard as it may be for you to grasp, considering the history of your attitude to most of your commanding officers"—Haroche tapped his comconsole—just *which* files had he been reading?— "I do want to do a good job. *Do your duty* is not enough. The lower ranks are filled with men who merely do their duty, and no more. I know I'm not a suave man—never have been—"

"Neither was Illyan's predecessor Captain Negri, I've heard," Miles offered.

Haroche smiled bleakly. "I didn't ask for this emergency. I will likely never be as smooth and polished as Illyan. But I mean to do as good a job."

Miles nodded. "Thank you, General."

⸻

Miles returned to the clinic level to relieve Ivan. Miles found him still sitting next to Illyan, though as far back in his chair as he would go, smiling in a pained way; one boot tapped softly on the floor in a nervous pattern.

Ivan rose hastily, and came to the door when he saw Miles leaning there watching. "Thank God. It's about time you got back," he muttered.

"How's it been going?"

"What d'you think? I can see why they sedated him, even without his trying to tear their heads off. Just so they didn't have listen to hour after hour of this. Miles, this is a nightmare."

"Yes. I know." He sighed. "I have some help on the way for this part, though. I've asked your mother to come in and sit with him."

"Oh," said Ivan. "Good idea. Better her than me, anyway."

Miles's mouth twisted. "You're not afraid it'll be too hard on her?"

"Oh. Um. Hell, she's tough."

"Tougher than you?"

"She'll be good at this," Ivan promised somewhat desperately.

"Take a break, Ivan."

"Yeah." Ivan didn't wait for a second invitation, but scooted past him.

"And Ivan?"

Ivan paused, suspiciously. "Yeah?"

"Thanks."

"Oh. No trouble."

Miles took a deep breath, and entered Illyan's room. It was still very warm. He took off his tunic, and folded it over the back of a chair, and rolled up his silk sleeves, and sat. Illyan first ignored him for a bit, then stared at him in puzzlement, then his face cleared. It began again, *Miles, what are you doing here . . . ? Simon, listen to me. Your chip has gone glitchy. . . .*

Over and over.

It was a little bit like talking to someone with multiple personalities, Miles decided after a while. The thirty-year-old Illyan gave way to the Illyan of forty-six, each man profoundly different from the Illyan of sixty. Miles waited patiently for the card he desired to be dealt again from the deck, endlessly repeating the date, the facts, the situation. Would it ever reach the point where all the Illyans had been informed, or would he continue to divide infinitesimally?

At last, the Illyan he was waiting for came around again.

"Miles! Did Vorberg find you? Shit, this is a nightmare. My damned chip has gone glitchy. It's turning to snot inside my head. Promise me—promise me by your word as Vorkosigan!—you won't let this go on."

"Listen, Simon! I know all about it. But I'm not bloody going to cut your throat. We've scheduled surgery instead, to take the chip out. No later than tomorrow, if I have anything to say about it, and I do. It can't be fixed, so we're going to remove it."

Illyan paused. "Remove . . . ?" His hand touched his forehead. "But how can I function without it?"

"Same as you did in the first twenty-seven years of your life before you ever had it installed, is the best medical guess."

Illyan's eyes were solemn, and afraid. "Will it take . . . all my memories? Will I lose my whole life? Oh, God, Miles." He was silent for a time, then added, "I think I'd rather have you cut my throat."

"That's not an option, Simon."

Illyan shook his head. And dissolved again, into another Illyan, another round of, "Miles! What are you doing here? What am *I* doing here?" He stared down at his bland civilian clothes; Illyan either favored really boring fashions, or else did not trust his own taste. "I'm supposed to be at the Council of Counts in full dress uniform *right now.* They must be told—they must be told. . . ."

Miles couldn't decide if it constituted informed consent or not, under the circumstances. Was it informed? Was it even consent? But it seemed the best he could do. He repeated the drill. Again. Again.

At length, Dr. Ruibal escorted Lady Alys into the room. He'd briefed her as Miles had requested; Miles could see it in her set, disturbed face.

"Hello, Simon." Her voice was quiet, a melodic alto.

"Lady Alys!" Illyan's face worked, as he searched his mind for Miles knew not what. "I am so sorry about the death of Lord Vorpatril," Illyan said at last. "If I had only known where you were in the city. I was trying to get Admiral Kanzian out. If only I'd known. Did you save the child?"

Apologies and condolences on the murder of her husband, thirty years ago. Kanzian had been dead of old age for half a decade now. Alys glanced in suppressed anguish at Miles. "Yes, Simon, it's all right," she said. "Lieutenant Koudelka brought us through Vordarian's lines. It's all right now."

Miles nodded, and repeated the orienting drill, as a model for Alys. She listened to the exchange carefully, and watched Illyan's face go through the usual array of emotions, startlement, denial, distraught dismay. Illyan's blunter barracks language disappeared abruptly from his speech in her presence. Miles slipped out of the chair beside Illyan's and offered it to her. She sat without hesitation, and took Illyan's hand.

Illyan blinked, and looked up at her. "Lady Alys!" His face softened. "What are you doing here?"

Miles withdrew to the doorway, where Ruibal watched.

"That's interesting," said Ruibal, checking a monitor readout on the wall. "His blood pressure dropped a bit, there."

"Yes, I'm . . . not surprised. Come out in the hall and talk to me. I want a word with Avakli, too."

———※◎※———

The three of them, Miles and Ruibal and Avakli all in shirt-sleeves now, sat at the medtech's station, and drank coffee. It was deep night outside, Miles realized. He was becoming as temporally confused as Illyan, tasting his mechanistic eternity.

"So you've convinced me the surgical facility here is adequate," Miles said. "Tell me more about the man."

"He's my second senior surgeon for installing and maintaining jump-pilots' neural implants," said Avakli.

"Why aren't we having your first senior surgeon?"

"He's good too, but this one is younger, more recently trained. I feel he's the optimum trade-off between most recent training and maximum practical experience."

"Do you trust him?"

"Let me put it this way," said Avakli. "If you've ever ridden in an Imperial fast courier vessel in the last five years, you've probably trusted him with your own life already, as surely as you've trusted it to the engineers who calibrated the ship's Necklin rods. He did the implant for the Emperor's personal pilot, too."

"Very good. I accept your choice. So how soon can we get him here, and how soon can he go to work?"

"We could fly him in from Vordarian's District tonight, but I think it's better to let him get a good night's sleep at home first. I'd allow a day at least for him to study the problem, and plan his surgical approach. After that—it will be up to him. We're likely looking at surgery the day after tomorrow at the earliest."

"I see. Very well." There was nothing more Miles could do to push that part of things along. "That gives Dr. Avakli's team two more days to play with their part of the problem. Let me know if you come up with any new approaches that won't involve putting Illyan through more of . . . this. And oh! I have a suggestion. When the surgery is complete, Dr. Avakli's team will become the chip coroners. I want an autopsy done on the damned thing, even if it is dead. What caused the malfunction? ImpSec and I both want to know. I thought of a man to add to the team who might be able to lend you some interesting galactic expertise. He has a lab in the Imperial Science Institute biofacility just outside of Vorbarr Sultana, where he does some secured work for the Imperium. Name's Vaughn Weddell." Once known as Dr. Hugh Canaba of Jackson's Whole. An early Dendarii mission had brought him incognito as a refugee to a new life, face, and name on Barrayar, along with some of the most secret genetic research in the galaxy. Sergeant Taura had been one of his earlier and more ambiguous projects. "He's a molecular biologist by trade and training, but his early experiences included an extraordinary range of . . . really oddball stuff. Kind of a wild card, and, ah, a bit of a prima donna in personality, but if nothing else, I think you'll find his ideas interesting."

"Yes, my lord." Avakli made a note. A Lord Auditor's suggestions had the weight of an Imperial command, Miles realized anew. He really had to watch his mouth.

And that seemed to be all he could do for today. He longed to flee back to Vorkosigan House and sleep.

Instead, he bedded down for four hours in one of the adjoining patient rooms, then relieved Alys Vorpatril in the night watch to take turn about. Lieutenant Vorberg, coming on duty, seemed pleased to cede them the place by Illyan's bedside, and took up his own post by the clinic door. Illyan slept only fitfully, waking about every twenty minutes in a new burst of confusion and fear. It was going to be a very long two days till the surgery.

EIGHTEEN

The two days stretched to three, agonizingly. For the last full day, Illyan was never coherent enough to beg for death, nor express his terror of the upcoming surgery, a respite to Miles of sorts. Illyan's flickering sequences of disorientation and distress passed too quickly now for reassurance; he became dumb, only his twitching face, not his words, reflecting the kaleidoscopic chaos inside his head.

Even Alys found it unbearable. Her rest breaks lengthened, and her visits to Illyan grew shorter. Miles stuck it out, wondering why he was doing so. Would Illyan remember any of this? *Will I ever be able to forget it?*

Illyan was no longer combative, but his lurching movements were abrupt and unpredictable. It was decided no attempt would be made to keep him conscious during the surgery. Monitoring of his higher neural functions would have to wait till after the fact. It was a profound relief to Miles when the techs came to anesthetize Illyan and prep him, and he became still at last.

As Gregor's appointed observer, Miles followed the procession right into the surgery, near the labs a few steps down the corridor from the patient rooms. No one even suggested he stay out. *Where does the forty kilo Imperial Auditor sit? Anywhere he wants to.* A tech assisted him into only slightly oversized sterile garb, and provided him with a comfortable stool with a good view of the holovid monitors that would record every aspect of the procedure, inside Illyan's skull and out, and a reasonable glimpse of the top of Illyan's head past the surgeon's shoulder. On the whole, Miles thought he would rather watch the monitors.

The tech depilated a little rectangular patch in the center of Illyan's scalp, almost unnecessary in the thinning hair. Miles felt he ought to be inured to bloodshed of all kinds by now, but his stomach still turned as the surgeon deftly cut through scalp and bone and peeled them back for access. The incision was tiny, really, a mere slot. Then the computer-aided microwaldoes were moved into place, concealing the cut, and the surgeon leaned into his vid enhancers, hunching over Illyan's head. Miles switched his attention back to the monitors.

The rest of it took barely fifteen minutes. The surgeon laser-cauterized the tiny arterioles that fed the chip with blood and kept its deteriorating organic parts alive, and swiftly burnt through the cilia-like array of neural connectors, finer than spider silk, across the chip's surface. The most delicate surgical hand-tractor lifted the chip neatly from its matrix. The surgeon dropped it into a dish of solution held out for it by the anxious Dr. Avakli, hovering nearby.

Avakli and his tech headed for the door, hustling the dead chip off to the lab. Avakli paused and glanced back at Miles, as if they'd expected him to follow *it*. "Are you coming, my lord?" Avakli inquired.

"No. I'll see you later. Carry on, Admiral."

Miles was barely able to interpret what he was seeing on the monitors, but at least he could read Dr. Ruibal, attending to Illyan's physiological state alongside the surgeon; Ruibal was attentive but relaxed. No emergencies yet, then.

The surgeon fitted the sliver of skull back into its place with biotic glue, and closed the incision and cleaned it. Nothing but a neat, thin red line showed on the pale scalp; Zap the Cat had left gorier-looking scratches on human flesh than this.

The surgeon stood, and stretched. "That's it, then. He's all yours, Dr. Ruibal."

"That was . . . simpler than I had anticipated," Miles commented.

"Several orders of magnitude simpler than installing it must have been," agreed the surgeon. "I had a horrible few minutes, when I first looked at the map of the thing, thinking that I was going to have to go in and remove all those neural connectors from their other ends, throughout the brain, until I realized they could just be left *in situ*."

"There won't be any consequences from leaving them all in there?"

"No. They'll just sit there, inert and harmless. Like any other sort of cut wire, there's no circuit now. Nothing flows."

The anesthetist inquired of Dr. Ruibal and the surgeon, "Are you ready for me to administer the antagonist now?"

Ruibal took a deep breath. "Yes. Wake him up. Let's find out what we've done."

A hiss of a hypospray; the anesthetist watched Illyan's quickening breathing, then at a nod from the surgeon removed the tubes from Illyan's mouth, and loosened the head-restraints. A little more color warmed Illyan's pale features, the death-warmed-over look of unconsciousness fading.

Illyan's brown eyes opened; he squinted, and his gaze flicked from face to face. He moistened his dry lips.

"Miles?" he husked. "Where the hell am I? What are you doing here?"

Miles's heart sank, momentarily, at this instant replay of the opening of most of Illyan's conversations of the last four days. But Illyan's gaze, though uncertain, remained steady on his face.

Miles shouldered forward through the medical mob, who gave way to him. "Simon. You're in surgery at ImpSec HQ. Your eidetic memory chip broke down, irreparably. We've just removed it entirely."

"Oh." Illyan frowned.

"What is the last thing you can remember, sir?" Ruibal asked, watching closely.

". . . remember?" Illyan winced. His right hand twitched, rose to the side of his head, waved forward, clenched, and fell back. "I . . . it's like a dream." He was silent a moment. "A nightmare."

Miles thought this an admirable demonstration of coherence and correct perception, though Ruibal's forehead wrinkled.

"Who," Illyan added, "decided . . . this?" A vague wave at his head.

"Me," Miles admitted. "Or rather, I advised Gregor, he consented."

"Did he. Gregor put you in charge here?"

"Yes." Miles quailed inwardly.

"Good," Illyan sighed. Miles breathed again. Illyan's eyes grew more intent. "And ImpSec? What's happening? How long . . . ?"

"General Haroche is flying your comconsole right now."

"Lucas? Oh, good."

"He has everything under control. No major crises aside from yours. You can rest."

"I admit," murmured Illyan, "I'm tired."

He looked absolutely beaten. "I'm not surprised," said Miles. "This has been going on for over three weeks."

"Has it, now." Illyan's voice went lower, even more tentative. Once more, his hand made that strange gesture beside his face, as if calling up . . . as if trying to call up a vid image that failed to appear, before his mind's eye. His hand jerked again, then closed; he almost seemed to force it back to his side.

Ruibal the neurologist stepped in then, and administered his first few tests; Illyan reported no worse overt effects than a slight headache, and some muscle pain. Illyan studied his own bruised knuckles with some bemusement, but did not inquire about them, nor about the marks on his wrists. Miles trailed after as they trundled Illyan back to the patient room in the clinic.

Ruibal briefed Miles in the corridor, after Illyan was put back to bed. "As soon as his physical recovery is established—as soon as he's eaten, eliminated, and slept—I'll start the battery of cognitive tests."

"How soon can he . . . no, I suppose it's too early to ask that," Miles began. "I was about to ask, how soon could he go home." Such as home was, for Illyan. Miles remembered his own long-ago sojourn in those windowless witness apartments downstairs, and shuddered inwardly.

Ruibal shrugged. "Barring new developments, I'd be willing to release him after two days of close observation. He would need to come back in for daily follow-up testing, of course."

"That soon?"

"As you saw, the surgery was not very invasive. It almost qualified as minor. Physically."

"And nonphysically?"

"We'll have to find that out."

Miles returned his sterile gear to a tech, and hunted up his tunic and its assorted decorations again. As soon as he'd dressed, he poked his head around the corner to a side office. Lady Alys Vorpatril sat patiently there; she looked up at the motion.

"All done," Miles reported. "It's all right so far. He seems to be back to something like normal, on track. Though he's a bit subdued. I don't see why you couldn't see him, if you want."

"Yes. I want." Lady Alys rose, and swept past him.

Miles paid a visit to the secured lab down the corridor that Avakli's team had taken over.

Avakli had the chip under a scanner already, but he'd not yet started to take it apart. A new face in the team, a tall lean man who hung back apart from the others, caught Miles's eye at once.

Dr. Vaughn Weddell, nee Dr. Hugh Canaba of Jackson's Whole, had paler skin now, darker hair, and light hazel eyes in place of the original dark brown color he'd sported when Miles had first met him. A higher arch to his cheekbones and nose lent him an even more distinguished look. His air of earnest intellectual superiority was still the same, though.

Weddell's eyes widened, seeing Miles. Miles smiled grimly. He hadn't thought the good doctor would have forgotten "Admiral Naismith." Miles stepped aside with him, and lowered his voice.

"Good morning, Dr. Weddell. And how are you enjoying your new identity these days?"

Weddell processed his surprise smoothly. "Well, thank you. And, uh . . . how are you enjoying yours?"

"This is my *old* identity, actually."

"Really?" Weddell's eyebrows rose, as he studied and decoded the meanings of Miles's Barrayaran House uniform and its decorations, and the flashy chain around his neck. "Hm. Do I understand then that you are the Imperial Auditor I have to thank for this interruption of my work at the Science Institute?"

"Correct. We subjects of the Imperium do have our surprise duties sometimes, you must realize by now. The price of being Barrayaran. One of the prices."

"At least," sighed Weddell, "your climate is an improvement."

Over Jackson's Whole, indeed. And Weddell was not referring only to the weather. "I'm very pleased things have worked out satisfactorily for you," said Miles. "If I had realized I was going to be seeing you, I'd have brought greetings from Sergeant Taura."

"My word, is she still alive?"

"Oh, yes." *No thanks to you.* "Admiral Avakli has presumably briefed you on the very delicate problem I've assigned to his team. I'm hoping, should it yield any interesting galactic connections, your somewhat eclectic background might help pick them out. Do you have any ideas yet?"

"Several."

"Do they tend to natural causes, or sabotage?"

"I'll be looking for signs of sabotage. If I can't find any, we may end up dubbing it natural causes by default. The analysis will take several days, if it's done thoroughly."

"I want you to be thorough. Molecule by molecule, if necessary."

"Oh, it will have to be."

"And, um . . . remember that while you are inside ImpSec's labs, and certainly part of a team, you are not inside ImpSec's chain of command. You'll be reporting directly to me."

Weddell's brows drew down, thoughtfully. "That's . . . very interesting."

"Carry on, then."

Weddell tilted his chin in slightly ironic acknowledgment. "Yes, my lord, ah . . . Vorkosigan, is it?"

"Or 'my Lord Auditor' would be correct, this week."

"Rarefied."

"I could scarcely go higher here without risking a nosebleed."

"Is that a warning to me?"

"Orientation only. A courtesy."

"Ah. Thank you." Weddell nodded, and drifted back to watch the proceedings over Avakli's shoulder.

Weddell/Canaba was still an ass at heart, Miles reflected. But he did know his molecular biology.

After a conversation with Admiral Avakli, Miles called Gregor to report the success of the surgery. He then returned to see Illyan one more time. He found the ImpSec chief sitting up in bed, dressed again, with Lady Alys seated nearby. Illyan actually smiled slightly as he entered, the first unharrowed expression Miles had seen on his features for days.

"Hello, sir. It's good to have you back."

"Miles." Illyan nodded, carefully, then touched his hand to his head as if to make sure it was going to stay on. "How long have you been here? Come over here."

"Only about four days, I guess. Or five." Miles went to his other side.

Illyan too studied his House uniform and its assorted ornaments. He reached out to lightly tick the gold Auditor's chain across Miles's shoulders. It rang with a faint, pure note. "Now that's . . . rather unexpected."

"General Haroche didn't want to let me in. Gregor decided this would save argument."

"How creative of Gregor." Illyan vented a brief surprised laugh, which Miles was not quite sure how to interpret. "I would never have thought of it. But waste not, want not."

"If you seem to be able to watch out for yourself now, sir, I thought I'd take a break, and go home for a bit."

"I'll stay for a while," Alys volunteered, then added, "You did a good job, Miles."

Miles shrugged. "Hell, *I* didn't do that much. Just got the tech boys into motion, I suppose." With an effort, he converted a parting salute into a more civilian polite nod, and half-bowed himself out.

————◆————

Back in his bedroom at Vorkosigan House, Miles hung up his House uniform to await attention from a laundry, and divested it of its decorations, which he put away carefully. It would likely be a long time before he wore them again, if ever. Still, they'd finally served a useful purpose. Lastly, he held up the gold chain of his ersatz Auditor's office, and let it turn in the light, studying its exquisite detail.

Well. That was amusing, while it lasted.

He supposed he ought to take the chain back promptly to the Residence, to be returned to the vault from which it had come. It seemed a little careless to leave an object of that much historical and artistic value lying around in one's bureau drawer. Still . . . a job was never over till the reports were written; a decade in ImpSec had taught him *that*, if nothing else. And until Avakli and his merry men turned in *their* report, Miles could not very well offer his final one to Gregor.

He tucked the chain away atop a stack of shirts.

NINETEEN

Reluctantly but firmly, Miles seated himself at his comconsole the next day and rang up the Imperial Military Hospital's veterans treatment division, and scheduled a preliminary examination for the diagnosis of his seizures. ImpMil was the most logical place to go; they had as much experience with cryo-revival cases as anybody else on Barrayar, and they had immediate and privileged access to all his medical records, classified or not. His Dendarii Fleet surgeon's notes alone should save weeks of repetitive horsing around. Sooner or later, Ivan would remember his threats to drag Miles bodily to the clinic of his choice, or worse, rat about Miles's foot-dragging to Gregor. This spiked Ivan's guns.

Mission accomplished, Miles sighed, pushed back from his comconsole, and rose for an aimless ramble around the echoing corridors and chambers of Vorkosigan House. It wasn't that he missed Ivan's company, exactly, it was just that . . . he missed company, even Ivan's. Vorkosigan House wasn't meant to be this quiet. It had been designed to host a full-time roaring circus, with its complement of guardsmen and staff, maids and grooms and gardeners, hurrying couriers and languid courtiers, Vor visitors trailing their retinues, children . . . with the successive Counts Vorkosigan as ringmasters, the hubs around which the whole great gaudy wheel turned. Counts and Countesses Vorkosigan. The party had been at its height in his great-grandparents' day, Miles supposed, just before the end of the Time of Isolation. He paused before a window overlooking the curving drive, and pictured horses and carriages pulling up below, officers and ladies disembarking with a glitter of swords and swirl of fabrics.

Running the Dendarii Mercenaries had been something like that, at least the roaring-circus aspect. Miles wondered if the Dendarii Fleet would outlast its founder by as long as Vorkosigan House had outlasted the first Count, eleven generations ago. And if it would be knocked down and completely rebuilt as often. Strange to think he might have created something so organic and alive that it would continue in his absence, without him to prop and push. . . . the way children went on living, without any further act of will on the parents' part.

Quinn was surely his worthy successor. He ought to give up any pretense of his return to the Dendarii and just promote her to Admiral, period. Or would personnel assignments now be Haroche's job? Miles would have trusted Illyan to handle Quinn. But did Haroche have the insight, the imagination required? He sighed unease.

His peregrinations brought him to the second-floor succession of rooms with the best view of the back garden, that had been his formidable grandfather's lair for the last years of the old man's life. Miles's father and mother had not chosen to move into them after the old Count's death, instead retaining their own extensive chambers on the floor above. But they'd had the old Count's rooms refurbished as a sort of Imperial-grade guest suite: bedroom, private bath, sitting room, and study. Even Ivan, a connoisseur of comfort, had not had the nerve to claim the elegantly appointed space on his recent sojourn. He'd taken instead a small bedroom down the hall from Miles, though that might have been for convenience in keeping an eye on his erratic cousin.

Staring around the silent chambers, Miles was seized with an inspiration.

———

"Kidnapping?" murmured General Haroche, eyeing Miles over Illyan's comconsole desk the following morning.

Miles smiled blandly. "Hardly that, sir. An invitation to Illyan to enjoy the hospitality of Vorkosigan House during his convalescence, offered by me in my father's name and place. I've no doubt he would approve."

"Admiral Avakli's team has not yet ruled out sabotage of the chip, though I find I'm drifting more and more to the natural explanation myself. But given that uncertainty, is Vorkosigan House really secure enough? Compared to ImpSec HQ?"

"If Illyan's chip was sabotaged, it may well have happened in ImpSec environs; that's where Illyan mostly *was*, after all. ImpSec is demonstrably no protection. And, ah . . . if Vorkosigan House is not securable by ImpSec, it will certainly be news to the former Lord Regent. I might even call it a major scandal."

Haroche bared his teeth. "Point taken, my Lord Auditor." He glanced at Ruibal, seated beside Miles. "And how does this removal look in your medical opinion, Dr. Ruibal? A good idea, or a bad one?"

"Mm . . . more good than bad, I think," said the pudgy neurologist. "Illyan is physically ready to return to normal light activity—that does not include work, of course. A little extra distance between him and his office might help prevent arguments about that."

Haroche's brows rose. He had apparently not considered this awkward possibility before.

Dr. Ruibal added, "Let him take medical leave, rest and relax, do a little reading or whatever . . . keeping a log of any further problems. I can give him his daily examination there as well as here, certainly."

"Further problems," Miles noted Ruibal's turn of phrase. "What are his current problems? How is he shaping up, now?"

"Well, he's physically fine, if understandably fatigued. Motor reflexes normal. But his short-term memory, to put it plainly, is shot to hell at present. His scores on cognitive tasks that involve short-term memory—and most of them do—are all well below his norms. His former norms, of course, were extraordinary. It's too early to tell if this will be a permanent condition, or if his brain will retrain itself over time. Or if some kind of medical intervention will be required. Or, God help me, what form that intervention might take. My prescription is for a couple of weeks of rest and varied activity, and then we'll see."

Thus buying time for Ruibal to scramble for solutions. "It sounds reasonable to me," Miles said.

Haroche nodded agreement. "On your head be it, then, Lord Vorkosigan."

———◦◉◦———

After another personal call on Avakli in his lab, Miles trooped over to the ImpSec clinic to pitch the invitation to Illyan. There he found an unexpected ally in his self-appointed mission of persuasion in Lady Alys, visiting Illyan again. She was impeccably turned out as usual, today in something dark red and Vorishly feminine, i.e., expensive.

"But it's a splendid notion," she said, as Illyan began to hesitantly demur. "Very right and proper of you, Miles. Cordelia would approve."

"Do you think so?" said Illyan.

"Yes, indeed."

"And the suite has windows," Miles pointed out helpfully. "Lots and lots of windows. That's what I always missed most, whenever I was stuck in here."

Illyan glanced around his blank-walled patient room. "Windows, eh? Not that they are necessarily an advantage. *You* were done in when Evon Vorhalas fired that gas grenade through your parents' bedroom window. I can remember that night. . . ." His hand twitched; he frowned. "It's like a dream."

The incident had occurred slightly over thirty years ago. "That's why all the windows in Vorkosigan House were subsequently force-screened," Miles said. "No problem now. It's pretty quiet there at present, but I have this new cook."

"Ivan mentioned your new cook," Illyan admitted. "At length."

"Yes," said Lady Alys, a faintly calculating look crossing her fine features—was she regretting that the days of horse, cattle, and serf raids upon neighboring lords' property were gone forever? "And it will be ever so much more convenient—and comfortable—for people to visit you there than in this dreadful depressing place, Simon."

"Hm," said Illyan. He smiled briefly at her, looking thoughtful. "*That's* true. Well, Miles . . . yes. Thank you. I accept."

"Excellent," said Lady Alys. "Do you need any help? Would you care to use my car?"

"I have my car and driver outside," said Miles. "I think we can manage."

"Then in that case, I believe I'll meet you there. I'm sure you haven't thought of everything, Miles. Men never do." Lady Alys nodded decisively, rose in a sweep of skirts, and hurried out.

"Whatever can she intend to provide that Vorkosigan House doesn't already have?" Illyan wondered in some bemusement.

"Flowers?" hazarded Miles. "Dancing maids?" *Er . . . soap and towels?* She was right, he hadn't thought of everything.

"I can hardly wait to find out."

"Well, whatever she comes up with, I'm sure it will be done right."

"With her, you can count on that," agreed Illyan. "Reliable woman." Unlike some men of Illyan's generation Miles knew, he did not seem to find this a contradiction in terms. He hesitated, and looked through narrowed eyes at Miles. "I seem to remember . . . she was here. At some rather unpleasant moments."

"That she was. In style."

"With Lady Alys, how else?" Illyan glanced around the little patient room, as if really seeing it for the first time in weeks. "Your respected aunt is right. This place *is* dismal."

"Then let's blow out of here."

They decamped from ImpSec HQ with only one valise and very little further fuss. Illyan had been traveling light for more years than Miles had been alive, after all.

⸺⸺◈⸺⸺

Martin wafted them back to Vorkosigan House in the fusty luxury of the old armored groundcar. They arrived at Illyan's new digs to find Alys directing a cleanup crew, who were just departing. Flowers, soap and towels, *and* fresh sheets had been laid on. If Miles ever made good his threat to turn Vorkosigan House into a hotel, he knew who he wanted to hire for his general manager. Martin spent all of five minutes distributing Illyan's meager belongings to their new storage, then was packed off by Alys to the kitchen.

Illyan's slight awkwardness at all these attentions was relieved by the return of Martin trundling a tea cart laden with a mighty afternoon snack a la Ma Kosti. He laid the spread on the sitting room's table, overlooking the back garden through an outcurving window. Lady Alys's hand was apparent in the service; all the correct trays and utensils seemed to have been found at last, and put to their proper uses. But after a round of tea and cream, little sandwiches, stuffed eggs, meatballs in plum sauce, the famous spiced peach tarts, sweet wine, and some decorated killer chocolate things with the density of plutonium that Miles didn't even know the name of, *everybody* was relaxed.

Into the replete and meditative silence that followed the demolishing of the tea, Miles at last dared to float a question.

"So, Simon. What's it like? What can you remember now, of the last few weeks, and, um . . . before?" *What have we done to you?*

Illyan, half-engulfed by the soft upholstery of the armchair in which he leaned back, grimaced. "The last few weeks seem very fragmentary. Before that . . . is fragmentary too." The hand twitch, again. "It feels like . . . as if a man who'd always had perfect vision had a glass helmet all smeared with grease and mud fastened over his head. Except . . . I can't get it *off*. Can't break it. Can't breathe."

"But," said Miles, "you do seem to be, I don't know, in possession of yourself. This doesn't seem like my cryoamnesia, for instance. I didn't know who I was . . . hell, I didn't even recognize *Quinn*." *God, I miss Quinn.*

"Ah, that's right. You've been through . . . worse, I suppose." Illyan smiled grimly. "I begin to appreciate it."

"I don't know if it was worse or not. I do know it was pretty disturbing." A *slight* understatement.

"I seem to be able to recognize things," Illyan sighed. "I just can't recall them properly. Nothing comes up, there's *nothing there*." His hand clenched to a fist, this time; he sat up.

Alys was instantly alert to Illyan's sudden rise in tension. "All the past is like a dream," she noted soothingly. "It's how most people remember all the time. Maybe you can think back to your youth, before old Ezar ever had the chip installed. If things come back to you about like those times do, why, that's perfectly normal."

"Normal for you."

"Mm." She frowned, and sipped the dregs of her tea, as if to mask her lack of an answer for this.

"I have a practical reason for asking," said Miles. "I'm not sure if anyone's explained it all to you, but Gregor appointed me an acting Imperial Auditor with the mandate to oversee your case."

"Yes, I was wondering how you engineered that."

"We needed something to top ImpSec, you see, and there's not much else that can. After Admiral Avakli's team gets done with their examination of the chip, I'm going to have to turn in a proper Auditor's report to the Emperor. If they deliver a verdict of natural causes, well, that's the end of it. But if they don't . . . I was wondering if you would be able to recall anything, any moment or event, that might have cloaked the administration of some form of biosabotage."

Illyan spread his hands, and placed them slowly to the sides of his head in a gesture of frustration. "If I had my chip . . . and a defined time-window, I could rerun every waking moment past my mind's eye. See every detail. It would take time, but it could be done. Nail the bastards dead to rights, no matter how subtly they'd slipped it to me . . . If this *was* sabotage, they've destroyed the evidence against themselves quite neatly." He snorted unhappily.

"Mm." Miles sat back, disappointed but not surprised. He poured himself a half cup of tea, and decided not to attempt that last peach tart, canted lonely and forlorn on the crumb-scattered doily. Pressing Illyan further would seriously agitate him, Miles sensed. Dead-end for now; time to change the subject. "So, Aunt Alys. How's the preparation for Gregor's betrothal ceremony coming along?"

"Oh"—she cast him a grateful look for the straight line— "quite well, all things considered."

"Who's in charge of security for it?" Illyan asked. "Is Haroche trying to handle it himself?"

"No, he's delegated Colonel Lord Vortala the younger."

"Oh. Good choice." Illyan relaxed again, and fiddled with his empty cup.

"Yes," said Alys. "Vortala understands the way things are done. The official announcement and ceremony will take place at the Residence, of course—I've been trying to help Laisa with the intricacies of Barrayaran traditional dress, though we are debating if Komarran styles might be appropriate for the betrothal. Barrayaran dress will be required for the wedding itself of course. . . ." She was off, on a lengthy dissertation of what Miles mentally dubbed the social-technical aspects of her job; the topic was soothing and happy, and both he and Illyan kept her going with leading questions for a while.

After Martin cleared away the tea things, Miles suggested a game of cards, to pass the time. It was not, of course, to pass the time, but to provide a private check of Illyan's neural function, a nuance Illyan did not miss. But Illyan went along with it.

Star-tarot One-up was a medium-complicated game, and required a certain amount of tracking of cards played, held in opponents' hands, and probably upcoming, to beat the odds. Miles had never in his life seen anybody win against Illyan over any lengthy series of rounds, except by overwhelming luck in a particular draw. After six rounds, Miles and Lady Alys had split the points between them, and Illyan pleaded fatigue. Miles gave way at once. Illyan did look weary, his face drawn and anxious, but Miles didn't think that was his real reason for quitting.

Ruibal hadn't exaggerated. Illyan's short-term memory and eye for detail were practically nonexistent. He seemed to hold his own in casual conversation, where one comment triggered the next in flowing succession, but . . .

"So what do you think of Haroche's appointment for security for Gregor's wedding?" Miles asked casually.

"Who did he appoint?" asked Illyan.

"Who would be your first pick?"

"Colonel Vortala, I think. He knows the capital scene as well as any man I have."

"Ah," said Miles. Alys, rising to take her leave, winced. Illyan frowned suddenly, his eyes narrowing, but he added nothing more. Faintly defiant, he waved Miles back to his seat and saw Lady Alys out to her car with courtly punctilio.

Miles stood and stretched, more tired than the day's accomplishments could justify. *This is going to be strange.*

⸺◦◉◦⸺

The new, if still rather quiet, household routine was quickly established. Miles and Illyan arose when they chose, and might or might not cross paths in the kitchen in the morning, cadging breakfast, though they met more formally for Ma Kosti's lunches and dinners. Miles went out daily to ImpMil, the vast Imperial Service hospital complex, on the other side of the river gorge which bisected the Old Town. The first day they kept him waiting in the corridors, like any other veteran seeking treatment; he casually dropped mention of his new status as an acting Imperial Auditor, and *that* didn't happen again. Well, Gregor's choke-chain had to be good for something.

Duv Galeni came the second evening. Illyan's new residency in the old Count's chambers seemed to catch Galeni by surprise; he tried to excuse himself from dinner, but Miles wouldn't let him. The Komarran-born officer was stiff and uncomfortable, dining with his formidable former chief; all that history weighing on his mind, Miles supposed. Galeni diplomatically pretended not to notice Illyan's frequent lapses of memory and attention, and swiftly picked up Miles's technique of sprinkling little reminder-remarks through his conversation, to help Illyan stay on track, or at least maintain the illusion he was doing so.

Lady Alys visited often, as promised, though the pace of her life was picking up as the Emperor's betrothal ceremony ap-

proached; she'd laid on not one but two new social secretaries in
her office in the Residence. Ivan dropped by, always just in time to
be invited for a meal. A half-dozen aging military acquaintances
of Illyan's generation stopped to say hello to him; they, too,
quickly learned to turn up around tea time. Their number included
ImpSec's Komarran Affairs section-chief Guy Allegre, but happily the man had the wit not to let Illyan agitate himself trying to
talk shop.

The courtesy-guard ImpSec had provided on the absent
Viceroy of Sergyar's residence was increased from one man per
shift to a more serious three, with the unfortunate side effect of
blocking Corporal Kosti's private box lunches; but he routinely
dropped by to visit in the kitchen after his shift, so Miles supposed he was in no danger of starving. Vorkosigan House's grocery bills were becoming nicely impressive, though they still had
a long way to go to equal the Count's former household's.

Miles called Admiral Avakli daily, for an update on his team's
progress. Avakli was scientifically guarded in his comments, but
Miles was able to construe that they were making steady progress
at least in the elimination of negative hypotheses. Miles did not
lean on Avakli for more definitive statements. This was one case
where they really couldn't afford hurried mistakes, in either direction. And there was no need for haste. Whatever harm was going
to be done, had been done, and there was no way Miles, Avakli, or
anyone else could undo it now.

═══◈═══

The medical breakthrough Miles was itching for came on the
sixth day, but not from Avakli's team. The ImpMil cryonicist and
neurologist who had teamed up to tackle his case at last managed
to trigger one of Miles's seizures in their lab.

Miles came up out of the all-too-familiar colored confetti and
blackness to find himself still lying on the examination table,
head clamped in a scanner half the size of the room, body wired
every which way. The three alert techs stationed around him had
perhaps been placed to keep him from spasming off the table, but
more likely to keep the monitors correctly adjusted. Colonel Dr.
Chenko, the neurologist, and Captain Dr. D'Guise, the cryonicist,
were bouncing up and down and chortling, loudly pointing out
fascinating readouts to each other. It was apparently the best show

since the bicycle-riding bear had come to the Hassadar Fair and spooked the horses. Miles groaned, but it did not gain him any immediate attention; the monitors were apparently much more engrossing.

The doctors didn't really start talking to him, instead of each other, until he was dressed again and awaited them in Dr. Chenko's office. Even his Imperial Auditor's status didn't rush them this time. Chenko, a fit and energetic middle-aged man who seemed a walking advertisement for the medical profession, came in at last, an assortment of data disks in his hand; his initial air of pleased excitement had by this time subsided to mere smugness. "We know what's happening with you, Lord Vorkosigan," he announced, seating himself at his comconsole. "As we'd guessed, the mechanism of your seizures was idiosyncratic. But we have it now!"

"Wonderful," said Miles flatly. "What *is* it?"

Undaunted by his tone, Chenko plugged the data disks into his comconsole, and made the holovid display models and graphs to illustrate his points as he talked. "Apparently, after your cryonic revival, your brain began generating an unusually high level of neurotransmitters. These build up over time in their neural reservoirs to a quite abnormal level of engorgement, as you see here, so. There's a layover view of a normal reservoir, by way of contrast, d'you see the difference? Then something happens to trigger some unusually heavy brain activity—stress or excitement of some kind, say—and the reservoirs cascade-release all at once. That's this spike in this graph, here. This shuts down your normal neural functions temporarily, and incidentally accounts for the hallucinatory effects you report. After a minute or two, your neurotransmitter reservoirs empty out to normal—actually, below-normal—levels. Thus the few minutes of unconsciousness that follow. Then equilibrium begins to re-assert itself, and you return to consciousness, though in a somewhat fatigued mode. And the cycle begins again. It is an entirely biochemical, rather than phase-electrical, form of epilepsy. Quite fascinating and unique. Dr. D'Guise wants to write it up for the ImpMil Medical Journal—your patient-anonymity will be protected, of course."

Miles digested the news of his upcoming place in medical history in silence. "So," he said at last. "What can you do about it?"

"Mm. The cause is global, spread throughout large parts of your brain. Though perhaps fortunately, it's concentrated in the frontal lobes rather than the brain stem, so the seizures don't kill you outright. It does not obviously lend itself to surgical treatments."

Nobody chops up my brain, you yo-ho. "I'm glad to hear it. What treatment *does* it lend itself to?"

"Ah." Dr. Chenko hesitated. Actually, he fell silent. "Ah. Hm," he added after a time.

Miles waited, clutching his fragile patience. Dr. Chenko's medical creativity would surely not be enhanced by having an Imperial Auditor launch himself over the comconsole and attempt to strangle him. Miles also wasn't sure if his Auditor's legal immunity extended to personal assault.

"One approach for phase-electrical epileptic defects," said Dr. Chenko after a time, "is to install a destabilization chip in the subject's brain. When a seizure begins to occur, the biochip senses it and generates a counter-surge of electrical impulses to dephase the offending brain-wave feedback pattern. Sort of a surge-suppressor in reverse. Not a cure, exactly, but it alleviates the major symptoms."

"I'm . . . not so sure I trust biochips," Miles mentioned. "Particularly neural ones."

"Oh, it's quite a reliable and mature piece of technology," Dr. Chenko assured him. "I just don't think it's right for your case."

There's a cure, but you can't have it. Right. "So what is?"

"Dr. D'Guise and I are going to have to consult on that one. Now that we have some proper data to work with, I think we may be able to evolve a couple of possible approaches. As your case is unique, they must of course be experimental. We may have to try several ideas before finding an optimum one."

Reasonable enough, Miles supposed. "So . . . are we talking days? Weeks? Months?" *Years?*

"No, not months. If it's any reassurance, after that seizure in the lab today, I think it will be some time before you are chemically primed for another episode. Which, in fact, gives me an idea. . . ." An abstracted look came over Dr. Chenko's face; he began to tap out a few notes on his comconsole, paused, then began tapping harder. Data displays fountained and folded. Miles watched him for a while, then rose and quietly tiptoed out.

"I'll call you tomorrow, my lord," Dr. Chenko called hastily after him as the door hissed closed.

⟾«◉»⟸

Miles entered the black-and-white paved foyer of Vorkosigan House to find Illyan sitting on the upholstered bench at the foot of the curving stairs. He was showered, shaved, combed, and wearing full dress greens with all his insignia and proper decorations. Miles suffered a horrible moment thinking, 1) Illyan had become confused, and thought he was off for a conference with the Emperor, or 2) *Miles* had become confused, and Illyan really *was* off for a conference with the Emperor.

"What's up, Simon?" he asked, with feigned casualness.

"Ah, there you are, Miles. Where did you say you'd gone? Oh, ImpMil, that was it. Sorry. Yes. Lady Alys has asked me to be her escort at a concert she wishes to attend this evening."

"A concert? I didn't know you had an interest in concerts. Where?"

"The Vorbarr Sultana Company Hall. I don't know if I have an interest in concerts or not. For all the times I've run security on that building for Gregor, when he attended, I never once had a chance to sit down and watch and listen to the show myself. Maybe I'll find out why all those pretty people like your aunt go there."

"To be pretty for each other, I suppose," said Miles. "Though that's probably not the only reason seats are sold out two years in advance. The Vorbarr Sultana Company *is* supposed to the best on Barrayar."

A concert, how unexpected. Illyan's first appearance in public since his breakdown would certainly have an interesting effect on the capital's rumor mills. He looked as sharp as he ever did, when he troubled to clean up and play the Imperial officer; the surgical scratch was almost healed, and with his thinning hair combed over the bare patch, hardly noticeable unless you knew what to look for. It was not even obvious that the new vague uncertainty in his eyes was different from the abstracted inward look he used to get when accessing his chip. But if it had been sabotage, some kind of attack . . . would somebody want to try again? Miles could imagine a depressed Illyan courting assassination, but it seemed unfair to take Miles's only aunt down with him.

"So . . . what are *you* doing for security, Simon?"

"Well, Miles . . . that's ImpSec's problem tonight. I think I'll leave it to them." An odd smile played around Illyan's lips. "Ah. Here she is."

The sound of Lady Alys's purring groundcar came from the porte cochere that sheltered the front door: the whine of the canopy lifting, the driver's tread, then Lady Alys's quick steps. Miles opened the door for his smiling aunt. Tonight she was wearing something beige, with subdued glitters winking from the fall of fabric, and *very* Vorish.

"Hello, Miles dear." She patted him on the shoulder, in passing; better than the regulation auntish peck on the cheek, Miles supposed. At least she didn't pat him on the head. "Simon."

Illyan rose, and bowed over her hand. "Milady."

Well . . . Lady Alys *probably* wouldn't let him wander off and get lost. Miles stepped back as she swept out bearing her prize, who seemed pleased enough to be captured. Illyan was a guest, not under house arrest, for heaven's sake. "Um . . . be careful," he called after them.

Illyan waved jauntily, then paused. "Wait. There was something . . . I forgot."

Alys waited. "Yes, Simon?"

"Message for you, Miles. It was important." His right hand rubbed his temple. "I put the message disk on your comconsole. What was it? Oh, yes. From your lady mother. She's just leaving Komarr, and will be here in five days."

Miles managed to keep an *oh, shit* from popping out of his mouth. "Oh? My father's not with her, is he?"

"I don't believe so."

"No, he's not," Alys put in. "I had a message from Cordelia myself this afternoon—she must have dispatched them all together. I shall be so glad to have her assistance for the betrothal— well, not *assistance*, exactly, you know how indolent your mother can become when presented with these little social challenges. But her moral support, anyway. And we have so much to catch up on."

Illyan's lips twitched. "You don't look overjoyed, Miles."

"Oh, I'll be glad to see her, I suppose. But you know the way she tries to take my emotional temperature, Betan-style. The thought of all that incoming maternal concern makes me want to duck and run."

"Mm," said Illyan, in judicious sympathy.

"Don't be childish, Miles," his Aunt Alys said firmly. Her poker-faced driver raised the canopy, and Illyan helped her settle herself and her dress neatly within. All those years of close observation of the Vor class had certainly taught him the moves, Miles had to admit.

And they were off, leaving Miles to another evening of wandering around Vorkosigan House talking to himself. So why didn't *he* take ladies to concerts? What was stopping him? Well, the thing with the seizures, of course. And the crisis with Illyan, hanging unresolved. But both looked to be ended soon, and then what? Not, dear God, more double dates with Ivan. Miles shuddered in memory of some historic disasters. He needed something new. He was still stuck somewhere in limbo, somehow, prisoner of old habits. He was too *young* to be retired, dammit. If only Quinn were here. . . .

He hoped his Aunt Alys would be careful tonight. He and Illyan had gone out for a walk one afternoon, Corporal Kosti trailing discreetly, and Illyan had become lost within two blocks of Vorkosigan House. He would have felt less nervous if Illyan and Lady Alys had stayed in and played cards again, a form of mild cognitive therapy Dr. Ruibal had approved.

Illyan and Lady Alys did not return till two hours after midnight, long past the end of the concert. Somewhat grouchily, Miles met his houseguest at the door.

Illyan seemed mildly surprised. "Hello, Miles. Are you still up?" Illyan *looked* all right, if slightly rumpled, and notably redolent of the esters of fine wine and perfumes.

"Where *were* you all this time?" Miles demanded.

"All what time?"

"Since the concert ended."

"Oh, we rode around. Had a late supper. Talked. You know."

"Talked?"

"Well, Lady Alys talked. I listened. I found it restful."

"Did you play cards?"

"Not tonight. Go to bed, Miles. I'm certainly going to." Yawning, Illyan headed up the stairs to his suite.

"So how do you like concerts?" Miles called after him.

Illyan's voice floated back: "Very well!"

Dammit, the rest of us are going crazy over this chip thing. Why aren't you? No, unfair to blame Illyan for declining to, well, to go into a decline. Perhaps the ImpSec chief had concluded the failure was natural, and was dealing with it. Or perhaps he was just more patient and subtle than Miles about stalking his stalker. *That* would not be news.

Anyway, why shouldn't Illyan have a normal night out? *He*

didn't fall over and have convulsions in public. Miles growled, and went to bed, but not to sleep; it was going to be a wearing wait for Chenko's call from ImpMil.

Dr. Chenko leaned intently into his comconsole pickup, and spoke.

"This is what we've managed to come up with so far, Lord Vorkosigan. We've ruled out the possibility of a purely medical approach, say, the administration of drugs to slow your production of neurotransmitters. If only one or a few related chemicals were involved, it might be possible, but you are apparently overproducing dozens or even hundreds—maybe even all of them. We can't suppress them all, and in any case, even if we could it would only reduce the frequency of the seizures, not eliminate them. And in fact, upon closer examination of the data, I don't think the malfunction is nearly so much on the production side, as it is on the reservoirs' molecular-release-mechanism side.

"A second approach looks more promising. We think we can microminiaturize a version of the neural stimulators we used in the lab to trigger your seizure the other day. This array could be permanently installed under your skull, along with feedback sensors that would report when your neurotransmitter reservoirs were becoming dangerously overloaded. You could use the stimulator to voluntarily trigger a seizure in a controlled time and place, and thus, so to speak, defuse yourself safely. Done on a schedule, the attacks ought to be milder and shorter in duration, too."

"Would I be able to drive? Fly?" *Command?*

"Mm . . . if the levels were properly monitored and maintained, I don't see why not. If it works."

After a short internal struggle—*against whom?*—Miles blurted, "I was medically discharged over these seizures. Would I be—could I be reinstated? Returned to duty?"

"Yes, I don't quite understand . . . you should have been sent to ImpMil *before* your discharge was finalized. Hm. Well. If you were a lieutenant still serving, you might be able to petition—or pull whatever strings you own—and arrange to be assigned to desk work. Since you are already discharged, you would . . . certainly need more strings." Chenko smiled in prudent unwillingness to underestimate Lord Vorkosigan's inventory of strings.

"Desk work. Not ship duty, not field command?"

"Field command? I thought you were an ImpSec galactic affairs operative."

"Ah . . . let's just say, I did not end up in that cryo-chamber as the result of a training accident." *Though it was surely a learning experience.*

"Hm. Well, that's most certainly not my department. ImpSec is a law unto itself; ImpSec's own medical corps would have to decide what you're fit for. As far as the rest of the Service goes, you'd need extraordinary mitigating circumstances to engineer yourself anything but office work."

I could provide some, I bet. But desk work was no temptation, no threat to the continued existence of Lord Vorkosigan. To spend the rest of his career in charge of the laundry, or worse, as weather officer on some backwater base, waiting forever for promotion—no, be sensible. He'd doubtless end up in a comfy cubicle down in the bowels of ImpSec, analyzing data garnered by other galactic affairs agents, collecting pay raises on a regular schedule—but spared the stresses of promotion to Department Head, or Chief of ImpSec. Going home every night to sleep in his own bed in Vorkosigan House, just like Ivan toddling off to his flat. Sleeping alone? Not even that, necessarily.

If only he hadn't falsified that thrice-damned report.

Miles sighed. "This is all entirely hypothetical, I'm afraid. As for the scheduled-seizures idea . . . it's not really a cure, is it."

"No. But while you're waiting for someone brighter than myself to come up with one, it will control your symptoms."

"Suppose no one brighter than yourself comes along. Will I have these damned things for the rest of my life?"

Chenko shrugged. "Honestly, I have no idea. Your condition is unique in my neurological experience."

Miles sat silent for a time. "All right," he said at last. "Let's try it. And see what happens." He smiled briefly at Gregor's habitual turn of phrase, a private joke.

"Very good, my lord." Chenko made a flurry of notes. "We'll need to see you again, mm, in about a week." He paused, and looked up. "Forgive my curiosity, my lord . . . but why in the world would an *Imperial Auditor* wish to be reinstated into the Service as a mere ImpSec lieutenant?"

ImpSec captain. I wanted to be reinstated as an ImpSec captain. "I'm only an acting Auditor, I'm afraid. My tenure ends when my case is closed."

"Um, and . . . what *is* your case?"

"Highly sensitive."

"Oh, quite. Sorry."

Shutting down his comconsole, Miles reflected on Chenko's very good question. He didn't seem to have a very good answer for it.

TWENTY

As the days slipped by without incident, Miles was with reluctance drawn more to Haroche's growing opinion, that the chip failure had been from natural causes. The new ImpSec acting chief was certainly acting less tense about it all. Yet why should Haroche remain twitchy, when there had been no follow-up, no other attack during the time-window of confusion? The transition of power had gone smoothly. If the putative plot had been intended to derail ImpSec's organization, instead of Illyan personally, it had been a notable flop.

Three days before Countess Vorkosigan was due to arrive at the capital, Miles's nerve broke, and he decided to flee to Vorkosigan Surleau. He had neither hope, nor, truly, desire to avoid her altogether on her visit home, he just wasn't quite ready to face her *yet*. Maybe a couple of days in the quiet of the country would help him marshal his courage. Besides . . . it would be good security for Illyan. Out in that thinly populated area, where strangers were immediately noticed, it was easier to spot trouble coming.

Miles's one doubt about the retreat to the country house was whether he could persuade his cook to accompany them. However, Martin proved a potent bribe to draw Ma Kosti out of her familiar city into the doubtful hinterlands. Miles began to consider raising not his cook's pay, but her son's, to entice him and therefore her to stay longer. But maybe soon he wouldn't need a driver.

Illyan was amenable to the proposed excursion, if not wildly enthusiastic.

"This week's probably the very last of the good fall weather down there," Miles pointed out; indeed, the capital was undergoing a succession of colder and rainier days, with a nasty hint of early snow.

"It will be . . . interesting, to see the place again," allowed Illyan. "See if it's as I remember."

More of Illyan's quiet self-testing; Illyan didn't talk much about it, perhaps because the results of so many of his little tests were so discouraging. Or perhaps because he lost track of the results too quickly.

A morning's very mild flurry of activity—both Miles and Illyan traveled light by training and habit—resulted in a restful afternoon tea taken on the long front porch of the lake house. It was impossible to stay tense in the warm afternoon, sitting in the shade and gazing down over the green lawn to the sparkling stretch of water cradled in the hills. The autumn trees were almost denuded of their colorful leaves, which opened up the view. And the demands of digestion cured the viewer of any remaining residue of ambition. If this went on, Miles thought, he was going to have to take up an exercise program, or end up looking like his clone-brother Mark, which would rather defeat Mark's purposes. He made a mental note to keep Mark and Ma Kosti separated for as long as possible.

During a lull in the arrival of delectables, Illyan glanced down over the lawn. "Huh. That's about the spot where Captain Negri died, isn't it. The opening shot in the War of Vordarian's Pretendership."

"So I'm told," said Miles. "Were you here then? Did you see it?"

"No, no. I was up in the capital, being taken by surprise by Vordarian's forces, along with almost everyone else." Illyan sighed meditatively. "Or so I construe. The only image I can call up is of one of my subordinates running in with the first word—I can't remember his *name*—and of going somewhere in a groundcar. And of being sick-scared. I remember *that*, vividly, how my guts felt. Odd. Why should I remember that, and not . . . all the more important facts?"

"I suppose," said Miles, "because you always did have to remember it. Did your chip record your emotions?"

"Not really. Though it was possible to reconstruct them, when I was recalling."

"Deduced. Not felt."

"More or less."

"That would be strange."

"I got used to it." Illyan smiled ironically, staring down across the sunlit grass. "Almost my first job, when your father promoted me to Chief of ImpSec, was to investigate the murder of my predecessor. Come to think of it, that could be said to have been Negri's first job too. Doubtless made easier by the fact that he helped engineer the murder of his predecessor, but still. Anything done twice on Barrayar is a tradition. I believe I got off lightly. I never thought I'd get out of this job alive, though your father's retirement, last year, was rather inspiring."

"Is that . . . when you started to think about targeting me for your successor?"

"Oh, I had you targeted long before that. Or Gregor and I did."

Miles wasn't sure he wanted to think about that. "So . . . after a week to reflect on it, do you now think your chip failure was natural?"

Illyan shrugged. "Nothing lasts forever. People, devices . . . Well, Admiral Avakli will advise in due course. I wonder what Lady Alys is doing today?"

"Triaging guest lists and choosing stationery, and prodding her new secretaries through calligraphy practice, or so she said." Lady Alys had told them both that, yesterday.

"Ah," said Illyan.

Pastries arrived, and silence fell for a time, broken only by the sound of munching, and little appreciative mumbles. "So," Illyan said at last. "What do a couple of retired officers and gentlemen do on a country weekend?"

"What they please. Sleep in?"

"We've been doing that all week."

"Do you have any interest in horseback riding?"

"Not really. Your grandfather the General insisted on giving me lessons, from time to time when I was down here. I can stay alive on a horse, but I don't recall its being what you would call a sybaritic pleasure. More in the masochistic line."

"Ah. Well, there's hiking. And swimming, though that might be imprudent for me . . . I could wear a float-jacket, I suppose."

"The water's a little cold by now, isn't it?"

"Not as bad as in the spring."

"I'll pass, I think. It all sounds a bit youthfully athletic."

"Oh, this was a great place to be a kid." Miles thought it over. "There's fishing, I suppose. I never did much of that. Sergeant Bothari wasn't fond of cleaning fish."

"That sounds sedate enough."

"Tradition is, you take the local beer from the village—there's a woman there who home-brews it, extraordinary stuff—and hang the bottles over the side of the boat to stay cold. When the beer gets too warm to drink, it's too hot to fish."

"What season is that?"

"Never, as far as I could tell."

"Let us by all means observe tradition," said Illyan gravely.

———⟨◍⟩———

It took half a day to get the power boat out of storage, which put them out on the lake in the hazy warmth of the next afternoon, instead of the foggy chill of the early morning. This suited Miles fine. The basic mechanics of fishing were not something Miles had forgotten, and he never had gone in for the refinements. The need for sticking hooks into wriggling unhappy live things had been technologically relieved by the invention of little protein cubes which, the package assured him, were guaranteed to attract fish in droves, or shoals, or whatever.

He and Illyan arranged their beer in a net bag over the side of the boat, and their awning overhead, and settled down to enjoy the peace and the view. The ImpSec guard on-shift, one of three assigned by HQ to trail Illyan around down here, got to sit on shore with a little pontoon-fitted lightflyer and watch from a distance, out of mind if not out of sight.

The two lines ploinked over the side nearly simultaneously, and the bait and sinkers disappeared into the water, gliding smoothly down. At this distance from the shore, the green view of the rocky bottom was replaced by a depth of black shadow. Miles and Illyan settled back in their padded chairs, and opened their first beers. The brew was smooth and nearly as dark as the lake waters, and doubtless swimming with vitamins. It slid down Miles's throat with a pleasantly bitter fizz, and its earthy aroma filled his nose.

"This would be more like a stakeout," Illyan remarked after a while, "if the fish were armed and could fire back. If fish fished for men, what kind of bait would they use?"

Miles pictured a line tossed onto the shore, tipped with a spiced peach tart. " 'Let's go manning?' I dunno. What kind of bait did you used to use?"

"Ah, the motivations of men. Money, power, revenge, sex . . .

they were almost never actually that simple. The screwiest case that I can recall . . . dear God, why can I remember *this*, when I can't . . . oh, well. In the event, then–Prime Minister Vortala was engaged in heavy negotiations with the Polians over the wormhole access treaty, and was trying anything he could think of to sweeten the deal. The Polian ambassador indicated to Vortala that what he'd really always secretly wanted most in his life was an elephant. To this day I don't know if he really wanted an elephant, or if it was just the most absurd and impossible thing to ask for he could think of on the spur of the moment. So anyway, the word came down. . . . It was really the Head of Galactic Affair's department, but I gave the assignment to my ImpSec agent personally, just so I could watch. I still can see this glazed look that came over his face, as he choked, 'And . . . and how big does this elephant have to *be*, Sir?' There aren't many moments like that in my job. I cherish 'em. It was before your time, or you know who would have been the first man I'd have thought of."

"Oh, thanks. So . . . did your agent locate an elephant?"

"He was ImpSec to the core; of course he did. A small one. I assigned myself to the detail the day Vortala delivered it to the Polian embassy, too. In that fruity, deadpan voice of his, 'A gift from my Imperial master, Gregor Vorbarra . . .' Gregor must have been about ten, then, and likely would have preferred to keep the beast himself. Your father prudently didn't let him know he'd ever given away an elephant."

"And did Vortala get his treaty?"

"Of course. I think the ambassador really did want an elephant, because after he got over being stunned and flummoxed, he was clearly delighted. They kept it in back of the embassy compound for about a year, and he used to bathe and groom it himself, till he took it home with him. It expanded my world view, ever after. Money, power, sex . . . and elephants."

Miles snorted. He wondered about his own motivations, which had driven him so hard, so long, so far. To death, and beyond. He was unexcited by money, he supposed, because he had never felt its lack, except in the astronomical quantities necessary to repair battle cruisers; Mark, by contrast, was in his own quiet way downright greedy. Power? Miles had no hankering for the Imperium, or anything like it. But it itched like fire when others had power over him. That wasn't lust for power; that was fear. Fear of what? Fear of being made victim of their incompetence? Fear of being destroyed for a mutant, if he could not constantly prove his superiority? There was a bit of that, underneath. Well . . . quite a lot, really. His own grandfather had tried to kill him for his deformities, he'd been told; and there had been a few other ugly little incidents during his childhood, usually, though not always, cut short by the timely intervention of Sergeant Bothari. But that was hardly a hidden motivation, not the un-self-aware kind that got you into deep trouble and you didn't know why.

He swallowed another chill and smoky slug of beer. *Identity. That's my elephant.* The thought came with certainty, without the question mark on the end this time. Not fame, exactly, though recognition was some kind of important cement for it. But what you were was what you did. *And I did more, oh yes.* If a hunger for identity were translated into, say, a hunger for food, he'd be a more fantastic glutton than Mark had ever dreamed of being. *Is it irrational, to want to be so much, to want so hard it hurts?* And how much, then, was *enough*?

Illyan too took another swig of home-brew, and wriggled the carbon-fiber high-strength fishing rod, which like Miles's had come from the boathouse's stores. "You sure there are fish down there?"

"Oh, yes. Have been for centuries. You can lie on the dock and watch the little ones, nosing around the rocks, or swim with them. This lake was actually first terra-formed long before the end of the Time of Isolation, in the old crude way, which was by dumping every kind of organic waste they could lay hands on into it, followed by stolen weeds and minnows, and hoping an earth-life-form-supporting ecosystem would result. There was a lot of argument over it, back about the time of the first Counts, since the local farmers also wanted the assorted shit for their fields. Since the Count-my-Grandfather's day there's been a string of fellows who work out of the Count's Office in Hassadar, in charge of scientifically terraforming and stocking the District's waters, so it's back to being safe to drink *and* the fish are genetically improved. Lake trout, bass, freshwater salmon . . . there's some good stuff down there."

Illyan leaned over and stared a little doubtfully down into the clear water. "Really." He wound up his line, and examined his hook. His bait-cube was gone.

"Did I put bait on this thing?"

"Yes. I saw you. Fell off, likely."

"Light-fingered fish." But Illyan resisted any impulse to make a more extended mutant-fish joke. He rebaited the hook more firmly and ploinked it into the water again. They opened another beer each. Miles perched on the edge of the boat, and cooled his bare feet in the water for a time.

"This is very inefficient," Illyan noted, after adjusting the awning to reposition the creeping shade.

"I've wondered about that myself. I don't think it was designed to be efficient. I think it was created to give the appearance of doing something, while actually doing nothing. To repel chore-bearing wives, perhaps."

"I've been doing nothing for a week." Illyan hesitated. "It hasn't seemed to help."

"Not true. You're doing better at One-Up. I've been tracking you."

"I thought you and Lady Alys had colluded to let me win, last time."

"Nope."

"Ah." Illyan looked slightly cheered, but only for a moment. "The ability to play One-Up without losing all the time is not enough to make me fit to return to ImpSec, I'm afraid."

"Give yourself time. You've scarcely begun rehabilitation." Miles's feet were getting wrinkled; he returned to his padded seat.

Illyan stared at the farther shore, all green and brown in the westering sun. "No . . . there is an edge to a performance. When you've balanced on that edge, played at the very top of your form . . . you can't go back to anything less. To invert your mother's old saying, anything that can't be done well is not worth doing. And . . . running ImpSec is about as far from *play* as anything I know. There are too many other peoples' lives on the line, every day."

"Mm," said Miles, covering his lack of useful comment in another swig of beer.

"I've had my twice-twenty-years in the Emperor's service," Illyan said. "Started when I was eighteen, in officer's training for old Ezar . . . not the Imperial Service Academy; you needed more points and money and syllables in front of your name to get in back then. I went to one of the regional schools. I never thought to make it to a three-times-twenty-years man. I knew I'd stop sometime before that, I just didn't know when. I've been serving Gregor since he was five years old. He's full-adult now, God knows."

"That's your achievement, surely," said Miles.

Illyan nodded. "Not mine alone. But I can't . . . be who I am—what I was—and not know that."

"I never made it to the end of my first twenty years," said Miles glumly. "Not even close."

Illyan cleared his throat, and studied his line. "Was that a nibble, there?"

"No, I don't think so. The rod would dip more. Just the current, playing with the weight of the line."

"I wouldn't have picked now to quit, mind you," said Illyan. "I would have liked to have seen Gregor through his wedding."

"And the next crisis after that," Miles twitted him. "And the next crisis after that, and . . ."

Illyan grunted resigned agreement. "So . . . maybe this isn't so bad." He added after a time, "Do you suppose all the fish in your lake have been stolen?"

"They'd have to catch 'em first."

"Ah. Good point." Illyan paused to fish up the net bag, and open another beer for himself, and hand one to Miles. He was halfway through the bottle when he said, "I . . . know how much the Dendarii meant to you. I'm . . . pleased you survived."

He did not say *I'm sorry*, Miles noted. Miles's disaster had been a self-inflicted wound. "Death, where is thy sting?" He jiggled his rod. "Hook, where is thy fish . . . ? No. Suicide wasn't an option for me anymore, I found. Not like good old adolescent angst. I'm no longer of the secret opinion that death will somehow overlook me if I don't do something personally about it. And given life . . . it seems stupid not to make the most of what I do have. Not to mention deucedly ungrateful."

"D'you think . . . you and Quinn . . . how to put this delicately. D'you think you will be able to persuade Captain Quinn to take an interest in Lord Vorkosigan?"

Ah. Illyan was trying to apologize for screwing up Miles's *love*-life, that was it. Miles drank more beer, and thought it over seriously. "I never was able to before. I want to try. . . . I have to try one more time with her. Again." *When? How? Where?* It hurt, to think of Quinn. It hurt still, to let himself think of the Dendarii at all. Therefore, he would not. Much. *More beer.* "As for the rest of it . . ."—he sipped, and smiled bitterly—"there is some convincing evidence that I was slowing down too much to play a moving target much longer. Really, my favorite missions lately scarcely engaged any military force."

"You were getting frigging clever, is all," opined Illyan, gazing at Miles's distorted form through the colored glass of his bottle. "Though even a war of maneuver requires a credible force to maneuver with."

"I liked the winning," Miles said softly. "That, I really liked."

Illyan chucked his bottle into the box with the rest of the empties, and leaned over to squint down into the lake water. He sighed, and got up and adjusted the awning again, and pulled up the string bag once more, in lieu of fish.

Miles held up his half-empty bottle, to repel the offered refill, and settled back, and watched his still white line, descending down and down into secret darkness. "I always got away with it somehow. Any way I could. On the table or under it, I won. This seizure thing . . . seems like the first enemy I couldn't out-smart."

Illyan's brows rose quizzically. "Some of the best fortresses were taken at the last by betrayal from within, they say."

"I was beaten." Miles blew thoughtfully across the top of his bottle, making it hum. "Yet I survived. Didn't expect that. I feel . . . very unbalanced about that. I *had* to win, always, or die. So . . . what else was I wrong about? . . . I'll take that other beer, now, thanks."

Illyan popped the cap for him, and handed it over. The lake water was getting nicely icy now, definitely too late in the year for swimming. Or drowning.

"Maybe," said Illyan after a very long while, "generations of fishermen have culled this population of all fish stupid enough to bite hooks."

"'S possible," Miles allowed. His guest was getting bored, he feared. As a proper host, he ought to do something about that.

"*I* don't think there *are* any fish down there. It's a scam, Vorkosigan."

"Naw. I've seen 'em. If I had a stunner, I could prove it to you."

"You walking around these days without a stunner, boy? Not bright."

"Hey, I'm an Imperial Auditor now. I get hulking goons to carry my stunners for me, just like the big boys."

"Anyway, you couldn't stun anything through all those meters of water," said Illyan firmly.

"Well, not a stunner. A stunner power pack."

"Ah!" Illyan looked immediately enlightened, then more doubtful. "You can bomb fish, can you? I didn't realize that."

"Oh, it's an old Dendarii hill-folk trick. *They* didn't have time to sit on their asses dangling strings into the water; that's a Vor perversion. They were hungry, and wanted their dinners. Also, the lake's lords considered it poaching in their preserve, so there was incentive to get in and out quickly, before the Count's Armsmen came riding along."

After about another minute, Illyan mentioned, "I happen to have a stunner on me."

Dear God, we let you get out armed? "Oh?"

Illyan put down his beer, and pulled the weapon from his pocket. "Here. I offer it as sacrifice. I have to see this trick."

"Ah. Well . . ." Miles put down his own beer, handed his rod to Illyan, and looked over the stunner. Regulation issue, fully charged. He pulled out the power pack and proceeded to bugger the cartridge, in the best approved ImpSec covert ops "How to Turn Your Stunner into a Hand Grenade" style. He took another swig of beer, counted a moment, and flipped the power cartridge overboard.

"You'd better hope that sinks," noted Illyan.

"It will. See." The metallic gleam vanished into the darkness.

"How many seconds?" asked Illyan.

"You never quite know, of course. That's one of the things that always made that maneuver so damned tricky."

A half a minute later, the darkness was lit by a faint radiant flash. A few moments after that, a roiling boil of water surfaced beside the boat. The noise it made could much better be described as a belch than a boom. The boat rocked.

Onshore, the ImpSec guard stood up abruptly, and studied them through his power-binocs. Miles gave him a cheery, beery, reassuring wave; slowly, he sat back down.

"Well?" said Illyan, peering down into the water.

"Just wait."

About two minutes later, a pale gleaming shape shimmered up from below. And then another. And another. Two more, silvery and sleek, popped to the surface.

"Goodness," said Illyan, sounding impressed. "Fish." He up-ended his beer bottle respectfully in a toast to Miles.

Fish and then some. The smallest was half a meter long, the largest nearly two-thirds of a meter; salmon and lake trout, including one that must have been lurking down there since Miles's grandfather's day. Their eyes were glassy and reproachful, as Miles leaned precariously overboard and tried to collect them with the net. They were cool and slippery, and Miles almost joined them in their watery grave before he managed to snag them all.

Illyan prudently hung on to one of his ankles as Miles swung and splashed. Their prey made an impressive row, laid out on the boat deck, scales iridescent in the late afternoon light.

"We have fished," Illyan announced, staring at the mass, which almost equaled Miles's own. "Can we go in now?"

"You got another stunner pack?"

"No."

"Any beer left?"

"That was the last."

"Then we might as well."

Illyan grinned malignantly. "I can hardly wait," he murmured, "till somebody asks me what we used for bait."

Miles managed to dock the boat without crashing it, despite a desperate need to pee and up-and-down sensations that had nothing to do with the waves in the water. He listed upslope toward the house lugging the two smaller fish on a line strung through their gills, and let Illyan struggle with the larger three.

"Do we have to eat all these?" Illyan wheezed in his wake.

"Maybe one. The rest can be cleaned and frozen."

"By whom? Will Ma Kosti mind? I really don't think you want to offend your cook, Miles."

"By no means." Miles stopped, and nodded upward. "What d'you think minions are for, anyway?"

Martin, attracted by the return of the boat—and probably about to angle for permission to take it out himself—was clumping down the path toward them.

"Ah, Martin," Miles caroled, in a tone of voice that would have made the more experienced Ivan turn and run. "Just the man I want to see. Take these to your mother"—he unloaded his burden into the appalled young man's arms—"and do what she tells you to do with 'em. Here, Simon."

Smiling blandly, Illyan handed over his own dead fishes. "Thank you, Martin."

They left Martin, ruthlessly not even looking back at his plaintive, "My lord . . . ?" and lurched on up toward the cool stone house. The greatest ambition in Miles's world right now was for a lavatory, a shower, and a nap, in that order. It would be enough.

—————⊷⊷⟨◉⟩⊶⊶—————

Miles and Illyan settled down at dusk to a fish dinner in the lake house's dining room. Ma Kosti had prepared the smallest lake trout, which was enough to feed the whole household, with a sauce that would have made baked cardboard delectable, and rendered the fresh fish a feast for minor gods.

Illyan was clearly amused at this proof of their prowess as primitive providers. "Did you do this often, down here? Feed your whole family?"

"Once in a great while. Then I figured out my Betan mother, who never eats anything but vat-protein if she can help it, was munching it down bravely and lying through her teeth about what a good boy I was, and I stopped, um, challenging her culinary preferences."

"I can just picture her." Illyan grinned.

"D'you want to go out again tomorrow?"

"Let's . . . at least wait until the leftovers are gone."

"The barn cats may help us out there. There are about four of them hanging around the kitchen door right now, trying to soften up my cook. When last seen, they were succeeding."

Miles made his glass of wine last, taking tiny sips. A great deal of water, the nap, and some medication had relieved his incipient beer-and-sun hangover. It was a strange and unfamiliar sensation, to be truly relaxed. Not going anywhere, on overdrive or at any other speed. Enjoying the present, the Now that partakes of eternity.

Martin trundled in, not bearing more food; Miles glanced up. "My lord? Comconsole for you."

Whoever it is, tell them I'll call back tomorrow. Or next week. No, it might be the Countess, landing early or calling from orbit. He was ready to face her now, he thought. "Who is it?"

"Says he's Admiral Avakli."

"Oh." Miles put down his fork, and rose at once. "I'll take it, thank you, Martin."

In the private comconsole chamber off the back corridor of the house, Avakli's lean face waited above the vid plate, a disembodied head. Miles slid into his seat and adjusted the vid pickup. "Yes, Admiral?"

"My Lord Auditor." Avakli nodded. "My team is ready to make our report. We can present it simultaneously to you and General Haroche, as you requested."

"Good. When?"

Avakli hesitated. "I would recommend, as soon as possible."

Miles's belly chilled. "Why?"

"Do you wish to discuss this over a comconsole?"

"No." Miles licked lips gone dry. "I . . . understand. It will take me about two hours to get back to Vorbarr Sultana." And for this conference, he'd better allow time to dress. "We could meet, say, at 2600 hours. Unless you would prefer first thing tomorrow morning."

"Your choice, my Lord Auditor."

Avakli wasn't objecting to a midnight meeting. A mild verdict of *natural causes* did not require such haste. Miles would get no sleep anyway, anticipating this. "Tonight, then."

"Very good, my lord." Avakli's parting nod was approving.

Miles shut down the comconsole, and blew out his breath. Life had just speeded up again.

TWENTY-ONE

It was late-night-quiet in the ImpSec HQ building; the clinic's conference chamber seemed almost like a tomb. The black vid projection table was ringed by five station chairs. Ah, yet another medical briefing. Miles was learning, these days, altogether more than he'd ever wanted to know about the insides of people's heads, including his own.

"We seem to be a seat short," Miles said to Admiral Avakli, nodding toward the table. "Unless you are proposing to have General Haroche stand?"

"I'll fetch another, my Lord Auditor," Avakli murmured back. "We weren't expecting . . ." His eyes shifted to Illyan, seating himself to the left of the place reserved for Miles, next to Colonel Ruibal and across from Dr. Weddell.

Miles had been uncertain about the wisdom of dragging Illyan along for this, but Avakli's obvious unease filled him with a cheery ruthlessness. "It will save my having to repeat it all to him later," Miles murmured back. "And offhand, I can't think of a man on the planet with a greater right to know."

"I can't argue with that, my lord."

You'd better not.

Avakli went out after the extra chair.

Miles was kitted out in his full brown-and-silver House uniform, though he'd left the military ornaments in his bureau drawer this trip. He didn't want the clutter to distract the eye from his Auditor's chain, formally draped across his chest. Illyan had chosen soft civilian clothing: an open-throated shirt, loose trousers and jacket, giving himself an off-duty and convalescent air. As a courtesy to his struggling replacement Haroche? Except Illyan had worn civvies on-duty so often that the message, if any, was a little ambiguous.

Avakli and Haroche arrived back in the briefing room together. Haroche's lips moved in startlement as he saw Illyan; Illyan turned his head and nodded greetings. "Hello, Lucas."

Haroche's deep voice softened. "Hello, sir. It's good to see you on your feet again." Though he turned aside and whispered to Miles, "Is he going to be all right? Is he up to this?"

"Oh, yes." Miles smiled, concealing his own clueless state on that score. At a brief negating hand-movement from Haroche, the company skipped the exchange of military salutes tonight; with Illyan present, there was perhaps some lingering confusion as to who ought to be saluting whom. There was a rustle and creak, as they seated themselves, serious and attentive. Admiral Avakli remained standing at the vid display podium.

"My Lord Auditor," began Avakli. "General Haroche, gentlemen. Chief Illyan." He gave Illyan a special, if slightly uncertain, nod. "I . . . don't expect it will come as any real surprise to you that we have found the damage to Chief Illyan's eidetic neural implant to have been an artificially created event."

Haroche vented a long sigh, and nodded. "I was afraid of that. I had hoped it would be something simpler."

Miles had hoped such hopes himself, on many occasions; he couldn't help but sympathize. He, too, had usually been disappointed.

"Simple," said Avakli, "is the last word I'd use to describe it."

"We're dealing with a case of deliberate sabotage, then," said Haroche.

Avakli sucked on his lower lip. "That, sir, is your department. I think I prefer to stand by my original wording, for the moment. An artificially created event. To explain this I will now turn you over to Dr. Weddell, who was"—a slight wrinkle passed over Avakli's high brow—"instrumental in assembling the chain of causality. Dr. Weddell, if you please."

By which wrinkle Miles deduced Weddell/Canaba was carrying on as usual, brilliantly and obnoxiously. If his brilliance ever failed, he'd doubtless be quite surprised at what a load of retribution his obnoxiousness had bought him. But Avakli was too honest a scientist to claim another's achievement as his own. Weddell took the podium, his patrician features weary, tense, and a little smug.

"If you would like to look at the culprit—the immediate culprit, that is—here is its portrait." Weddell fiddled with the holovid control; the plate projected a bright green, topologically complex blob, which turned slowly in air. "The color is a computer enhancement, of course—I took a little artistic license there—and the magnification several million times. That, gentlemen, is a bioengineered apoptotic prokaryote. Or so I have reconstructed it."

"A what?" said Miles. "Simplify, please."

Weddell flashed a pained smile, doubtless searching his mind for words of one syllable. Miles regretted his last four beers. "A little bug that eats things," Weddell essayed, by way of further translation.

"Not that simplified," said Miles dryly. The Barrayarans around the table, knowing the power of an Imperial Auditor, cringed at his tone; immigrant Weddell did not. *Never argue with a pedant over nomenclature. It wastes your time and annoys the pedant.* Miles let it go. "A prokaryote. So. Reconstructed?"

"I'll get to that in a moment, my Lord Auditor. It barely qualifies as a life-form, being smaller and simpler than the smallest bacterium, but it does perform two life-functions. In a manner of speaking it 'eats.' Specifically, it manufactures a proteolytic enzyme that breaks down the protein matrix found in the eidetic chip and several related galactic neuroenhancement applications. It destroys that and nothing else. And, after absorbing the resulting nutrients, it reproduces, by simple binary fission. A population of these prokaryotes, presented with a field, as it were, of chip proteins upon which to graze, will double and redouble in the usual geometric progression—up to a point. After a number of doublings, the prokaryote is programmed to self-destruct. By the time we obtained the chip for analysis, almost all of them had done so, leaving me a pretty jigsaw puzzle of fragments to play with. Another week, and there would have been nothing left to analyze."

Haroche winced.

"So," said Miles, "was this engineered for Illyan specifically? Or is it a commercial product, or what?"

"Your first question I cannot answer. But I could read much of its product history off its molecular structure. First of all, whoever made this did not begin from scratch. This is a modification of an existing, patented apoptotic organism originally designed to destroy neural plaque. The galactic patent code for that perfectly legitimate medical application was still readable on some of the molecular fragments. The modified prokaryote, however, bore no identifications of laboratories of origin, licensing, or patent markings. The original patent is about ten years old, by the way, which gives you the first point in your time-window problem."

"That was going to be my next question," said Miles. "I hope we can narrow things down more than that."

"Of course. But you see how much we learn already, just from the codes and their absences. The original medical prokaryote was pirated for the new purpose, and the people who modified it were obviously not concerned with legitimizing it for mass trade. It has all the signs of being a one-off job for a one-time customer."

"Illegal Jacksonian work, by chance?" asked Miles. *You would know.*

"The kind of shortcuts taken in its design strongly suggest it. I'm not personally familiar with it, unfortunately."

Not something from Bharaputra Labs, Weddell/Canaba's former employer, then. *That* would have been a happy chance. But there were a dozen other Jacksonian houses who might have taken on small work like this. For a fee.

"So how much did this cost to make? Or rather, to have made?"

"Mm . . ." Weddell stared thoughtfully into space. "Actual lab costs, something under fifty thousand Betan dollars. Who knows what the markup might have been. Any special demand for secrecy on the part of its purchasers would have driven the cost up, oh, about fivefold. Or more, depending on what the market would bear."

Not the work of a lone nut, then, unless he were a fabulously rich lone nut. An organization, perhaps. Komarran terrorists sprang to mind—they always did, unfortunately.

"Could this be Cetagandan work?" asked General Haroche.

"Oh, no, I don't think so," said Weddell. "It's not in their style at all. Genetically speaking. Cetagandan work is distinguished by its quality, originality, and, how shall I put it, *elegance.* This is, by comparison, slapdash. Effective, mind you, but slapdash. On a molecular level."

Illyan's lips twisted, but he said nothing.

"The self-destruct sequencing," Weddell went on, "could have been a safety-check, simply left over from the original design. Or . . . it could have been deliberately intended to destroy the evidence."

"Can you tell which?"

"There were some slight modifications in it, compared to the original medical prokaryote . . . it was deliberately left in the design, anyway. I can give you facts, my lord; I cannot give you the intentions of unknown persons."

That's my job, right. "So . . . when was it administered to Illyan? And how?"

"*Administered* is an assumptive term, though under the circumstances probably allowable. The first gross symptoms of breakdown were when, again?"

"Four weeks ago," said Haroche. "At the all-departments briefing."

"About a week before that, actually," said Miles. "According to my informant."

Haroche gave him a sharp look. "Really."

Illyan stirred, as if about to add something, but then kept his peace.

"Hm. The prokaryote does not reproduce very rapidly. Much depends on how large a dose was initially introduced."

"Yes, and how was it done?" Miles put in. "For that matter, how is this stuff stored and transported? What's its shelf life? Does it require any special conditions?"

"It's stored dry, in an encapsulated form, at room temperature, though it would not be harmed by mild freezing. Shelf life—heavens. Years. Though it's obviously less than a decade old. It is activated by wetting, presumably upon administration, which requires moist contact. Through mucous membranes—it could have been inhaled as a dust—injected as a solution, or introduced as a contaminant into a scratch. Broken skin and moisture would do it. It wouldn't have to be a large scratch."

"Swallowed?"

"Most of the prokaryotes would be destroyed by stomach acids. It could be done, but would require a larger initial dose, to be certain enough entered the bloodstream to be carried to the chip."

"So . . . when? What's the maximum possible time-window for exposure? Can't you use its reproductive rate to calculate when it was administered?"

"Only crudely. That's one of the several variables, I'm afraid, my lord. Administration must have been between ten weeks and one week before the appearance of the first symptoms."

Miles turned to Illyan. "Can you remember anything like that?"

Illyan shook his head helplessly.

Haroche said, "Is there any way . . . could it . . . is it possible the exposure might have been accidental?"

Weddell screwed up his mouth. "Possible? Who can say? Likely? That's the question." And he looked as if he was glad he didn't have to answer it.

"Have there been"—Miles turned to Haroche—"any reports of anyone else on Barrayar who possesses related chip technologies undergoing a mysterious breakdown?" For that matter, *did* anyone else on Barrayar possess a related chip?

"Not that I know of," said Haroche.

"I would like ImpSec to double-check that, please."

"Yes, my lord." Haroche made a note.

"The jump-pilots' neural implants use an altogether different system," put in Avakli. "Thank God." He blinked, presumably at an inner vision of the chaos that would result from some sort of pilot-plague.

"This prokaryote is not communicable by ordinary means," Weddell assured them, rather offhandedly, Miles thought.

"We must assume a worst-case scenario, I think," said Miles.

"Indeed," sighed Haroche.

"It looks like sabotage to me," Miles went on. "Pinpoint deliberate, knowledgeable, and subtle." *And cruel, lord, something cruel.* "We now know what, and how. And some of when. But who, and why?" Ah, the motivations of men again. *I have touched the elephant, and it is very like a . . .* what were the six answers?— *rope, tree, wall, snake, spear, fan. . . .* "We have the method. The motive remains obscure. You have too many enemies, Simon, and none of them are personal. I don't think. You weren't . . . sleeping with anyone's wife or daughter or anything like that, that we don't know about, were you?"

Illyan's mouth twisted in bleak amusement. "Alas, no, Miles."

"So . . . it had to be someone who was mad at ImpSec generally. Political motivations? Damn, that still leaves too wide a field. Though they did have money to burn, and, um, patience—how long would you estimate it took to develop that microbeastie, Dr. Weddell?"

"Laboratory time, oh, a couple of months. Unless they paid for a rush job. A month at least."

"Plus travel time . . . this plot has to have started at least six months ago, I'd think."

Haroche cleared his throat. "It appears probable that it came from off Barrayar. I'd like to know what laboratory it came from, and when. With your permission, my Lord Auditor, I'll immediately alert Galactic Affairs to put their agents onto the Jacksonian end of this tangle. With an eye to other possible sources for bio-work on this order—Escobar, for example. Jackson's Whole does not possess a *complete* monopoly on shady deals, after all."

"Yes, please, General Haroche," said Miles. It was exactly the sort of tedious legwork ImpSec could do much better than Miles. A real Imperial Auditor normally possessed a staff of his own to whom to delegate such jobs. He'd have to check the reports personally, to be sure. Ah, he was going be stuck down in the bowels of ImpSec HQ after all. He must be fated.

"And," added Haroche, "I'll review of all of Chief Illyan's movements for the last, say, sixteen weeks to five weeks ago."

"I was mostly here at HQ," said Illyan. "Two trips out of the city . . . I think . . . I know I never left Barrayar in that time."

"There was Gregor's State dinner," Miles pointed out. "And a few other events you personally supervised."

"Yes." Haroche made another note. "We'll need a list of every galactic visitor Chief Illyan could have physically encountered at those functions. The list will be large, but finite."

"Is there anything else you can do to narrow the time-window?" Miles asked Avakli and Weddell.

Weddell spread his hands; Avakli shook his head and said, "Not with our current data, my lord."

"Is there anything else at all you can add?" asked General Haroche.

Head shakes all around. "Not without moving into realms of speculation," said Avakli.

"It's such an odd attack," said Miles. "Targeting Illyan's function, yet not his life."

"I'm not sure you can rule out murderous intent, my lord," put in Dr. Ruibal. "If the chip had not been removed, he might well have died eventually of exhaustion. Or met some accident during his periods of confusion."

Haroche sucked in his breath. *Quite*, Miles thought. And if someone was targeting ImpSec chiefs for assassination, Haroche could well be next on the list.

Haroche sat up straight. "Gentlemen, you have all done an outstanding job. My personal commendation will be added to all your secret files. As soon as you have your final report ready to turn in, you may return to your regular duties."

"Tomorrow, most probably," said Avakli.

"Can I go home tonight?" put in Weddell. "My poor laboratory has been in the hands of my assistants for a week. I shudder to think of what awaits me upon my return."

Avakli glanced at Miles, tossing this one his way—*You foisted him on me, you deal with him.*

"I don't see why not," said Miles. "I do want a duplicate copy of the report."

"Certainly, my Lord Auditor," said Admiral Avakli.

"And anything else your office generates, General Haroche."

"Of course." Haroche started to say more, then opened his hand to Miles. "My Lord Auditor? You called this meeting."

Miles smiled, and rose. "Gentlemen, dismissed. And thank you all."

In the corridor outside, Illyan paused with Haroche, and Miles waited for him.

"Well, sir," Haroche sighed, "you've bequeathed me an ugly puzzle, I must say."

Illyan grinned. "Welcome to the hot seat. I was telling Miles . . . yesterday?—that *my* first job as chief of ImpSec was to investigate the assassination of my predecessor. The triumph of tradition."

You were telling me that this afternoon, Simon.

"You weren't murdered, at least," said Haroche.

"Ah." Illyan's smile thinned. "I . . . forgot." He glanced at Haroche, and his voice fell to a murmur that Haroche had to bend his head to hear. "Get the bastards for me, will you, Lucas?"

"I'll do my best, sir. We all will." Gravely, and despite Illyan's civilian garb, Haroche saluted him as they turned to leave.

———※———

Miles did not fall asleep easily that night, or rather morning, despite replacing his expected insomnia of anticipation with . . . what? Information-indigestion, he supposed.

He turned in his bedsheets, and stared into a darkness considerably less opaque than the problem that had just landed in his lap. When he had leapt at the chance of playing Imperial Auditor, he'd expected it to be exactly that, a charade, acted out just long enough to spring Simon Illyan from ImpSec's clumsy medical clutches. Not that difficult a task, really, in retrospect. But now . . . now he faced a problem that would give a *real* Auditor, with all his staff and support, galloping insomnia.

The hollowness of his office, issued to him merely on Gregor's whim, echoed in his head. He missed his Dendarii backup. If he'd thought for a minute this appointment was going to go real, even temporarily, he'd have started building a staff of suitable experts, raided from, though independent of, all other Barrayaran organizations. He knew a number of good fellows from ImpSec, for instance, close to their twenty-year anniversaries, who might be willing to retire and lend their training to his use. Study the other Auditors' staffs, and model his from theirs. Pin Lord Auditor Vorhovis to the nearest wall, and not let him go until he'd disgorged everything he knew about doing his job. A new apprenticeship. *I'm doing it backwards again, dammit.* A familiar unfamiliarity. *You'd think I'd learn.*

So. What should he do next, or rather, first? His one piece of physical evidence, the bioengineered prokaryote, appeared to lead back to Jackson's Whole, if he could trust Weddell's technical expertise, which he did. Should he go haring off to Jackson's Whole, to supervise the search? The thought made him shudder.

That sort of fieldwork was just the sort of thing to delegate to a team of field agents, of the kind he'd formerly been himself. Speaking of expertise. So the obvious thing to do was delegate it, except . . . if ImpSec *itself* was tainted with suspicion . . .

If the production of the prokaryote had been a purely commercial enterprise, there was no motivation to be found on Jackson's Whole. Well, maybe revenge. "Admiral Naismith" had seriously annoyed several Jacksonian Great Houses there on his last visit: if they'd finally figured out who he was working for . . . Yet House Fell, which could command the resources for this nasty piece of sabotage, had not been seriously discommoded by him; House Bharaputra, which had been more upset, was perhaps not crazy enough to start a private war with Barrayar— there was no obvious profit in it, after all; House Ryoval, which both had the resources and was crazy enough, was dismembered, Baron Ryoval dead.

No. The weapon might have come from Jackson's Whole, but the crime had been committed *here. Intuition, boy?* So what was he supposed to do, lie in wait trying to ambush his own subconscious? He'd go quietly mad.

Maybe he needed to give his intuition demon more to chew on. Stir up ImpSec? *Stir up your own assassination, maybe?* At least it would be entertaining, and less frustrating than this blankness.

Do you really think it's an inside job? The intuition demon, as usual, was too coy to give him a straight answer. But there was this; anyone could go scope out Jackson's Whole. Only an Imperial Auditor could get inside ImpSec HQ. Solving this puzzle was not going to be a one-man job, but it was all too apparent what his part in it must be.

ImpSec it is, then.

———— ⊚ ————

The crack of noon found Miles up, fully uniformed in his House brown-and-silver and his Auditor's chain. He was sipping the last of his coffee, sitting on the padded bench in the black-and-white paved front vestibule and waiting for Martin to bring the Count's groundcar around, when a commotion arose out in the porte cochere too great to be Martin—at least, Miles hadn't heard a crunch, as of a groundcar hitting a pillar. But there were several groundcars, and canopies opening, and voices, and scuffling footsteps. He set down his coffee and stood up to answer the door, but it swung open on its own. *Oh. Of course.* Countess Vorkosigan and her retinue had evidently made orbit this morning, while he still slept.

Two brown-and-silver uniformed Armsmen preceded her into the vestibule, bowing her inside before turning to salute Miles. She sailed through the mob of guards, secretaries, maids, servitors, drivers, porters, dependents, and more guards like a fine yacht cutting through choppy water, and they parted around her like a bow wave, spinning aside in little eddies to their various appointed directions. She was a tall, red-haired woman of quiet presence, dressed in something cream-colored and sweeping, enhancing the nautical effect. *Well preserved* did not do her idiosyncratic beauty justice; she was, after all, Betan, and in her mid-sixties had barely reached middle-age by that planet's standards. A secretary, tugging at her elbow, was waved aside as Countess Vorkosigan saw her son.

"Miles, love!"

He abandoned his coffee cup and bowed over her hand, trying to short-circuit a maternal embrace. She took the hint, saying only, "My, how formal for this hour of the morning."

"I'm on my way to work," Miles explained. "More or less."

"You'll enlarge upon that, of course. . . ." She took him by the arm, and towed him out of the traffic pattern of arriving luggage that reminded Miles of a column of army ants. They ducked into the next room, the antechamber to the great library; her minions carried on competently without her.

She stood him at arm's length, and looked him over. "How are you?" Her smile did not quite conceal an anxious edge.

Coming from her, that was a question of potentially dangerous depth; he floated a "Fine, thanks."

"Really?" she asked quietly.

"Really."

"You actually look . . . better than I'd expected. Not so zombielike as in some of your, ahem, exceedingly brief communiqués."

"I . . . had a few bad days, right after, you know. I got over it."

"Your father and I almost came home. Several times."

"I'm glad you didn't. Not that I'm not glad to see you now," he added hastily.

"Hm. I thought that might be how the wind lay."

"I might still have had my head up my ass," he admitted ruefully, "but events intervened. You've heard about Simon."

"Yes, but not all about Simon. Though Alys has been more helpful than either you or Gregor. How is he?"

"He's fine. He's here. Sleeping in. We had a late night last night. I think . . . I'd better let him tell you about it. As much as he can." He added cautiously, "He's physically recovered, but he's a little . . . well, he's a lot vaguer than the Simon you're used to, I'm afraid. You'll figure it out pretty quickly when you talk to him."

"I see." She frowned faintly. "As soon as possible. I have a brunch meeting with Alys in an hour. I'm extremely anxious to meet Laisa."

"So did you succeed in soothing her parents, where Lady Alys says she could not?"

"Oh, Alys did a good job of laying the groundwork. Laisa's parents' feelings are naturally mixed, of course. As *those* Toscanes, they are understandably excited by the prospect of gaining more influence, both for themselves and their company, and, to their credit, for Komarr generally."

"They're mistaken there, if that's what they think. Gregor's too conscious of the need to appear evenhanded to do too many open favors for his wife's relations."

"So I gently let them know. They're not without wit, I am happy to say. Their excitement was dampened by a genuine concern for their daughter's safety and personal happiness, though they are certainly as puzzled how this is to be achieved as any other set of parents." She smiled dryly at him.

Was that to his address? Unquestionably. "So . . . how is Father? How did he take . . . all this?" A shrug of Miles's shoulder in no particular direction indicated his new civilian life.

She cleared her throat. "Mixed feelings, mixed reactions. He gave me all sorts of logically conflicting assurances for you, which I think I shall simply boil down to: you have his support. Always."

"I knew *that.* That wasn't the question, exactly. Was he . . . very disappointed?"

She shrugged in turn. "We all know how hard you worked for what you had achieved, and in the face of what odds."

She evades the answer, dammit.

She added, "He was more worried about what would happen to you afterwards, left at loose ends." One long finger tapped his chain of office. "This was very clever of Gregor, I must say. The boy's growing quite gratifyingly subtle, in his maturity."

"Wait'll Simon explains to you what load I'm expected to tow with this damned chain."

Her brow rose, but she did not press him. He reflected for a moment upon Countess Vorkosigan's cool maternal style, in contrast to the hands-on attempted arrangements of Lady Alys versus—and it was versus—Ivan. On the whole, he found the Countess's quiet respect a hell of a lot more daunting than any overt interference could possibly have been. One found oneself wishing to be worthy of it. The Countess played the disinterested observer almost convincingly, a style Gregor had no doubt learned from her.

Martin stuck his face around the door frame, his expression awed as he took in the Countess. "My lord? Um, your car's ready and all. . . ."

The Countess waved Miles away. "If you need to go, go along. I'll tackle Simon next."

"It's going to be my job to prod his former"—he disliked the taste of that *former*—"department, it seems. Haroche has been slow to get into gear on this problem. Though I don't suppose I can fault ImpSec for refusing to reason in advance of its data."

"Why not? They have before, often enough."

"Now, now. Don't be snide. Milady Mother." Miles bowed himself out, very Vorishly.

She called after him, "I'm glad to find you here, anyway."

"Where else?"

She hesitated, then admitted wryly, "*I* bet Aral that you would choose the little Admiral."

TWENTY-TWO

Miles haunted Haroche's office for the rest of that day, rechecking everything ImpSec had done since last night, and monitoring the new orders flying out. He devoured the detailed log of Illyan's locations and movements for the past three months, till he was cross-eyed and beginning to be afraid he'd miss something. Haroche patiently endured his nervous kibitzing. It would be weeks before anything could come back from the galactic inquiries. Haroche was concentrating mainly on the Jackson's Whole connection, their one physical lead, which exactly suited Miles's theories, or prejudices.

Any side-branch Haroche missed, Miles pointed out, and Haroche promptly mended the oversight. By the end of the afternoon there seemed nothing more to do with Jackson's Whole short of Miles going there in person, an idea that occurred independently to Haroche.

"You do seem to have had an extraordinary amount of experience dealing with the Jacksonian Houses," Haroche observed.

"Mm," said Miles neutrally, concealing the pull of the idea on his own imagination. Returning to Jackson's Whole in his new persona of an Imperial Auditor, with all the Barrayaran Imperial warships he cared to requisition as backup, made a delightful little power-fantasy. "No," he said vaguely, "I don't think so." *The answer is here, inside ImpSec. I just wish I knew how to phrase the question.*

Restless and frustrated, Miles left Jackson's Whole to the agents assigned there, and Haroche to himself for a while, and set off for a rambling tour of the building. He'd thought he'd memorized ImpSec HQ, but there were nooks and crannies he'd never penetrated before, whole departments he'd never needed-to-know. Well, he certainly had the run of the place *now*.

He poked into a couple of such offices at random, thoroughly alarming their inhabitants, then decided to make his tour systematic. He would inspect every department from the top floor down, not excepting Physical Plant and Food Service.

He left behind a trail of disruption and dismay, as every department head frantically searched his conscience for a reason why the Imperial Auditor might be visiting *him*. *Ha. Guilty, every one of 'em*, Miles thought dryly. Several made a point of explaining their budgetary expenditures in what Miles felt was excessive detail, though one blurted out a wholly unasked-for defense of his recent galactic vacation. Watching these normally closemouthed men babble in panic was highly entertaining, Miles had to admit. He led them on with lots of well-timed neutral noises, like "Um," and "Hm?", but it seemed to bring him no closer to formulating his right question.

Enough of the departments ran on Barrayar's whole 26.7-hour diurnal cycle that Miles could have continued his tour all night, but in the late evening he broke it off. ImpSec was a big building. Care, not speed, was called for now.

Miles woke the next morning to find Vorkosigan House full of the unaccustomed bustle of his mother's retainers. They were reordering the place: whisking away the furniture covers, efficiently taking over care of his houseguest, Illyan, and blocking his path with inquiries of what they might do for him, m'lord, as he attempted to wander the place half-dressed, thinking and drinking his morning coffee. It was the way it should be, but . . . still he was inspired to go off to work early. As long as he was being official, or officious, about it all, Miles decided to begin with a personal report to Gregor at the Imperial Residence, in his best Auditor's style. Besides, Gregor might have an idea. Miles felt particularly empty of ideas just now.

His Auditor's style melted rapidly into his usual style, once he reached Gregor's office and they were alone. They sat in the comfortable chairs overlooking the garden window, and Miles put his feet up on the low table and scowled at his boots.

"Anything new?" inquired Gregor, leaning back in his own chair.

"Not so far. What has Haroche told you?"

Gregor rattled off a tolerably complete précis of the midnight meeting, and of the orders and inquiries Haroche's office had disgorged under Miles's eye yesterday. "He said Illyan was awfully quiet at your briefing," Gregor added. "I gather Haroche believes that Illyan's a lot more damaged than he lets on."

"Mm. Illyan thinks he is too. I'm not sure he's damaged so much as he is out of practice. It's like he's forgotten how to pay attention. The inside of his head . . . must be a strange world for him right now. I think Lady Alys could probably give you better observations than Haroche on that score."

"So what have you done?"

Miles grimaced. "Nothing. I'm stuck twiddling my thumbs till the galactic reports start coming back. I've been poking through closets at ImpSec HQ, playing Inspector General. It provides some amusement, while I wait. And wait."

"You've only been waiting one day."

"It's the anticipation."

"Are you any happier with Haroche now?"

"Yes, in fact. He's doing all he should. And he learns fast, and doesn't make the same mistake . . . well, more than twice at most. It's the situation I'm not happy with. It seems singularly devoid of handles, strings . . . there are no loose ends to yank and see what happens. Or none I've found yet."

Gregor nodded in sympathy. "You've just started the real investigation."

"Yeah." Miles hesitated. "This thing has blown up a lot bigger and more complicated than I was anticipating, back when I was just being pissed at the way ImpSec was handling Illyan's medical treatment. It's no joke now. Are you sure you . . . don't want to put a real Auditor on the case? Vorhovis, for example."

"Vorhovis is still on Komarr. It would take a week to recall him. And I want him there."

"Or one of the others."

"What is this, funk?" Gregor studied Miles through narrowed eyes. "Do you want me to relieve you?"

Miles opened his mouth, closed it, and finally said, "I thought you should have an opportunity to change your mind."

"I see." Gregor sucked on his lower lip. "Thank you, Lord Vorkosigan. But no."

I hope you're not making a major mistake, Gregor. But he didn't say it out loud.

The coffee Gregor had ordered upon Miles's arrival appeared at last, borne on a tray not by Gregor's majordomo, but by Lady

Alys Vorpatril herself. She had Laisa Toscane in tow. Gregor's face lit.

"Are you ready for a break, gentlemen?" Lady Alys inquired, setting the tray down with a flourish and frowning at Miles's boots. He hastily removed his feet from the table and sat up straight.

"Yes," said Gregor, holding out his hand to Laisa, who took it and sat—snuggled—in beside him. Miles felt a momentary pang of envy.

"We're actually done, I think," added Miles. "For today." *My report is, there's nothing to report. Feh.*

A concerned and quizzical half-smile curved Laisa's lips. "Gregor and Lady Alys have told me about Illyan. I suppose I feel . . . sorry? No, that's not the right word. Awed, maybe, that such an icon has fallen. He was such a legend on Komarr. And yet when I finally met him, he seemed just an ordinary fellow."

"Hardly that," said Lady Alys.

"Well, not really ordinary, but that's the impression he seemed to want to give. So quiet. He was not . . . what I expected."

Not a monster? Laisa was a polite Komarran; you had to give her credit for that. "Real monsters," observed Miles, answering her thought instead of her words, "often *are* just ordinary men. Only more confused in their thinking. Illyan was one of the least confused men I know."

Laisa colored faintly. On her, it looked good. She cleared her throat, and forged on. "We actually came in for a reason, Lord Vorkosigan."

"You may as well start calling me Miles, in private."

She glanced for approval to Gregor, who nodded. "Miles," she went on. "Lady Alys has proposed a reception and dance here at the Residence next week, for Gregor's and my particular friends. There's nothing political about it, for a change."

Or so you can wish. But Lady Alys nodded confirmation. If not politically, it was certainly socially calculated. Was this a reward, for Laisa working so hard to be a good apprentice Vor?

Laisa went on, "Won't you come, Lo—Miles, your duties permitting? As a friend to us both."

Miles, seated, half-bowed to his future Empress. "My duties permitting, I'd be honored." It was likely he'd have time on his hands then, still waiting for the galactic reports.

"And you're welcome to bring a guest, of course," Laisa

added. She glanced again at Gregor, and they exchanged one of those maddening private smiles. "Do you *have* a regular . . ."—she groped for a proper Barrayaran term—"young lady?"

"Not at this time."

"Hm." She gave him a speculative look; Gregor, who still held it, squeezed her hand. If she'd had a younger sister, Miles would have known exactly how to interpret that glance. Love, it seemed, was not only contagious, it was *aggressively* contagious.

"Miles has proven immune to our Vor ladies," put in his Aunt Alys, not approvingly. Good God, was she about to give up on trying to alter Ivan's single state and start in on him instead, in sheer frustration?

Laisa looked as if she was trying to work out whether Lady Alys had meant to imply Miles preferred boys, without being so rude as to ask, or at least, not till she was alone again with her mentor.

"Not immune," Miles put in hastily. "Only unlucky, so far. My former travel schedule was pretty disruptive to romance." *At home, anyway.* "Now that I'm based in Vorbarr Sultana permanently, who knows. Um . . . maybe I'll ask Delia Koudelka."

Laisa smiled her pleasure. "I'd love to see her again."

Alys poured the coffee all around; Laisa watched carefully. She didn't scribble notes, but Miles bet she would remember, next time, that he took his black. Alys led the conversation into lighter concerns for the time it took to drink one cup, no refills, then rose to usher Laisa back out again. Off to the ladies' lavatory, to dissect Miles *in absentia*? *Don't be so twitchy, boy.* Under Alys's tutelage, Laisa seemed to be making rapid connections with the Vor women's world, and unlike Haroche she did not seem to be underestimating its importance to her future.

Gregor released Laisa with obvious reluctance. "Lady Alys," he added, looking thoughtful. "If you think he's up to it, why don't you bring Simon to the lunch Laisa and I are having with you and Lady Vorkosigan. I find I miss his conversation." He caught Miles's eye, and smiled wryly.

"I thought Simon's conversations with you were mostly reports," Miles said.

"It's rather fascinating to find out what all those reports were displacing, all these years," Lady Alys remarked. "Certainly, Gregor. I think it will be good for him." She shepherded Laisa out; Miles followed shortly.

Miles continued his self-inflicted inspection of ImpSec HQ where he'd left off. Personally, he would have preferred a pinpoint rapier thrust to this brute-force bludgeoning of the data, but when you didn't know what the hell you were looking for, you had to look at *everything*. Cryptography proved cryptic; their overt cooperation turned into a slyly technical explanation of their doings that lost him on the third turn. *If you can't dazzle 'em with daring, hang 'em up with horseshit.* Miles smiled through it all, and made a mental note to recheck this department again later. Finance seemed simply delighted that somebody *cared*, and threatened to go on forever. Miles fought his way clear of the spreadsheets, and escaped.

Housekeeping and Physical Plant proved unexpectedly fascinating. Miles had known the headquarters building was highly secured, but he hadn't realized in detail just how this was accomplished. He now learned where all the steel-reinforced walls and floors were, and just how much thought had gone into questions of blast containment, air circulation and filtration, and water purification. His respect for the building's late mad architect rose a notch. The building wasn't merely designed by a paranoid, it was *well* designed. Every room had its own biolab grade filtration system, in addition to the central unit that filtered and flash-cooked all returning air to destroy possible poison gases or microbes, before it was recirculated or vented. The heat generated was also used to distill the water, which explained its peculiar flat taste. Miles had seen spaceships with systems less tight. No colds were going to be transmitted among personnel *here*.

The janitorial staff were all serving soldiers, veterans of at least ten years' standing. They were also, he discovered, the best paid of their classification of any such men in the Imperial Service. Morale was high among them; once they'd realized his visit implied no criticism of the quality of their work, they became not merely cooperative but downright friendly. It seemed no inspecting officer had actually been willing to crawl through the ductwork in person with them for quite some time; but then, most senior inspectors were a lot older, stiffer, and stouter than Miles. He also discovered, along the way, what had to be the most boring job in ImpSec HQ—checking the vid monitors of all the kilometers of ductwork and piping in the building. He could only marvel that it had never fallen to his lot before, during one of his earlier periods of semidisgrace.

Janitorial was quite pleased with their Imperial Auditor by the time he reluctantly departed, and vice versa. Their combination of competence and camaraderie put him in mind for a brief and breathtakingly painful moment of the Dendarii, till his mind shied away from the comparison.

His busyness blocked excessive morbid reflection on the general weirdness of his current situation. On the whole, Miles thought he preferred it that way. He was an ImpSec outsider, a civilian, for the first time in his adult life, and yet he was obtaining a better view of the organization he'd so passionately served than he'd ever had before. Was this some sort of final good-bye? *Enjoy it while it lasts.*

Conscience-prodded, he broke off early enough that night to actually go home and have dinner with his mother and Illyan, a welcome touch of human civility. He successfully kept the conversation focused on the progress of the Imperial colony on Sergyar, about which, indeed, the Countess had much of interest to tell. He returned to HQ early the next morning, and breathed down Haroche's neck for a bit, till Haroche began once more to wistfully enumerate the benefits of a jaunt to Jackson's Whole. Miles grinned, and continued his inspection.

Miles's visit to Analysis took the most time that day. Among other things, he stopped in to talk with Galeni, and with the analysts now assigned to this internal ImpSec problem; they too were mostly waiting for the return of galactic reports. He checked on the men working other problems as well. The high priority of Illyan's chip sabotage did not mean that all other crises went on hold. Miles had a long and interesting chat with Komarran Affairs chief General Allegre, which understandably tended to turn to Gregor's betrothal, a topic Miles had carefully avoided with Galeni. Miles wondered if it would be worth a trip at least as far as Komarr to talk in person with Allegre's counterpart in Galactic Affairs stationed there. Colonel Olshansky, in Sergyaran Affairs, inquired politely after the Countess; Miles invited him to dinner with her, a courtesy the colonel seemed to find a bit daunting, but which he accepted with alacrity.

What Miles had been thinking of as the dessert of his inspection thus fell, not by accident, the last thing that afternoon.

The ImpSec Evidence Rooms were sited in the sub-sub-basement, occupying the chambers of the old prison block—chambers of horrors, Miles had always thought of them. The block had been the best modern dungeon, in Mad Emperor Yuri's blatant last days, with a distinctly medical flavor that Miles found more chilling than dripping walls and spiderwebs and chains and scuttling vermin. Emperor Ezar had used it too, much more discreetly, for his political prisoners—starting with Yuri's own gaolers, a grace note of cosmic justice in a generally ruthless reign. Miles felt it was one of the better quiet achievements of his father's Regency that the sinister prison had then been converted into, effectively, a museum. It really ought to feature a lifelike tableau in wax of old Mad Yuri and his goon squads.

But as evidence storage rooms went, it had to be one of the most secure on the planet. It now housed all the most interesting trinkets and toys ImpSec had collected in the course of its many investigations. The several rooms were stuffed with documentation, weapons, biologicals—*well* sealed, Miles trusted—drugs, and even more bizarre items confiscated from the evil and the unlucky, awaiting prosecutions, further investigations, or reclassification and culling as obsolete matter.

He fancied a meditative visit to the weapons room. It had been a couple of years since he'd last been down here, bringing home some interesting goodies from one of his Dendarii missions. On one of the back shelves he'd discovered a corroded metal crossbow and some emptied soltoxin gas canisters. They were the last physical remains aside from himself of the poisoning attempt upon the then-new Imperial Regent Lord Aral Vorkosigan and his pregnant wife, thirty years and a few months ago. *Alpha and omega, boy, beginnings and endings.*

The sergeant in charge at the front desk, sited in the old prisoner-processing chamber at the section's only entrance, was a pale young man with the mild air of a monastic librarian. He shot up out of his comconsole station chair when Miles entered, and stood at attention, obviously uncertain whether to bow or salute. He ducked his head, by way of compromise. "My Lord Auditor. How may I assist you?"

"Sit down, relax, and cycle me in. I want a tour," Miles told him.

"Certainly, my Lord Auditor." He reseated himself as Miles, experienced in the procedures, approached the desk and laid his palm on the read-pad, and stretched his neck to catch the retina scan. He smiled a little gratefully at Miles for thus relieving him of having to decide whether an Imperial Auditor was above standard security or not, and if not, how the devil he was to attempt to enforce his rules.

His relief was short-lived, as his panel lights blinked red, and his comconsole made disapproving noises. "My lord? You are explicitly listed as not-cleared, by order of General Haroche."

"What?" Miles trod around the comconsole desk to look over his shoulder. "Ah. Check the date. That's a leftover from . . . a few weeks back. If it bothers you, call Haroche's office and get the change authorized. I'll wait."

Nervously, the sergeant did so. While he was negotiating with Haroche's secretary, who sped the authorization back along with an apology the moment he understood the problem, Miles stared at the flat readout screen projected above the vid plate. It listed the dates and times of every visit he'd ever made down here, going back nearly a decade, together with codes for the items he'd carried in and out, mostly in. There was the safely lobotomized zvegan smart bomb, ah yes. And those strange Cetagandan genetic samples, now undergoing further investigation under the aegis of Dr. Weddell, he suspected. And . . . what the *hell . . . ?*

Miles leaned closer. "Excuse me. This comconsole lists me as visiting the evidence room twelve weeks ago." It was the date of his return from his last Dendarii mission, in fact, the fatal day Illyan had been out of town. The time logged was . . . right after he'd reported in to, and out of, Illyan's office; about the time he'd been walking home, in fact. His eyes widened, and his teeth snapped shut. "How . . . *interesting*," he hissed.

"Yes, my lord?" said the sergeant.

"Were you on duty that day?"

"I don't remember, my lord. I'd have to check the roster. Um . . . why do you ask, sir?"

"Because I didn't come down here that day. Or any other day since year before last."

"You're listed, sir."

"I see that." Miles grinned, his lips peeling back.

He'd found what he'd been subliminally looking for the last three days, all right and tight. The loose end. *This is either the jackpot or a trap. I wonder which?* So was he meant to find it? Was *he* meant to find it, *now*? Could any seer have predicted this subterranean visit? *Assume nothing, boy. Just go on.*

Carefully.

"Open a secured channel to Ops on your comconsole," he told the sergeant. "I want Captain Vorpatril, and I want him *now.*"

━━━━◉━━━━

Ivan made good time, coming over from the Operations building on the other side of the city; by luck, Miles had caught him on a day he hadn't skinned out of work early. Miles, sitting on the edge of the evidence room entry port's comconsole desk, one booted leg swinging, smiled grimly at Ivan's entrance, shaking off his ImpSec internal escort—"Yes, yes, see, I'm not lost. You can go away now. Thank you." The evidence room sergeant and his supervisor, a lieutenant, waited on the Lord Auditor's pleasure. The lieutenant was green and shaking.

Ivan took one look at Miles's face, and his brows rose. "So, Lord Auditor Coz. Did you find some fun?"

"Do I look cheerful?"

"More like manic."

"It's a joy, Ivan, an absolute joy. The ImpSec internal security system is lying to me."

"Tricky, that," said Ivan cautiously. "What's it saying?"

"It thinks I visited the evidence room, here, on the day of my return from my last mission. Furthermore, the entry desk log upstairs has been altered to match—it lists me as having left the building half an hour later than I really did. The security records at Vorkosigan House still show the actual time of my arrival, though—just enough time in the gap for me to have taken a groundcar home. Except that I walked that day. Furthermore—and this is the cream—the evidence room's internal vid monitor cartridge for that day was found to be, guess what?"

Ivan glanced at the obviously distraught ImpSec lieutenant. "Missing?"

"Got it in one."

Ivan's face screwed up. "*Why?*"

"Why, indeed. The very question I propose to answer next. I *suppose* this could be totally unconnected with Illyan's sabotage. Want to take a side bet?"

"Nope." Ivan stared at him glumly. "Does this mean I need to cancel my dinner plans?"

"Yes, and mine too. Call my mother and give her my apologies, but I won't be home tonight. Then sit down here at this desk." He pointed to the sergeant's station chair; the sergeant scrambled out of it. "I declare this evidence room sealed. Let no one in, Ivan, no one at all, without my Auditor's authorization. You two"—his arm swung to point at the two ImpSec men, who flinched—"are my witnesses that I, personally, did not enter the storage areas today." He added to the lieutenant, "Tell me about your inventory procedures."

The lieutenant swallowed. "The comconsole records are continually updated, of course, my Lord Auditor. We do physical inventory once a month. It takes a week."

"And the last one was done when?"

"Two weeks ago."

"Anything turn up missing?"

"No, my lord."

"Anything missing in the last three months?"

"No."

"The last year?"

"No!"

"Do the same fellows always do the inventory?"

"It rotates. It's . . . not a popular chore."

"I'll bet not." Miles glanced at Ivan. "Ivan, while you're sitting here, call Ops and requisition yourself four men with top security clearances, who have never worked for or with ImpSec. They're going to be your team."

Ivan's face screwed up in dismay. "Oh, God," he groaned. "You're not going to make *me* inventory the whole damned thing, are you?"

"Yes. For obvious reasons, I can't do it myself. Somebody's planted a red flag here, with my name on it. If they wanted my attention, they've certainly got it."

"Biologicals too? The cold room too?" Ivan shuddered.

"All of it."

"What will I be looking for?"

"If I knew that, we wouldn't have to do an inventory, now, would we?"

"What if, instead of something taken out, something was added? What if it's not a lead you've got hold of, but a fuse?" Ivan asked. His hand flexed in nervous pantomime.

"Then I trust you will stamp it out." He gestured the two ImpSec men into his wake. "Come with me, gentlemen. We're going to go see General Haroche."

———◦⊙◦———

Haroche too came on the alert the minute he saw Miles's face, as Miles and his little train marched into his office. Haroche sealed his doors behind them, shut down his comconsole, and said, "What have you found, my lord?"

"Approximately twenty-five minutes of revised history. Your comconsoles have been buggered."

Haroche's face grew unhappy indeed as Miles explained his discovery of the added time, with corroboration from the evidence room supervisor. It darkened further with the news about the missing vid record.

"Can you show where you were?" he asked when Miles had finished. "Prove you walked home?"

Miles shrugged. "Possibly. I passed plenty of people in the street, and I am, ah, a bit more memorable than the average man. Scrounging for witnesses ages after the fact is the sort of thing the municipal guard has to do all the time, investigating their civil crimes. I may put them on it, if it seems necessary. But as an Imperial Auditor, my word is not on trial." *Yet.*

"Er. Right."

Miles glanced at the evidence room men. "Gentlemen, will you wait for me in the outer office, please. Go nowhere and speak to no one."

He and Haroche waited until they'd cleared the room, then Miles continued, "What *is* certain, at this point, is that you have a mole in your internal security systems. Now, I can play this one of two ways. I can shut ImpSec down entirely while I bring in outside experts to check them. There are certain obvious disadvantages to this method."

Haroche groaned. "A *slight* understatement, my lord."

"Yes. Taking all of ImpSec off-line for a week—or more— while people unfamiliar with your system attempt to learn and then check it seems to me an invitation to disaster. But running an internal check using internal personnel also has, um, obvious drawbacks. Any ideas?"

Haroche rubbed his forehead. "I see your point. Suppose . . . suppose we set up a team of men to do the checking. At least three, who must work together at all times. They watch each other that way. One mole I must grant, but three, chosen at random . . . they can freeze the system in sections, with the minimum disruption to ImpSec's ongoing duties. If you like, I can give you the list of qualified personnel, and you can select the men."

"Yes . . ." said Miles slowly. "That works. Good. Do it."

Haroche breathed obvious relief. "I'm . . . grateful you are reasonable about this, my lord."

"I'm always reasonable."

Haroche's lip twitched, but he didn't argue. He sighed. "This thing is growing uglier all the time. I despise internal investigations. Even if you win, you lose. But what . . . I confess, I don't understand this business with the evidence room. What do you make of it?"

Miles shook his head. "It *looks* like it's meant to be a frame. But most frames come with pictures in them. This one's empty. It's all . . . very backwards. I mean, usually, you start with the crime and deduce the suspects. I'm having to start with the suspect and deduce the crime."

"Yes, but . . . who would be fool enough to try to frame an Imperial Auditor? It seems just short of insane."

Miles frowned, and paced the room, back and forth in front of Haroche's desk. How many times had he paced like this in front of Illyan, as they'd hammered out his mission plans? "That depends . . . I want your systems analysts to look particularly for this. That depends on how long this thing has been sitting down there in the evidence room comconsole. It was a buried mine, set to go off only when touched. *When* were the changes made in the records? I mean, it could have been any time between the day I arrived downside, and this morning. But if they were done more than a few weeks back—somebody maybe didn't think they *were* framing an Imperial Auditor. I don't see how they could have foreseen my getting that appointment, when I didn't myself. They were framing, bluntly, a cashiered junior officer who had departed ImpSec under a cloud. The obscure son of a famous father, and some kind of demimutant to boot. I might have been tailor-made to be an easy target." *Then.* "I don't like being a target. I'm downright allergic to it, anymore."

Haroche shook his head in wonder. "You confound me, Lord Vorkosigan. I believe I'm finally beginning to understand why Illyan always . . ."

"Why Illyan what?" Miles prodded after a long moment.

A lopsided smile lightened Haroche's heavy face. "Came out of your debriefings swearing under his breath. And then promptly turned around and sent you out again on the stickiest assignments he had."

Miles essayed a short, ironic salaam in Haroche's direction. "Thank you, General."

TWENTY-THREE

Ivan found it two hours before dawn, not *quite* by chance.

It was in the fifth aisle of the second room he'd tackled, Weapons IV. He'd placed Biologicals, Poisons, and the Cold Room last on his list for this very contingency, in the hope that he might not have to do them at all. Miles would have chosen to knock off the worst rooms first; sometimes, he had to admit, Ivan was not such an idiot as he feigned.

Ivan trod out to the reception area. Miles had been cross-checking the inventory lists on the comconsole there for the last several hours, ever since he'd overseen Haroche's three-man security systems analysis team selected and put to work upstairs.

"I'm in a Weapons Room, right?" Ivan demanded, waving his inventory sheaf of plastic flimsies.

Miles tore his attention away from the chemical description of the nine-hundred-and-ninth item in alphabetical order in the Poisons Room: Ophidian Scrapings, Polian, Three Grams. "If you say so."

"Right. So what's a little box labeled 'Komarran virus' doing on Aisle Five, Shelf Nine, Bin Twenty-Seven? What the hell is it, and shouldn't it be in Biologicals? Did somebody misclassify it? I'm not unsealing the damned thing till you find out what it is. It might make me break out in green fungus, or bloat up like those poor suckers with the Sergyaran worm plague. Or worse."

"The worm plague has to have been the most disgusting in recent history," Miles agreed. "But it wasn't very lethal, as plagues go. Let me look. Was it on the Weapons Room listing?"

"Oh, yes, right where it should be. They think."

"So it's got to be a weapon. Maybe." Miles marked his place and refiled the poisons list he'd been examining on the Evidence Rooms' library comconsole, and pulled up that of the weapons section instead. The "Komarran virus" had a code classification that blocked access to its description and history to any but men of the very highest security clearances. ImpSec HQ was crammed with such men. Miles smiled slightly, and overrode the lockout with his Auditor's seal.

He hadn't read more than the first three lines before he began to laugh, very softly. He would swear, but he couldn't think of any invective foul enough.

"*What*?" snapped Ivan, craning around to peer over Miles's shoulder.

"Not a virus, Ivan. Somebody in Classification needs a lecture from Dr. Weddell. It's a bioengineered apoptotic prokaryote. A little bug that eats things, specifically, neurochip proteins. *The* prokaryote, Illyan's prokaryote. It's no danger to you at all, unless you've acquired a neurochip I don't know about. Oh, God. *This* is where it came from . . . or rather, this is where it came from last." He settled in and began to read; Ivan, hanging over the back of his station chair, knocked his hand aside when he tried to advance screens before Ivan had finished too.

This was it, hidden in plain sight, buried in an inventory of tens of thousands of other items. It had been sitting here demurely in Bin Twenty-Seven, Shelf Nine, collecting dust for nearly five years, ever since the day it was delivered to the ImpSec Evidence Room by an officer from Komarran Affairs. It had been picked up at that time by Imperial Counterintelligence right here in Vorbarr Sultana, on an arrest-sweep of Komarran terrorist cells associated with . . . the late Ser Galen, killed on Earth while trying to launch his last complicated, dramatic, and futile plot for bringing down the Barrayaran Imperium and freeing Komarr. The plot for which Galen had created Miles's clone-brother Mark.

"Oh, hell," said Ivan. "Has your damned clone got something to do with this?"

"Brother," corrected Miles, swallowing the same fear. "I don't see how. He's been on Beta Colony for almost the last half-year. My Betan grandmother can confirm it."

"If you want confirmation," said Ivan, "then you must be thinking what I'm thinking. *Could* he have been pretending to be you again?"

"Not without going on one hell of a crash diet."

Ivan grunted half-assent. "Could be done, with the right drugs."

"I don't think so. I promise you, the last thing Mark wants is to be me, ever again. I'll have his whereabouts formally checked anyway, just to stop everyone from galloping down a blind alley. The ImpSec office at the embassy on Beta Colony keeps him in their sights just because Mark is . . . who he is."

Miles read on. The Jacksonian connection was quite real too. The chip-eating prokaryote had indeed been made to order there for the Komarran terrorists, by one of the Houses Minor more usually known for its tailored drugs. And Illyan had been its intended target from the beginning; the disruption of ImpSec had been timed to coincide with the assassination of then–Prime Minister Count Aral Vorkosigan. The ImpSec investigation of five years ago had traced the prokaryote right back to its building of origin, and the Komarran payment to the Jacksonian biochem team's bank accounts. The new search, just launched, must sooner or later turn up the exact same data: later, if they had to totally reconstruct the first tedious investigation; sooner, if the organization overcame its collective amnesia and spotted the data in its own files. Three to eight weeks, depending, Miles estimated.

"This explains . . . the frame, at least," Miles muttered.

Ivan cocked an eyebrow. "How so?"

"I came at it in the wrong order. My ersatz visit here was meant to be found, yes, inevitably, but it wasn't meant to be found first. This data . . ."—Miles waved at the comconsole—"when it finally arrived here, would have focused attention on the Evidence Rooms. Instead of starting with the comconsole records, and then checking the inventory, the investigators would have begun with Bin Twenty-Seven and then checked the security records of people going in and out. Where they would have been quite pleased with themselves for finding me, a recently cashiered officer with no business here. Gone at that way, it would have been a *much* more convincing frame."

Miles sat for a moment, ordering his thoughts. Then he called ImpSec Forensics and requisitioned the senior officer on call. After that he put through a call to Dr. Vaughn Weddell's home console.

The machine blocked him, and tried to take a message; Weddell didn't care to have his beauty sleep interrupted, it appeared. He tried once more, with the same results, waited a full three seconds to recover his patience, and then called the Imperial Guards.

Miles had the duty officer dispatch a couple of their largest uniformed men to Weddell's flat with instructions to wake him up by
whatever means were required, and bring him at once to ImpSec
HQ, carried bodily if necessary.

It still seemed an eternity—almost dawn outside, Miles
gauged—before Miles had his team assembled, and marched
them all before him into Weapons Room IV. Weddell was still
whining under his breath about being awakened so rudely in the
middle of the night; as long as he prudently kept his complaints
sotto voce, Miles chose to ignore them. Neither he nor Ivan had
gotten any sleep at all, not that Miles was the least tired right now.

The forensics man was given first crack at the exterior of the
little sealed biocontainer.

"It's been moved a few times," he reported. "Some finger-
prints, some smudges, none very fresh . . ." He duly recorded
them by laser-scan, for cross-match with Evidence Rooms personnel, and the rest of the population of the Empire if necessary.
"The screamer-signal circuit to detect the container's removal
from the Evidence Rooms has never been activated. No hairs or
fibers. I wouldn't expect much dust, given the air filters here.
That's all I can say. It's all yours, gentlemen."

He stepped back; Ivan stepped forward, drew the box from its
shelf, and positioned it on the lighted examination board brought
in for the purpose. The box was sealed with the simplest of nu-
meric code-locks, designed more to keep it from popping open if
accidentally dropped than for any real security—for one thing, the
access-code was listed right in the inventory description. Ivan re-
ferred to the flimsy, and tapped in the sequence. The little lid
swung up.

"Right," drawled Ivan, peering inside, and then at his
inventory-flimsy again. The box was lined with a shockproof gel-
pack, scored by six parallel slots. Three slots were filled with tiny
brown capsules, small enough for a child to swallow. The other
three were empty. "Six sealed vector-delivery units—that's what
they're called on here, anyway—to start with, one taken out for
examination five years ago and listed as destroyed. Five supposedly left—only now there are three." He opened his hand with a
flourish; the forensics man again stepped forward, and bent over
the box to begin checking the seal from the inside.

Right, right! Miles howled inwardly, with a small mental
reservation for that one capsule removed five years back. *That* was

going to complicate things, but perhaps the laboratory records would help, once retrieved.

"You mean," moaned Weddell, "I racked my brains for a week reassembling that damned crap, and a whole undamaged sample was sitting downstairs all that time?"

"Yep." Miles grinned. "I hope you like irony."

"Not at this hour of the morning."

The forensics man looked up and reported, "The lock has never been forced."

"All right," Miles said. "The box goes to Forensics for a full examination. Ivan, I want you to go with it. Don't let those weasels up there sneak it out of your sight. Weddell, you take one of those samples for a molecular analysis—I want you to confirm it *is* the same crap you flushed out of Illyan's chip, and I want to know anything else you can figure out about it. It and you don't leave the building—you can have the same lab in the clinic again, and any supplies you care to requisition, but no one—*no* one—but you is to touch the sample. You report to no one but me. The last two units go back into the new box on the shelf, locked under my Auditor's seal. I trust it will stay there this time." *Though I'm beginning to think it would be safer in my pocket.*

Haroche, the rat, had gone home to sleep last night after the systems team was assigned, an hour after midnight. While waiting for his return, Miles took a break for breakfast in the ImpSec HQ cafeteria. This was a mistake, he realized, catching himself dozing off into his coffee mug. He dared not stop. Somehow, getting started again was a lot harder than it used to be.

He was yawning in Haroche's outer office when the ImpSec chief entered, also yawning. Haroche blearily swallowed his yawn, and motioned Miles to follow into his inner sanctum. Miles pulled up a chair and sat as Haroche settled behind his desk. "So, Lord Vorkosigan. Any progress?"

"Oh, yes." Rapidly, Miles brought Haroche up to speed on the events of the last hours. Haroche, hunching forward on the edge of his station chair, wasn't yawning by the time he finished.

"Damn," Haroche breathed, leaning back again. "Damn. There goes the last hope of this being anything other than an inside job."

"I'm afraid so."

"So now we have another list. How many men could have known the samples were down there?"

"Five years' worth of Evidence Rooms inventory teams, for starters," Miles said.

"The men who captured and delivered it," Haroche added.

"And anyone working here at the time who might have been close friends with the men who captured and delivered it." Miles began to tick off the count on his hands. He wondered if he was going to have enough fingers. "It was filed under the seal of the Komarran Affairs chief who preceded Allegre. Allegre himself was still working on Komarr itself at that time, as the local section head. I checked. Also . . . any Komarrans in those revolutionary groups who escaped capture at the time, or who were imprisoned and have been recently released. People they might have talked to in prison . . . That list had better be checked too, I suppose, though, as you say . . . the comconsole tampering compels me to believe it's an inside job too."

Haroche made a note. "Right. Not a short list yet, I'm afraid, by any means."

"No. Though it's a lot shorter than the three planets full of people we started with." Miles hesitated, then added reluctantly, "I don't know if my brother Lord Mark—my clone, that is—knew about this stuff or not. It will be necessary to check, I suppose."

Haroche's gaze rose to meet Miles's, his expression arrested. "Do you suppose—"

"Not physically possible," Miles asserted. "Mark has spent the last six months on Beta Colony. Been to school every day since the term began." *I hope.* "His whereabouts are eminently provable."

"Hm." Haroche reluctantly subsided.

"Do *you* remember anything about that period?"

"I was still assistant Domestic Affairs section-chief. It was just before my last promotion. I remember the flurry of activity over Komarrans in Vorbarr Sultana. The case that had riveted Domestic's attention right about then had to do with an antigovernment group in Vorsmythe's District suspected of trying to import proscribed weapons."

"Ah. Well, I hope your data boys can help triangulate this," Miles went on. "Whoever did this must have had recent access to ImpSec's internal systems, plus a lot of wit and nerve. The short list is going to consist of the men who are on both lists."

"Why are you assuming it's only one man?" asked Haroche.

"Oh." Miles deflated. "Right. Thank you." Haroche, Miles reminded himself, was not without experience in this sort of thing.

"Not that I wouldn't prefer it that way," admitted Haroche. "I'd much rather find myself dealing with one than a conspiracy."

"Mm. But one man or a group, the motivation is growing . . . complex. Why me? Why was I picked to be the goat? Is there some special hatred at the bottom of this, or was it chance—was I simply the only ImpSec officer to be cashiered in the right time-window?"

"If I may presume to advise you, my lord, motivations are a slippery thing in this sort of business. Too wispily cerebral. I always got further faster following the facts. You can spin theories about motivation later, over your victory beer. When you know who, you'll know why. I admit, that's a philosophical preference."

When I know why, I'll know who. "It's true, there may be nothing personal in it. As soon as the crime was discovered . . . to *be* a crime, the, the . . . I can't call him a killer, I suppose. . . ."

Haroche half-smiled, not happily. "We're short a body, for one thing."

Illyan, for all his new vagueness, was hardly a zombie. But Miles remembered that hoarse distraught voice, begging him earnestly for a clean death. . . . "The assassin," he went on, "was absolutely required to supply a goat to take the heat off himself. Because this is not a case that can ever be closed except by being solved. No 'Hold pending further data' till it's dusty and forgotten this time. He had to know ImpSec would never rest."

"You're damned right," Haroche growled.

"That crap downstairs was carefully arranged to be found, because it was inevitable. Once the hunt was up, too many records existed in too many places for it to just be made to disappear. All I've done . . ." Miles's voice slowed, "was alter the timetable."

"Three days." Haroche smiled crookedly. "You went through all of ImpSec in just three days."

"Not all of ImpSec, just the headquarters building. And it was more like four days. Still . . . somebody must be squirming. I hope. If they meant to hook ex-Lieutenant Vorkosigan, and instead got Lord Auditor Vorkosigan . . . it must have felt like putting in your line for a trout, and pulling up a shark. I may have arrived just in time downstairs after all. Given the several more weeks of lead time he was expecting, our assassin might well have thought to yank his plant in the evidence room and try something else. God, I'd love to know."

Who hates me, and works here? Could Lieutenant Vorberg have found out who Admiral Naismith really was . . . ? Vorberg couldn't possibly be so twisted as to destroy Illyan just to destroy Miles, could he? *Surely I was a secondary target.* He had to be a secondary target. The alternative was too horrible to think about.

"Nonetheless, you've made extraordinary progress, Lord Vorkosigan," said Haroche. "I've cracked cases which started with far less data than what you've uncovered. It's good, solid work."

Miles tried not to be too pleased with Haroche's measured praise, though he felt his face warm anyway. Haroche was such a contained man, his brief words were clearly the meaningful sort men might strive to win. Surely it was not disloyal to Illyan to hope his successor might yet grow to fill his place, not the same, but as well.

"It's a shame," Haroche sighed, "that so many men in ImpSec HQ are fast-penta-proofed."

"It's much too early to think of starting to pull out people's fingernails," said Miles, nibbling on one of his own. "Tempting as it is. I suppose . . . that we now wait on the reports from your systems analysis team. I suppose . . ."—another yawn cracked his face—"that I might as well go home and get some sleep while I wait. Call me the minute they have anything to report, please."

"Yes, my Lord Auditor."

"Oh, hell, will you just call me Miles? Everyone else does. This Lord Auditor stuff is only fun for the first twenty minutes, after that it's just work." Not *quite* true, but . . .

Haroche gave him wave that nearly qualified as an analyst's salute, as he departed.

———※———

Martin returned Miles to the front door of Vorkosigan House in the midmorning. Seductive visions of his soft bed filled his head. Dutifully, he went first to find his lady mother and say goodmorning, or good-night.

Two or three retainers' conflicting directions eventually brought him to one of the downstairs sitting rooms on the east side, filled with unusually pleasant morning light for this chill early winter. The Countess was sipping coffee and leafing through an old leather-bound tome Miles thought he recognized from

Lady Vorpatril's Imperial wedding history assignment, the one
that he had ducked. *Better her than me.*

"Hello, love," she answered his greetings. She indulged herself by planting a maternal kiss upon his forehead; he stole a gulp
of her coffee. "You were out late. Any progress on your case?"

"I think so. The first crack, anyway." Miles decided not to disturb her morning by explaining that the first crack consisted of
discovering himself being framed for the crime.

"Ah. I wasn't sure if the abstracted look was that, or lack of
sleep."

"Both. I'm on my way to bed, but I want to talk to Illyan first.
Is he up yet, do you know?"

"I think so. Pym just took him up his breakfast."

"Breakfast in bed halfway to noon. What a life."

"I think he's earned it, don't you?"

"The hard way." He sucked up some more of her coffee, and
rose to go upstairs.

"Oh. Knock, first," she advised him as he passed the doorway.

"Why?"

"He's having breakfast with Alys."

That explained the book; Lady Alys had delivered it. He wondered what piece of Vorish history she was making poor Illyan read.

As advised, he knocked politely on the door of the second-
floor guest suite. No response: he knocked again. Pym had not lingered to serve the breakfast, it appeared, because instead of the
retainer opening it, Illyan's voice finally floated through the wood:
"Who is it?"

"Miles. I have to talk to you."

"Just a minute."

The minute became two or three or four, as he leaned against
the door frame and scuffed his boot on the patterned carpet. He
knocked again. "C'mon, Simon, let me in."

"Don't be so impatient, Miles," his aunt's voice admonished
him firmly. "It's a bit rude."

He closed his teeth on a snappish reply, and scuffed the carpet
some more, and fingered his Auditor's chain, and while he was
about it unfastened the high collar of his brown-and-silver tunic.
Some shuffling and clinking noises came from within, and a low
laugh. At long last, Lady Alys's light step approached the door; a
click, as she unlocked it, and it swung aside.

"Good morning, Aunt Alys," he said dryly.

"*Good* morning, Miles," she responded, much more cheerfully than he'd been expecting. She waved him inside to the sitting room. The cluttered breakfast tray was jammed onto the little table in the bay window overlooking the back garden. Only crumbs left, alas. Lady Alys was dressed oddly formally for this hour of the day, Miles thought, in a gown more suitable for dinner than breakfast, and was apparently experimenting with her hairstyle; it was loose, brushed in burnished black and silver waves down her back.

Illyan appeared from the direction of the bathroom, shrugging on a tunic over his shirt and trousers, and still wearing bedroom slippers. "Good morning, Miles," he echoed Lady Alys, right down to the repellent morning-person chirp in his voice. His smile faded as he took in Miles's rumpled up-all-night look. His tone flattened. "What's happening?"

"I found some very interesting things at ImpSec HQ last night."

"Progress?"

"Two steps forward, three sideways. Um . . ." He frowned at his aunt, wondering how to throw her out politely. She failed to take a hint, instead seating herself on the little sofa beside the table and attending to him with sharpened interest. Illyan sat beside her. Miles decided cravenly to let Illyan do the dirty work. "This is all highly classified, or it's going to be."

He waited a beat, while they both looked at him. "Do you really think it's appropriate for Lady Alys's ears?" he added.

Bad choice of phrasing; Illyan merely replied, "Certainly. Out with it, Miles, don't keep us in suspense."

Well, if *Illyan* thought it was all right . . . Miles took a breath, and began a fast-forward description of his last day-cycle's investigation at ImpSec. Neither of his listeners interrupted him, though Lady Alys muttered, "Good for Ivan," when he got to the description of finding their prize needle in the haystack of Weapons Room IV.

Illyan's cheerful air had vanished altogether; he sat tensely. Lady Alys watched his profile in concern, and took his hand; he squeezed hers in turn.

"What I need to know," Miles finished, "is if you remember anything, anything at all, about the time that sample was brought in, during the thwarting of that last Komarran fling."

Illyan rubbed his forehead. "It's . . . pretty blank. I remember Ser Galen's plot, of course, and that initial horrific fuss over discovering the existence of Lord Mark. The Countess was very upset, in her most Betan style. Drove your father to distraction. I re-member your report from Earth. A masterpiece of its literary genre. That Sector Four adventure where you smashed both your arms was . . . right after that, right?"

"Yes. But surely *someone* must have reported on the prokary-ote to you. I can see why you might not have risked inspecting it in person."

"I'm sure someone did." Illyan's right hand released Lady Alys's, and clenched into a fist. "They doubtless gave me all the details. And I doubtless put them where I always put the details. But there's nothing *left* now."

Lady Alys frowned irritatedly at Miles, as if it were somehow all his fault.

"Who ought to have given you that report?" Miles pushed on.

"General Diamant, I suppose. Komarran Affairs chief before Allegre, you remember him? Died just two years after he retired, the poor sod. Miles, I really *can't* . . . I would surely have been re-minded before this, if it were in here!" He clutched his head in frus-tration. Lady Alys recaptured his hand, and stroked it soothingly.

"Does your friend Captain Galeni have any ideas?" Illyan went on more calmly. "He might have some inside track. It was his father's plot, after all."

Miles smiled unhappily.

Illyan's eyes narrowed. "You know he's going to turn up on your short list, as soon as it's generated."

"Yes."

"Did you tell Haroche?"

"No."

"Why not?"

"It would have been redundant. Duv will be checked along with everyone else. And . . . I've done him enough bad turns lately."

"Aren't you . . . prejudging your data—my Lord Auditor?"

"*You* know Galeni."

"Not so well as you do."

"Just so. I'm not judging data at all, here. I'm judging the man's character. Motivations, if you like."

"Hm," said Illyan. "Just watch your own motivations there, old son."

"Yes, yes, I know. I not only have to be impartial, I have to ap-pear so. *You* taught me that one," he added rather nastily. "In a way I'm not likely to forget."

"I did? When?"

"Never mind." He pressed the bridge of his nose. He was not only exhausted, he was getting a fatigue headache. It was time to quit for the night, or he'd be unable to function properly on the next round.

"All right," he sighed. "Last thing. Do you remember, at any time in the last four months, anyone ever giving you a small brown capsule to swallow?"

"No."

"There's two missing. He might have taken one himself at the same time, right along with you." Whoever *he* was.

"No." Illyan sounded more certain than usual. "I haven't taken any medication in the past thirty years except what my personal physician gives me with his own hands."

Miles recalled Haroche's more-than-one-man theory. "It might even have *been* your own physician. It's the small brown capsule I'm trying to track."

Illyan shook his head.

Miles levered himself up, and made polite farewells, and staggered off to bed.

He woke in the midafternoon, and spent a futile half-hour trying to return to sleep, while his mind worried his new problems. He gave up, rose, and checked in with Haroche by comconsole; the systems analysis team had not yet offered their report. A call to Weddell in the ImpSec clinic labs elicited mostly snarls at the interruption, but also a promise of more information soon. Soon, but not yet.

His restless prowling around his room was interrupted in turn by a call from a very bleary Ivan, who reported the original biocontainer box had been duly examined and returned by Forensics, and could he for God's sakes give the damn thing to somebody else and go off-duty and go to bed now? Miles flinched guiltily, glad Ivan could not detect sleep on his breath over a comconsole, and ordered him to return the box to the guardianship of the Evidence Rooms, and take the rest of the day off.

He was just stepping into the bath when his comconsole chimed again. This time it was Dr. Chenko, from the Imperial Military Hospital's veterans clinic.

"Lord Vorkosigan." Chenko ducked his head in cheery greetings. "My apologies for taking so long. These micro-engineering challenges always prove a little more complex in the execution than the planning. But we've worked up a device small enough to insert under your skull to, we hope safely, trigger your seizures, and we're finally ready to test it on you. If it works properly, we can go ahead with the final calibrations and schedule surgery to install it."

"Oh," said Miles. "Good work." *Bad timing*.

"When can you come in? Tomorrow?"

Haroche might call with the systems team's report at any time, and when that happened, Miles suspected, things would start to move very quickly. And . . . somewhere in Vorbarr Sultana was a very clever ImpSec-trained man who had made Miles his special target. Did Chenko's experimental gizmo use any protein circuits, and what *had* happened to that missing capsule? The thought of people he didn't know very well installing devices he didn't understand into his brain gave him cold chills, just now. "I . . . probably not tomorrow. I'll have to get back to you on scheduling, Doctor."

Chenko looked disappointed. "Have you had any more episodes since the one we forced in the lab?"

"Not so far."

"Hm. Well, I'd advise you not to wait too long, my lord."

"I understand. I'll do my best."

"And avoid stress," Chenko added as an afterthought, as Miles reached for the disconnect.

"Thank you, Doctor," Miles growled at the empty vid plate.

He was halfway through his shower when he suddenly recalled that this was the night of Laisa's party. His attendance had been just short of Imperially commanded; and his duties, it appeared, were going to permit. At the very least, it would be well to seize the chance beforehand to get in an interim report to Gregor. All he needed was to dredge up a dance partner.

He dressed carefully, and called Delia Koudelka.

"Hi," he greeted her blondness. At least he didn't get a crick in his neck looking up, over a comconsole. "What are you doing tonight?"

"I'm . . . rather busy," she responded politely. "Why do you ask?"

"Oh." Damn. His own fault, for waiting till the last minute, and just assuming . . .

"Or—this doesn't have anything to do with your Imperial Auditor thing, does it?" she added in worry.

A vision of a splendid opportunity to abuse his new powers danced in his head, briefly. Regretfully, he pushed it aside. "No. Just a Miles-thing."

"Sorry," she said, sounding sincere.

"Um . . . is Martya in?"

"She's busy tonight too, I'm afraid."

"And Olivia?"

"Her, too."

"Ah. Well, thanks anyway."

"Whatever for?" She cut the com.

TWENTY-FOUR

Miles's verbal report to Gregor made them both late for the party; Gregor had dozens of questions, most of which Miles could not yet answer. He chewed on his lip in frustration as they paused in the shadowed vestibule opening onto one of the Imperial Residence's smaller reception rooms. It was already bright and crowded with people. In the chamber next to it, visible through arched doors thrown open, a small orchestra was tuning up.

Colonel Lord Vortala the younger, in charge of the Residence's security tonight, had escorted Miles and the Emperor there personally. Vortala, who looked both neat and harried simultaneously, now saluted and broke away back into the hallway, already answering some subordinate though his headset.

"It's hard to get used to not having Illyan at my back," sighed Gregor, staring after him. "Though Vortala's doing a fine job," he added hastily. He glanced down at Miles. "Try not to look so grim. Even without your Auditor's chain, it will make people curious what we've been up to, and then we'll both have to spend the rest of the evening trying to squelch gossip."

Miles nodded. "Same goes for you." He couldn't think of any good, or even awful, jokes just at the moment. "Think of Laisa," he advised.

Gregor's face lightened right up; smiling dryly in turn, Miles followed him into the chamber. There they completed Gregor's happiness by finding Dr. Toscane, under Lady Alys's wing as usual. Countess Vorkosigan also stood with them, chatting amiably.

"Oh, good," said the Countess. "Here they are." Gregor captured Laisa's hand, and placed it on his arm, possessively; she smiled up at him with starry eyes. The Countess continued, "Alys, now that her proper escort is here, why don't you let me play Baba for a while. You ought to relax and enjoy yourself at one of these things for a change." A slight inclination of her head: Miles followed the nod to notice Illyan, quite sharp in a dark and unusually well cut civilian-style tunic and trousers, yet managing by pure habit to look not-quite-there, as if light parted to flow around him.

"Thank you, Cordelia," murmured Lady Alys. After Gregor greeted his former security chief, and they exchanged some standard how-are-you-feeling, fine, Sire, you-look-well party chat, Alys determinedly bore Illyan off, before he could slip back into any kind of attempted work-mode.

"His convalescence does seem to be going well," said Gregor, watching this byplay in approval.

"You can thank Lady Alys for that," Countess Vorkosigan told him.

"Your son too."

"So I understand."

Miles bowed slightly, and not altogether ironically. He glanced after Illyan and his aunt, who were apparently heading for the refreshment tables. "Not that I'm intimately familiar with the contents of Illyan's closet, but . . . there's something different about the way he's dressed, I swear. Conservative as hell, as always, but . . ."

Countess Vorkosigan smiled. "Lady Alys finally persuaded him to let her recommend a tailor. His taste, or lack of it, in clothing has made her tear her hair for years."

"I always thought it was part of his ImpSec persona. Blandly invisible."

"That, too, certainly."

Gregor and Laisa began comparing what they had been doing for the interminable four hours since they'd last met, a conversation mainly absorbing to its principals; Miles, having spotted Ivan across the room, left them together under his mother's indulgent eye. Ivan was escorting Martya Koudelka, ah ha.

Martya was a younger, shorter, and tawnier version of Delia, though no less striking in her own way. She wore something pale green tonight, in a shade perfectly calculated to complement Imperial dress uniforms.

As Miles neared them, Martya poked her partner and said, "Ivan, you twit, stop watching my sister. You asked *me* to this dance, remember?"

"Yes, but . . . I asked her first."

"You were too slow off the mark. Serve you right if I step on your boots and spoil the shine." She glanced aside at Miles, and added to him, "I'm going to be so glad when Delia finally picks someone, and moves out. I'm getting as tired of hand-me-down men as I am of hand-me-down clothes."

"As well you should be, milady." Miles bowed over her hand, and kissed it.

That got Ivan's attention; he repossessed Martya's hand, and patted it soothingly. "Sorry," he apologized. But his eyes shifted left for one more surreptitious glance.

Miles looked too, and spotted the bright blond head at once. Delia Koudelka was seated on one of the little sofas next to Duv Galeni; they were apparently sharing the plate of hors d'oeuvres balanced on Galeni's knee. The dark head and the blond bent together for a moment, then Delia laughed. Galeni's long teeth flashed in one of his more saturnine smiles. Galeni's knee was touching Delia's, Miles noted with unexpectedly keen interest.

A servitor with a tray of glasses circulated near. "Would you care for a drink?" Ivan asked Martya.

"Yes, please, but not that red stuff. White, please." Ivan departed in pursuit of the servitor, and Martya confided to Miles, "*When* I dribble it on myself, it won't show that way. I don't know how Delia does it. She never spills anything. Some days I feel like she's practicing to be Lady Alys."

Galeni hadn't mentioned he would be here—with Delia— when they'd spoken at ImpSec HQ . . . only yesterday? "How long has this been going on?" Miles asked Martya, with a jerk of his head in Galeni's direction.

Martya smirked. "Delia told our Da a month ago that Duv was going to be the one. She likes Duv's style, she says. I think he's all right, for an old fellow."

"I have style, too," Miles pointed out.

"One all your own," Martya agreed blandly.

Miles prudently decided not to follow up on that straight line. "Um . . . and when did old Duv find out?"

"Delia's working on it. Some fellows you have to hit with a brick to get their attention. Some you have to hit with a *big* brick."

As Miles was trying to figure out which category she thought he fell into, Ivan returned, balancing beverages. A few minutes later the first strains of music sounded from the next room; Ivan rescued Martya's gown from its rendezvous with spiced wine and bore her away for the dancing. If the civilian strangers' faces here were work-friends of Laisa's from the shipper's consortium, there was quite a sprinkling of other Komarrans in the crowd. Nothing political about this party, hah. Galeni's presence, Miles suspected, must be due to Laisa's hand in the guest list. Her best old friend, of course.

Miles grazed for a time on the hors d'oeuvres, splendid as always, then drifted into the next room to listen to the music and watch the dancers. He became keenly aware that his failure to pack along his own partner left him odd man out, and not the only one; the ratio of men to women present was easily ten to nine, if not ten to eight. He cadged one or two dances with women who knew him well enough not to mind his height, such as Henri Vorvolk's Countess, but all of them were depressingly married or attached. The rest of the time he practiced his best sinister Illyanesque holding-up-the-wall pose.

Illyan himself danced past with Alys Vorpatril. Ivan, pausing beside Miles to fortify himself with a cup of hot spiced wine, stared in astonishment.

"I didn't know old Illyan could dance," he commented.

"I sure didn't know he could dance that well," Miles agreed. Ivan was not the only one doing a double-take. Henri Vorvolk's wife, watching Alys and her partner sail by, whispered some comment in her husband's ear; he looked up with a bemused smile. "I've never seen Illyan do anything like that before. I suppose he was always on-duty." *Always.* Dr. Ruibal had mentioned personality changes as well as cognitive changes as a possible side effect of the chip removal . . . hell, just removing that thirty-year burden of crushing responsibility could account for it.

A wisp of hair escaped Lady Alys's elaborate beflowered coiffure, and she brushed it back from her forehead. The image of her *en deshabille* at breakfast burst in Miles's memory, and he had the sudden sensation of being hit with a *big* brick. He choked on his own wine.

Good God. Illyan's sleeping with my aunt.

And vice versa, or something. He wasn't sure if he should be indignant or pleased. The only clear thought that came to him was a suddenly renewed admiration for Illyan's cool nerve.

"Are you all right?" Ivan asked him.

"Oh, yes." *I think I will let Ivan figure this one out for himself.* He hid an uncontrollable grin by knocking back another gulp of wine.

He escaped Ivan and retreated into the reception room. At the buffet there he ran into Captain Galeni, selecting snacks for Delia, who waited demurely nearby. She favored Miles with a little, distant wave of her fingers.

"You, ah . . . found a new dance partner, I see," Miles commented to Galeni's ear.

Galeni smiled, like a pleased fox with its mouth full of feathers. "Yes."

"*I* was going to ask her to this thing. She said she was busy tonight."

"Too bad, Miles."

"Is this some kind of skewed symmetry?"

Galeni's black brows twitched. "I don't pretend I'm above a little revenge, but I'm an honorable man. I asked her first if she thought you were serious about her. She said no."

"Oh." Miles pretended to nibble on a fruit pastry. "And are you serious about her?" He felt like a stand-in for Commodore Koudelka, demanding to know Galeni's intentions.

"Deathly," Galeni breathed, his smile, for a moment, utterly gone from his eyes. Miles almost recoiled. Galeni blinked, and continued more lightly, "With her background and connections, she'd make a superb political hostess, don't you think?" The slow smile widened. "The brains and beauty don't hurt, either."

"No fortune," Miles pointed out.

Galeni shrugged. "I can do something about that myself, if I put my mind to it."

Miles had no doubt of it. "Well . . ." It would not quite do to say, *Better luck this time.* "Would you, ah . . . like me to put in a good word for you with her da the Commodore?"

"I hope you won't take this in bad part, Miles, but I would *really* rather you didn't try to do me any more favors."

"Oh. I can see that, I guess."

"Thank you. I don't care to repeat mistakes. I'm going to ask her tonight, on the way home." Galeni nodded in determination, and abandoned Miles without a backwards look.

Duv and Delia. Delia and Duv. They made an alliterative couple, anyway.

Miles fended off queries from two acquaintances who had heard garbled rumors about his Imperial Auditor's appointment, then ducked back into the music chamber, where conversation was more difficult. His brain, inexorably, began turning over last night's data, as he leaned and watched with unseeing eyes as the dancers swirled past. Ten or so minutes of this aimless glowering, and people were beginning to stare at him; he pushed off from the wall and went to beg a dance from Laisa while there was still time. Gregor would surely claim the last couple of rounds for himself.

He was absorbed in keeping the beat to a rather fast-paced mirror dance with Laisa, and trying not to appreciate his Emperor's fiancée's well-padded figure too openly, when he caught a glimpse of Galeni through the arched doors into the reception room. An ImpSec colonel and two enlisted guards in ordinary undress greens had accosted him; Galeni and the colonel stood arguing in some fierce undertone. Delia stood a little away from them, blue eyes wide, her hand touching her lips. Galeni was stiff-backed, his face set in that blank and burning look that suggested well-suppressed but dangerous rage. What ImpSec emergency could be dire enough to send them to fetch their top Komarran analyst out of a party? Worried, he slid and dipped and turned so as to put Laisa's back to the archway.

The colonel, gesturing urgently, put his hand on Galeni's sleeve; Galeni shook it off. One of the guards went for a grip on his stunner, loosening it in his holster.

Laisa, breathless, froze with him, then realized this was not a move of the dance. "Miles, what's wrong?"

"Excuse me, milady. I have to attend to something. Please go back to Gregor now." He bowed hastily and slipped around her; inevitably, her gaze followed him as he walked, a little too quickly, through the archway.

"What seems to be the trouble, gentlemen?" Miles asked quietly, coming up to the tense little group. If he couldn't alter the tone of the proceedings, he might at least lower the volume. Half the people in the room were staring already.

The colonel gave him an uncertain nod—he wasn't wearing his Auditor's chain, but the ImpSec man had to know who he was. "My lord. General Haroche has ordered the arrest of this man."

Miles concealed shock, and kept his voice down. "Why?"

"The charge was not specified. I'm required to remove him immediately from the Imperial Residence."

Galeni hissed to Miles, "What the hell is this, Vorkosigan? Do you have a hand in it?"

"No. I don't know. I didn't order this—" Was this connected with his case? And if so, how dare Haroche make a move on it that blindsided him?

Ivan and Martya drifted up too, looking concerned; the colonel looked increasingly rigid, watching his doubtless ordered-to-be-quiet arrest slipping out of his control.

"You got any unpaid traffic fines I don't know about, Duv?" Miles continued, trying to lighten the tone. Both guards had their hands on their stunners now.

"No, goddammit."

"Where is General Haroche right now?" Miles demanded of the colonel. "HQ?"

"No, my lord. He's following on. He'll be here shortly."

To report to Gregor? Haroche had better have an explanation for this. Miles sucked in his breath. "Look, Duv . . . I think you'd better go along quietly. I'll look into it."

The colonel shot him a grateful look; Galeni, one of baffled suspicion and enormous frustration. It was a lot to ask of Galeni, to eat this moment of public humiliation, but it could be worse; letting him get stunned or knocked around for resisting arrest at the Emperor's reception sprang to Miles's mind. That would capture the attention of *all* the people in the room.

Galeni glanced at Delia, a flash of agony in his dark eyes, then at Ivan. "Ivan, will you see Delia gets home all right?"

"Of course, Duv."

Delia was biting her lip; ten more seconds and *she* was going to mix into this, explosively, Miles gauged from some experience of her.

At Miles's hasty nod, the colonel and the guards eased Galeni out of the room, wisely letting him travel under his own steam, not touching him. Miles waved Ivan away, and followed down the corridor. As he'd feared, the minute they turned the corner, the two guards jammed Galeni up against the nearest wall, and began frisking and binding him.

Miles raised his voice a split second before Galeni rounded and swung on them. "That's not necessary, gentlemen!"

They paused; Galeni, with visible effort, unclenched his fists, if not his jaw, and shrugged them off rather than attempting to throw them bodily across the corridor.

"He'll go like a brother officer if you'll just permit it." His stern glance added silently, *Won't you, Duv*. Galeni brushed his tunic straight again, and nodded stiffly. "Colonel—what is Captain Galeni charged with *really*?"

The colonel cleared his throat. He dared not evade answer to an Imperial Auditor, regardless of what orders for public discretion Haroche might have given him. "Treason, m'lord."

"What?" Galeni bellowed, as Miles snapped, "Horseshit!" Miles's cautionary hand on Galeni's sleeve stopped more physically violent denial.

Miles took three breaths, for control, and to set Galeni a good example, and said, "Duv, I'll come see you as soon as I've talked to Haroche, all right?"

Galeni's nostrils flared, but he echoed, "All right." His teeth set, fortunately, on any further comment. He managed a reasonably dignified stride down the corridor as the arrest-squad escorted him out.

Miles boiled back toward the reception rooms. In the corridor just outside he was intercepted by a posse consisting of Gregor, Laisa, Delia, and his mother.

"What's going on, Miles?" Gregor asked.

"Why did those men take Duv away?" Laisa added, her eyes wide and alarmed.

"Miles, *do* something!" Delia demanded.

Countess Vorkosigan just watched, one arm crossed over her torso, the other hand to her mouth.

"I don't know. And I bloody should know!" Miles sputtered. "Galeni's just been arrested by ImpSec on"—he stole a glance at Laisa—"some vague charge. By order of Lucas Haroche himself, apparently."

"I must assume he had a reason . . ." began Gregor.

"I must assume he made a mistake!" said Delia hotly. "Cordelia, help!"

Countess Vorkosigan's gaze flicked up, past Miles's shoulder. "If you want your information ungarbled, go to the source. Here he comes now."

Miles wheeled to see Haroche round the corner, led by one of Gregor's Armsmen. Haroche's face was no less heavy than his tread. He strode up to the group and gave Gregor a formal nod, "Sire," and a more abbreviated one to Miles, "My Lord Auditor. I came as quickly as I could."

"What the hell is going on, Lucas?" Gregor said quietly. "ImpSec has just arrested one of my guests from the middle of my reception. I trust you can explain why." Did Haroche know Gregor well enough to detect the anger under that slight emphasis on the *mys*?

"My profound apologies, Sire. And to you too, Dr. Toscane. I fully appreciate the awkwardness. But ImpSec's mandate is to keep you—and yours"—a small nod to Laisa—"safe. I was given reason just this evening to suspect the loyalty of the man, and then discovered to my alarm that he was actually in your presence. I may err on the side of caution many times, but I dare not err on the side of carelessness even once. My first priority had to be the physical removal Captain Galeni; everything else, including explanations, could wait." He glanced at the women, and meaningfully away. "For those, I am now at your disposal, Sire."

"Oh." Gregor turned to Countess Vorkosigan, and made a vague frustrated gesture at Delia and Laisa. "Cordelia, would you . . . ?"

Countess Vorkosigan smiled very dryly. "Come, ladies. The gentlemen need to go talk."

"But I want to know what's going on!" protested Laisa.

"We can get it later. I'll explain the system to you. It's really stupid, but it can be made to work. Which, come to think of it, could also sum up a great many other Vor customs. In the meantime, we need to keep the show going out there"—she nodded toward the reception rooms—"and repair what damages we can from this, ah"—a sharp glance at Haroche, which should have made him wince—"unfortunate exercise in caution."

"Repair damages, how?" asked Laisa.

"Lie, dear. Alys and I will show you the drill. . . ." Countess Vorkosigan shepherded them away; Delia looked back over her shoulder at Miles, and mouthed, *Do something, dammit!*

"We'd better continue this in your office, Sire," Haroche murmured. "We'll want the comconsole. I brought copies of my security system team's report for each of you." He touched his tunic, and smiled grimly at Miles. "I figured you'd want to see it as soon as possible, my Lord Auditor."

"Oh. Good. Yes," admitted Miles. He fell in behind the two men as they paced down the corridor, and descended the turning stairs at its end; the Armsman brought up the rear, and took up his post outside Gregor's office. Gregor sealed the door behind them.

"My short list shrank abruptly, and unexpectedly," said Haroche. "If you will, Sire . . ." He nodded to the comconsole; Gregor turned it on. Haroche slotted one secured data card into the read-slot, and handed its twin to Miles. "I'm sure you'll want to study this in more detail later, but I can give you the quick synopsis now.

"As frames go, Miles, yours was very nearly perfect. The insertion of your false visit into the Evidence Rooms' log was extremely well executed; my team had the damnedest time finding any trace of how it was done. I was really starting to wonder. Then it occurred to me to have them recheck your retina scan. Your retina scan was subtly altered by your cryo-revival, were you aware?"

Miles shook his head. "Though I'm not surprised." *A lot of me was subtly altered by my cryo-revival.*

"It's said that every criminal makes one mistake. In my experience, this isn't necessarily true, but it happened this time. The retina scan on the Evidence Rooms' log was a copy from one made last year, not identical to your current one. As you can see on this overlay." Haroche made the two scans coalesce above the vid plate of Gregor's comconsole; the alterations sprang out, highlighted in purple, a malignant hungover cyclops stare. "And so you are cleared, my Lord Auditor." Haroche opened his hand.

"Thanks," growled Miles. *I was never accused.* "What does this have to do with Duv Galeni?"

"Bear with me. From the evidence, or lack of it, my team says that the Evidence Room comconsole record had to have been altered by a mole program Galeni physically inserted via its read-slot. That machine is one of the isolated ones. There was no other way."

"Galeni or someone," Miles corrected.

Haroche shrugged. "That's not how we tagged Galeni, however. The other point of attack I turned them loose on was of course the building's own admittance-log. That proved more fruitful. The log was *not* altered on-site, but at a remove, via its data links to other ImpSec HQ systems. My team had to peel it right down to the undercode level to find this one; I commend their dedication and patience to you, Sire, as well as their expertise." Haroche zipped though screen after screen of logic-links. "The significant items are highlighted in red; you can follow it out yourselves. They traced the alteration through to the section-head level—the system has lockouts in sections up to that level, y'see. Which the section-heads can override—myself, or rather my second-in-charge at Domestic Affairs, now—Allegre, Olshansky, the Galactic Affairs chief when he's here. They traced it *through* Allegre's comconsole, down to his Analysts' level. To Captain Galeni's comconsole."

Haroche sighed. "The affairs analysts in all our departments have an enormous amount of discretion as to the data they can access. I can't say *too much*, in all honesty; it's their job to review everything, since vital decisions are taken at higher levels based upon their reports and recommendations and opinions. I spent a couple of years in that job myself, in Domestic. But Galeni apparently used his analyst's codes to gain access to his superior's comconsole, and from there to leapfrog into the larger system."

"Or somebody using Galeni's comconsole did," Miles suggested. He felt sick to his stomach. The highlights on the vid display looked like smears of blood. "Is this really evidence?" *If one frame, why not two?* Or . . . as many as necessary, till they came up with a suspect Miles neither knew nor liked?

Haroche looked glum. "It may be all we can get. I'd give my arm to be able to question the man under fast-penta, but he was given the allergy treatment when he was promoted to his current position. Fast-penta would kill him. So we have to build our case the old hard way. Any physical evidence for the crime went up in smoke long ago. We're back to your motivations after all, my Lord Auditor. Which men in the Komarran Affairs analysis department had both access to knowledge of the bioengineered prokaryote, and some reason to do this? He had the access; he met with his father, Ser Galen, on Earth just before the original Komarran plot came to grief."

"I know," said Miles shortly. "I was there." *Oh, God, Duv . . .*

"I don't know how much weight to give the fact that your clone-brother shot Galeni's father—"

"If that were going to be a problem, it would have been a problem before this."

"Perhaps. But it must have left some residue of feeling. Then, on top of that, you recently became instrumental in destroying his marital plans."

"He's over that."

"What marital plans?" asked Gregor.

Miles gritted his teeth. *Haroche, you idiot.* "At one time, Duv was rather interested in Laisa. Which is how he came to escort her to your ambassadorial reception, where you met. Duv has since, um, found another love interest."

"Oh," said Gregor, looking stricken. "I didn't quite realize . . . things were that serious between Laisa and Galeni."

"It was one-sided."

Haroche shook his head. "I'm sorry, Miles. But the man called *you*, and I quote, a 'smarmy goddamn little pimp.'" Haroche's gaze grew abstracted, his expression for a moment so like Illyan giving one of his verbatim quotes from his chip that Miles drew in his breath. "And went on to declaim quite passionately, 'Vor does mean thief. And you goddamn Barrayaran thieves stick together all right. You and your fucking precious Emperor and the whole damn pack of you.' And you seriously expect me to construe he merely felt mild inconvenience?"

Gregor's eyebrows rose.

"It was to my face," snapped Miles. From the look on Gregor's, the Emperor did not see why this remark constituted a defense. "Not to my back," Miles tried to explain. "Never to my back, not Galeni. It's . . . not his style." He added to Haroche, "Where the hell did you get that? Does ImpSec have all its analysts' private comconsoles monitored, now? Or had someone targeted Galeni before Illyan ever went down?"

Haroche cleared his throat. "Not Galeni's comconsole, in fact, my lord. Yours."

"What!"

"All the public channels in Vorkosigan House are monitored by the ImpSec chief's own office, for security. They have been for decades. The only three that are not are the Count and the Countess's personal machines, and your personal machine. Surely your parents mentioned this to you before. They knew."

Monitored by Illyan, of course. His father and mother would not have objected to that. And he'd taken Galeni's call that night in . . . the comconsole station in the guest suite, right. Miles subsided, seething, but mostly with his mind whirling, trying to remember everything he'd said in the last three months to anyone over any comconsole in Vorkosigan House.

"Your loyalty to your friend does you great credit, Miles," Haroche went on. "But I'm not so sure he's any friend of yours."

"No," said Miles. "No. I *know* what Galeni paid to get here. He wouldn't piss it down the wind for some . . . personal ire. This is a trail of smoke and mirrors. And anyway, even granted Galeni has some motivation to frame me, what about the original crime? What motive did he have to take out Illyan in the first place?"

Haroche shrugged. "Political, perhaps. There are thirty years of bad blood between ImpSec under Illyan, and some Komarrans. I agree the case is not complete by any means, but it should be easier to pursue now that we have a real direction."

Gregor looked almost distraught. "I had hoped my marriage might do some little part toward healing things with Komarr. A truly unified empire . . ."

"It will," Miles assured him. "Doubly so, if Galeni ends up marrying a Barrayaran." *If he doesn't get jailed first on some trumped-up treason charge, that is.* "You know how Imperial fashions go; you're sure to start a big fad in cross-planetary romances. And given the shortage of Barrayaran girl babies our parents created in our generation, a mob of us are going to have to import wives anyway."

Gregor's lips crooked up, in sad appreciation of Miles's attempted humor.

Miles gripped his copy of the report. "I want to review this."

"Please do," said Haroche. "Sleep on it. And if you can find anything in it that I haven't, let me know. I'm not happy to find any of my ImpSec people are disloyal, regardless of their planet of origin."

Haroche took his farewells; Miles followed immediately, sending a residence servant to find Martin and have his car brought around. If he went back to the party, he'd be jumped by women demanding explanations and action, neither of which he could offer right now. He did not envy Gregor his task of returning and having to socialize as if nothing had happened.

———※※※———

He was in the Count's groundcar, halfway between the Imperial Residence and ImpSec, when his view through the canopy of some dilapidated buildings, with brightly lit towers behind, suddenly sharpened. They took on an abrupt unreal reality, as if grown denser, overpowering, as if about to be outlined in green fire. He had just time to think, *Oh shit oh shit oh shi*—before the whole scene dissolved into the familiar colored confetti, then darkness.

He returned to consciousness laid out on the car's backseat, with Martin's panicked form looming over him in the dim yellow light. His tunic was ripped open. The canopy was raised to the night mist, and he shivered in the cold.

"Lord Vorkosigan? My lord, oh hell, are you dying? Stop it, stop it!"

"Unh . . ." he managed. It came out a muffled groan to his ringing ears. His mouth hurt; he touched his wet lips, and his fingers came away smeared, red-brown in this light, with fresh blood.

" 'S all right, Martin. Only, uh, seizure."

"Is *that* what they look like? I couldn't think but what you'd been poisoned or shot or something." Martin looked only slightly relieved.

He tried to sit up; Martin's big hands opened in hovering uncertainty whether to help him up or shove him back down. Both his tongue and his lower lip were bitten, and bleeding freely over his best House uniform.

"Should I take you to a hospital or a doctor, my lord? Which one?"

"No."

"Let me take you back home, at least, then. Maybe . . ." Martin's harried face brightened with hope. "Maybe your lady mother will be there soon."

"And take me off your hands?" Miles grunted a pained laugh. *She's not going to kiss it and make it well, Martin. No matter how much she might like to.*

He wanted desperately to go on to ImpSec HQ. He'd promised Galeni. . . . But he hadn't properly reviewed the new data, and the team of men he'd want to question about it when he had were undoubtedly gone home to a well-earned night's rest. And he was still shaken, and dizzy with the postseizure lassitude.

The military medical people were all too right. The stress-triggered aspect of the damned seizures virtually *guaranteed* they would always occur at the most inconvenient possible moment. Unfit for duty indeed, any duty. Unfit.

I hate this.

"Home, Martin," he sighed.

TWENTY-FIVE

Miles woke the next morning with what he was coming to recognize as a postseizure hangover. A couple of painkiller tablets helped only slightly. If anything, the symptoms were getting worse with time, not better. Or maybe he was simply becoming more accurate in identifying them, now that they were not masked by a stunner-migraine or suicidal depression. *I have to see Chenko soon.*

He carried a carafe of coffee up to his room, and locked himself in with his comconsole and Haroche's report. He spent, or wasted, the rest of the morning reviewing it, then re-reviewing it.

The very scantiness of the data made it all the more convincing. If this was supposed to be a double-frame, there ought to be *more* of it. It was strongly suggestive, but not quite proof. But try as he might, he could spot no flaw in its reasoning, no break in the flow of its logic.

With nothing more optimistic to report than this, he dreaded seeing Galeni again. ImpSec had held the Komarran-born officer overnight in the temporary cells at ImpSec HQ, a small section which had replaced the more extensive downstairs dungeons of Ezar's times. There Galeni sat, pending the formal leveling of charges, after which he would presumably be moved to some more official, and dreary, military prison. *Held on suspicion.* Barrayaran military law was a trifle unclear just how *long* one could be held on suspicion. *Held on bloody paranoia is more like it.*

His sour meditations were interrupted by a call from Dr. Weddell, plaintively demanding to know when *he* could go home.

Miles promised to come take his report and let him out; if he couldn't spring one ImpSec prisoner, he at least might spring another. He donned a fresh, if second-best, House uniform and his Auditor's chain, daubed more stim-salve on his lacerated lip, and called Martin to bring his car around.

The medicinal and chemical odors of the ImpSec HQ clinic still gave Miles unpleasant fluttering sensations in his belly. He entered and found the laboratory chamber Weddell had taken over. A rumpled cot in the corner gave evidence that the galactic bioexpert was following orders, and had not left the sample or his data unattended. Weddell himself was still wearing his same clothes from yesterday morning, though he'd obviously managed to shave between times. He was somewhat less bleary than Miles, which wasn't saying much.

"Well, my Lord Auditor. You probably won't be surprised to learn I have positively identified your find as the same prokaryote that was used on Chief Illyan. It's even the same batch." He led Miles to the lab's comconsole, and embarked on a detailed comparison of the two samples, with visual aids and highlights, and mild self-congratulations when the silent Imperial Auditor was not forthcoming with any.

"I spoke with Illyan," said Miles. "He reports no memory of ever having swallowed a small brown capsule in the last four months. Unfortunately, his memory isn't what it used to be."

"Oh, it wasn't *swallowed*," Weddell stated positively. "It was never designed to be swallowed."

"How do you know?"

"The capsule was neither permeable nor soluble. It was meant to be broken—a pinch of the fingers would do—and the sample mixed with air and breathed. The vector encapsulation design is obviously meant to be airborne. It's quite sporelike."

"The which what?"

"Here." Weddell banished the vid of the molecular chain presently occupying the vid plate, and brought up an image of an object that looked for all the world like a spherical satellite, bristling with antennae. "The actual prokaryotes would have been unmanageably tiny, if someone had simply attempted to load them naked into those large capsules. Instead, they are contained in these hollow sporelike particles"—Weddell pointed to the vid plate—"which float in air until they contact a wet surface, such as mucous membrane or bronchia. At that point, the delivery units dissolve, releasing their load."

"Could you see them in the air, like smoke or dust? Smell them?"

"If the light was strong I suppose one might see a brief puff as they were initially distributed, but then they would appear to vanish. They would be odorless."

"How long . . . would they hang in the air?"

"Several minutes, at least. Depending on the efficiency of the ventilation."

Miles stared in fascination at the malignant-looking sphere. "This is new information." Though he did not, offhand, see how it helped much.

"It was not possible to reconstruct it from the eidetic chip," noted Weddell a bit stiffly, "as no part of the vector encapsulation would ever reach the chip. There were several other potential means of administration."

"I . . . quite understand. Yes. Thank you." He pictured himself going back to Illyan: *Can you remember every breath you took in the last four months?* Once, Illyan might have.

A bleep from the comconsole interrupted his thoughts; the delivery-spore vanished and was replaced by the head of General Haroche.

"My Lord Auditor." Haroche nodded diffidently at Miles. "My apologies for interrupting you. But since you're in the building, I wonder if you could stop in and see me. At your convenience, of course, when you're done in the labs and so on."

Miles sighed. "Certainly, General." At least it gave him an excuse to put off seeing Galeni for a few more minutes. "I'll be up to your office shortly."

Miles took possession of the code-card containing Weddell's report, and the resealed residue of the sample, and released the man, who departed gratefully. Miles's step quickened as he paced down the too-familiar hallways of ImpSec HQ, up and around to Illyan's old office, Haroche's new one. Maybe, pray God, Haroche had found something fresh to share, something to render this whole tangle less painful.

————※◎※————

Haroche locked his office door behind Miles, and courteously pulled up a chair for the Imperial Auditor, close to his comconsole desk. "Have you had any second thoughts since last night, my lord?" Haroche inquired.

"Not really. Weddell has identified the sample, all right. You'll probably want to make a copy of this."

He handed Weddell's data card across to Haroche, who nodded and ran it through his comconsole's read-slot. "Thank you." He handed the original back to Miles and went on, "I've been taking a closer look at the other four senior Komarran Affairs analysts in Allegre's department. None were as well positioned as Galeni to know of the existence of the Komarran sample, and two can be eliminated outright by that very test. The other two lack any motivation that I can uncover."

"The perfect crime," muttered Miles.

"Almost. The truly perfect crime is the one which is never discovered at all; this came very close. Your frame, now, was by all indications a backup plan of some kind, and necessarily less than perfect."

"I never rammed a perfect tactical plan through to reality in my whole time with the Dendarii Mercenaries," Miles sighed. "The best I ever did was *good enough*."

"You can be assured, Domestic Affairs never did much better," Haroche admitted.

"This is all very circumstantial, without a confession."

"Yes. And I'm not sure how to elicit one. Fast-penta is out. I wondered . . . if you might be able to help in that regard. Given your knowledge of the man. Use your noted powers of persuasion on him."

"I might," said Miles, "if I thought Galeni was guilty."

Haroche shook his head. "We may want more evidence, but I'm not optimistic that we're going to get more. You often must proceed with the imperfect, because you must proceed. You can't stop."

"Let the juggernaut roll on, regardless of what gets squashed underneath?" Miles's brows rose. "How *are* you planning to proceed?"

"A court-martial, probably. The case must be closed properly. As you pointed out, this one can't be left hanging."

What would a court-martial make of this, with ImpSec breathing down its neck urging swift decision? Guilty? Not guilty? Or a more foggy, Not proven? He must find a top military attorney, to evaluate the case. . . . "No, dammit. I don't want a panel of military judges guessing, and then going home to dinner. If the outcome is to be guessed, I can guess myself, all day long. I want to *know*. You have to keep looking. We can't just stop with Galeni."

Haroche blew out his breath, and rubbed his chin. "Miles,

you're asking me to unleash a witch-hunt, here. Potentially very damaging to my organization. You'd have me turn ImpSec upside down, and for what? If the Komarran *is* guilty—and I'm provisionally convinced he is—you'll have to go very far indeed to produce a suspect more to your taste. Where will you stop?"

Not here, for damn sure. "The Empress-to-be is not going to be happy with you. Or with me."

Haroche grimaced. "I'm aware. She seems a very nice young woman, and it gives me no pleasure to think this may cause her distress, but I took my oath to *Gregor*. So did you."

"Yes."

"If you have nothing more concrete to offer, I'm ready to lay the charges and let the court-martial sort it out."

You can lay the charges, but I'll not light the fuse. . . . "I could decline to close my Auditor's case."

"If the court-martial convicts, you'll have to close it, my lord."

No, I won't. The realization made him blink. He could keep his Auditor's inquiry open *forever* if he so chose, and there wasn't a damned thing Haroche could do about it. No wonder Haroche was being so exquisitely polite today. Miles could even veto the court-martial. . . . But Imperial Auditors were traditionally circumspect with their vast powers. From a large pool of experienced men, they were chosen not for the glory of their former careers, but for their long records of utmost personal probity. Fifty years of life's tests were normally considered barely enough to smoke out the likely candidates. He ought not to screw with ImpSec's internal rules any more than the bare minimum necessary to—

Haroche smiled wearily. "We may end up having to agree to disagree, but try to see my view. Galeni was your friend once, and I sympathize with your dismay at the turn things have taken. This is what I can do. I can drop the treason charge, and reduce it to assault on a superior officer. Minimize the distress. A year in prison, a simple dishonorable discharge, and Galeni walks away. You might even use whatever pull you have to gain him an Imperial pardon, and spare him the prison. I've no great objection, as long as he's gotten out of *here*."

Thus destroying Galeni's career, and any future political ambitions . . . and Galeni had been an ambitious man, anxious to serve Komarr in that new and more peaceful future Gregor had envisioned, immensely conscious of his opportunities there. "A pardon is for the guilty," said Miles. "It's not the same thing as an acquittal."

Haroche scratched his head, and grimaced again, or maybe that was intended to be a smile. "I . . . really had another reason for asking you up here, Lord Vorkosigan. I'm looking to the future on more than one front." Haroche hesitated for a long moment, then went on, "I took the liberty of requisitioning a copy of your Imp-Mil neurologist's medical reports on your condition. Your seizure disorder. I thought his plan of treatment sounded promising."

"ImpSec," Miles murmured, "always was ubiquitous as cockroaches. First tap my comconsole, then my medical files . . . remind me to shake out my boots, tomorrow morning."

"My apologies, my lord. I think you'll forgive me. I had to know the particulars, before I could say what I'm about to say. But if this controlled-seizure device proves to work as you hope . . ."

"It only controls the symptoms. It's not a cure."

Haroche opened his hand, dismissing the difference. "A matter of medical definition, not practical use. I'm a practical man. I've been studying the reports of your Dendarii missions for ImpSec. You and Simon Illyan made an extraordinary team."

We were the best, oh yes. Miles grunted, neutrally, suddenly uncertain of just where Haroche was leading.

Haroche smiled wryly. "Filling Illyan's place is a damned big challenge. I'm reluctant to give up any advantage. Now that I've had a chance to work with you in person, and look over your records in real detail . . . I'm increasingly sure that Illyan made a serious mistake when he discharged you."

"It was no mistake. I more than deserved what I got." His mouth was growing dry.

"I don't think so. I think Illyan overreacted. A written censure appended to your records would have been enough, in my view." Haroche shrugged. "You could have added it to your collection. I've worked with your sort before, willing to take risks no one else is willing to take, to get results no one else is able to obtain. I like results, Miles. I like them a lot. The Dendarii Mercenaries were a great resource, for ImpSec."

"They still are. Commodore Quinn will take your money. And deliver your goods." His heart was beginning to pound.

"This woman Quinn is unknown to me, and not Barrayaran. I'd much prefer—if your medical treatment is successful—to reinstate you."

He had to swallow, in order to breathe. "Everything . . . to be as it was before? Take up where I left off?" *The Dendarii . . . Admiral Naismith . . .*

"Not exactly where you left off, no. By my calculations you were about two years overdue for your promotion to captain, for one thing. But I think you and I could be a team just as you and Illyan were." A small twinkle lit Haroche's eye. "You will perhaps forgive me my touch of ambition if I say, maybe even better? I'd be proud to have you on board, Vorkosigan."

Miles sat stunned. For a moment, all he could think, idiotically, was *I'm sure glad I had that seizure last night, or I'd be rolling on this carpet again right now.* "I . . . I . . ." His hands were shaking, his head exploding with joy. *Yes! Yes! Yes!* "I'd . . . have to close this case first. Give Gregor back his choke-chain. But then . . . sure!" His injured lip split again as it stretched, painfully, into an unstoppable grin. He sucked salt blood from it.

"Yes," said Haroche patiently, "that's exactly what I've been saying."

An ice-water wash seemed to pour down through the middle of Miles's chest, quenching his hot exaltation. *What?* He scarcely felt able to think straight. A memory filled his inner vision, of a docking bay crammed wall-to-wall with Dendarii troopers chanting, *Naismith, Naismith, Naismith!*

My first victory.

. . . Do you remember what it cost?

His grin had become fixed. "I . . . I . . . I . . ." He swallowed twice, and cleared his throat. As if echoing from some far-off tunnel he heard his voice—which *him*?—saying, "I'm going to have to think about this, General."

"Please do," said Haroche genially. "Take your time. But don't leave me in suspense forever—I can already imagine a use for the Dendarii in a certain situation which looks to be looming out near Kline Station. I'd love to discuss it with you, if you're in. I'd like your advice."

Miles's eyes were wide and dilated, his face pale and damp. "Thank you, General," he choked out. "Thank you very . . ."

He scrambled out of his chair, still smiling with bleeding lips. He almost caromed off the door frame like a drunken man; Haroche keyed the door open for him just in time. A mumbled word to Haroche's secretary had Martin and the groundcar waiting for Miles by the time he reached the building's exit.

Miles waved Martin away, and sat alone in the rear compartment. He silvered the canopy, and wished he might as easily blank out the shocky expression on his face. He felt as if he was fleeing a battlefield. But where was the wound in all this grinning glory?

He didn't stop retreating till he was back at Vorkosigan House. He ducked past his mother's retainers, and swung wide around Illyan's guest suite. He locked himself in his own bedroom, and began to pace, till he found his gaze fixated on his comconsole. It seemed to stare back at him with Horus eyes. He fled up one floor further, to the little spare room with the old wing chair. It felt small enough at last to contain him, soothing as a straitjacket. He didn't bring the brandy or the knife, this time. They would have been redundant.

He locked the door, and flung himself into the wing-chair. Not just his hands but his whole body was shaking.

His old job back. Everything to be as it was before.

Tell me about denial now, huh? He'd thought he was over Naismith. Lord Vorkosigan had the upper hand, right. Pretend not to care Naismith was gone. Pretend to walk on water, while he was about it, why not? *So that's why I feel like I'm drowning. The truth comes out.*

You want it? Want the Dendarii back?

Yes!

But was he medically fit for it, *really?* So, he'd have to stay in the damned tactics room, and not go out with the squads anymore. What was new about that? He could manage the thing. He'd been defying his disabilities all his life; this was just another one in a long string. He knew how. *I can do it. Somehow.*

He could have Quinn back. And Taura, for all the precious bit of time she had left.

Except for the small, sly, demonic whisper at the back of his brain, *There's just one little hitch. . . .*

Finally, painfully, he sidled around to look at it, out of the corner of his eye, then square-on.

Haroche wants me to sacrifice Galeni. Miles closing his case, and letting Haroche get on with running ImpSec unimpeded, was to be Miles's ticket back to the Dendarii. An Imperial Auditor had broad powers, but they surely stopped short of ordering ImpSec to reemploy one. That authority was wholly at Haroche's discretion.

He rocked in his chair, his feet tapping in a fractured rhythm. But what if Galeni *was* guilty? Speaking of denial. Haroche's witch-hunt fears were very compelling. Miles and Galeni had been friends. If it had been any other man accused, someone he didn't know, would he be so picky about it right now? Or would he have been quite content with Haroche's evidence?

Dammit, this wasn't about friendship. It was about knowledge. Character judgment. *I used to be good at personnel, I thought.* Was he to doubt that judgment now? But hell, people were strange. Subtle and twisty. You never *really* knew everything about them, even after years of friendship. Relatives even less.

His hands flexed on the chair arms. He found himself suddenly thinking of that jump-pilot he'd ordered Sergeant Bothari to question, on his very first encounter with the Dendarii and his destiny, thirteen years ago. It bothered him extremely that he could not now remember the man's name, though he had spoken, hypocritically, at his funeral. They'd desperately needed the pilot's access-codes, to save lives. And Bothari had got them, through the roughest of ready means, and they had saved lives, Miles supposed. Though not the jump-pilot's.

His first military career had begun with a human sacrifice. Maybe another one was required for its renewal. He'd sacrificed friends enough before, God knew, led them into one bloody good cause or another but not led them back out. And they hadn't all been volunteers.

I want, I want . . . Had Haroche read the naked longing in his face? Yes, of course; Miles had seen the knowledge in Haroche's smug eyes, in the easy certainty of his smile, in his casually tented hands reflected darkly in the black glass. Powerful hands, that could give or withhold so much at will. *He sees me, oh yes.* Miles's eyes narrowed, and his sore lips parted. His breath puffed on the chill air of the tiny room, as if he'd just been rabbit-punched in the stomach.

Oh, God. This isn't just a job offer. This is a bribe. Lucas Haroche had just tried to bribe an Imperial Auditor.

Tried? Or succeeded?

We'll get back to that.

And what a bribe. What a *sweet* bribe. Could Miles even prove it *was* a bribe, and not sincere admiration?

I'm sure. Oh, I'm sure. Lucas Haroche, you subtle son of a bitch, I underestimated you from Day One. So much for Miles's vaunted character judgment.

He should not have underestimated Haroche. Haroche was just as much Illyan's handpicked man as Miles was. Illyan liked weasels. But Illyan had a knack for keeping them under control. Haroche's bland, controlled, former-noncom style was a mask for a razor-sharp mind. Haroche, too, got results, any way he could, or he would not have risen to head of Domestic Affairs, not under Illyan.

Haroche would not have dared to float his suggestion unless he was sure of Miles. And why not? With access to all of Illyan's files, he'd had ample opportunity to study Admiral Naismith's career from end to end. *Especially this end.* Haroche knew what a fellow weasel the little Admiral was. He could confidently predict Miles would sacrifice everything up to and including his integrity to keep Naismith, because he'd already done it once. No virgins here.

His captaincy. His *captaincy. Haroche certainly had no trouble figuring out where my on-switch was located.* But Haroche was a loyal weasel, Miles would swear, loyal to Gregor and the Imperium, a true brother in arms. If money meant anything to the man, Miles had seen no hint of it. His passion was his ImpSec service, like Illyan himself, like Miles too. The work he had taken over from Illyan.

Miles's breath stopped; for a moment, he felt as frozen as any cryo-corpse.

No. The work Haroche had taken *away* from Illyan.

Oh.

Miles bent double in his chair, and began to swear, softly and horribly. He was dizzy with fury and shame, but mostly with fury. *I'm blind, blind, blind! Motive! What's an elephant got to do around here, to advance and be recognized?*

It was Haroche, Haroche all the time, had to be. Haroche who'd blown out Illyan's brains, in order to steal his *job.*

Of course the comconsole records were all beautifully choreographed. Haroche had *all* of Illyan's override codes, lots of time to play, and a decade's knowledge of the ImpSec HQ internal system. Miles shot out of his chair, and began to pace, practically running from side to side in the tiny room, slapping his palm into the wall hard enough to sting at every second turn. This elephant was very like a snake, all right.

It's Haroche, dammit, I know it is.

Oh, yeah? Prove it, Imperial Auditor-boy.

All the physical evidence had gone up in smoke, and all the documentation was entirely under Haroche's control. Miles had a hell of a lot less on Haroche than Haroche had on Galeni.

He couldn't just accuse the man out of thin air; he'd be counteraccused of God-knew-what, hysteria at the very least. An Imperial Auditor had power, but so did the Chief of ImpSec. He'd get one chance only, then Haroche would turn on him. *Real strange things could start to happen to me. Untraceable things.* In fact, the moment he failed to come back with an acceptance of Haroche's fantastic bribe, Haroche would know Miles knew. *There's not much time.*

Motivation. Judgment. Proof. Smoke.

He flung himself to the floor and lay glaring at the ceiling; his clenched fists pounded, once, on the worn and frayed carpet.

But . . . suppose he played along with Haroche. Took his bribe and lay in wait, to get him later, at some better opportunity. Miles could have the Dendarii *and* justice.

Yes!

Haroche and Miles would belong to each other, for a time, or Haroche could be lulled into thinking so. . . . Belatedly, it occurred to Miles that if this was a bribe, Haroche's oily flattery of him back in Illyan's office, all that *You and Illyan were such a great team*, was pure horseshit. Haroche was not in love with Admiral Naismith. And how long would it be till Haroche arranged Miles's "accidental" death, and no cryo-revival this time? An ImpSec field agent's life was a gamble anyway. Honor among thieves, hah. It would be a fascinating race, to see who could get the other first. Death, the traditional reward of treason, on a slow fuse, burning from the middle toward both ends. *What a life we'd lead, for a little while. Highly stimulating.*

A knock at the door derailed his thoughts, crashingly. He flinched in place, on his back on the floor, hyper-reactive. "Who is it?" he gasped.

"Miles?" came his mother's low alto, vibrant with concern. "Are you all right in there?"

"You're not having one of your seizures, are you?" Illyan's voice seconded the Countess.

"No . . . no. I'm all right."

"What are you *doing*?" the Countess asked. "We heard a lot of footsteps, and a thump through the ceiling. . . ."

He fought to keep his words even. "Just . . . wrestling with temptation."

Illyan's voice came back, amused. "Who's winning?"

Miles's eye followed the cracks in the plaster, overhead. His voice came out high and light, on a sigh: "I think . . . I'm going for the best two falls out of three."

Illyan laughed. "Right. See you later."

"I'll be down soon, I think."

Their footsteps receded, voices muted and gone.

Lucas Haroche, I believe I hate you.

But suppose Miles could know in advance that Haroche was going to play straight with him. It was possible. Suppose the offer had been only and exactly what it had seemed, no knife to the back later? What answer then? What answer ever?

Haroche had Admiral Naismith figured, all right, forward and back. Naismith would cry *Yes!*, and try to weasel out of the deal after. But Haroche didn't know Lord Vorkosigan. How could he? Practically no one did, not even Miles. *I just met the man myself.* He'd known a boy by that name, long ago, confused and passionate and army-mad. Properly, that boy had been left behind by Admiral Naismith, striking out for his larger identity, his wider world. But this new Lord Vorkosigan was someone else altogether, and Miles scarcely dared guess his future.

Miles was abruptly weary, sick to death of the noise inside his own head. Haroche the puppet-master had him running in circles, trying to bite himself in the back. What if he didn't play Haroche's dizzying game? What if he just . . . stopped? What other game was there?

Who are you, boy?

. . . Who are you who asks?

On the thought a blessed silence came, an empty clarity. He took it at first for utter desolation, but desolation was a kind of free fall, perpetual and without ground below. This was stillness: balanced, solid, weirdly serene. No momentum to it at all, forward or backwards or sideways.

I am who I choose to be. I always have been what I chose . . . though not always what I pleased.

His mother had often said, *When you choose an action, you choose the consequences of that action.* She had emphasized the corollary of this axiom even more vehemently: when you desired a consequence you had damned well better take the action that would create it.

He lay drained of tension, not moving, and content to be so. The oddly stretched moment was like a bite of eternity, eaten on the run. Was this quiet place inside something new-grown, or had he just never stumbled across it before? How could so vast a thing lay undiscovered for so long? His breathing slowed, and deepened.

I elect to be . . . myself.

Haroche dwindled, to a tiny figure in the distance. Miles hadn't realized he could make his adversary shrink like that, and it astonished him.

But my future's gonna be short, unless I do something.

. . . Truly? In fact, Haroche had killed no one, so far. And the death of an Imperial Auditor in the middle of an unclosed case would arouse the wildest suspicions; in Miles's empty place would arise, hydra-headed, a half-dozen other Auditors at least, experienced, annoyed, and immune to horseshit of all kinds. Haroche could not possibly control them all.

It was *Galeni's* life which would not be worth spit. What was more traditional than for a disgraced officer to commit suicide in his cell? It was the Vorish thing to do. It would be taken as a confession of guilt, a gesture of expiation. Case closed, oh yeah. It would doubtless be a very well-staged suicide; Haroche had lots of practical experience in such things, and would not make amateurish mistakes. As soon as Haroche knew Miles knew, it would be a race against time. And all Miles had was a trail of mirrors and smoke.

Smoke.

Air filters.

Miles's eyes widened.

—◆— TWENTY-SIX —◆—

A scant hour before ImpSec HQ quitting time, at least for those men there so fortunate as to work day shift, Miles marshaled his little troop at the side door for what he mentally dubbed *The Assault on Cockroach Central.* He was grateful at last for the embarrassing dimensions of the Count's old groundcar, because he'd been able to fit everyone in the rear compartment, and finish his mission briefing on the way over from the Imperial Science Institute, thus saving a few more precious minutes. He'd pressed Ivan into service again, and Simon Illyan himself, in the undress greens with full insignia Miles had insisted he wear. Dr. Weddell followed, carefully carrying an old shipping carton labeled, but not containing, *Petri-mice, frozen, lot #621A, 1 dozen.* Last but by no means least important, Delia Koudelka swung out her long legs, and hurried to catch up.

The corporal on duty at the front desk looked up anxiously as Miles entered. Miles strode up to him, and smiled tightly. "General Haroche has left your station orders to report to his office when I go in and out, has he not?"

"Why . . . yes, my Lord Auditor." The corporal glanced around Miles and saluted Illyan, who returned the courtesy.

"Well, don't."

"Uh . . . yes, my Lord Auditor." The corporal looked faintly panicked, like a grain of wheat foreseeing itself about to be ground between two stones.

"It's all right, Smetani," Illyan assured him in passing; the corporal relaxed gratefully.

The cavalcade continued on into the corridors of ImpSec.

Miles's first stop was the new detention area, now located in an inner quadrant of the second floor. Miles braced the officer in charge.

"In a short time, I'm coming back here to interview Captain Galeni. I expect to find him alive when I arrive, an outcome for which I will hold you personally responsible. In the meanwhile, Miss Koudelka here will be visiting him. You will permit no one else—*no* one, not even your own superiors," *especially your own superiors*, "to enter the prisoner's block until I return. Is that crystal clear?"

"Yes, my Lord Auditor."

"Delia, don't leave Duv alone for so much as a second till I get back."

"I understand, Miles." Her chin rose firmly. "And . . . thanks."

Miles nodded.

He hoped this blocked any chance of a last-minute convenient "suicide" attempt upon Galeni. Haroche had to be ready by now to move on that plan at a moment's notice; the trick was to deny him the moment. Miles led the rest of his people onward, to Janitorial, where he cornered the department head, an aging colonel. Once the man was reassured that Miles's intense interest in the schedule of air filtration maintenance was no adverse reflection upon his department's services, he became very cooperative. Miles brought him along.

Miles wanted to be in four places at once, but the thing had to be taken in as strict an order as any proof in 5-space math. Inspiration was one thing, demonstration quite another. After collecting a tech from Forensics, he hurried his team along to the sub-sub-basement, and the Evidence Rooms. In a very few more minutes he had his array of impeccable witnesses lined up in Aisle 5, Weapons Room IV. Weddell set his box down and leaned against the shelf frame, arms crossed, his air of skeptical intellectual superiority for once almost masked by his fascination with the proceedings.

Shelf 9 was inconveniently out of reach; Miles had to have Ivan hand him down the familiar little bio-sealed box. His Auditor's seal was unbroken. The two remaining brittle brown capsules waited demurely. He picked up one and rolled it between his thumb and forefinger.

"All right. Watch closely, all. Here goes." He pressed firmly, and the capsule snapped; he waved it twice over his head. A smoky tan comet's-trail of exquisitely fine powder hung a moment in the air, then dissipated. A little smudge clung to his fingers. Ivan was holding his breath, Miles noticed.

"How long should we wait?" Miles asked Dr. Weddell.

"I'd give it at least ten minutes to get all over the room," Weddell advised.

Miles attempted to compose his soul in patience. Illyan stared at the air, his expression hard. *Yes*, thought Miles, *here is the weapon that murdered you. You can't touch it, but it can touch you. . . .* Brick-colored, Ivan gave up, and started breathing again before he turned altogether purple and passed out.

At last, Weddell bent down and opened his box. From it he drew a small transparent bottle of clear fluid, and an atomizer dispenser, which he filled. For custom-designing that precious liquid on three hours' notice, Miles was ready to forgive him all his sins of pride for the next five years, and kiss him to boot. Weddell himself seemed to regard it as trivial. Scientifically, perhaps it was. *A simple chelation solution,* he'd dismissed it. *The vector encapsulation's exterior structure is nicely regular, specific, and unique. If you wanted something to detect the presence of the prokaryotes themselves, that would be a real challenge.*

"Now," said Miles to the colonel in charge of Janitorial, "we go to the return-air vent and filters."

"This way, my Lord Auditor."

They all filed through the aisle and around to the far wall, where a small rectangular grille, about the size of a standard plastic flimsy, at ankle-height marked the return-air duct. "Go ahead and pull off the outer cover," Miles instructed the colonel. "It's the very top filter I'm interested in."

The whole crew of them ended up on their knees, watching over the colonel's shoulder. He pulled off the outer grille to reveal the sealed rectangle of fiber designed to catch dust, dirt, hairs, mold, spores, smoke particles, and the like; the tiny prokaryotes themselves, if freed from their sporelike cases, would have slipped right through this barrier and gone on, possibly, even to penetrate the electrolytic resin barrier behind it, only to be destroyed at the last when they reached the central flash-unit.

At Miles's nod the colonel gave way to Dr. Weddell, who sat cross-legged on the floor and earnestly saturated the air around the vent with his atomizer.

"So what's he doing?" the colonel whispered to Miles.

Miles suppressed the reply, *We're spraying for traitors. Pesky vermin this time of year, don't you find?* "Watch and see."

Weddell then pulled an ultraviolet hand-light from his box, and directed it at the filter. A pale red fluorescence slowly grew more brilliant as the black light played over the surface.

"There you are, my Lord Auditor," Weddell said. "The vector encapsulations were caught in the filter, all right."

"Just so." Miles scrambled to his feet. "That's our baseline, then. On to the next. You there"—he pointed to the forensics tech—"document, bag, label, and seal all that, and follow as quickly as you can."

The parade took their positions and followed him once more. This time he led them to the Department of Komarran Affairs, where Miles asked the disturbed General Allegre to join the procession. They all fetched up crowded into Captain Galeni's cubicle-sized office, fourth door down the Komarran analysts' corridor.

"Do you remember ever personally visiting Galeni in here in the last three months?" Miles asked Illyan.

"I'm sure I stopped in a few times. I came down here almost every week, to discuss items in his reports of particular interest."

As soon as the forensics tech arrived, out of breath, the colonel from Janitorial repeated his performance with the cubicle's return-air vent, identical to the one in Weapons Room IV. Weddell sprayed again, liberally. This time, Miles held *his* breath. The results of this test could force a major fork in his planned strategy. If Haroche had anticipated him—there had been *two* missing capsules, after all.

Weddell, on one hand and his knees, played his black light over the filter. "Huh." Miles's heart seemed to stop. "There's nothing here that I can see. Do you see anything?"

Miles inhaled, gratefully, as the other men bent to examine the filter also. It remained a slightly dirty and now-damp white.

"Can you ascertain that this hasn't been changed since the last scheduled maintenance at Midsummer?" Miles asked the colonel.

The colonel shrugged. "The filters are not individually numbered, my lord. They're interchangeable, of course." He checked the report panel he carried. "No one in *my* department has done so, anyway. It's not due to be changed again till next month at Winterfair. It looks to have about the normal amount of accumulation for this point in its cycle."

"Thank you, Colonel. I appreciate your precision." He rose, and glanced at Illyan, who was watching stony-faced. "Your old office is next, Simon. Would you care to lead the way?"

Illyan shook his head, politely declining. "There isn't much joy for me in this, Miles. Either way your results come out, I lose a trusted subordinate."

"But wouldn't you rather lose the one who's actually guilty?"

"Yes." Illyan's snort was not wholly ironic. "Carry on, my Lord Auditor."

They trooped up three floors and down one to the level of Illyan's old office. If Miles had managed to surprise Haroche with his arrival in force, the general showed no sign of it. But was there maybe just a little discomfort in his eyes, as Haroche greeted his old boss and offered Illyan a chair?

"No, thanks, Lucas," said Illyan coolly. "I don't think we'll be here very long."

"What are you doing?" Haroche asked, as the colonel, practiced, went straight for the grille low on the wall to the right of his comconsole desk. The increasingly burdened forensics tech followed him.

"Air filters," said Miles. "You didn't think of the air filters. You've never been on space duty, have you, Lucas?"

"No, unfortunately."

"Believe me, it makes you very conscious of things like air circulation systems."

Haroche's brows rose as Weddell began vigorously spraying around the vent. He rocked back in his station chair, as-if-casually. He sucked thoughtfully on his lower lip, and did not ask, *Have you considered my offer, Miles?* He was a cool hand, and patient, and perfectly capable of waiting for the answer to emerge. No reason for him to flinch yet; whether the filters here were jammed full of vector encapsulations or not, it would prove nothing. Lots of people went in and out of Illyan's office.

"No," said Weddell after a moment. "Take a look for yourselves, gentlemen." He passed the black light along to Ivan and General Allegre.

"You'd think it would be here," commented Allegre, peering over Ivan's shoulder.

Miles had given it about a twenty-five-percent chance, personally, though he'd upped the odds after finding Galeni's vent clear. That left one of the conference chambers, or . . .

"Find anything?" asked Haroche.

Miles made a small show of going over and borrowing the hand-light from Ivan. "Not in here, dammit. I was hoping it would be simple. If the prokaryote vectors are caught in the filters, they show up bright red, y'see. We tested one, downstairs."

"What are you going to do next?"

"There's nothing for it but to start at the top of the HQ building and check every filtered air vent till I get to the basement. Tedious, but I'll get there in the end. You know I said if I knew why, I'd know who. I've changed my mind. I now think if I know *where*, I'll know who."

"Oh, really. Have you tried Captain Galeni's office?"

"First place we looked. It's clear."

"Hm. Perhaps . . . one of the briefing rooms?"

"I'd give odds." *Bite, Haroche. Bite my hook. Come on, come on. . . .*

"Very good."

"If you want to save steps," put in Ivan, on cue, "you ought to start with the places Illyan went most, and work out from there. Rather than from the top down."

"Good thinking," said Miles. "Shall we start with the outer office? Then—excuse me, General Allegre, but I must be complete—the offices of the department heads. Then the briefing rooms, then *all* the affairs analysts' offices. We should probably have done the whole of Komarran Affairs while we were first down there. After that we'll see."

From the look on the forensics tech's face, he was mentally kissing his dinner good-bye, a regret perhaps blunted by his obvious fascination with the proceedings. Allegre nodded; they all straggled back out, and the colonel began the drill again with the grille in the outer office. Miles wondered if anyone had noticed yet that Weddell didn't have nearly enough chelation solution to check every air filter in ImpSec HQ. Illyan exchanged abstracted greetings with his old secretary. After a few moments, General Haroche excused himself. Illyan did not look up.

Miles watched out of the corner of his eye as Haroche exited into the corridor. *Hook set, yes, now the line plays out. . . .* He began counting in his head, timing out how a man in a suppressed panic might walk to one room, then another. He motioned Weddell to desist with his spray; when he reached one hundred, he spoke. "All right, gentlemen. If you will follow me one more time. Quietly, please."

He led them out into the corridor and turned left, and right again at the second intersection. In the middle of that hallway, he met the commodore who had taken over Domestic Affairs from Haroche.

"Oh, my Lord Auditor," the commodore hailed him. "How fortunate. General Haroche just sent me to get you."

"Where did he tell you to look for me?"

"He said you'd gone down to the Evidence Rooms. You've just saved me some steps."

"Oh, yes. Tell me, was Haroche carrying anything?"

"A flimsy-folder. Did you want it?"

"I rather think so. He's just in here, eh? Come along. . . ." Miles led the way back up the corridor and into the Domestic Affairs outer office. The door to Haroche's old inner office was locked. Miles overrode its codes with his Auditor's seal. It hissed aside.

Haroche was crouched to the left of his old comconsole desk, just levering the vent grille out of the wall. In the opened flimsy-folder on the floor by his side lay another fiber filter. Miles laid a small bet with himself that they would find a disemboweled grille awaiting Haroche's return in one of the briefing rooms on a direct line between Illyan's old office and this one. A quick switch, very cool. *You think fast, General. But this time I had a head start.*

"Timing," said Miles, "is everything."

Haroche jerked upright, on his knees. "My Lord Auditor," he began quickly, and stopped. His eye took in the small army of ImpSec men crowding into the doorway behind Miles. Even then, Miles thought, Haroche might have been capable of some brilliantly extemporized explanation, to Miles, to the whole damned mob, but then Illyan shouldered forward. Miles fancied he could almost see the glib lies turning to clotted ashes on Haroche's tongue, though the only outward sign was a little twitch at the corner of his mouth.

Haroche had avoided facing his victims, Miles had noticed. He'd never once visited Illyan in ImpSec's own clinic, had tried unsuccessfully to avoid Miles back when he'd doubtless been planning the original version of the frame-up, and had been careful to enter the Imperial Residence only after Galeni had been arrested and removed. He was not, perhaps, an evil man, but only an ordinary smart man tempted to one evil act, and then overwhelmed when its consequences proliferated beyond control. *When you chose an act, you chose the consequences of that act.*

"Hello, Lucas," Illyan said. His eyes were amazingly cold.

"Sir . . ." Haroche scrambled up, and stood, empty-handed.

"Colonel, Dr. Weddell, if you please . . ." Miles waved them forward, and motioned the forensics tech in their immediate wake. He himself stood back a little, on the other side of the group from where Haroche stood. When he looked up, their eyes accidentally met, and both looked quickly away, avoiding an unfortunate intimacy. *This is my moment of triumph. Why isn't it more fun?*

The motions were all as choreographed and practiced as a dance, by now. The colonel finished dislodging the grille, Weddell sprayed. An excruciating few seconds' wait. Then the red fluorescence glowed, bright and malicious, as the black light transmuted the invisible into something resembling blood.

"General Allegre," Miles sighed, "you are now the acting chief of ImpSec, pending Emperor Gregor's approval. I am sorry to inform you that your first duty is the arrest of your predecessor, General Haroche. By my order as an Imperial Auditor, on the serious charge of . . ." What? Sabotage? Treason? Stupidity? *The criminal secretly wants to get caught*, so ran the popular wisdom. Not true, Miles thought; the criminal just wants to get away. It was the sinner who sought to be brought to light, on the long crawl back through confession, to absolution and some sort of grace, however shattered. Was Haroche a criminal or a sinner?

"On the capital charge of treason," Miles finished. Half the men in the room flinched at that last word.

"Not treason," Haroche whispered hoarsely. "Never treason."

Miles opened his hand. "But . . . if he is willing to confess and cooperate, possibly a lesser charge of assault on a superior officer. A court-martial, a year in prison, a simple dishonorable discharge. I think . . . I will let the Service court sort that one out."

By the looks on their faces, both Haroche and Allegre caught the nuances of *that* speech. Allegre was Galeni's superior, after all, and doubtless had been following the case against his subordinate in detail. Haroche's jaw tightened; Allegre smiled in acid appreciation.

"May I suggest," Miles went on to Allegre, "that you march him downstairs and have him trade places with your top analyst, for the moment, while you play catchup."

"Yes, my Lord Auditor." Allegre's voice was firm and determined, though he had a moment's pause when he realized he had no husky sergeants to do the official hands-on arresting. Miles thought eight-to-one was odds enough, but he forbore making suggestions. It was Allegre's job now.

Allegre, after a quick glance at Illyan gave him no clues, solved his problem by drafting Ivan—what *was* it about Ivan?—

the colonel, and the commodore. "Lucas, are you going to give me
any trouble?"

"I think . . . not," sighed Haroche. His eyes surveyed the room,
but there were no handy high windows inviting a quick resolution,
four floors headfirst to the pavement. "I'm too old to be that athletic anymore."

"Good. Me too." Allegre escorted him out.

Illyan watched them go. He remarked in an undertone to
Miles, "This is a damned sad business. ImpSec really needs to
start some new traditions for changing its chiefs. Assassination
and retribution is so disruptive to the organization."

Miles could only shrug agreement. He led the way for a quick
survey of nearby briefing rooms, and found the opened vent, missing its filter, in the second they tried. He oversaw the forensics
tech's careful bagging and documenting of the last pieces of evidence, and sealed the whole set with his Auditor's seal, and sent
them down to wait in the Evidence Rooms for whatever after-
maths eventually unfolded.

Everything from here on out was, thank God, beyond his mandate as an acting Imperial Auditor. His responsibilities ended with
his report to Gregor, and the turning over of any evidence he'd accumulated to the proper prosecuting authorities, in this case, in all
probability, the Service court. *I only have to find the truth. I don't
have to figure out what to do with it.* Though, he supposed, any
recommendations he made would bear weight.

Finished in the Office of Domestic Affairs, and unhurried at
last, he and Illyan strolled side by side down the corridor after the
tech. "I wonder how Haroche will try to play this?" Miles wondered aloud. "Hope to be assigned a good defender and try to
tough it out? He spent so much time and effort himself doctoring
the comconsole evidence—which was, I think, all that distracted
him from thinking of those damned filters before I did—I thought
he'd cry *Plant!* first thing. Or will he fall back on the Old Vorish
solution? He looked . . . pretty pale, there at the end. He folded
quicker than I thought he would."

"You hit him harder than you thought you had. You don't know
your own strength, Miles. But no. I don't think suicide is Lucas's
way," said Illyan. "And anyway, it's difficult to arrange without
cooperation from his jailers."

"Do you believe . . . I ought to hint for such cooperation?"
Miles asked delicately.

"Dying's easy." Illyan's drawn features grew distant. How

much did he remember of his agonized pleading to Miles for an easy death, so few weeks ago? "Living's hard. Let the son of a bitch stand his court-martial. Every last eternal minute of it."

"Ah," breathed Miles.

The new ImpSec HQ detention area was a lot smaller than the old one, but shared the design of a single entrance and prisoner processing area. At the front comconsole desk they found Captain Galeni, Delia Koudelka by his side, just completing his exit documentation under the eye of General Allegre and the duty officer. Ivan looked on. Haroche, it appeared, had already been processed in; Miles hoped he'd been given Galeni's cell.

Galeni was still in the dress greens he'd worn to Gregor's reception, now very rumpled. He was unshaven, red-eyed, and pale from lack of sleep. A dangerous tension still hung about him, like a fog.

He swung on his heel to face Miles, as he and Illyan entered. "Goddammit, Vorkosigan, where were you all this time?"

"Ah . . ." Miles ticked his Auditor's chain, to remind Galeni he was still on duty.

Galeni snapped, "Goddammit, my Lord Auditor, where the *hell* were you all this time? You said last night you'd follow on. Thought you were going to let me out. Then I didn't know what the hell to think. I'm quitting this frigging paranoid *stupid* organization just as soon as I get out of this rat-tank. No more."

Allegre winced. Delia touched Galeni's hand; he grasped hers, and his roiling boil visibly settled to a milder simmer.

Well, I had this seizure, and then I had to sort through Haroche's misdirection with the comconsole report, and then I had to get Weddell from his lab at the Imperial Science Institute, and he took forever, and I didn't dare contact anyone by comconsole from Vorkosigan House, I had to go in person, and . . . "Yes. I'm sorry. I'm afraid it took me all day to assemble the evidence to clear you."

"Miles . . ." said Illyan, "it's only been five days since this was discovered to be sabotage. It's going to take you longer to assemble your Auditor's report than it did for you to solve the case."

"Reports," sighed Miles. "Yech. But Duv, see, it wasn't enough for me to order your release. I'd have been accused of favoritism."

"*That's* true," murmured Ivan.

"At first I thought Haroche was just being clumsy, to have you arrested at the Imperial Residence in front of so many people. Ha. Not him. It was beautifully choreographed to destroy your reputation. After that, neither release nor acquittal for insufficient evidence would have removed suspicion from most men's minds. I *had* to nail the real culprit. It was the only way."

"Ah . . ." Galeni's brows drew down. "Miles, just who was the real culprit?"

"Oh, didn't you tell him yet?" Miles asked Delia.

"You *told* me not to say anything about it till you were done," Delia protested. "We just now got out of that dreadful little cell."

"They aren't as dreadful as the *old* cells," Illyan objected mildly. "I remember those. Spent a month under arrest in 'em myself, thirteen years ago." He cast a slightly sour smile at Miles. "Something about the Lord Regent's son's private army, and a certain treason charge."

"With all the things you've forgotten, I could wish you'd have forgotten that," murmured Miles.

"No such luck," Illyan murmured back. "I had them converted to evidence storage and the new detention area built right after. Much upgraded. Just in case I ever ended up in them again."

Galeni stared at Illyan. "I'd never heard that story."

"In retrospect—much later—I came to consider it a salutary experience. I fancied afterwards that every senior ImpSec officer ought to undergo something similar, for the same reason every doctor ought just once to be a patient. It sharpens one's perspectives."

Galeni was silent a moment, obviously processing this. His dangerous air of rage was almost fully dissipated. Ivan covertly let out his breath. Allegre, after directing a grateful half-smile at Illyan, looked on.

"It was Haroche," Miles added. "He wanted a promotion."

Galeni's brows shot up; he wheeled to General Allegre, who nodded confirmation.

"As soon as those bioengineered prokaryotes were discovered," Miles went on, "Haroche lost his chance of his sabotage passing undetected, which I'm sure was his first-choice scenario. At that point, he had to have a goat. It didn't have to be a perfect goat, as long as he was able to generate enough fog to justify stopping the search for another. He disliked me, you had the right profile, he hit upon a way to take us both down at once. Sorry I made Delia keep you in the dark, but arresting the acting head of ImpSec in the middle of ImpSec HQ proved to be a bit tricky. I didn't want to make any promises till I was sure how it was going to come out."

Galeni's eyes were wide. "Forget . . . what I said."

"Does that include the part about resigning your commission?" Allegre asked anxiously.

"I . . . don't know. Why *me?* I'd never thought Haroche was particularly prejudiced against Komarrans. How much longer am I going to have to wade through this kind of crap, what more do they *want* from me to prove my loyalty?"

"I expect you'll be wading for the rest of your life," Illyan answered seriously. "But every Komarran who follows you will have less crap to deal with, because of you."

"You've come so far," Miles pleaded. "Don't let a cockroach like Haroche waste your sacrifices. The Imperium needs your perspectives. ImpSec particularly desperately needs your perspectives, because it's part of ImpSec's job to give much of the Imperial government its picture of the world. If we get straight truth in, *maybe* we've got half a chance of getting good judgment out. No damn chance otherwise, that's for sure."

Allegre seconded this with a nod.

"Besides"—Miles glanced at Delia, who was following all this in deep alarm—"Vorbarr Sultana is a very nice posting for any ambitious officer. Look at the people you meet here, for one thing. And the opportunities." Ivan nodded vigorously; Miles went on, "Um . . . not to interfere in ImpSec's internal business or anything, but I think the department of Komarran Affairs is going to need a new head man very soon." He glanced at Allegre. "The old one being about to inherit a much worse job, y'see."

Allegre looked startled, then thoughtful. "A Komarran, to head Komarran Affairs . . . ?"

"Radical," Miles purred, "but it just might work."

Both Allegre and Illyan gave him the same quelling look. Miles subsided.

"Besides," Allegre went on, "I think you're premature, Lord Vorkosigan. It's by no means assured that Gregor will confirm me as permanent chief of ImpSec."

"Who else is there?" Miles shrugged. "Olshansky isn't seasoned enough yet, and the Galactic Affairs head likes his old job very well, thank you. With this Imperial marriage coming up, at long last, your depth of experience in Komarran matters makes you nearly ideal, I'd say."

"Be that as it may." Allegre looked a little daunted; were the full implications just starting to seep in? "That's tomorrow's worry. I have enough for today. Gentlemen, will you excuse me. I think I had better start with a quick survey of Haroche's . . . Illyan's . . . of whatever's waiting in the in-file of that comconsole upstairs. And . . . and a meeting of department heads, to apprise them of, hm, events. Any suggestions, Simon?"

Illyan shook his head. "Carry on. You'll be fine."

"Duv," Allegre continued to Galeni, "at least go home and get dinner, and a good night's sleep, before you make any important decisions, will you promise me that?"

"All right, sir," said Galeni, in a neutral tone. Delia squeezed his hand. He had not loosened his grip upon her, Miles noticed, the whole time they'd been standing there talking. He wasn't risking letting this one get away. Once he relaxed a bit, he would perhaps realize that it would take at least four large men with hand-tractors to pry her off his arm. *Foolhardy* large men. Ivan, noting this byplay at last, frowned faintly.

"Do you wish to report to Gregor first, my Lord Auditor, or shall I?" Allegre added.

"I'll take care of it. You should check in with him as soon as you've triaged your situation upstairs, though."

"Yes. Thank you." They exchanged sketchy salutes, and Allegre hurried out.

"Are you calling Gregor now?" asked Galeni.

"Right from here," Miles said. "It's urgent I let him know what's happened, since I couldn't give him any hint of it earlier. The ImpSec chief's office monitors all of his communications."

"When you do . . ." Galeni glanced at Delia, and away, though his grip on her hand tightened again, "will you be sure to . . . will you please ask him to be sure to let Laisa know that I am no traitor?"

"First thing," Miles promised. "My word on it."

"Thank you."

Miles detailed a guard to make sure Galeni and Delia got to the outer door without any last-straw harassment, and lent Delia the use of Martin and the groundcar to convey them to Galeni's nearby flat. Miles retained Ivan, spiking Ivan's ingenuous offer to see Galeni settled and take Delia on to her home by pointing out that Ivan's groundcar was still parked at Ops HQ. Then he booted the duty officer from his comconsole station and took it over. Illyan drew up another station chair by his side to look on. Miles entered a particular code-card into the comconsole's read-slot.

"Sire," Miles said formally, when Gregor's upper body appeared over the vid plate; the emperor was wiping his mouth with a dinner napkin.

Gregor's brows twitched up at the officiality; Miles had all his attention. "Yes, my Lord Auditor. Progress? Problems?"

"I'm finished."

"Good God. Ah . . . would you care to elaborate on that?"

"You'll get all the details"—Miles glanced aside at Illyan— "in my report, but briefly, you're out one provisional chief of ImpSec. It was never Galeni. It was Haroche himself. I figured out that the prokaryote vector encapsulations had to be trapped in the air filters."

"Did he confess this?"

"Better. We caught him trying to switch the filter in his old office, which was where he'd apparently dosed Illyan."

"I . . . take it this event did not occur by chance."

Miles's lips drew back in a wolfish grin. "Chance," he intoned, "favors the prepared mind, as somebody or another said. No. Not by chance."

Gregor sat back, looking very disturbed. "He delivered my ImpSec daily report to me in person just this morning, and all the time, he knew. . . . I was almost ready to confirm him as ImpSec's permanent chief."

Miles's lips twisted. "Yeah. And he would have been a good one, almost. Look, um . . . I promised Duv Galeni I would have you tell Laisa he was no traitor. Will you redeem my word for me?"

"Of course. She was extremely distressed by last night's scene. Haroche's explanations threw us all into the most painful doubt."

"Lucas always was smooth," murmured Illyan.

"Why did he do it?" asked Gregor.

"I have a great many questions I still want answers to before I sit down to assemble my report," said Miles, "and most of them seem to start with *why*. It's the most interesting question of all."

"And the hardest to answer," Illyan warned. "Where, what, how, who, for those I could at least sometimes make physical evidence speak. *Why* was almost theological, and often proved beyond my scope."

"There's so much that only Haroche can tell us," said Miles. "But we can't use fast-penta on the bastard, more's the pity. I think . . . we might get something out of him, if we hit him tonight, while he's still off-balance. By tomorrow, he'll have recovered his considerable wits, and be demanding a military defender, and standing pat. No . . . not *we*. It's clear he hates my guts, though once again *why* . . . Simon, can you . . . are you up to running an interrogation for me?"

Illyan rubbed his hand over his face. "I can try. But if he was willing to take me out, I don't see why he won't be willing to stand up to any moral pressure I can bring to bear."

Gregor seemed to study his hands, interlaced before him on his comconsole, then looked up. "Wait," he said. "I have a better idea."

TWENTY-SEVEN

"Do I really have to watch this?" Ivan muttered to Miles's ear, as their little party trod down the heavily monitored corridor to Haroche's cell. "It promises to be pretty unpleasant."

"Yes, for two reasons. You have been my official witness throughout, and will doubtless have to give all kinds of testimony under oath later, and neither Illyan nor I are physically capable of overpowering Haroche if he decides to go berserk."

"You expect him to?"

"Not . . . really. But Gregor thinks the presence of a regular guard—one of Haroche's own former men—would inhibit his, um, frankness. Tough it out, Ivan. You don't have to talk, only listen."

"Too right."

The ImpSec guard coded open the cell door, and stood back respectfully. Miles entered first. The new ImpSec detention cells were not exactly spacious, but Miles had seen worse; they did have individual, if monitored, bathrooms. The cell still smelled like a military prison, though, the worst of both worlds. Two bunks lined the narrow chamber on either side. Haroche was seated upon one, still in the uniform trousers and shirt he'd been wearing a scant half-hour ago, not yet degraded to prisoner's-orange smock and pajama pants. But he was without his tunic and boots, stripped of all signs of his rank, and minus his silver eyes. Miles could feel the absence of those eyes, like two burning scars on Haroche's neck.

Haroche's face, as he looked up and saw Miles, was closed and hostile. Ivan followed, and took up a stand beside the door, present but detached. As Illyan entered Haroche's expression grew embarrassed and even more closed, and Miles was suddenly reminded that the root word of *mortification* meant *death*.

Only when Emperor Gregor, tall and grave, ducked inside did Haroche's face escape control. Shock and dismay gave way to a flash of open anguish. Haroche took a breath, and tried to look cold and stern, but only succeeded in looking congealed. He scrambled to his feet—Ivan tensed—but only said, "Sire," in a cracked voice. He had either not enough nerve, or better sense, than to salute his commander-in-chief under these circumstances. Gregor did not look likely to return it.

Gregor motioned his pair of personal Armsmen to wait outside. Miles didn't expect to be of much direct use if Haroche exploded into some attack on the Emperor, but at least he might throw himself between the two men. By the time Haroche stopped to kill him, the reinforcements would arrive. The cell door slid closed. Miles imagined he felt pressure in his ears, like an air lock. The silence and sense of isolation in here were profound.

Miles, after a thoughtful calculation of the angles and forces, took up a stance like Ivan's on the opposite side of the cell door, on the extreme available edge of Haroche's personal space. They would be quiet as a mismatched pair of gargoyles, and in time Haroche would forget their presence. Gregor would see to that. Gregor seated himself on the bunk opposite Haroche; Illyan, arms folded, leaned against the wall as only he could do, an eye-of-Horus personified.

"Sit down, Lucas," said Gregor, so quietly Miles had to strain to hear.

Haroche's hands opened, as if in anticipation of protest, but his knees buckled; he sat heavily. "Sire," he murmured again, and cleared his throat. Ah, yes. Gregor was right in his estimations.

"General Haroche," Gregor went on, "I wanted you to give me your last report in person. You owe me that, and for the thirty years of service you have given me—nearly my whole life, my whole reign—I owe you that."

"What . . ." Haroche swallowed, "do you want me to say?"

"Tell me what you have done. Tell me why. Begin at the beginning, go on to the end. Put in all the facts. Leave out all the defenses. Your time for that will come later."

It could scarcely be simpler, or more overwhelming. Miles had seen Gregor quietly socially charming, quietly bravura-fey, quietly desperate, quietly determined. He'd never before seen him quietly angry. It was impressive, a weight all around like deep seawater. You could drown in it, still trying to strike upward to the air. *Weasel out of that, Haroche, if you can. Gregor is not our master only in name.*

Haroche sat silent for as long as he dared, then began, "I . . . had known about the Komarran prokaryotes for a long time. Since the beginning. Diamant of Komarran Affairs told me; we were co-ordinating on the sweep of Ser Galen's little group of saboteurs, lending men and help back and forth in the crisis. I was with him the day he put the capsules away downstairs. Didn't think anything more about it for years. Then I won my promotion to head of Domestic Affairs, the *Yarrow* case, do you remember that . . . sir?" This to Illyan. "You said my work on it was superb."

"No, Lucas," Illyan's voice was falsely pleasant. "Can't say as I do."

The silence after *that* threatened to extend itself for rather a long time. "Continue," said Gregor.

"I . . . began to be more and more aware of Vorkosigan, in and out of ImpSec HQ. There were rumors about him, some pretty wild stories, that he was some sort of galactic affairs hotshot, that he was being groomed as Illyan's successor. It was very clear that he was Illyan's pet. Then last year he was suddenly killed, though as it turned out . . . not quite dead enough."

A slight tic of his lip was all the expression Gregor allowed himself. After a glance at him, Haroche hurried on, "For whatever reason, during that period Illyan reorganized his chain of command, clarified his line of succession. I was made second-in-command of ImpSec. He told me he was thinking of choosing a new successor, in case anyone actually succeeded in dropping him in his tracks, and I was it. Then Vorkosigan turned up alive again.

"Didn't hear anything more about him one way or another, till this last Midsummer. Then Illyan asked me if I thought I could stand to work with Vorkosigan as my second in Domestic Affairs. Warned me he was hyperactive, and insubordinate as hell, but that he got results. Said I'd either love him or hate him, though some people did both. He said Vorkosigan needed a dose of my experience. I said . . . I'd try. The implication was pretty clear. I wouldn't have minded training my replacement. Being asked to train my boss was a little hard to swallow. Thirty years of experience, jumped over . . . But I swallowed it."

Gregor's attention was wholly on Haroche, and Haroche's, perforce, wholly on Gregor. It was as if Gregor generated his own little personal force-bubble, just like those used by a Cetagandan haut-lady, with only the two of them inside. Haroche grew more intense, leaning forward, his knee almost touching Gregor's.

"Then Vorkosigan . . . shot his foot off. So to speak. Good and proper. I didn't have to do him, he did himself, better than I could ever have imagined. He was out, I was in. I had my chance back, but . . . Illyan was good for another five years, maybe ten. There's more young hotshots coming up all the time. Now, while I was still at my peak, I wanted my chance. Illyan was getting stale, you could see it, feel it. Getting tired. He kept talking about retiring, but he never did anything. I wanted to serve the Imperium, serve you, Sire! I knew I could, if I got my chance. In time, in my time. And then . . . I thought of that damned Komarran powder."

"Just when did you think of it?"

"That afternoon, when Vorkosigan came stumbling out of Illyan's office with his eyes torn off. I went down to the Evidence Rooms on another matter, walked right by that shelf, as I'd done a hundred times before, but this time . . . I opened the box, and pocketed two capsules. It was no trouble walking out with them; it was the box that was screamer-tagged, not its contents. Of course I wasn't searched. I knew I'd have to do something about the monitors, eventually, but even if someone had visually checked them, all they would see was me, authorized to take anything I wanted."

"We know where. When did you administer the prokaryotes to Illyan?"

"It was . . . a few days later. Three, four days." Haroche's hand jerked in air; Miles could imagine the stream of tan smoke spinning from his fingers. "He was always popping into my office, to check out facts, to get my opinion."

"Did you use both capsules then?"

"Not then. Nothing seemed to be happening for about a week, so I dosed him again. I hadn't realized how slowly the symptoms were going to show. Or . . . how severely. But I knew it wouldn't kill him. I thought it wouldn't, anyway. I wanted to be sure. It was an impulse. And then it was too late to back out."

"An impulse?" Gregor raised his eyebrows, devastatingly. "After three days of premeditation?"

"Impulse," Miles broke his own long silence, "does work as slowly as that sometimes. Particularly when you're having a really bad idea." *I should know.*

Gregor motioned him to desist; Miles bit his tongue. "When did you decide to frame Captain Galeni?" Gregor asked sternly.

"I didn't, not then. I didn't want to frame anyone, but if I had to, I wanted to get Vorkosigan. He was perfect for it. There was a kind of justice in it. He'd damn near got away with murder, in that business with the courier. I'd have court-martialed the hyper little dwarf, but he was still Illyan's pet, even after all that mess. Then he turned up on my front doorstep with that damned Auditor's chain around his neck, and I realized he wasn't just Illyan's pet." Haroche's eyes, meeting Gregor's at last, were accusing.

Gregor's eyes were very, very cool. "Go on," he said, utterly neutral.

"The little git wouldn't leave it alone. He pushed and pushed—if I'd been able to hold him off one more week, I'd never have had to frame anyone at all. It was Vorkosigan forced my hand. But it was clear by then Vorkosigan was fireproof; I'd never make it stick to him. Galeni was around him, he caught my attention, I realized his suspect profile was even better than Vorkosigan's. He wasn't my first choice, but . . . he was a lot more disposable. He was a potential embarrassment to the Empress-to-be, if nothing else. Who would miss him?"

Gregor had grown so neutral as to seem almost gray. *So, that's what rage looks like on him.* Miles wondered if Haroche realized what Gregor's extreme lack of expression meant. The general seemed caught up in his own words, indignant, speaking faster now.

"The little git *still* wouldn't give it up. Three days—he found those capsules in the evidence room in *three days*. It was supposed to have taken him three *months*. I couldn't believe it. I thought I could get him to run all the way to Jackson's Whole and back, but he stuck tight to me, all hours of the day or night I'd turn around and there he'd be, under my elbow, all over my building. I had to get rid of him before I strangled him, so I advanced the timetable on Galeni as much as I dared and delivered him gift-wrapped. And the little git *still* wouldn't give it up! So I gave him the bait he was hungry for, I was sure he'd swallow *that* one, I practically stuffed it down his throat but he was salivating so hard by that time, the next thing I turn around he's back in my office with that damned arrogant galactic biobird with those frigging filters apart, and I'm down here and he's . . . up." Haroche paused for breath.

Gregor blinked. "What bait?"

Aw, hell, Haroche, you don't have to go into that, really. . . .

When Haroche did not reply, Gregor's gaze turned to Miles. "What bait?" he asked, with deceptive mildness.

Miles cleared his throat. "He offered me the Dendarii. He said

I could go back to work for him on the same terms I used to work for Simon. Oh, better. He threw in a captaincy."

Three nearly identical astonished stares seemed to pin him to the wall.

"You did not mention this to me," said Illyan at last.

"No."

"You didn't mention it to me, either," said Gregor.

"No."

"You mean you didn't say yes?" asked Ivan, in a stunned voice.

"No. Yes. Whatever."

"Why not?" said Illyan, after what seemed like a full minute.

"Didn't think I could prove it was a bribe."

"No. I mean, I know what a bribe it is, God knows you don't have to demonstrate that to *me*," said Illyan. "Why didn't you take it?"

"And give up Galeni to him as a goat? And let *him* run ImpSec for the next ten, twenty years, knowing what I knew about him? How long d'you think it would have been before he stopped just reporting to Gregor, and began manipulating him through his reports, or more directly? For his own good, of course, and the good of the Imperium."

"I would not. I would have served you well, Sire," Haroche insisted, his head bent, his voice low.

Gregor frowned, deeply.

Hell, let him have his denial. Miles would no more have tried to wrest it from him than he would have tried to take a log from a drowning man. He didn't want anything more from Haroche, not more confession, not even revenge. He didn't even need to hate him back. Miles might grieve for the honest Haroche of Midsummer, now lost; the Haroche of Winterfair had chosen his fate. *You have no mass, and cannot move me. I'm tired, and I want my dinner.* "Are we done yet?" he sighed.

Gregor sat back. "I'm afraid so."

"You're acting like it was murder, and it wasn't. It wasn't treason," Haroche insisted. "You must see that, Sire."

Try, "I'm sorry." Give up on justification, go for mercy. You'd be surprised what can happen.

"Simon wasn't even hurt!"

Very deliberately, Gregor rose and turned his back on him. Haroche's mouth opened on more desperate defenses, which did not emerge, but seemed to clot there. Illyan, famous for silken verbal venom, looked as if he couldn't think of anything to say scathing enough.

As soon as Gregor motioned the door open and ducked through, Ivan scooted out after him. Illyan waited for Miles, by sheer habit not letting him turn his back on a potential hazard unguarded, and followed him into the corridor. The door hissed closed on Haroche's last choked protests, cutting them off as abruptly as a blade to his throat.

They were all silent, until they reached the processing area again. Then Illyan remarked, "I'd thought that crack about wrestling with temptation was a joke."

"Best two falls out of three, Simon. It was that close. I . . . really don't want to talk about it."

"He did try to bribe one of my Auditors, then," said Gregor. "It's a capital charge."

"I don't think I want to try to explain it to a military court, Sire. Haroche has enough on his plate. He can scarcely be more ruined. Let it go. Please."

"If you wish. My Lord Auditor." Gregor had a strange look on his face, staring down at Miles; Miles shifted uncomfortably. It wasn't surprise or amazement, which would have unraveled to an insult, after all. Awe? Surely not. "What stopped you? I too want to know why, you know. You owe me that much."

"I don't . . . quite know how to put it." He searched for, and rather to his surprise found, that odd calm place inside, still there. It helped. "Some prices are just too high, no matter how much you may want the prize. The one thing you can't trade for your heart's desire is your heart."

"Oh," said Gregor.

———※《()》※———

Illyan had estimated the time to compose the Auditor's report would be equal to the time it had taken to crack the case. This turned out to be optimistic; he hadn't factored in the interruptions. Miles spent most of the following week holed up in his bedroom, shoving masses of data files and words around on his comconsole. After identifying all the missing pieces, he trudged back and forth to ImpSec HQ to confer with Forensics, the clinic, and a half-dozen other departments, to record depositions, or to closet himself with General Allegre. He made one trip out of Vorbarr Sultana to collect extra medical testimony from Admiral Avakli. He rechecked everything. This was one report he didn't want to see floating back on a tide of clarification queries, even if they would lack Illyan's acerbic marginalia.

Miles was in deep concentration composing a brief, neutrally worded account of Haroche's stonewalling and misdirection during the peak of Illyan's medical crisis, and cursing himself for every clue he had missed—oh, Haroche had *handled* him all right, handled them all—when Ivan barged in, unannounced, to demand loudly, "Do you realize what's been going on in your guest suite?"

Miles groaned, and ran his hands through his hair, waved Ivan to silence, tried and failed to remember the brilliant way he'd been going to finish that paragraph, gave up, and shut down his comconsole. "You don't need to bellow."

"I am not bellowing," said Ivan. "I'm being firm."

"Could you please be firm at a lower volume?"

"No. Simon Illyan is sleeping with *my mother*, and it's your fault!"

"I . . . don't think it is, somehow."

"It's happening in your house, anyway. You've got some kind of responsibility for the consequences."

"What consequences?"

"I don't know what consequences! I don't know what the hell I'm supposed to do about it. Should I start calling Illyan *Da*, or challenge him to a duel?"

"Well . . . you might start by considering the possibility that it's none of your business. They are grown-ups, last I checked."

"They're *old*, Miles! It's, it's, it's . . . *undignified*. Or something. Scandalous. She's high Vor, and he's, he's . . . *Illyan*."

"In a class by himself." Miles grinned. "I shouldn't anticipate much scandal, if I were you. I had the impression they were being reasonably, um, discreet. Your mother does everything in good taste. Besides, her being her, and him being him, who would dare comment?"

"It's *embarrassing*. After Gregor's betrothal ceremony, and before things start to gear up for the wedding, Mama told me they're going to take a vacation on the south coast for a half-month. Together. Some middle-class prole resort I never heard of, that Illyan picked because he'd never heard of it either, and any place that's never once come to the attention of ImpSec was all right by him. She says after the betrothal she wants to sit in a beach chair in the sun all day and not do anything, and drink those

disgusting drinks with the fruit on a stick in them, and all night—
she said—she's sure they'll be able to think of something to do.
Good God, Miles, my own mother!"

"How did you think she got to *be* your mother? They didn't
have uterine replicators on Barrayar back then."

"That was thirty years ago."

"Time enough. South coast, huh? It sounds . . . relaxing.
Downright placid, in fact. Warm." It was sleeting in Vorbarr Sultana this morning. Maybe he could persuade Illyan to tell him the
name of the place, and once he had this bloody report off his
hands . . . but Miles had no one to go on holiday with but Ivan,
just at present, and that wasn't the same thing at all. "If it really
bothers you, I suppose you could talk to my mother."

"I tried. She's Betan. She thinks it's just great. Good for your
cardiovascular system, and endorphin production, and all that.
She and my mother probably plotted it all out together, come to
think of it."

"Possibly. Look on the bright side. Chances are Aunt Alys'll
be so occupied with her own love-life, she won't have any attention left over for trying to arrange yours. Isn't that what you said
you always wanted?"

"Yes, but . . ."

"Think back. In the last month, how much has she harassed
you about courting eligible girls?"

"In the last month . . . we've all been pretty busy."

"How many of her acquaintances' children's betrothals, weddings, or new babies has she described in detail?"

"Well . . . none, now you mention it. Except Gregor's, of
course. Longest she's ever gone without inflicting the high Vor vital statistics roll call on me. Even when I was doing duty at our
embassy on Earth, she'd message twice a month."

"Count your blessings, Ivan."

Ivan's mouth screwed up. "Fruit," he muttered. "On little
sticks."

It took Miles a full hour to recover his concentration, after
evicting Ivan. He did make practical use of the disruption by calling Dr. Chenko at ImpMil, and finally setting up his appointment
to calibrate the seizure-control device. Chenko seemed quite anxious to find out if it was going to work. Miles tried not to feel like
a large bipedal lab rat.

He was getting ready to step out the front door of Vorkosigan

House for that appointment the next afternoon, when he encountered Illyan, just coming in. It was snowing, and white flakes
clung to Illyan's civilian jacket, and dusted his thinning hair. His
face was red with cold, and exhilarated. He appeared to be alone.

"Where have you been?" Miles asked. He craned his neck as
the door swung shut, but didn't see Lady Alys, or a guard, or any
other companion departing the entryway.

"I took a walk around town."

"By yourself?" Miles tried to keep the alarm out of his voice.
After all this, to lose the man, and have to rout out the municipal
guard to go hunting for him, to find him wandering frightened or
bewildered and embarrassed in some oddball corner of the
city . . . "You got back all right, it seems."

"Yes." Illyan positively grinned. He held out his hand, and displayed the holocube clutched there. "Your lady mother gave me a
map. It has the entire North and South Continents and all the populated islands, every city and town and street and mountain range
down to the one-meter scale. Now whenever I get lost, I can find
my own way back."

"Most people use maps, Simon." *I'm an idiot! Why didn't I
think of that before this?*

"It's been so long since I had to, it didn't even occur to me. It's
like an eidetic chip you can hold in your hand. It even remembers
things you never knew before. Wonderful!" He unfastened his
jacket, and pulled a second device from an inner pocket, a perfectly ordinary, though obviously best-quality, business audionote
filer. "She gave me this, too. It cross-references everything automatically by key word. Crude, but perfectly adequate for ordinary
use. It's nearly a prosthetic memory, Miles."

The man hadn't had to even think about taking notes for the
past thirty-five years, after all. What was he going to discover
next, fire? Writing? Agriculture? "All you have to remember is
where you put it down."

"I'm thinking of chaining it to my belt. Or possibly around my
neck." Illyan started up the curving stairs toward the guest suite,
chuckling under his breath.

The following evening Miles broke away from his now almost
cross-eyed rechecking of his comconsole data, to attend a quiet
dinner at home, just himself, the Countess, and Illyan. He spent

the first half of the meal firmly squelching the Countess's broad hints that perhaps Ma Kosti might be made interested in emigrating to Sergyar, in which case a place for her could certainly be found on the Viceroy's household staff.

"She'll never leave Vorbarr Sultana while her son's posted here," Miles asserted.

The Countess looked thoughtful. "Corporal Kosti could be transferred to Sergyar. . . ."

"No fighting dirty," he said hurriedly. "I found her first, she's mine."

"It was an idea." She smiled fondly at him.

"Speaking of Sergyar, when is Father arriving from there?"

"The day before the betrothal. We'll leave together shortly afterwards. We'll return for the wedding at Midsummer, of course. I'd love to stay longer, but we really both need to get back to Chaos Colony. The shorter his stay in Vorbarr Sultana, the less likely he'll be to get nailed for new jobs by old political comrades. That's one advantage of Sergyar; they have a harder time getting at him there. One still turns up about every month, full of ideas for things Aral can do in his nonexistent spare time, and we have to wine and dine him and shove him gently back out the door." She smiled invitingly across the table at him. "You really should come and visit us there soon. It's perfectly safe. We have an effective treatment for those revolting worms now, you know, much better than the old surgical removal. There's so much to see and do. Especially do."

There was something universal, Miles reflected, about the sinister light in the eye of a mother with a long list of chores in her hand. "We'll see. I expect to have my part of this Auditor's investigation wrapped up for Gregor in a few more days. After that . . . I'm not quite sure what I'm going to do with myself."

A short silence fell, while everybody applied themselves appreciatively to the dessert course. At length Illyan cleared his throat, and announced to the Countess, "I signed the lease on my new flat today, Cordelia. It will be ready for occupancy tomorrow."

"Oh, splendid."

"I want to thank you both, especially you, Miles, for your hospitality. And your help."

"What flat?" asked Miles. "I'm afraid I've been living inside my comconsole this week."

"Quite right. Lady Alys helped me find it."

"Is it in her building?" And a very exclusive venue that was, too. Could Illyan afford it? A vice-admiral's half-pay was merely decent, though, come to think of it, he had to have amassed considerable savings by now, given the enforced simplicity of his work-devoured former life.

"I feel I am less of a menace to my neighbors than I used to be, but just in case some old enemy has bad aim . . . it's a couple of streets away from her. It might not be a bad idea to float a few rumors that I am more mentally incapacitated than I actually am, should you get the chance. It will make me a less exciting target."

"Do you think you'll be continuing any ImpSec service, if not as chief, then . . . I don't know . . . consultant or something?"

"No. Now that my, hm, peculiar assassination has been solved, I'll be opting out. Don't look so shocked, Miles. Forty-five years of Imperial service does not qualify as a career cut tragically short."

"I suppose not. Gregor will miss you. We all will."

"Oh, I expect I'll be around."

⸺※⸺

Miles finished his Auditor's report late the following afternoon, including the table of contents and the cross-referenced index, and sat back in his comconsole chair, and stretched. It was as complete as he could make it, and as straightforward as his indignation with the central crime would allow. He only now realized, looking over the finished product, just how much subtle spin he used to put on even his most truthful Dendarii field reports, making the Dendarii and Admiral Naismith look good to assure the continued flow of funding and assignments. There was a dry serenity in not having to give a damn what Lord Auditor Vorkosigan looked like, that he quite enjoyed.

This report was for Gregor's eyes first, not for Gregor's eyes only. Miles had been on the other end of that stick, having to devise Dendarii missions on the basis of all sorts of dubious or incomplete intelligence. He was determined that no poor sod who had to make practical use of the report later would have cause to curse him as he had so often cursed others.

He decanted the final version onto a code-card, and called Gregor's secretary to arrange a formal appointment the following morning to turn it, and his chain of office and seal, over to the Emperor. He then rose for a muscle-unkinking stroll around Vorkosigan House, with an eye to checking his lightflyer. Chenko had promised the final surgical installation of his seizure-control device possibly as early as tomorrow afternoon. Martin, whose long-awaited birthday had gone by unnoticed by Miles sometime during the recent crisis, had delayed his application to the Imperial Service an extra couple of weeks, to save Miles having to break in an interim driver. But Miles knew exactly how anxious the boy was to be gone.

Illyan and his scant belongings had been carried off, most helpfully, by Lady Alys in her car this morning, and the Countess's household staff had restored the guest suite to its original, if slightly sterile, order. Miles wandered through it, to stare out onto the snowy back garden and be glad he wasn't frozen in a cryochamber. This really was the most splendid set of rooms in Vorkosigan House, with by far the best windows. Miles remembered the chambers from his grandfather's day, jammed with military memorabilia, thick with the formidable scent of old books, old leather, and the old man. He gazed around the suite's clean-swept emptiness.

"Why not?" he murmured, then more loudly, "Why the hell not?"

His mother found him half an hour later, leading a press-ganged troop consisting of Martin and half her retainers. They were carrying all Miles's possessions down one flight and around the corner from the other wing, and spreading them through the bathroom, bedroom, sitting room, and study under Miles's somewhat random direction. "Miles, love, what are you doing?"

"Taking over Grandfather's rooms. Nobody else is using them now. Why not?" He waited, a little nervously, for some objection from her, mentally marshaling his defensive arguments.

"Oh, good idea. It's about time you got out of that little room upstairs. You've been in it since you were five, for heaven's sake."

"That's . . . what I thought."

"We only picked that one for you because Illyan calculated it had the most disadvantageous angle for anyone trying to lob a projectile through the window."

"I see." He cleared his throat, and, emboldened, added, "I thought I'd take over the whole second floor, the Yellow Parlor, the other guest rooms, and all. I might . . . entertain, have people in, something."

"You can have the whole place, when we're off to Sergyar."

"Yeah, but I want a space even when you're here. I never needed it before. I was never around."

"I know. Now you're here and I'm gone. Life is odd like that, sometimes." She wandered away, humming.

With that many porters, the moving job only took an hour. Spread out into a more reasonable area, his life made a thin layer. There was at least a metric ton of Admiral Naismith's possessions back with the Dendarii Fleet, which Miles supposed he ought to retrieve somehow. No one else was likely to be able to use his clothing or his customized space armor, after all. He wandered about, rearranging things, trying to guess how he would use them here. It was all wonderfully unconstrained. He felt a sympathetic twinge of identification with those root-bound plants that had waited too long to be moved to bigger pots, not that he was exactly planning to vegetate. Spacer Quinn would call him a dirt-sucker. Quinn would be . . . half-right.

He owed her a message. He owed her several, and a major apology, for setting her couple of more recent queries aside in the rush of recent events. He settled himself at his newly moved com-console. The city lights reflected in an amber haze from the cloudy sky. The back garden, seen out his wide study window, was luminous and soft in the snowy night.

He composed his face and his thoughts, and began. He recorded cheerful reassurances, medical and otherwise, and sent it by tight-beam; she'd receive it in a week or so, depending on where the Dendarii fleet was now. Rather to his surprise, a task that had seemed impossible earlier came easily now. Maybe he'd only needed to free his brain.

TWENTY-EIGHT

Miles decided to make a little ceremony out of returning his Auditor's chain and seal to Gregor, along with the report. The traditional dignity of the office seemed to demand something more than just handing them back through the Residence door in a plastic bag. So he dressed in his brown-and-silver House uniform again, with all due care. He hesitated a long time before attaching his military decorations to his tunic, perhaps for the last time. But he was planning to ask Gregor for a very personal favor, and he would rather the decorations spoke for him than having to speak for himself.

He had qualms about that favor. It was only a little thing, taken all in all, and he felt obscurely that he ought to be rising above such petty concerns. But it mattered to him, like that extra centimeter of height that no one else noticed. He had Martin deliver him to the Residence's east portico, as before. Martin missed clipping Gregor's gates, this time; his handling of the Count's old groundcar was really vastly improved. Miles was ushered once again into Gregor's office in the north wing by Gregor's majordomo.

Gregor too must have had some ceremonial duties on his agenda this morning, for he was turned out in his Vorbarra House uniform, in his usual sharp style that was the envy of all Vor lords with less superior valets. He was waiting for Miles at his blank comconsole, his attention undivided by any data display.

"Good morning, my Lord Auditor." Gregor smiled.

"Good morning, Sire," Miles responded automatically. He laid down the data card in its security case on the smooth black glass of the desk, carefully pulled the chain and seal over his head, and let the heavy links spill through his hands before clinking them gently to the surface. "There you go. All done."

"Thank you." At a motion from the Emperor, the majordomo brought Miles a chair. Miles seated himself, and licked his lips, mentally thumbing through the several choices of opening lines he'd rehearsed for his request. But Gregor waved a small wait-please to both Miles and his majordomo, and both, necessarily, waited. He opened the security case, and ran the data card through his comconsole's read-slot. Then he handed it in its opened case to his majordomo, saying, "You can take this next door, now, please."

"Yes, Sire." The majordomo departed carrying the report on a small plate, like a servitor delivering some strange dessert.

Gregor sped through a scan of Miles's Auditor's report, saying nothing more to indicate his opinion than a muttered "Huh," now and then. Miles's brows rose slightly, and he settled back in his chair. Gregor went back to the beginning, and examined selected sections more slowly. At last he finished, and let the data display fold back into itself, and disappear. He picked up the Auditor's chain, and let it turn in the light, fingering the Vorbarra arms incised into the gold. "This was one of my more fortunate snap decisions, I must say, Miles."

Miles shrugged. "Chance put me in a place where I had some useful expertise."

"Was it chance? I seem to recall it was intent."

"The sabotage of Illyan's chip was an inside job; you needed an ImpSec insider to unravel it all. A lot of other men might have done what I did."

"No . . ." Gregor eyed him, measuringly. "I think I needed a former ImpSec insider. And I can't offhand think of any other man I know with both the passion and the dispassion to do what you did."

Miles gave up arguing about it; he only needed to be polite, not ingenuous. Besides, he might never get a better straight-line upon which to open his plea. "Thank you, Gregor." He took a breath.

"I've been thinking about an appropriate reward for a job well done," the Emperor added.

Miles let out his breath again. "Oh?"

"The traditional one is another job. I happen to have an opening for a new Chief of Imperial Security, this week."

Neutrally, Miles cleared his throat. "So?"

"Do you want it? While it has traditionally been held by a serving military officer, there is no law whatsoever saying I can't appoint a civilian to the task."

"No."

Gregor raised his brows at this concise certainty. "Truly?" he asked softly.

"Truly," Miles said firmly. "I'm not playing hard-to-get. It's a desk job stuffed with the most tedious routine, in between the terror-weeks, and the chief of ImpSec not only almost never gets off-planet further than Komarr, he scarcely ever gets out of Cockro—out of ImpSec HQ. I would hate it."

"I think you could do it."

"I think I could do almost anything I had to do, if you ordered it, Gregor. Is this an order?"

"No." Gregor sat back. "It was a genuine question."

"Then you have my genuine answer. Guy Allegre is much better fitted than I am for this job. He has the downside and the bureaucratic experience, and he's well respected on Komarr as well as on Barrayar. He is fully engaged with his work, and cares a lot about it, but he's not distorted by ambition. He's the right age, neither too young nor too old. No one will question his appointment."

Gregor smiled slightly. "That's what I thought you'd say, actually."

"What is this, then, some sort of spiritual exercise?" *I think I've had all of those I want for a while, thanks.* His heart still seemed to ache, the way an overstrained muscle twinged when one put weight on it. Like muscle strain, it would pass with a little rest, he suspected.

"No," said Gregor. "Just a courtesy. I wanted to give you first refusal."

He did not ask again, which saved Miles the embarrassment of refusing him again. Instead he leaned forward, and put down the gold chain and played with it a moment, arranging the links in a smooth oval pattern. Then he asked, "Would you like some coffee? Tea? Breakfast?"

"No, thanks."

"Something stronger?"

"No. Thanks. I have a spot of brain surgery scheduled for this afternoon. Dr. Chenko is ready to install his controlled-seizure chip. It looks like it's going to work. I'm not supposed to eat anything beforehand."

"Ah, good. It's about time."

"Yes. I can hardly wait to get back in my lightflyer."

"Will you miss the egregious Martin?"

"A little, I think. He grew on me."

Gregor glanced again at his office door. Was he waiting for something? Now was a good time for Miles's request. "Gregor, I wanted to ask you—"

The door to Gregor's office slid aside, and the majordomo entered. At Gregor's nod, he turned back to the corridor and said, "If you will, my lords." He stepped back respectfully.

Four men entered Gregor's office. Miles recognized them at once; he was Barrayaran enough that his first thought was a conscience-stricken, *My God, what have I done wrong?* Good sense reasserted itself; his feats of evil would have had to have been downright heroic to rate the attention of *four* Imperial Auditors at one time. Still, it was unusual, as well as unnerving, to see so many Auditors in one room. Miles cleared his throat, and sat up straighter, and exchanged polite Vorish greetings with them as Gregor's majordomo hurried to arrange seats for them all around Gregor's desk.

Lord Vorhovis was back from Komarr, it appeared. In his early sixties, he was the youngest of the crowd, but with a formidable career behind him nonetheless; soldier first, then diplomat, planetary ambassador, and onetime assistant minister of finance. He might be a model for Duv Galeni to emulate. He was a cool, lean, sophisticated man, very much in the modern style of Vor lord—Miles wondered if he shared Gregor's tailor—and he carried Miles's data card case in his hand.

Dr. Vorthys was one of the two recent appointees of Gregor's who was not in the military mold. He was a professor emeritus of engineering failure analysis from Vorbarr Sultana University, and had written the text on his subject. Several of them, in fact. He looked a professor, stout, white-haired, smiling, rumpled, with a noble nose and big ears. Late in his career he had become philosophically interested in the connections between sociopolitical and engineering integrity; his addition to Gregor's array of Auditors had brought in some welcome technical expertise, not that the Auditors exactly worked as a team.

Lord Vann Vorgustafson, chatting amiably with him, was the other civilian, a retired industrialist and noted philanthropist. He was short, and stouter than Vorthys, with a bristling gray beard and pink choleric face that alarmed observers about the state of his cardiovascular system. Surely the most financially unbribable of Gregor's Auditors, he routinely gave away money in lumps larger than the average man saw in his lifetime. One wouldn't guess his wealth to look at him, for he dressed like a workman, if there were any workmen so lacking in color-sense.

Admiral Vorkalloner was an Auditor of the more traditional type, retired from the Service after a long and impeccable career. He seemed socially bland, and was notably unaffiliated with any political party, conservative or progressive, as far as Miles had heard. Tall and thick, he seemed to take up a lot of space.

He nodded cordially to Miles, before taking a chair. "Good morning. So, you're Aral Vorkosigan's boy."

"Yes, sir," Miles sighed.

"Haven't seen you around much in the last ten years. Now I know why."

Miles tried to work out whether that was a positive or negative statement. Seeing so many of them together, Miles gained a renewed sense of what an *odd* lot the Auditors were. All were experienced, accomplished, wealthy in their own right. In other ways they were downright eccentric, outside or perhaps above the norms. More than fireproof, they were Gregor's firemen.

Vorhovis seated himself on the Emperor's left.

"So," Gregor said to him, "what do you gentlemen think?"

"This"—Vorhovis leaned forward, and laid the data case containing Miles's Auditor's report on the comconsole—"is an extraordinary document, Gregor."

"Yes," seconded Vorthys. "Concise, coherent, and complete. Do you know how rare that is? I congratulate you on it, young man."

Do I get a good grade, professor? "Simon Illyan trained me. He didn't have much tolerance for slop. If he didn't like my field reports, he'd fire them back to me for additions. It got to be something of a hobby with him, I think. I could always tell when ImpSec HQ was having a really slow week, because my report would come back shot full of little query boxes with these dryly worded corrections for grammar and style. Ten years of that, and you learn to do it right the first time."

Vorkalloner smiled. "Old Vorsmythe," he noted, "used to turn in handwritten plastic flimsys. Never more than two pages. He insisted anything important could always be said in two pages."

"Illegibly handwritten," muttered Gregor.

"We used to have to go and squeeze the footnotes out of him in person. It became somewhat irritating," added Vorkalloner.

Vorhovis, with a gesture at the data case, went on to Miles, "You appear to have left the military prosecutor with very little to do."

"Nothing, in fact," said Gregor. "Allegre reported to me last night that Haroche has given up and is going to plead guilty, trying to reduce his sentence through cooperation. Well, he could hardly have confessed to Us and then turned around and tried to pretend innocence to a Service judge."

"I wouldn't have bet on that. He did have nerve," said Miles. "But I'm glad to hear it's not going to be dragged out."

"It was a truly bizarre case," Vorhovis went on. "I'd been worried something might be very wrong when I first heard that Illyan had gone down. But I could not have unraveled the events as you did, Lord Vorkosigan."

"I'm sure you would have unraveled them in your own way, sir," said Miles.

"No," said Vorhovis. He tapped the data case. "By my analysis, the critical juncture was when you brought in that galactic biochemist, Dr. Weddell. It was from that point that Haroche's plans began to go irretrievably wrong. I would not have known of Weddell's existence, and would have left the selection of the chip autopsy team entirely to Admiral Avakli."

"Avakli was good," Miles said, uncertain if this was a criticism. The biocyberneticist had done his best, certainly.

"We"—a circular wave of Vorhovis's finger indicated the Auditors there assembled—"do not often work directly together. But we do consult with one another. 'What resources do you know of that I don't, that might have a bearing on this problem?' It increases our access to odd knowledge fivefold."

"Five-fold? I thought there were seven of you."

Vorthys smiled faintly. "We think of General Vorparadijs as a sort of Auditor Emeritus. Respected, but we don't make him come to meetings anymore."

"In fact," muttered Vorgustafson under his breath, "we don't even mention them to him."

"And Admiral Valentine has been too frail for some years to actively participate," Vorhovis added. "I would have urged him to resign, but as long as the gap left by the death of General Vorsmythe was still unfilled, there seemed no need to beg his space."

Miles had been dimly aware of the loss two years ago of the eighth Auditor, the elderly Vorsmythe. The position of ninth Auditor, which Miles had lately held, was by tradition always left open for acting Auditors, men with particular expertise called up at the Imperium's need, and released again when their task was done.

"So we four here," Vorhovis went on, "constitute a quorum of sorts. Vorlaisner couldn't be here, he's tied up on South Continent, but I've kept him apprised."

"That being so, my lords," said Gregor, "how do you advise Us?"

Vorhovis glanced around at his colleagues, who gave him nods, and pursed his lips judiciously. "He'll do, Gregor."

"Thank you." Gregor turned to Miles. "We were discussing job openings, a bit ago. It happens I also have a place this week for the position of eighth Auditor. Do you want it?"

Miles swallowed shock. "That's . . . a permanent post, Gregor. Auditors are appointed for life. Are you sure . . . ?"

"Not necessarily for life. They can resign, be fired, or impeached, as well as be assassinated or just drop dead."

"Aren't I a little young?" And he'd just been feeling so old. . . .

"If you take it," said Vorhovis, "you'll be the youngest Imperial Auditor in post Time-of-Isolation history. I looked it up."

"General Vorparadijs . . . will surely disapprove. As will like-minded men." *Hell, Vorparadijs thinks I'm a mutant.*

"General Vorparadijs," said Vorhovis, "thought *I* was too young for the job, and I was fifty-eight when I was appointed. Now he can switch his disapproval to you. I shall not miss it. And along with ten years of quite unique ImpSec training, you have more galactic experience than any three out of four of us in this room right now. Rather odd experience, but very wide-ranging. It will add a great deal of scope to our mutual data store."

"Have you, ah, read my personnel files?"

"General Allegre was kind enough to lend us complete copies, a few days ago." Vorhovis's glance swept Miles's chest, and the commendations there. Fortunately for the hang of his tunic, the Imperial Service did not also give out material symbols for one's demerits.

"Then you know . . . there was a little problem with my last ImpSec field report. A major problem," he corrected himself. He seached Vorhovis's face for whatever judgment lurked there. Vorhovis's expression was grave, but free of censure. Didn't he know? Miles looked around at all of them. "I almost killed one of our courier officers, while I was having one of my seizures. Illyan discharged me for lying about it." There. That was as bald and flat and true as he could make it.

"Yes. We and Gregor spent several hours yesterday afternoon, discussing that. Chief Illyan sat in." Vorhovis's eyes narrowed, and he regarded Miles with the utmost seriousness. "Given your falsification of that field report, what kept you from also taking Haroche's extraordinary bribe? I can almost guarantee no one would ever have figured it out."

"Haroche would have known. Galeni would have known. And I would have known. Two can keep a secret, if one of them is dead. Not three."

"You would certainly have outlived Captain Galeni, and you might have outlived Haroche. What then?"

Miles blew out his breath, and answered slowly. "Someone might have survived, with my name, in my body. It wouldn't have been me, anymore. It would have been a man I didn't much . . . like."

"You value yourself, do you, Lord Vorkosigan?"

"I've learned to," he admitted wryly.

"Then so, perhaps, shall we." Vorhovis sat back, an oddly satisfied smile playing about his lips.

"Note," said Gregor, "as the most junior member of this rather eclectic group, you will almost certainly be awarded the worst jobs."

"So true," murmured Vorhovis, a light in his eye. "It will be nice to pass that position off to someone more, ah, *active*."

"Every assignment," Gregor went on, "may be totally unrelated to any other. Unpredictable. You'll be tossed in to sink or swim."

"Not entirely unsupported," objected Vorthys. "The rest of us will be willing to call advice from shore, now and then."

For some reason Miles had a mental flash of the whole lot of them sitting in beach chairs holding drinks with fruit on little sticks, awarding him judiciously discussed points for style as he went under, frantically gulping and splashing, the water filling his nose.

"This . . . wasn't the reward I'd been planning to ask for, when I came in," Miles admitted, feeling horribly confused. People never followed your scripts, never.

"What reward was that?" asked Gregor patiently.

"I wanted . . . I know this is going to sound idiotic. I wanted to be retired retroactively from the Imperial Service as a captain, not a lieutenant. I know those post-career promotions are sometimes done as a special reward, usually with an eye to boosting some loyal officer's half-pay grade during retirement. I don't want the money. I just want the title." Right, he'd said it. It did sound idiotic. But it was all true. "It's been an itch I couldn't scratch." He'd always wanted his captaincy to come freely offered, and unarguably earned, not something begged as a favor. He'd made a career out of scorning favor. But he didn't want to go through the rest of his life introduced in military reminiscence as *Lieutenant*, either.

Belatedly, it occurred to Miles that Gregor's job offer wasn't another first-refusal courtesy. Gregor and these serious men had been conferring for nearly a week. Not a snap decision this time, but something argued and studied and weighed. *They really want me. All of them do, not just Gregor. How strange.* But it meant that he had a bargaining chip.

"Most other Auditors are p—" his tongue barely cut the accustomed adjective *portly* "—retired senior officers, admirals or generals."

"You *are* a retired admiral, Miles," Gregor pointed out cheerfully. "Admiral Naismith."

"Oh." He hadn't thought of it like that; it stopped him cold for a full beat. "But . . . but not publicly, not on Barrayar. The dignity of an Auditor's office . . . really needs at least a captaincy to support it, don't you think?"

"Persistent," murmured Vorhovis, "isn't he?"

"Relentlessly," Gregor agreed. "Just as advertised. Very well, Miles. Allow me to cure you of this distraction." His magic Imperial finger—index, not middle, thank you Gregor—flipped down to point at Miles. "Congratulations. You're a captain. My secretary will see that your records are updated. Does that satisfy you?"

"Entirely, Sire." Miles suppressed a grin. So, it was a touch anticlimactic, compared to the thousand ways he'd dreamed this promotion over the years. He was not moved to complain. "I want nothing more."

"But *I* do," said Gregor firmly. "My Auditors' tasks are, almost by definition, never routine. I only send them in when routine solutions have fallen short, when the rules are not working or have never been devised. They handle the unanticipated."

"The complex," added Vorthys.

"The disturbing ones that no one else has the nerve to touch," said Vorhovis.

"The really bizarre," sighed Vorgustafson.

"And sometimes," said Gregor, "as with the Auditor who

proved General Haroche's strange treason, they solve crises absolutely critical to the future of the Imperium. Will you accept the office of eighth Auditor, my Lord Vorkosigan?"

Later, there would be formal public oaths, and ceremonies, but the moment of truth, and for truth, was now.

Miles took a deep breath. "Yes," he said.

The surgery to install the internal portion of the controlled-seizure device was neither as lengthy nor as frightening as Miles had expected; for one thing, Chenko, who was getting used to his star patient's slightly paranoid world-view, let him stay awake and watch it all on a monitor, carefully positioned above his head-clamp. Chenko allowed him to get up and go home the next morning.

Two afternoons later, they met again in Chenko's ImpMil neurology laboratory for the smoke-test.

"Do you wish to do the honors yourself, my lord?" Dr. Chenko asked Miles.

"Yes, please. I might have to."

"I don't recommend doing this by yourself as your routine. Particularly at first, you ought to have a spotter by you."

Dr. Chenko handed Miles his new mouth guard, and the activation unit; the device fit neatly in the palm of Miles's hand. Miles lay back on the examination table, checked the settings on the activator one last time, pressed it to his right temple, and keyed it on.

Colored confetti.

Darkness.

Miles popped open his eyes. "Pfeg," he said. He wriggled his jaw, and spat out his mouth-guard.

Dr. Chenko, hovering happily, retrieved it, and pressed a hand to Miles's chest to keep him from sitting up. The activation unit now sat on top of a monitor beside him; Miles wondered if he'd caught it on the fly. "Not yet, please, Lord Vorkosigan. We've a few more measurements." Chenko and his techs busied themselves around their equipment. Chenko was humming, off-key. Miles took it for a good sign.

"Now . . . now you did encode the activation signals, as I asked you, Chenko? I don't want this damned thing being set off by accident when I walk through a security scan, or something."

"Yes, my lord. Nothing can possibly set off your seizure-stimulator but the activator," Chenko promised him, again. "It's required, to complete the circuit."

"If I get my head banged around for some reason, I don't know, a lightflyer crash or something, there's no chance this thing will switch on and not switch off?"

"No, my lord," Chenko said patiently. "If you ever encounter enough trauma to damage the internal unit, you won't have enough brains left to worry about. Or with."

"Oh. Good."

"Hm, hm," sang Chenko, finishing with his monitors. "Yes. Yes. Your convulsive symptoms on this run were barely half the duration of your uncontrolled seizures. Your body movements were also suppressed. The hangoverlike effects you reported should also be reduced; try to observe them over the next day-cycle, and tell me your subjective observations. Yes. This should become a part of your daily routine, like brushing your teeth. Check your neurotransmitter levels on the monitor-readout panel of the activation unit at the same time every day, in the evening before bed, say, and whenever they exceed one-half, but before they exceed three-quarters, discharge them."

"Yes, Doctor. Can I fly yet?"

"Tomorrow," said Chenko.

"Why not today?"

"Tomorrow," repeated Chenko, more firmly. "After I examine you again. Maybe. Behave yourself, please, my lord."

"It looks . . . like I'm going to have to."

"*I* wouldn't bet Betan dollars," Chenko muttered under his breath. Miles pretended not to hear him.

⟫⟫⟨●⟩⟪⟪

Lady Alys, prodded by Gregor, set the Emperor's formal betrothal ceremony as the first social event of the hectic Winterfair season. Miles wasn't sure if this represented Imperial firmness, bridegroomly eagerness, or a sensible terror that Laisa might wake at any moment from her fond fog to an appreciation of her dangers, and run away as far and as fast as possible. A bit of all three, perhaps.

The day before the ceremony, Vorbarr Sultana and the three surrounding Districts were hit with the worst Winterfair blizzard in four decades, closing all the commercial shuttleports and severely reducing activity at the military one, and stranding the ar-

riving Viceroy of Sergyar in orbit. Wind-whipped snow sang past
the windows of Vorkosigan House in a hard horizontal line, and
drifts piled up with the speed of sea-foam as high as second-story
windows in some blocks in the capital city. It was prudently decided that Viceroy Count Vorkosigan would not land until the following morning, and would go straight to the Imperial Residence
when he did.

Miles's intention to take himself off to the Residence in his
own lightflyer was scratched in favor of accompanying the Countess and her retinue in their groundcars. His master plan to get
them all out the door early met its first check of the day when he
opened his closet door to discover that Zap the Cat, having penetrated the security of Vorkosigan House through Miles's quisling
cook, had made a nest on the floor among his boots and fallen
clothing to have kittens. Six of them.

Zap ignored his threats about the dire consequences of attacking an Imperial Auditor, and purred and growled from the dimness
in her usual schizophrenic fashion. Miles gathered his nerve and
rescued his best boots and House uniform, at a cost of some high
Vor blood, and sent them downstairs for a hasty cleaning by the
overworked Armsman Pym. The Countess, delighted as ever to
find her biological empire increasing, came in thoughtfully bearing a cat-gourmet tray prepared by Ma Kosti that Miles would
have had no hesitation in eating for his own breakfast. In the general chaos of the morning, however, he had to go down to the
kitchen and scrounge his meal. The Countess sat on the floor and
cooed into his closet for a good half-hour, and not only escaped
laceration, but managed to pick up, sex, and name the whole batch
of little squirming furballs before tearing herself away to hurry
and dress.

The convoy of three groundcars from Vorkosigan House took
off at last in billowing clouds of snow flung up from their fans.
After a couple of checks from blocked streets, they lumped and
bumped over the last snowbanks and wound around through the
wrought-iron gates of the Residence, where a squadron of soldiers
and Residence servitors were working frantically to keep the
paths clear. The wind, though still a nuisance, had fallen from its
dangerous velocities of last night, and the sky, Miles fancied
hopefully, was lighter.

They were not the only late arrivals; government ministers and
their wives, high-ranking military officers and *their* wives, and
counts and countesses continued to straggle in. The fortunate were

escorted by spiffy-shiny Armsmen in their many-colored House uniforms; the less so by Armsmen harried, bedraggled, and half-frozen after freeing their groundcars from ice-choked air intakes or predatory snowdrifts, but triumphant upon learning they were not the last to arrive. Since some of the Armsmen were as old or older than the counts they served, Miles felt conscience-stirred to watch them closely for fear of incipient coronary collapse, but only one had to be sent to the Residence's infirmary with chest pains. Happily most of the important Komarrans, including Laisa's parents, had arrived safely downside earlier in the week and been put up in the Residence's extensive guest quarters.

Lady Alys had either passed beyond panic to some sort of smiling whiteout overload, or was so experienced with arranging Gregor's social affairs that nothing could disturb her equanimity, or possibly some odd combination of both. She moved without haste, but without stopping, greeting and sorting guests. Her tension grew less edged when she saw the Countess and Miles arrive, last-but-one of her missing principals for the coming ceremony. Her face lit with open relief a few minutes later when they were followed through the door from the east portico by Viceroy Count Aral Vorkosigan himself, shaking off snow and solicitous Armsmen. Judging from the neat and glittering appearance of his retainers, they'd managed to avoid close personal acquaintance with any drifted ditches between the shuttleport and the Residence.

The Count exchanged a hard hug with the Countess, half-dislodging the flowers from her hair, as if it had been a year instead of weeks since they'd parted on Sergyar. A little "Ah," of pleasure rumbled in his chest, like a man eased of some burden. "I trust," he said to his wife, holding her at arm's length and devouring her with his eyes, "Gregor's weatherman has been sent to Kyril Island for a time, to practice his trade until he can get it right."

"He did say snow would fall." Miles grinned, looking on. "He just missed the part about it falling sideways. I gather he felt under some pressure to produce an optimistic forecast for the date."

"Hello, boy!" In this public arena, they exchanged only a hand-grip, but the Count managed to make it an eloquent one. "You look well. We *must* talk."

"I believe Lady Alys has first claim on you, sir. . . ."

Lady Alys was stepping down the stairs, her heavy blue afternoon-skirt floating about her legs with the speed of her passage. "Oh, Aral, good, you're here at last. Gregor's waiting in the Glass Hall. Come, come. . . ."

As distracted as any other artist in the throes of creation, she swept up the three Vorkosigans and herded them before her to their appointment with tradition, a mere hour late off the mark.

Due to the huge mob of witnesses—the betrothal was the foremost, as well as the first, social event of Winterfair—the ceremony took place in the largest ballroom. The bride-to-be and her party were arranged in a line opposite the groom-to-be and his party, like two small armies facing off. Laisa was elegant in Komarran jacket and trousers, though in a fine shade of Barrayaran Winterfair red, a compromise nicely calculated by Lady Alys.

Spearheading the two groups, Laisa was flanked by her parents, and a Komarran woman-friend as her Second; Gregor had his foster parents the Count and Countess Vorkosigan, and Miles as his Second. Laisa clearly had inherited her body-type from her father, a small, round man with an expression of cautious courtesy plastered on his face, and her milk-white skin from her mother, an alert-eyed woman with a worried smile. Lady Alys was of course the go-between. The days were long past when the duties of a Second legally included an obligation to marry the surviving fiancée if some unfortunate fatal accident occurred between the betrothal and the wedding. Nowadays the Seconds were limited to marching a collection of ceremonial gifts back and forth between the two sides.

Some of the gifts were obvious in their symbolism—money in fancy wrappers from the bride's parents, rather a lot of different food items from the groom's, including a bag of colored groats tied up with silver tinsel, and bottles of maple mead and wine. The silver-gilt mounted bridle was a little baffling, since it did not come with a horse. The gift of a small scalpel-like knife with a blunted edge from the bride's mother as pledge of her daughter's genetic cleanliness had been quietly eliminated, Miles was glad to see.

Next came the traditional reading of the Admonishments to the Bride, a task that fell to Miles as Gregor's Second. There were no reciprocal Admonishments to the Groom, a gap that Elli Quinn would have been swift to point out. Rising to the occasion, Miles stepped forward and unrolled the parchment, and read in a good clear voice and with a poker-straight face, as if he were giving a briefing to the Dendarii.

The Admonishments, though traditional in form and content, had been subtly edited too, Miles noted. The comments on the Duty to Bear an Heir had been reworded so as not to imply any particular obligation to do so in one's own body using one's real womb, with all the inherent dangers that entailed. No question whose hand was at work there. As for the rest of them . . . Miles's imagined Quinn's suggestions of how to roll the parchment and in what part of the Admonisher's anatomy he might lodge it for storage thereafter, and how hard. Dr. Toscane, less vigorous in her vocabulary, only cast one or two beseeching looks at Countess Vorkosigan, to be reassured with a few covert palm-down don't-take-it-too-seriously-dear gestures. The rest of the time, fortunately, she was so occupied with smiling at Gregor smiling at her, the Admonishments slithered past without objection.

Miles stepped back, and the fiancées had their hands joined in the last gesture of the ceremony, or rather, each was permitted to grasp one of Lady Alys's hands, and at this well-chaperoned remove exchange their promissory pledges. *And if you think this was a circus, just wait till the wedding at Midsummer.* Then the ceremony was over, and the party started. Since everyone was feeling more or less snowed-in, the party went on, and on. . . .

Gregor had first claim on Miles's father, so Miles took himself off to one of the buffets. There he encountered Ivan, tall and splendid in his parade red-and-blues, filling a single plate.

"Hello, Lord Auditor Coz," said Ivan. "Where's your gold leash?"

"I get it back next week. I take my oath before the last joint session of the Counts and Ministers, before they break for Winterfair."

"The word is out, you know. All sorts of people have been asking me about your appointment."

"If it gets too thick, direct 'em to Vorhovis or Vorkalloner. Though not, I think, to Vorparadijs. Did you bring a dance partner I might borrow?"

Ivan grimaced, and looked around, and lowered his voice. "I tried to do one better. I asked Delia Koudelka to marry me."

Miles thought he already knew the lay of things, but this was, after all, Ivan. "I figured this stuff would be contagious. Congratulations!" he said with synthetic heartiness. "Your mother will be ecstatic."

"No."

"No? But she likes the Koudelka girls."

"Not that. Delia turned me down. The first time I ever proposed to a girl, and—*squelch*!" Ivan looked quite indignant.

"She didn't take you, Ivan! What a surprise."

Ivan, awakening to his tone of voice, eyed him suspiciously. "And all my mother said was, *That's too bad, dear. I told you not to wait so long.* And wandered away to see Illyan. I saw them a couple of minutes ago, hiding out in an alcove. Illyan was rubbing her neck. The woman's besotted."

"Well, so she did tell you. Hundreds of times. She knew the demographic odds."

"I figured there would always be room at the top. Delia says she's marrying Duv Galeni! The damned Komarran . . . um . . ."

"Competition?" suggested Miles, as Ivan groped for a noun.

"You knew!"

"I had a few clues. You'll enjoy your untroubled single existence, I'm sure. Your next decade will be just like your last, eh? And the next, and the next, and the next . . . happy and carefree."

"*You're* not doing any better," Ivan snapped.

"I . . . didn't expect to." Miles smiled grimly. That was perhaps enough Ivan-twitting, on this topic. "You'll just have to try again. Martya, maybe?"

Ivan growled.

"What, two rejections in—you didn't ask both sisters on the same day, did you, Ivan?"

"I panicked."

"So . . . who's Martya marrying?"

"Anyone but me, apparently."

"Really. So, um . . . did you see where the Koudelkas went?"

"The Commodore was here a bit ago. He's probably gone off with your da by now. I expect the girls will be up in the ballroom as soon as the music starts."

"Ah." Miles started to turn away, but then added absently, "Do you want a kitten?"

Ivan stared at him. "Why in God's name would I want a kitten?"

"It would brighten your bachelor digs, you know. A bit of life and movement, to keep you company on your long, lonely nights."

"Get stuffed, Lord Auditor Coz."

Miles grinned, popped an hors d'oeuvre in his mouth, and departed, munching thoughtfully.

He spotted the Koudelka clan in the ballroom, in a cluster on the far side. The three sisters were minus their fourth, Kareen, who was still on Beta Colony but who would, he'd been informed, be returning for the Imperial wedding at Midsummer. So would Lord Mark, presumably. Captain Galeni stood engaged in serious conversation with his prospective father-in-law the Commodore,

Delia by his side in her favorite blue. Upon reflection, and some quiet campaigning from his fiancée, Galeni had decided not to resign his commission, to Miles's immense relief. Miles was staying out of ImpSec's internal business this week, but he'd had a whiff through Gregor of just how seriously Galeni was being considered for head of Komarran Affairs, and hoped to congratulate him soon.

Madame Koudelka looked on benignly. It made a nice tableau, and would do much toward repairing whatever damages still lingered to Galeni's reputation from Haroche's calculatedly clumsy arrest of him here a few weeks ago. With four sisters in all, Galeni was on his way to gaining an array of major Barrayaran clan connections by marriage. . . . Miles wondered if anyone had apprised Galeni yet that he stood in some danger of acquiring Miles's clone-brother Mark as his next brother-in-law. If not, Miles wanted to be there when somebody told him, just to savor the look on his face. Also, he wondered if kittens would make good wedding presents. . . .

A rich, raspy baritone voice over his shoulder said, "Congratulations on your promotion, sir."

Miles grinned dryly, and turned around to greet his father. "Which one, sir?"

"I admit," said Viceroy Count Aral Vorkosigan, "I was thinking of your Imperial Auditorship, but I understand from Gregor you slipped a captaincy in there somehow as well. You hadn't mentioned it. Congratulations on that, too, though . . . that has to be the most roundabout method of acquiring a set of blue tabs I've ever heard of."

"If you can't do what you want, do what you can. Or how you can. The captaincy . . . completed something, for me."

"I'm glad you survived long enough to finally grow into yourself. So, you're not losing your forward momentum with age, are you, boy?" The Count refrained from following this up with one of those we're-getting-so-old complaints mainly designed to invite the listener to offer a contradiction.

"I don't think so." Miles's eyes narrowed in a brief moment of introspection. His new calmness was still there, inside, but it did not feel at all weary. Quite the opposite. "It's just taking another direction. Vorhovis tells me I'm the youngest Imperial Auditor since the Time of Isolation. It's not a post you ever held, I understand."

"No. I missed that one, somehow. Your grandfather never held it, either. Nor your great-grandfather. In fact . . . I'll have to look it up, but I don't think any Count or Lord Vorkosigan has ever been an Auditor."

"I did. None has. I'm the first in the family," Miles informed him smugly. "I am unprecedented."

The Count smiled. "This is not news, Miles."

TWENTY-NINE

Miles stood in the concourse just outside Customs Processing on one of Komarr's larger orbital transfer stations. *Smells like a space station, oh, yeah.* It was not a sweet perfume, that odd acridity compounded of machinery, electronics, humanity and all its effluvia, and chill air run through filters which never quite succeeded in reducing its complexity. But it was familiar, universal, and an enormously nostalgic odor for him: Admiral Naismith's atmosphere, subliminally electrifying even now.

The station was one of a dozen orbiting the system's only semihabitable planet. Three more deep-space stations circled Komarr's feeble star, and each of the six wormhole exits they all served boasted both a military station and a commercial one. In this far-flung network cargo and passengers loaded, unloaded, and shuffled, bound not only for Barrayar but for Pol, the Hegen Hub, Sergyar, Escobar beyond it, and a dozen other connecting routes. The reopened trade route to Rho Ceta and the rest of the Cetagandan Empire, uneasy neighbors though they were, also supported a growing stream of traffic. The fees and taxes generated here were a vast source of income for the Barrayaran Imperium, far beyond anything squeezed out of poor backcountry groat farmers on the homeworld. This too was part of Barrayar, he must remember to point out to space-bred Elli Quinn.

Quinn might be almost happy on Komarr. Its domed cities were reminiscent of the space station upon which she had been born. True, most of Lord Vorkosigan's duties would keep him in a tight little circuit around Vorbarr Sultana. The capital drew all ambitious men like a gravity well. But one might maintain a second domicile on one of the stations here, a cozy little deep-space dacha. . . . *It is far from the mountains.*

He'd seen the Count and Countess off from this station yesterday, on their way back to Sergyar, having hitched a ride with them as far as Komarr in their government courier ship. Five days in the relatively uninterrupted confines of a jump-ship had actually given them time enough to talk, for a change. He had also seized the opportunity to beg an Armsman for himself from his father, the comfortable Pym by choice. The Countess grumbled they should have held out for Ma Kosti in exchange, but gave up her favorite Armsman to him nonetheless; the Count promised to send him a couple more in due time, chosen from those whose wives and families had been the most bitterly unhappy at having been forcibly transplanted from their familiar city to the wilds of Chaos Colony.

The crowd around the exit door from Customs Processing thickened, as inbound passengers began to spill through and hurry to their further destinations, or greet waiting parties with businesslike decorum or familial enthusiasm. Miles rose on his toes, futilely. Nine-tenths of this outrush dissipated before Quinn came striding through the doors, conservatively incognito in Komarran civilian fashion, a white padded silk jacket and trousers. The outfit set off her dark curls and brilliant brown eyes; but then, Quinn made anything she wore look great, including ripped fatigues and mud.

She too craned to look for him, murmured a "Heh," of satisfaction upon spotting him waving a hand behind a few other shoulders, and wove through the crowd. Her stride stretched as she neared; she dropped the gray duffel she swung and they embraced with an impact that nearly knocked Miles off his feet. The scent of her made up for any number of defective space station atmospheric filters. *Quinn, my Quinn.* After a dozen or so kisses, they parted just far enough to permit speech.

"So why did you ask me to bring *all* your stuff?" she demanded suspiciously. "I didn't like the sound of that."

"Did you?"

"Yes. It's stuck back in Customs. They choked on the contents, particularly all the weapons. I gave up arguing with them after a while—you're a Barrayaran, *you* sort them out."

"Ah, Pym." Miles gestured to his Armsman, like Miles dressed in discreet streetwear. "Take Commodore Quinn's receipts, and rescue my property from our bureaucracy, please.

Readdress it to Vorkosigan House, and send it by commercial shipper. Then go on back to the hostel."

"Yes, my lord." Pym collected the data codes, and plunged back through the doors into Customs.

"Is that all your personal luggage?" Miles asked Quinn.

"As ever."

"Off to the hostel, then. It's a nice one." The best on the station, in fact, luxury class. "I, ah, got us a suite for tonight."

"You'd better have."

"Have you had dinner?"

"Not yet."

"Good. Neither have I."

A short walk brought them to the nearest bubble-car terminal, and a short ride to the hostel. Its appointments were elegant, its corridors wide and thickly carpeted, and its staff solicitous. The suite was large, for a space station, which meant nicely cozy for Miles's present purposes.

"Your General Allegre is generous," remarked Quinn, unloading her duffel after a quick reconnoiter of the sybaritic bathroom. "I may like working for him after all."

"I think you will, but this is on my bill tonight, not ImpSec's. I wanted someplace quiet where we could talk, before your official meeting with Allegre and the Galactic Affairs chief tomorrow."

"So . . . I don't quite understand this setup. I get one lousy message from you with you looking like a damned zombie, telling me Illyan caught up with you about poor Vorberg, and didn't I tell you so. Then a resounding silence, for weeks, and no answers to my messages to you, you rat. Then I get another one with you all chipper again, saying it's all right now, and I sure don't see the connection. Then I get this order to report to ImpSec on Komarr without delay, no explanations, no hint of what the new assignment is, except with this postscript from you to bring your whole kit with me when I come and put the freight charges on ImpSec's tab. Are you back in ImpSec, or not?"

"Not. I'm here as a consultant, to get you up and running with your new bosses, and vice versa. I, ah . . . have another job, now."

"I *really* don't understand. I mean, your messages are usually cryptic—"

"It's hard to send proper love letters, when you know everything you say is going to be monitored by ImpSec censors."

"But this time, it was frigging incomprehensible. What is going on with you?" Her voice was edged with the same suppressed fear Miles was feeling, *Am I losing you?* No, not fear. Knowledge.

"I tried to compose a message a couple of times, but it was . . . too complicated, and all the most important parts were things I didn't want to send tight-beam. The edited version came out sounding like gibberish. I had to see you face-to-face anyway, for, for a lot of reasons. It's a long story, and most of it is classified, a fact that I am going to completely ignore. I can, you know. Do you want to go down to the restaurant to eat, or order room service?"

"*Miles,*" she said in exasperation. "Room service. And explanations."

He distracted her temporarily with the hostel's enormous menu, to buy a little more time to compose his thoughts. It didn't help any more than the previous weeks he'd spent composing those same thoughts, in their endless permutations. Miles put in their order and they settled side by side, facing one another, on the suite's smaller couch.

"To explain about my new job, I have to tell you something about how I acquired it, and why Illyan isn't Chief of ImpSec anymore. . . ." He told her the story of the past months, beginning with Illyan's breakdown, doubling back to explain about Laisa and Duv Galeni, growing excited and jumping up to gesture and pace when he described how he'd nailed Haroche at last. His seizure treatment. Gregor's job offer. All the easy stuff, the events, the facts. He did not know how to explain his inner journey; Elli was not, after all, Barrayaran. The food arrived, stopping Elli's immediate reaction. Her face was tense and introspective. *Yes. We should all think before we speak tonight, love.*

She did not take up her thread until the hostel's human servitor finished arranging the meal on their table, and bustled out again.

It was three bites before she spoke; Miles wondered if she was tasting her soup as little as he was tasting his. When she did, she began obliquely, in a carefully neutral tone. "Imperial Auditor . . . sounds like some kind of an accountant. It's not you, Miles."

"It is now. I took my oath. It's one of those Barrayaran terms that doesn't mean what you think it does. I don't know. . . . Imperial Agent? Special Prosecutor? Special Envoy? Inspector General? It's all of those things, and none of them. It's whatever . . . whatever Gregor needs it to be. It's extraordinarily open-ended. I can't begin to tell you how much it suits me."

"You never once mentioned it before, as your ambition."

"I never imagined the possibility. But it's not the sort of job that should ever be given to a man who is too ambitious for it. Willing, yes, but not ambitious. It . . . calls for dispassion, not passion, even with respect to itself."

She sat frowning over this for a full minute. At last, visibly gathering her courage, she took a more direct cut. "So where does it leave me, leave us? Does it mean you're never coming back to the Dendarii? Miles, I might never see you again." Only the smallest quaver edged her controlled voice.

"That's . . . one of the reasons I wanted to talk to you tonight, personally, before tomorrow's business overwhelms everything else." Now it was his turn to pause for courage, to keep his voice in an even register. "You see, if you were . . . if you stayed here . . . if you were Lady Vorkosigan, you could be with me all the time."

"No . . ." Her soup would have cooled, forgotten, if not for the stay-warm circuit in the bottom of the bowl. "I'd be with Lord Vorkosigan all the time. Not with you, Miles, not with Admiral Naismith."

"Admiral Naismith was something I made up, Elli," he said gently. "He was my own invention. I'm an egotistical enough artist, I suppose, I'm glad you liked my creation. I made him up out of me, after all. But not all of me."

She shook her head, tried another tack. "You said the last time, you wouldn't ask me that Lady Vorkosigan thing anymore. You said it the last three times you asked me to marry Lord Vorkosigan, in fact."

"One more last chance, Elli. Except this time it really is. I . . . in all honesty, I have to tell you the other half, or rather, the other side, the counteroffer. What's coming up tomorrow, along with the Dendarii's new contract."

"Contract, hell. You're changing the subject, Miles. What about us?"

"I can't get to us, except this way. Full disclosure. Tomorrow, we, that is, Allegre and ImpSec and I, Barrayar if you will, we're offering you the admiralcy. Admiral Quinn of the Dendarii Free Mercenary Fleet. You'll go on working for Allegre in exactly the same capacity that I worked for Illyan."

Quinn's eyes widened, lit, fell. "Miles . . . I can't do your job. I'm not nearly ready."

"You have been doing my job. You're half-past ready, Quinn. *I* say so."

She smiled at the familiar forward-momentum passion in his voice, that had so often driven them all to results beyond reason. "I admit . . . I wanted a share of command. But not so soon, not like this."

"The time is now. Your time. My time. This is it."

She stared intently at him, baffled by his tone of voice. "Miles . . . I don't want to be stuck on just one planet for the rest of my life."

"A planet's a damned big place, Elli, when you get down to the details. And anyway, there are three planets in the Barrayaran Imperium."

"Three times worse, then." She leaned across the table, and grasped his hand in both hers, hard. "Suppose I make you a counterproposal. Screw the Barrayaran Imperium. The Dendarii Fleet does not require its Imperial contracts to survive, though I admit, thanks to you, they have been very fine and favorable. The Fleet existed before Barrayar ever came over our event horizon, it can go on existing after they sink back into their damned gravity well. We spacers, we don't need planets sucking us down. You—come with me, instead. Be Admiral Naismith, shake the dirt off your boots. I'd marry Admiral Naismith in a heartbeat, if that's what you want. We can be such a team, the two of us, we'll make legends. You and me, Miles, out there!" She waved one arm in a random circle, though the other did not release her grip.

"I tried, Elli. I tried for weeks. You don't know how hard I tried to go. I was never a mercenary, not ever. Not for one single minute."

A flash of anger sparked briefly in her brown eyes. "Do you figure that makes you morally superior to the rest of us?"

"No," he sighed. "But it makes me Miles Vorkosigan. Not Miles Naismith."

She shook her head. Ah, denial. He recognized the hollow reverberation of it. "There always was a part of you I could never touch." Her voice was edged with pain.

"I know. I worked for years to extinguish Lord Vorkosigan. I couldn't do it, not even for you. You can't *select* from me, Elli, take the parts you favor and leave the rest on the table." He gestured in frustration to their drying dinner. "I don't come a la carte. I'm all or nothing."

"You could be anything you chose, Miles, anywhere! Why insist on this place?"

He smiled, grimly. "No. I have discovered I am constrained on other levels." This time, his hands enclosed hers. "But maybe you can choose. Come to Barrayar, Elli, and be . . . and be desperately unhappy with me?"

Her breath puffed on a laugh. "What is this, more full disclosure?"

"There is no other way, for the long haul. And I'm talking about a very long haul."

"Miles, I *can't*. I mean, your home is very pretty, for a planet, but it's dreadful down there."

"You could make it less dreadful."

"I can't . . . I can't be what you want, can't be your Lady Vorkosigan."

He looked away, looked back, opened his hands to her. "I can give you everything I have. I can't give you less."

"But you want everything I am in return. Admiral Quinn annihilated, Lady Vorkosigan . . . rising from the ashes. I'm not good at resurrection, Miles. That's your department." She shook her head, helplessly. "Come away with me."

"Stay here with me."

Love does not conquer all. Watching the struggle in her face, he began to feel horribly like Admiral Haroche. Perhaps Haroche had not enjoyed his moment of moral torture either. *The one thing you can't trade for your heart's desire . . .* He gripped her hand harder, willing then not love but truth, and with all his heart. "Then choose Elli. Whoever Elli is."

"Elli is . . . Admiral Quinn."

"I rather thought she was."

"Then why do you do this to me?"

"Because you have to decide now, Elli, once and for all."

"You're forcing this choice, not me!"

"Yes. That's just exactly right. I can go on with you. I can go on without you, if I have to. But I can't *freeze*, Elli, not even for you. Perfect preservation isn't life, it's death. I know."

She nodded, slowly. "I understand that part, anyway." She began spooning her soup, watching him watching her watching him. . . .

———※◎※———

They made love one last time, for old times' sake, for goodbye, and, Miles realized halfway through, each in a desperate last-ditch effort to please and pleasure the other so much, they would change their mind. *We'd have to change more than our minds. We'd have to change our whole selves.*

With a sigh, he sat up in the suite's vast bed, disentangling their limbs. "This isn't working, Elli."

"'L make it work," she mumbled. He captured her hand, and kissed the inside of her wrist. She took a deep breath, and sat up beside him. They were both silent for a long time.

"You were destined to be a soldier," she said at last. "Not some kind of, of, superior bureaucrat."

He gave up trying to explain the ancient and noble post of Imperial Auditor to a non-Barrayaran. "To be a great soldier, you need a great war. There doesn't happen to be one on, just now, not around here. The Cetagandans are quiescent for the first time in a decade. Pol is not aggressive, and anyway, we're in good odor in the whole Hegen Hub these days. Jackson's Whole is nasty enough, but they're too disunited to be a military threat at this distance. The worst menace in the neighborhood *is* us, and Sergyar is absorbing *our* energies. I'm not sure I could lend myself to an aggressive war anyway."

"Your father did. With remarkable success."

"Mixed success. You should study our history more closely, love. But I am not my father. I don't have to repeat his mistakes; I can invent bright-new ones."

"You're turning into such a political animal, these days."

"It goes with my territory. And . . . they may also serve who only stand and wait, but life is short enough already. If the Imperium ever wants me in a military capacity again, they can forward a bloody comconsole message."

Her brows rose; she sat back, and plumped pillows around them. He drew her head down, to rest on his scored chest, and stroked her hair, curling it around his fingers; her free hand idled up and down his body. He could feel the letting-go in them, with the easing of the tension and the terror, with the slowing of every pulse of their blood. Not pain, or not so much pain, but only a just sadness, a due measure of melancholy, quiet and right.

"Now . . ." he said at last, "that's not to say there won't be need for the odd rescue mission or whatever, from time to time. Mind you, as Admiral Quinn, the place for your sweet ass is in a nice soft tactics room chair. Don't you be going out with the squads all the time. It's not appropriate for a senior staff officer, and it's way too dangerous."

Her fingernails traced the spider-nest lines of his most spectacular scars, making the hairs stand up on his arms. "You are a howling hypocrite, my love."

He elected prudently not to quibble over that one. He cleared his throat. "That . . . brings up another thing I wanted to ask you. A favor. About Sergeant Taura."

She stiffened slightly. "What?"

"Last time I saw her, I noticed she's getting some gray in her hair. You know what that means. I talked recently to old Canaba about it, you remember him. He gives no more than two months between the time she starts to go into serious metabolic failure, and the end. I want you to promise me, you'll let me know in time, time to get out there with the Fleet, or wherever she is, before she goes. I . . . don't want her to be alone, then. It's a promise I made to myself once, that I mean to keep."

She settled back. "All right," she said seriously. After a moment she added, "So . . . *did* you sleep with her?"

"Um . . ." He swallowed. "She was before your time, Elli." After another minute he was compelled to add, "And after, from time to time. Very rarely."

"Hah. I thought so."

As long as we're being morbid . . . "How . . . about you? Was there ever anyone else, when I was gone?"

"No. *I* was good. Huh!" She added after a moment, "Now, before *your* time, that's another Quinn."

That dig, he decided, was within her rights; he let it go by. "It should go without saying, but just in case . . . you do know you are free of any personal obligation to me hereafter?"

"So you can be too? Is that what this is all about?" She touched his face, and smiled. "I don't need you to free me, love. I can free myself, any time I choose."

"That's part, I think, of what I've always loved about you." He hesitated. "But can you choose any time you choose?"

"Well. That's the other question, isn't it," she said softly. They each of them gazed long at the other, as if memorizing the image for some interior cache. After a time she added, with unerring perceptiveness and wry goodwill, "I hope you find your Lady Vorkosigan, Miles. Whoever she is."

"I hope so too, Elli," he sighed. "I dread the search, though."

"Lazy," she murmured.

"That, too. You were a drunkard's dream, Quinn. You've quite spoiled me, you know."

"Shall I apologize?"

"Never."

She came up for breath from the long kiss that followed this to ask, "Till your search prospers, shall we have flings? From time to time?"

"Perhaps . . . I don't know. If we're ever on the same planet at the same time. It's a big universe."

"Then why do I keep running into the same people over and over?"

They fell then to unhurried caresses, without agenda; no future, no past, just a little bubble in time containing Miles and Elli. After that things went much better.

——※——

In the afterglow, Elli murmured into his hair, "Do you think you'll like your new job as much as I'll like mine?"

"I'm beginning to suspect so. You are ready, you know. I've lately had some sharp lessons on what a bad idea it is to leave competent subordinates unpromoted for too long. Watch out for that in"—he almost said, *my*—"your staff."

"So is there, like, a top spot you can go for? Work your way up to First Auditor from Eighth Auditor, say?"

"Only by longevity. Which, come to think of it, could happen; I'm the youngest by three decades. But the Auditors are numbered for convenience. It doesn't denote rank. They all seem to be sort of equal. When they meet, they sit in a circle. Very unusual for hierarchy-conscious Barrayar, really."

"Like the Knights of the Round Table," Elli suggested.

Miles choked on a laugh. "Not if you could see them. . . ." He hesitated. "Well, I don't know. Those original Round Table knights competed for honors, obsessively. I mean, that's why old Arthur had to make the table round in the first place, to defuse all that. But most of the Auditors are . . . I can't say, not ambitious, or they wouldn't all have achieved what they have. Post-ambitious? These old Barrayaran paladins are an amazingly disinterested lot. I'm actually looking forward to getting to know them better." He provided her with a few giggles, by giving a vigorously worded description of his new colleagues' odder quirks.

She ran a hand through her dark curls, grinning despite herself. "Dear godlings, Miles. I begin to think you're going to fit right in after all."

"Have you ever come home, to a place you've never been before? It feels like that. It's . . . very odd. But not at all unpleasant."

She kissed his forehead, for benediction; he kissed her palm, for luck.

"Well, if you insist on being a civilian, you be a good bureaucrat-paladin, then," she told him firmly. "Do me proud."

"I will, Elli."

———※◎※———

Miles's return from Komarr to Barrayar was uneventful. He arrived back at Vorkosigan House in the quiet of a late winter evening, to find it warm and lit and ready for him. Tomorrow he would formally invite company to dinner, he decided, Duv and Delia and the rest of the Koudelkas, by choice. But tonight he dined in the kitchen with his Armsman and Ma Kosti; his cook was a little scandalized, either by his stepping out of his role or by his invading her territory. But he told her a string of jokes until she laughed, and snapped at him with a towel as if he were one of her boys, which amused Pym no end. Corporal Kosti ducked in at the end of his guard shift, to be properly fed as well, and to play with the kittens who now lived in, or rather, obsessively escaped from, a rag-padded box near the stove. The corporal and Ma Kosti caught Miles up on all the news from Martin, now suffering through basic training with all the bragging complaints that entailed.

After his late supper, he took himself off to his wine cellar. Ceremoniously, he selected a bottle of his grandfather's oldest and rarest. Upon opening it, he discovered it was going more than a bit off. He considered drinking it anyway, for the symbolism's sake. Then, decisively, he dumped it down the bathroom sink in his new suite and went back for a bottle from a much more recent batch that he knew to be very good.

With a wineglass of the best crystal this time, he sat in the incredibly comfortable chair by the bay window, to watch a few fat snowflakes dance past in the garden lights, and to hold his own private wake. He toasted his ghostly night-reflection in the window. This was what, Admiral Naismith's third death? Once on Jackson's Whole, once in Illyan's office, third and last and astonishingly painful, resurrected and dispatched again by Lucas Haroche. On his first death he'd been in no position to enjoy a proper wake—frozen lost luggage, he'd been—on the second, his grandfather's dagger, opener for a redder wine, had held more blandishment than the brandy. He settled back, and prepared to ration himself one hour of self-pity along with his wine, and be done with it.

Instead, he found himself leaning back in the warm chair, laughing softly. He swallowed the laugh, wondering if he'd lost his grip at last.

Just the opposite.

Haroche was no miracle-worker. He wasn't even a stage magician. He'd had no power then or ever to give or withhold Naismith, though Miles felt a cryonic chill, thinking how close he'd come to delivering *himself* into Haroche's hands.

No wonder he was laughing. He wasn't mourning a death. He was celebrating an escape.

"I'm not dead. I'm *here*." He touched his scarred chest in wonder.

He felt strange and single, not to be in pieces anymore. Not Lord Vorkosigan ascendant, not Naismith lost, but all of him, all at once, all the time. *Crowded in there?*

Not particularly.

Harra Csurik had been almost right. It wasn't your life again you found, going on. It was your life anew. And it wasn't at all what he'd been expecting. His slow smile deepened. He was beginning to be very curious about his future.

MILES VORKOSIGAN/NAISMITH: HIS UNIVERSE AND TIMES

Chronology	Events	Chronicle
Approx. 200 years before Miles's birth	Quaddies are created by genetic engineering.	*Falling Free*
During Beta-Barrayaran War	Cordelia Naismith meets Lord Aral Vorkosigan while on opposite sides of a war. Despite difficulties, they fall in love and are married.	*Shards of Honor*
The Vordarian Pretendership	While Cordelia is pregnant, an attempt to assassinate Aral by poison gas fails, but Cordelia is affected; Miles Vorkosigan is born with bones that will always be brittle and other medical problems. His growth will be stunted.	*Barrayar*
Miles is 17	Miles fails to pass physical test to get into the Service Academy. On a trip, necessities force him to improvise the Free Dendarii Mercenaries into existence; he has unintended but unavoidable adventures for four months. Leaves the Dendarii in Ky Tung's competent hands and takes Elli Quinn to Beta for rebuilding of her damaged face; returns to Barrayar to thwart plot against his father. Emperor pulls strings to get Miles into the Academy.	*The Warrior's Apprentice*

Chronology	Events	Chronicle
Miles is 20	Ensign Miles graduates and immediately has to take on one of the duties of the Barrayaran nobility and act as detective and judge in a murder case. Shortly afterwards, his first military assignment ends with his arrest. Miles has to rejoin the Dendarii to rescue the young Barrayaran emperor. Emperor accepts Dendarii as his personal secret service force.	"The Mountains of Mourning" in *Borders of Infinity* *The Vor Game*
Miles is 22	Miles and his cousin Ivan attend a Cetagandan state funeral and are caught up in Cetagandan internal politics.	*Cetaganda*
	Miles sends Commander Elli Quinn, who's been given a new face on Beta, on a solo mission to Kline Station.	*Ethan of Athos*
Miles is 23	Now a Barrayaran Lieutenant, Miles goes with the Dendarii to smuggle a scientist out of Jackson's Whole. Miles's fragile leg bones have been replaced by synthetics.	"Labyrinth" n *Borders of Infinity*
Miles is 24	Miles plots from within a Cetagandan prison camp on Dagoola IV to free the prisoners. The Dendarii fleet is pursued by the	"The Borders of Infinity" in *Borders of Infinity*

Chronology	Events	Chronicle
	Cetagandans and finally reaches Earth for repairs. Miles has to juggle both his identities at once, raise money for repairs, and defeat a plot to replace him with a double. Ky Tung stays on Earth. Commander Elli Quinn is now Miles's right-hand officer. Miles and the Dendarii depart for Sector IV on a rescue mission.	*Brothers in Arms*
Miles is 25	Hospitalized after previous mission, Miles's broken arms are replaced by synthetic bones. With Simon Illyan, Miles undoes yet another plot against his father while flat on his back.	*Borders of Infinity*
Miles is 28	Miles meets his clone brother Mark again, this time on Jackson's Whole.	*Mirror Dance*
Miles is 29	Miles hits thirty; thirty hits back.	*Memory*

SFBC 50th
ANNIVERSARY COLLECTION

1 *The Door Into Summer,* Robert A. Heinlein
2 *The Space Merchants,* Frederik Pohl & C.M. Kornbluth
3 *The City and the Stars,* Arthur C. Clarke
4 *Three Hearts and Three Lions,* Poul Anderson
5 *City,* Clifford D. Simak
6 *Under Pressure,* Frank Herbert
7 *The End of Eternity,* Isaac Asimov
8 *The Stars My Destination,* Alfred Bester
9 *To Your Scattered Bodies Go,* Philip José Farmer
10 *Norstrilia,* Cordwainer Smith
11 *The Man in the High Castle,* Philip K. Dick
12 *The Dream Master,* Roger Zelazny
13 *Stand on Zanzibar,* John Brunner
14 *A Canticle for Leibowitz,* Walter M. Miller, Jr.
15 *The Left Hand of Darkness,* Ursula K. LeGuin
16 *Rite of Passage,* Alexei Panshin
17 *Rendezvous with Rama,* Arthur C. Clarke
18 *Gloriana,* Michael Moorcock
19 *The Forever War,* Joe Haldeman
20 *Her Smoke Rose Up Forever,* James Tiptree, Jr.
21 *Wild Seed,* Octavia E. Butler
22 *The Snow Queen,* Joan D. Vinge
23 *The Mote in God's Eye,* Larry Niven and Jerry Pournelle
24 *Deathbird Stories,* Harlan Ellison
25 *Ender's Game,* Orson Scott Card
26 *The Anubis Gates,* Tim Powers
27 *Blood Music,* Greg Bear
28 *Mythago Wood,* Robert Holdstock
29 *Courtship Rite,* Donald Kingsbury
30 *Good Omens,* Neil Gaiman and Terry Pratchett
31 *Schismatrix Plus,* Bruce Sterling
32 *Startide Rising,* David Brin
33 *Snow Crash,* Neal Stephenson
34 *Rats and Gargoyles,* Mary Gentle
35 *Memory,* Lois McMaster Bujold
36 *Only Begotten Daughter,* James Morrow
37 *Doomsday Book,* Connie Willis
38 *Steel Beach,* John Varley
39 *The Iron Dragon's Daughter,* Michael Swanwick
40 *A Fire Upon the Deep,* Vernor Vinge